SHE WANTED TO DENY EVERYTHING—BUT
THE WHITE MAN WOULD NOT LET HER
FORGET WHO SHE WAS. . . .

Lying in his bed of sand, Flann O'Phelan could feel
the grains in his fingers. Above his head, stars twinkled.
The steady swish he heard was caused by Kitchigami's
waves licking the shore near him. The smell of burning
wood filled his nostrils. With Birch Leaf's help, Flann
propped himself into a sitting position with his back
braced against driftwood.

Flann stared at her, remembering what Fire Grass
had said of Birch Leaf's origins.

"Birch Leaf," he said, "you're adopted. Soft Willow
adopted you as her daughter when the warriors brought
you home from a raid on the Sioux. You're white, Birch
Leaf, not Indian at all."

She sank back on her heels, bringing a hand to her
heart. Her lips moved but no words came out.

"Birch Leaf?" Flann asked, reaching toward her. He
was able to move and bend forward quite easily now,
and he touched her shoulder.

"Car-o-line," she whispered. "Car-o-line."

CHIPPEWA DAUGHTER

JANE TOOMBS

CHIPPEWA DAUGHTER

JANE TOOMBS

A Dell/Standish Book

Published by
Miles Standish Press, Inc.
37 West Avenue
Wayne, Pennsylvania 19087

Copyright © 1982 by Jane Toombs

All rights reserved. No part of this book may be
reproduced in any form or by any means without the
prior written permission of the Publisher,
excepting brief quotes used in connection
with reviews written specifically for inclusion
in a magazine or newspaper.

Dell ® TM 681510, Dell Publishing Co., Inc.

ISBN: 0-440-01270-8

Printed in the United States of America

First printing—February 1982
Second printing—November 1982

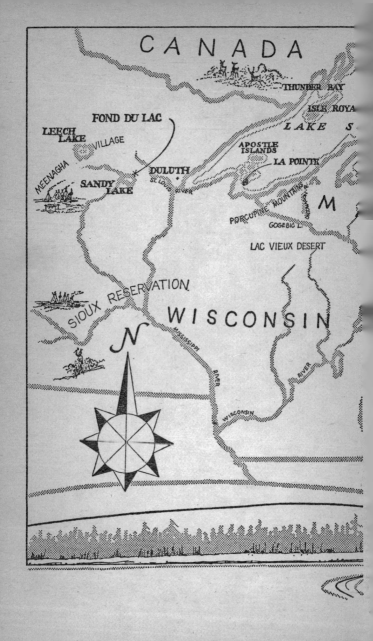

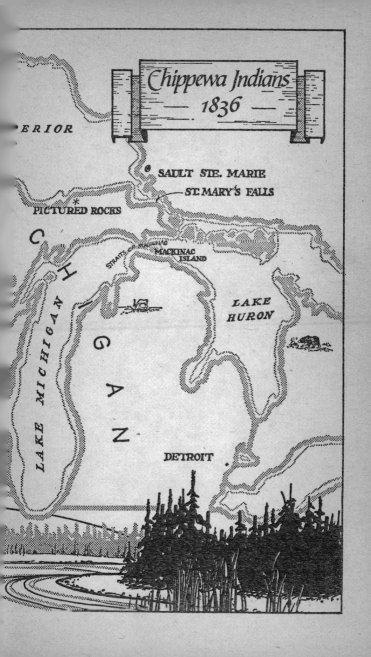

Chippewa Indians
1836

SUPERIOR

SAULT STE. MARIE
ST. MARY'S FALLS

PICTURED ROCKS

MICHIGAN

STRAITS OF MACKINAC

MACKINAC
ISLAND

LAKE MICHIGAN

LAKE
HURON

DETROIT

Chapter 1

Flann O'Phelan shifted his weight from one foot to the other, glancing nervously about at the flames in the marble-faced fireplace and then at the gilt wallpaper between the arched windows. In a mirror, he glimpsed his red hair flaring above the sober black of his frock coat.

On the small writing table beside him lay a reed-stemmed pipe with a red stone bowl. Flann tried to focus his attention on it. This must be the famous Indian pipe he'd heard about, the bowl made from catlinite quarried in the Minnesota Territory, the red stone all the Indian tribes used for their calumets.

Walking along Pennsylvania Avenue on his way to the White House, he had seen an Indian out for a stroll, wearing buckskin clothes decorated with beads and a bonnet of feathers atop his head. Flann had stopped to stare, only to earn a laugh from a store-keeper in the doorway of his shop.

"There's painted Indians on this street all the time, always visiting the Great White Father, or trying to," the man said. "It's plain to see you're not from these parts or you'd pay no mind."

Flann heard a noise in the hall and pulled himself to rigid attention, recalling a conversation. "I've known General Jackson for ten years," his Uncle Whitney had told him two days earlier, in Boston. "He can take a man's measure in a matter of minutes. Be yourself and he'll warm to you, I'm certain of it."

Two men came into the room, a tall, thin, white-haired man supported on the arm of a shorter, younger man. Flann took a step forward, thinking to himself that President Jackson was a sick man, he needed help.

Andrew Jackson drew himself up and smiled at the man who had assisted him into the room. "Thank you, Jack. I'll do fine now."

That was Jack Donelson, Flann thought as the man left them. The president's secretary as well as his foster son. Jackson turned to look at Flann. He seemed to hold himself erect with effort and Flann saw that he and the President were roughly the same height, over six feet.

"So you're a redhead," Jackson remarked, touching his own white hair. "Your uncle didn't tell me that. You know, I used to be a redhead myself. Do you have the temper to go with the hair?"

"I try not to be hasty," Flann replied. "I don't always succeed." He bowed slightly. "I'm most honored to meet you, sir."

Jackson nodded and seated himself in the high-backed chair by the writing table. He reached for the pipe. "Sit down, young man," he invited as he began to tamp tobacco into the bowl. "Do you smoke?"

"No, sir."

"You'll have to learn. The pipe is a courtesy with

2

the Indians. A ceremony. You won't get anywhere unless you puff a pipe with them."

"Yes, sir."

Jackson's light blue eyes, keen in his drawn and lined face, examined Flann. "You look healthy at any rate," he declared finally. "Tell me, do you want to go?"

"Very much, sir." Flann's voice was earnest. He did want the appointment, despite having to postpone the wedding, despite the fact he would owe still another favor to Uncle Whitney.

"Whitney McNeil tells me you've a talent for languages," Jackson continued. "Says you speak French, German and Spanish as well as knowing Latin and Greek. Learning the Chippewa tongue should pose no problem for you. Now Whitney and I've been friends a long time but he's your relative and I've got to know whether you're what he made you out to be. He says you left West Point against your father's wishes because you felt your calling was in medicine. Is this correct?"

Flann hesitated. Jackson pulled papers from a pocket and toyed with them as he waited for Flann's answer.

"It's true I seem to have a gift for languages," Flann finally responded. "As for West Point, I didn't like military life. I'll fight when and if I have to as well as I can. I don't want to be a professional soldier." He leaned forward. "I want to heal, not kill." He paused, then went on. "My superiors at West Point also felt I was insubordinate," he added stiffly.

Jackson stared at him, then grinned. "I suspect you were, with that red hair. But you do like doctoring?"

"More than anything I've ever done."

3

"Ever see an Indian? Not many in Boston, I'll wager."

"I saw the Sauk and Fox Indians dance on the Boston Common three years ago and those are the only ones I've ever set eyes on except for passing an Indian on Pennsylvania Avenue as I came here."

"What are your feelings about Indians?" Jackson queried.

"The Indian is a natural man. He's been called noble, but that's the wrong word. He's natural, from the Latin, *naturalis*, of nature. As we all were once. We can't expect him to take up civilized ways overnight, we must be patient, give him. . . ."

He broke off, face flushing as he remembered he was talking to the President. General Andrew Jackson had fought alongside Indians against the British in 1812. Some said he had taken an orphaned Indian baby and raised him as he would a son.

He had also fought against the Seminoles in 1818. Who was he, Flann O'Phelan, to be telling General Jackson about Indians?

He saw Jackson was smiling.

"You're quite right, sir," Flann agreed. "I've never really met an Indian. I hope that won't disqualify me."

"No reason why it should." Jackson's smile faded. He sat in silence, drawing on the red stone pipe, weighing matters. The young fellow wanted to go and Whitney McNeil had been a good friend when Andy Jackson needed friends. He owed Whit. He recalled their conversation a month earlier in this same study.

"I haven't asked you for anything," Whitney had said. "I wouldn't ask you now if my nephew, Flann, wasn't qualified for this gunrunning investigation. His problem is a woman, an adventuress who Flann thinks is a lily-white maid. If I try to influence him against her he won't listen. And he'll hate me after he's married to her and discovers I was right. I can't think of any other way to save him from a foolish mistake except to have him sent off where she can't go. And quick, before she manages to marry him." He had shaken his head. "If she loved the boy, it'd be different. She doesn't."

Jackson had nodded. The wrong woman could play hell with a man's life.

"It'll be out of sight, out of mind with her," Whitney McNeil had continued. "I'm certain of that."

Jackson put down his pipe and looked again at Flann O'Phelan. "About the Indians, I've always thought my predecessor put it well," he said. "Perhaps, Mr. O'Phelan, you remember President Adams' choice of words. 'What is the right of a huntsman to the forest of a thousand miles over which he has accidentally ranged in quest of prey? Shall the fields and valleys, which a beneficent God has formed to teem with the life of innumerable multitudes, be condemned to everlasting barrenness?' "

"No, sir, I've never heard that speech."

"Mr. Adams saw clearly that the Indian must give way as our nation grows." Jackson's brows drew together in a formidable frown. "For the United States is a nation and will remain one in spite of those disgruntled South Carolinians who threaten her unity."

"Yes, sir."

The President picked up the papers again. "You're to report to Charles Madden, chief clerk in the Office of Indian Affairs, for complete instructions in the matter of the Lake Superior Chippewa tribes." He glanced at Flann.

"I talked briefly with Mr. Madden last week. I'll go again to his office immediately," Flann said.

"Those damn Canadian rebels." Jackson's vehemence started a coughing spell which left him gray-faced as he went on. "Stirring up trouble in New York and now trying the same tactics among the Chippewas. You're to see that it's stopped. Do you understand?"

"I'll do my best, sir."

"If I didn't think you would, I wouldn't send you. There's also the matter of metals in that north country you're headed for. Copper. We know there's copper. But I hear rumors lately of silver, and that's more interesting. You keep your eyes peeled for silver sources along Lake Superior and you report back here in the fall to. . . ." He paused. "To my successor, President Van Buren. I'll brief him on your mission before he takes over this coming March."

"As for the Indian herbs you might learn of, that's your own business and can be eliminated from your official report." Jackson coughed again. "Though I might as well be swallowing what the Indians concoct for all the good any medicine does me these days."

"I appreciate the appointment, sir, and I'll do everything possible to carry it out to your satisfaction."

The President pulled a card from among the papers and wrote his name at the bottom. "Give this to Mr. Madden."

Flann took the card, rose, checked his impulse to salute, and bowed slightly. "It's been a great honor to meet you, sir."

Jackson rose slowly and held to the back of the chair. "I'd like to be there when you meet your first Indian. Well, good-bye, Mr. O'Phelan. And good luck to you."

Flann smiled. "Good-bye, sir." He walked from the room, along the hall and down the stairs to the first floor. A servant returned his hat and let him out. He stood for a moment on the steps of the White House, looking between the trees. A pale January sun flickered on the Potomac River. A brisk, chilly breeze ruffled his hair. He restrained himself from giving a whoop of joy.

The wilderness. Indians. A chance to learn how they treated sickness in addition to the important part of the mission, namely, preventing Canadian rebels from arming the Chippewas.

If father were alive, he'd be proud of me, Flann thought. Perhaps he'd even forgive me for leaving the military.

Andrew Jackson eased himself back into his leather chair and tapped the dottle from his pipe onto a bronze tray.

When I was his age I was fighting on the Tennessee frontier, he thought. Hell, I was only thirteen when I first came up against the British in '80. God grant those Canadian rebels don't involve us in another war with them. Young O'Phelan will do all right. That red hair has to mean there's something solid there. After all, I was once a redhead myself, wasn't I?

As far as the Indians go, he'll learn.

Chapter 2

The forest of white pine and hardwoods swept down the flanks of the Porcupine Mountains, halting where the waves of Lake Superior, the great Kitchigami, washed the sand and pebble beach. At the mouth of Iron River the pines fell back and the dark green leaves of white birch trembled in the lake breeze. It was July, the Raspberry Moon, and the day was pleasantly warm.

Birch-bark wigwams were fitted among the birch trees. The smoke of cooking fires drifted to the southeast.

Birch Leaf sat cross-legged on the work shelf outside her mother's wigwam, bone needle slack in her fingers, an incomplete moccasin forgotten, as she stared at the long, domed *midewigan*, three times the size of an ordinary wigwam. The *mide*, those with medicine power, had put new birch bark on their lodge this spring. Only the uncovered west end showed its framework of saplings.

Birch Leaf knew a hide-covered *jizikun*, taking

the shape of a tepee, had been built inside the west end of the midewigan. She shivered in eager and frightened anticipation of the mide ceremonies to come, when Crouching Fox, the shaman, would shut himself inside the jizikun.

She had chosen well when she picked this day to begin her spirit quest. Surely the spirits summoned by the mide today would linger afterwards to enter into her *apawa*, her vision dream. Birch Leaf heard her mother come out of the wigwam and pushed the needle into the moccasin in her lap.

Soft Willow paused beside her. "I dreamed you'd have a true vision this time," she said.

Birch Leaf smiled. Her mother's dream was a good omen. As she watched Soft Willow walk toward the midewigan, dogs began to bark, running from the wigwams down to the beach. Children raced after the dogs. Birch Leaf slid off the shelf and followed them. When she passed the chief's wigwam, Snowberry came out and joined her.

"Are you still going into the woods tonight?" Snowberry asked.

"Yes."

"What is it now? Your fifth try or your sixth?"

I will not let her rile me, Birch Leaf told herself. Not today. "My fourth," she replied, aware that Snowberry knew exactly how many times she had fasted in the woods, hoping for a vision.

"I dreamed on my first night," Snowberry persisted, rearranging her dark braids so they fell over her breasts. She wore a new blue tunic with beads set in leaf and flower designs.

Birch Leaf glanced at Snowberry's gleaming dark eyes and round, brown face. The chief's daughter was the prettiest maiden in the Bear Clan. Too bad her attitude was not as pleasant as her appearance. Snowberry was Birch Leaf's own age. She was not really her friend.

When they reached the sand beach at the river mouth, Birch Leaf shaded her eyes against the shimmer of the summer sun on the lake. Seven canoes approached from the east. Kitchigami was ruffled by choppy waves made by the cool northwest breeze, and the men paddled hard. Almost the whole Meenagha Bear Clan village, except for the mide, gathered on the sand to welcome their brothers of the Loon Clan from Ontonagon.

Birch Leaf, watching to learn who of the Ontonagon braves had come, noticed Snowberry had edged in front of her. Birch Leaf shifted so that if Black Rock wished to see her instead of Snowberry, he'd be able to.

Black Rock was in the first canoe to reach the river mouth. Birch Leaf decided he was the tallest and strongest and bravest. She felt her heart beat faster when Black Rock displayed easy grace as he moored the canoe. The children laughed and jabbered. They crowded about the visitors. However, it would have been immodest for her to come forward or speak because she wasn't a child, even though she had not managed to dream.

Black Rock smiled at both women as he passed by with the other Ontonagon braves, but Birch Leaf thought his eyes rested longest on her. Evidently Snowberry had not noticed because she chattered quite cheerfully as they walked back to the village.

"Did you hear about Wood Lily?" Snowberry asked. "That Moosefoot, her husband, threw the moccasins she made for him from the wigwam, yelling they were fit only for a Sioux to wear."

"Wood Lily was always clumsy with her needle," Birch Leaf allowed. "But she works hard and she's agreeable. I don't think her husband has much complaint. If he's such a great warrior, where are his scalps? And their wigwam doesn't have a copper kettle, so that means Moosefoot's no great trapper either, if he can't take enough furs for even one kettle."

In the clearing beside the midewigan, Snowberry's father, Copper Sky, the chief, greeted Buoy, the Ontonagon chief, and they sat on mats to smoke. No mide was in sight. Birch Leaf knew this meant the mide had gone to the sweat lodge to purify themselves for the ceremony to come. Because Soft Willow was a mide, there was a separate small sweat lodge for her use as the spirits would have been offended if she went in with the men.

Rarely did a woman qualify to join the Midewiwin Society and never until she had stopped having a blood course each moon. Everyone knew the moon blood of women was unlucky and dangerous. Even though there were no men in their wigwam, Birch Leaf went to the special tepee in the woods each moon at her blood time and she was careful not to touch Soft Willow's *wayan* at any time. The woman's mide bag was inviolate.

Crouching Fox was the chief mide, the shaman of the Bear Clan, and Birch Leaf was somewhat afraid of him, as was everyone else. He possessed tremendous powers to be able to call spirits into the jizikun. Who knew when a shaman's power might be turned against you?

The rich meat smells from the cooking kettles

11

made Birch Leaf's mouth water, but she would have to
miss the feasting. She hadn't eaten or had anything to
drink since sunup, and she would fast until she had her
dream. Perhaps this time the spirits wouldn't reject her,
for the omens were good. Wasn't she Anishinabe, one
of the People, even if her eyes were leaf green and her
skin paler than any other of the People.

I'll search until I find the mountain ash with red
berries and make my dream nest in it, she vowed.
Surely the spirits will come to a sacred tree.

"What if you fail again?" Snowberry spoke from
behind her.

Birch Leaf controlled her surprise. "What happens doesn't concern you," she sniffed coolly. It would,
however. How much longer would Black Rock wait to
take a wife?

Soft Willow had warned often that the young
woman could not marry until she had her dream.
Kitchi Manito, the Great Spirit, might doom both Birch
Leaf and her husband to a life of misfortune.

Birch Leaf gasped when the moose-skin flap of
the sweat lodge shifted. Others in the waiting crowd of
villagers gasped also.

"*Na ge!*" Copper Sky exclaimed and the others
took up his cry. "Hail, hail!"

The three mide emerged from the sweat lodge.
Soft Willow came from hers and joined the men.
Crouching Fox advanced until he stood before the east
door of the midewigan. His face was painted red with a
green line drawn from his left temple across his nose and
down his right cheek. Two dark lines were painted upward from his eyes, signifying he could foretell the future. The lines from his ears meant he knew what was
happening far away. He wore a white buckskin

12

auzeum. This special breechcloth was embroidered with porcupine quills and decorated with silver and copper ornaments. His arms and hands had two red lines painted on them to show his touch was lethal. The *megis* at his throat, the white seashell from the great ocean called Atlantic, indicated great power. Birch Leaf caught her breath once more as he turned and looked at the gathering. He extended his hands and began to sing:

> From the daylight land
> From the east
> From the sun's home
> From the daylight land
> I walk.

Beside him the mide pole planted in front of the midewigan rose into the air, twice as tall as the shaman. As Crouching Fox continued to chant, Birch Leaf thought for a moment that the eyes of the carved and painted owl atop the post turned to look at him.

> I walk like a white bear,
> Like my colleague, the Bear
> My colleague, the White Bear
> Like him
> I walk from the daylight land.

The other three mide, Soft Willow among them, responded, "*We! Ho, ho, ho!*"

Crouching Fox turned his back to the crowd, still chanting. Then he advanced toward the midewigan. The three mide followed, chanting "Na, na!" as they followed him inside.

The crowd surged toward the uncovered west end of the midewigan where the small moose-hide jizikun showed between the bent poles. From here they could see into the midewigan.

Crouching Fox now held a mide drum, which he tapped gently with a padded stick as he walked toward the jizikun within the lodge.

Birch Leaf knew what the shaman would ask the Great Turtle when that special spirit came to him. For all the year, ever since Boiling Moon when they made maple sugar, the People had talked of The Move. No one could understand why the white men wanted them to move, but everyone agreed the Sioux would certainly try to kill them all if they moved west into Sioux country. Besides, this was their home, the woods along Kitchigami, their name for the great lake. Crouching Fox intended to ask the Great Turtle what they must do to prevent such a move.

The shaman dropped to his knees and crawled under the moose hides and disappeared from sight into the jizikun. At first there was silence while the other three mide inside the midewigan kindled four small fires around the outside of the jizikun, then the sound of rapid drumbeats came from beneath the moose skins.

The drumming stopped and the jizikun began to shake violently. Birch Leaf gasped as animals howled and voices screamed from inside. Silence fell again.

A tiny voice cried out. Birch Leaf thrilled to the feeble tones. One of the mightiest spirits the shaman could evoke was the Great Turtle and that spirit had the weakest voice of all spirits. But Turtle spoke truth. He could not lie. She listened eagerly, even though she knew she wouldn't understand the spirit language. There came a roar as Thunderbird cut into Turtle's speech, drowning him out.

The jizikun began to shake again, so hard the moose skins flapped in the air. Thunderbird continued shouting until the harsh call of Owl sounded. Thunderbird quieted. Owl called once more and the deep grunt of Bear answered. The skins settled into place. Now no voices spoke.

Birch Leaf heard a feeble yipping, almost like that a newborn puppy would make, and she held her breath. Turtle was back.

But what was that other noise, that faint splashing? She realized it came from the lake, not the midewigan, and she glanced toward the water. Far offshore the white man's great wheeled vessel, the Walk-in-the-Water, its white paint gleaming in the sun, hurried past Meenagha on its way west toward La Pointe to the stores of the trader.

What a strange ship, much larger than even the voyageurs' big transport canoes. And so noisy! Braves could power a canoe so not a sound was heard, not even the drip of water from a paddle. Still she wondered. What would it be like to ride on that fast white boat? Would she feel she flew on the back of Thunderbird himself?

The Great Turtle Spirit was still speaking as the splash of the Walk-in-the-Water faded and was gone. Was he warning them they must move west? To leave their own land? Copper Sky had told them the Indian agent spoke of the move as maybe coming in a few moons' time. Birch Leaf knew that the agent, though white, had married a woman of the People. Would they move, too?

At last the tiny, shrill voice ceased. A few moments later, Crouching Fox crawled from under the moose skins, weak and trembling. The other mide helped him to stand and Soft Willow passed him a container of medicine to drink. The shaman was led out of the midewigan through the west door and brought to stand before Copper Sky. Everyone formed a circle around them.

"The message of my colleague, Turtle, is good," Crouching Fox reported in a tired voice that strengthened as he went on. "His counsel is wise, words we must heed. What we are to do is keep those who are not of us, not of the Anishinabe, from living in our villages and speaking in our councils. If we hear and obey, Turtle says we shall live and die along Kitchigami, that we shall never move from our land."

"*Hoy!*"

The cry came from the lake where a canoe stood off the mouth of Iron River. Dogs yelped and howled as the canoe approached. Birch Leaf saw that the man in the middle of the canoe wore a black robe. The other two were *metis*, half-French, half-Indian. She recognized one of them and she remembered the priest, the Black Robe who had been in the village last summer. This was the same man. Copper Sky had been courteous then. What would his manner be now? She turned back to Crouching Fox, but he was hidden from her view.

The Black Robe came up the path and greeted Copper Sky in the fashion of the French. "*B'zoi.*" He spoke the language of the People imperfectly but she could understand what he said. Standing next to Copper Sky, the Black Robe looked as small as a child.

"Hail Copper Sky, chief of the Meenagha Chippewa," the Black Robe said.

Chippewa. One of the names the whites used for them, taken from what other tribes called them. It sounded like it might be the word for roasting until

16

puckered. Sometimes they said Ojibway, the word for those who draw pictures. Not once did the whites ever use Anishinabe, which is what they called themselves.

"You may speak, Black Robe," Copper Sky invited.

Birch Leaf saw the priest wore the silver ornament she remembered hanging about his neck, that of two sticks crossed. His eyes were as blue as the lake water. She looked quickly away lest he see her own eyes and ask Copper Sky again, as he had the summer before, about her. She was not different as he had observed then. She was one of the People.

Birch Leaf turned and hastened toward her mother's lodge. Before the sun hid in its western home, she had to find the right place in the woods to build her tree nest. The Black Robe and the two metis were no concern of hers. She heard a step behind her.

"Birch Leaf," Black Rock called, catching up. "Why the hurry?"

She looked at him, then down at her beaded moccasins. "I make my vision quest."

"I shall miss you at the feast. And afterward."

Her heart thudded in her chest as she smiled up at him. Black Rock had intended to court her tonight, away from the fires of the village, in the pine shadows. He had as much as said so, if she could have evaded Soft Willow's vigilance, that is. Soft Willow thought maidens should stay maidens until they married.

"I think I shall probably have my dream this time," Birch Leaf said.

"I'll wait in the village for you," Black Rock told her. He touched her hand and left.

Birch Leaf went to the doorway of Soft Willow's wigwam. Before she could lift the skin to enter, a man

17

stepped around from behind the lodge, one of the metis. She had seen him in the village before. He wore a red scarf about his neck and white man's clothes except for his moccasins.

"You know me, eh, Birch Leaf?" he said in Chippewa. "Henri Fontenac."

He had called her by name. She became uneasy, displeased that he knew her name.

He reached out and grasped her arm. "You want to go with me, be my woman?"

She pulled back from him. "No! I'd never do such a thing. Go away." She was afraid to enter the lodge lest he follow her in. Metis were untrustworthy, like whites.

"I have watched you a long time," Henri leered. "I give you many goods, beads, all you want if you come with me."

"No."

He grinned at her. "You think about what I say, eh? Maybe you change your mind."

Birch Leaf looked beyond him, seeing her mother approach.

"What do you want here?" Soft Willow's voice was as hard and cold as winter ice.

Henri whirled around to stare at Soft Willow. She was still in her mide paint, carrying the wayan, her mide bag made from the skin of a mink with head, tail and feet intact.

"Talking to Birch Leaf, that's all. A very pretty girl." Birch Leaf could see the tension in Henri's back.

Soft Willow's fingers touched the mink bag. "She's my daughter and I tell you now to leave. Don't bother her again."

"No offense meant," Henri apologized, easing

away sideways. He turned and walked away, disappearing from view.

Soft Willow watched him go. "Better to be courted by a snake," she observed, going into the wigwam.

Birch Leaf stayed outside, trying to recapture the excitement of Black Rock's words, but remembering instead the revulsion she'd felt when Henri Fontenac touched her.

Chapter 3

The northwest wind ruffled Flann O'Phelan's red hair as he stood forward on the side-wheeler looking out over the cold blue water of Lake Superior. Gulls circled in the air, screeching plaintively. There were no other boats in sight, neither the planked bateaux of the American Fur Company nor Indian birch-bark canoes. He didn't expect to see another ship. The vessel carrying him, the *John Jacob Astor*, was the only vessel of her kind sailing Lake Superior.

There was beauty in the rugged, desolate country, but the sight of rock cliffs and pine forests grew monotonous. Since the ship had come around the Keeweenaw Peninsula there had been no sign of habitation, Indian or otherwise.

The *Astor*'s Captain Tobias Stannard hailed Flann. "We should be able to set you at the mouth of the Ontonagon River by early afternoon."

"That's good news. I'll be glad to see a settlement."

Captain Stannard smiled. "Pretty lonesome in this

neck of the woods. Some Indians, some French. Most of the French are part Indian by now, they call them metis. Half-breed, it means."

Flann nodded.

"Then there's the fur traders, they're white. And that Catholic priest, Father Baraga, he comes from someplace in the old country. But if you travel in the woods you can go weeks and months without ever seeing a human being, not even an Indian."

"Do you think this . . ." Flann waved a hand toward the shore where woods sloped to the water ". . . will be settled someday?"

"Well, now. Not for farming. I can tell you that. But there's copper up here. You see Indians wearing ornaments of copper. It might be the copper could be mined if anyone figures a way to ship it out of here once it's dug up. You saw St. Mary's Falls there at The Soo where Lake Superior water drops down into Lake Huron. No ship can navigate those falls."

"I saw Indian canoes shoot the rapids at Sault Ste. Marie," Flann offered.

"Yes, and they get killed sometimes, too. You can't get anything bigger than a canoe down the rapids. But water navigation isn't the only problem to mining copper up here. There were some Englishmen tried mining copper on the Keeweenaw back in 1780 or thereabouts. First their shaft caved in and then they got caught by ice in the lake and had to spend the winter on Keeweenaw. Damn near killed all of them and they got out fast the next spring and never came back. Winter's something fierce around here."

"I can imagine."

Captain Stannard glanced at him. "No, I don't think you can. You've only been up here in good weather. The lake forms an ice crust and, thick as it may be, storms break the crust and toss slabs of ice onto the shores. They pile up like logs. There's no navigation possible before May or after October."

Flann raised his eyebrows. He'd be out of the region before the coming winter, so he had never known if it really was worse than he could imagine.

The captain pointed off starboard. "Isle Royale lies out there about seventy miles and she's full of copper. The fur company has a fishery on Isle Royale in the summer but no one's tried to mine the copper. The island's a forty-five mile long slab of rock covered with trees and tricky to approach by ship because of hidden reefs."

Flann remained near the bow after the captain returned to his duties. Lake Superior seemed almost like the Atlantic. Although the *Astor* sailed close to the south shore, the lake was so wide the north shore could not be seen. Flann imagined himself sailing on the ocean, except the wind carried no salt-water tang. It certainly was as cold as the Atlantic in July. Flann thought, I should have put on that jacket made of blanket wool I bought from the fur company at Mackinac.

In April, when he had disembarked from the steamer in Detroit, a flood of settlers had poured off the ship with him, hoping to find land in this new state of Michigan. The lower peninsula did have good farm land, the soil rich even to Flann's city eyes. The country was flat or gently rolling. The woods were mixed with meadows. Lilacs bloomed around some of the houses. But once he'd boarded the schooner and sailed north on Lake Huron toward the Straits of Mackinac, the wilder the countryside appeared. Soon he saw no white settlements. Pine forests crowded up to the shore of the lake. The April air felt more like January.

By the time Flann reached Mackinac Island he thought the upper peninsula would be a pine wilderness where no lilacs bloomed.

The Army fort on Mackinac Island attracted Flann with its whitewashed stone buildings and walls climbing the green hill. He also remembered the British had had little trouble recapturing the fort from the Americans in 1812 since its builders had ignored a nearby hill higher than the one they selected as the site. It was easy enough to land at night and haul cannon up that higher hill under cover of darkness, then demand surrender at dawn.

British General Brock had done just that.

The rest of the island settlement was small and dominated by the great rambling building of the American Fur Company. Inside, the odors of any general store mixed with the pungency of undressed fur. Ramsey Crooks, the former factor here, now owned this Great Lakes department of the company, having bought it from Astor when he sold out in 1834.

Flann found Crooks' factor, Samuel Abbott, skeptical of anyone "botanizing" with the Chippewas, as he put it, but too polite to scoff openly.

"If Henry Rowe Schoolcraft says you're permitted to do it, why go right ahead," Abbott allowed. "I thought maybe you were just another easterner coming up to try to buy that copper boulder from the Ontonagon Chippewas."

Again, Flann observed that Mackinac Island was damned cold for April. Patches of snow still dotted the woods. The Indian agent, Schoolcraft, invited Flann to stay with his family, and Flann was grateful to find their quarters snug against the chill winds. The hospitality was warm, too.

"My wife, Jane," Schoolcraft said, his face alight with affection as he introduced the dark-haired attractive woman to Flann. She was dressed as any lady of fashion might be in Boston, but also wore leggings of black silk, ruffled at the ankles.

"My husband tells me you are to further your knowledge of Chippewa while you stay with us," she affirmed. "I'll be glad to help." Her eyes crinkled in silent laughter. "To begin, and from now on, I shall try to speak only in the language of the People with you. You'll learn quickly."

During the days Flann spent with the couple, Schoolcraft too spoke only Chippewa, fluently.

Under two masters, Flann's grasp of the language developed rapidly. Nonetheless, he frequently made errors, causing Jane to hoot with laughter.

"My father, John Johnston, was red haired," she told Flann when he'd mastered Chippewa well enough for conversation. "He was Irish, as you are, and he took me to visit Ireland and Europe when I was seventeen. Do you know the Duchess of Devonshire wanted to adopt me? Imagine. Ireland is a beautiful land. Though not more beautiful than here, my home."

"And your mother?" Flann inquired.

"Neengay became her name after she married and bore us. When she was a maiden and lived with her father, Waubojeeg, chief of all the Lake Chippewa, she had another name—Oshaguzcodayqua." Jane watched as Flann mentally translated the long name into English.

Neengay meant "Mother." Oshaguzcodayqua meant "Daughter of the Green Mountain."

24

"When you go to Sault Ste. Marie, The Soo we call it, you must meet her. She still lives there and she'll probably sell you some of her famous maple sugar, if I know mother."

Schoolcraft took Flann to his office, where he dealt daily with the Indians who lived on Mackinac. "My area overlaps Lawrence Taliaferro's," Schoolcraft said. "He's the Indian agent for the Chippewas in Wisconsin and the Minnesota Territory, as well as being the Sioux agent. I'm responsible for all the Lake Superior Chippewa clans, and since I'm closer to northern Wisconsin than he is, I keep track of clans that are officially in his district."

"Madden said I was to be guided by you," Flann told him, "not Taliaferro."

"The only band I'm completely certain of is the one at Keeweenaw Bay," Schoolcraft said. "They have no new guns and I doubt they'd listen to a Canadian rebel." He thought for a moment. "The Chippewas at The Soo and Mackinac are so close to 'me I'm sure they're not involved. There's a subagent at La Pointe now, Daniel Bushnell. He's keeping an eye out there. What you should do is stop first at Ontonagon. I've had previous trouble with their chief, Buoy. I thought I'd put the fear of God into him in 1831 about killing whites but I'm never certain. The Chippewas are traditionally warriors. While you're meeting Buoy and his shaman, Star-in-Cedar, you can keep your eye peeled for new guns."

"Just new ones?"

Schoolcraft nodded. "The fur factor at La Pointe, Dr. Borup, tells me he hasn't had a shipment of new guns yet this year. And Borup supplies these bands with their guns. After you 'botanize' a bit with Star-in-Cedar, go up the lake to the Meenagha village at Iron

River. Their chief is Copper Sky and their shaman, Crouching Fox. Copper Sky's getting old and keeps to himself. I've heard one of his braves was seen with a new gun.

"You can get acquainted there for a bit, then make a visit to Great Chief Buffalo at La Pointe. The reason for the hurry is, Buffalo's making a trip down the Mississippi this summer for treaty signing and I'd like you to talk to him before he goes."

"These are the only bands you think I should visit?" Flann asked.

"There's a Lynx Clan at Lac Vieux Desert you might see if you have time. I don't think they're involved, but you might learn a bit of Indian medicine there." Schoolcraft smiled.

"You don't seem particularly worried about the Canadian rebels infiltrating the Lake Chippewa."

"The only band I ever have real trouble with is a Pillager group between Sandy Lake and Leech Lake. That group is split from Flat Mouth's Pillager village at Leech Lake. Both Leech and Sandy Lakes are in the Minnesota Territory, so actually Taliaferro is their agent. At any rate, you won't be going there, which is good. I never trust the Pillagers. As for the other Chippewas, you're right, I don't think they'd help the Canadian whites fight one another for any amount of new guns. The Sioux, now, are another matter. The Chippewas will fight the Sioux any time. And that hostility is a continual headache for us."

"Do you want me to report back to you on what I find?" Flann inquired.

"First report to Bushnell at La Pointe. Then to me when you pass by on your way back east this fall. We're going to The Soo next week to open our summer home there and I'll put you aboard the *Astor* above the falls."

Abbott had already told Flann how every last plank of oak and the machinery for the *Astor* had been hauled up to Lake Superior so the side-wheeler could be built on those shores. The little ship could never leave Lake Superior because it could not navigate the rushing cascade of the tremendous falls that carried Lake Superior water down to Lake Huron.

Schoolcraft's parting words as he saw Flann off carried a warning about the Chippewas. "They're reserved and solitary. Don't presume or try to be too friendly at first. When they get to know you, they'll either accept you or they won't. If they do, then you'll see humor and feeling. If not. . . ." Schoolcraft shrugged.

Standing on the forward deck of the *Astor* now, Flann reviewed those words. He could easily see how a man living in this wilderness would have to draw in on himself to survive. He had until October, less than four months, to complete his mission. Then he'd be back in Boston with Lynette and they'd celebrate their postponed wedding. Lynette would be his then, all his. Flann had not liked the way she smiled at the lawyer who was trying to straighten out his father's estate, but that kind of thing would be over when she was his wife.

As for Schoolcraft, he'd been friendly. But Flann had the feeling the Indian agent thought the men in Washington were unduly agitated over the Canadian rebel rumors in the Lake Superior region and that whatever was going on, he, Schoolcraft, could handle it.

He's got me going in and out of those villages like

a whirlwind, Flann thought. How does that square with his advice to let them take time to know me?

Well, if there's nothing to the rumors, maybe I'll learn about Chippewa medicine, the trees and plants they use as cures. That would be a real bonus.

"Mr. O'Phelan," Captain Stannard called, coming to stand beside him again. "See those hills way up ahead, they look like blue smoke from here. That's what the Indians call *Kaug Wudju*, the Porcupine Mountains, on account of they look like a crouching porcupine with its tail going into the lake. And just along the shore there. See that smudge of smoke? That's where you're going, that's the Ontonagon."

The *Astor* crew put a boat over the side to bring Flann to shore. He saw that the river had formed a small bay at its mouth, and on the west side of the Ontonagon was a cluster of the hemispheric wigwams he'd seen at Mackinac and The Soo. Hills rose behind, but at the mouth the land was almost level. Stands of hardwood grew among the pines on both sides of the river.

When he got out of the boat he was greeted on the beach by a bunch of lean, barking dogs, a few naked toddlers and two old men. He kicked at the dogs and they backed away, snarling.

"I come in peace to speak to your chief," he said to the men, speaking carefully in Chippewa.

They stared at him, saying nothing. He stared back. Although old, they stood straight, almost as tall as he was. Both wore their hair in two braids. Finally the taller one spoke.

"The chief is not here."

Flann heard the splash of oars behind him. The boat was heading back to the *Astor*. He looked at the man who'd spoken, being careful not to smile. Schoolcraft had warned him that the Chippewas, like many other Indians, didn't trust smiling strangers.

"I would talk with Star-in-Cedar," he ventured.

"He's not here."

"Who, then, may I speak to?"

"We are here. You see us."

Schoolcraft had told him not to ask too many questions at first, but he had no choice.

"If I wait for the chief, how long will it be?"

"Maybe the next sun, maybe not."

"How about Star-in-Cedar?"

"Who can tell?" The old man shrugged. "Not this sun."

Flann looked along the bank toward the wigwams under the birches. Smoke rose from a fire between the lodges, but there was no sign of anyone except for the two old men and the children. He had an idea.

"Do the villagers feast with friends at Meenagha?" Flann asked.

"It is true," the old man answered reluctantly.

"I would go to Meenagha," Flann told him. The village was only fifteen miles west. He could reach it in no time with a canoe. "I'll pay for a canoe and a man to paddle," he added.

The old men looked at one another, then out at the lake before returning their gaze to Flann.

"Kitchigami is too rough now. Maybe next sun," the taller man said. The other grunted in affirmation.

"How about a canoe, then?" Flann said, trying not to appear impatient. "I'll pay well."

He'd handled a canoe before, paddling in the Charles River at home. He could certainly manage a few miles up the lake. Superior didn't look too rough, and the ship's boat hadn't had any trouble putting into

29

shore. Maybe these braves didn't want to admit their paddling days were over.

"You speak the language of the People," the spokesman said.

Flann decided to say nothing. A bit of mystery would not hurt. He folded his arms, waiting. One of the little boys came up and, with a show of mock daring, touched his pants leg. Flann looked down at him and smiled. He hoped it was all right to smile at children, if not adults. The child grinned at him.

"Water Flower has a canoe," the spokesman said. He pointed at the wigwams.

By the time Flann had met the old woman named Water Flower and negotiated with her to buy the canoe, he had used up all his patience. He handed each of the men a twist of tobacco for their help, pushed off into the Ontonagon River and, with quick strokes, was soon out into the lake.

The birch-bark canoe was lighter than planked Boston canoes. He had to kneel in the bottom, for there was no board to sit on. Water Flower had warned him to take off his boots or he would break a hole in the fragile craft. He was barefoot, his boots and socks on the bottom of the canoe with his two rifles and a pack of supplies.

All too quickly he discovered what the old men had meant. The lake was choppy and each wave rocked the canoe. Not only that, the waves constantly pushed him toward shore. He had to paddle hard to stay off the beach and keep going west at the same time. Far ahead on the lake, he saw the *Astor* sailing for La Pointe.

Flann was no longer chilled by the brisk wind. Sweat gathered on his forehead as he struggled to keep the canoe moving ahead smoothly. Though overheated, he found his toes were cold. He cursed. Water had begun to seep into the canoe bottom.

A damned leaky canoe. That was all he needed. He dug the paddle into the water viciously. That was a mistake. The canoe tipped. He fought to keep it upright as his rifles slid off the seat and landed with a thud on the bottom of the canoe.

He might find something in his pack to bail with, but he couldn't bail and keep the boat from swamping. And he couldn't keep afloat with water leaking into the bottom. He swore again and pointed the canoe toward shore.

When he'd beached it, he took out his possessions, then overturned the canoe to look at the bottom. There was a hole, near the bow, a small tear in the bark.

All right, O'Phelan, he muttered, we walk the rest of the way. He squeezed water from his socks and pulled them on. They were chill and clammy. His boots were wet, too. He wiped the rifles dry. He slung his pack onto his shoulders. At least I can't get lost, he thought as he started off. All I have to do is walk along the shore until I come to Iron River and there will be the Meenagha village. Meenagha. The word means "blueberry," and right now I could use a few blueberries. I hope this group is more hospitable than those old people at Ontonagon. I'm hungry.

I wonder if Water Flower knew the canoe wasn't seaworthy? I suppose the muzzle of one of the rifles could have made the hole. I should have thought to secure them. Ontonagon means, "I lost my bowl." Well, I lost more than that. I lost my whole damned canoe.

Flann realized the first river he came to could not be the right one since he had not been walking long enough. It was too small, besides. It was a creek, really. He walked across its mouth, the water scarcely up

31

to the top of his boots. But he found that the fifteen-mile stretch between Ontonagon and Meenagha had a tiresome number of streams and rivers to cross. None was as simple as the first to ford.

Finally he stopped at the widest river mouth he had come to yet. He looked across, hoping to spot wigwams, but saw only pines growing all the way down to the sand of the beach. Along the beach there was only bleached driftwood. Not Iron River yet. He watched the swift flow of water pouring into Lake Superior. It was clear water, but deep amber in color. It looked deep. He didn't dare get into deep water flowing this fast or he would risk losing his rifles and pack. Worse luck, there were no fallen logs nearby to use as a bridge. As for stones, Michigan rivers did not seem to have convenient boulders in them to use for bridges. There was nothing for him to do but hike upstream and find a safe place to cross.

Flann pushed his way through a thicket of birch saplings and came into the gloom of the forest of white pines. Overhead the great trees rose well over a hundred feet, the dark gray trunks free of branches two-thirds of the way up, the green branches then spreading out to form a canopy to shut out the sun. Dry brown needles crackled under his boots with each step he took. The aromatic scent of pine filled his nostrils. It was quieter and warmer among the trees. Small, golden bits of sunlight trickled in from above and the soughing of the wind through the needles above him was a soft counterpoint sound to the waves washing onto the shore.

Flann walked among the trees easily, for the shade prevented smaller shrubs or saplings from growing and there was little underbrush. He climbed a rise. A spot of lavender caught his eye and he stopped to examine the flower. It was a single plant, with one bloom, a delicate shade of pink varying into lavender. He knew it was a variety of orchid commonly called Lady's Slipper.

Orchids were the last flowers he had expected to find in this northern wilderness. Flann bent over and plucked the flower, inserting it into the flap of his pack. A few moments later he came to a clearing and saw below him a crisscross of fallen trees. A tangle of bushes blocked his way down the hill that led to the river, but he plunged into the growth, hoping the fallen logs would provide him with bridges.

The bank was muddy. He slid down the last few feet, stumbling and falling to his knees as he broke free of the brush.

A loud, grunting snort raised the hair on his nape. He readied one of his rifles, as he came erect.

"Lord," he gasped. He found himself face to face with a black bear. Worse, he could see her cub behind her, chewing at a fish the mother bear must have flipped out of the river.

She roared angrily and rose on her hind legs. He tried to get the rifle into firing position. The bear dropped to all fours again and charged straight at him.

He pulled the trigger.

The gun didn't fire.

Chapter 4

Birch Leaf put on deerskin leggings, tying them around her legs just under her knees. She changed her blue cloth dress for a buckskin garment that came to her calves. Soft Willow spoke as Birch Leaf lifted the skin flap of the wigwam.

"The spirits have told me you'll dream. Dream well, my daughter."

Birch Leaf smiled at her, then left the wigwam, carrying no food or water. Her stomach cramped as she smelled the stew in the steaming kettles, but she ignored her hunger pangs and strode from the village into the pines. She walked some distance upstream along Iron River until she came to the place where a dead pine bridged the stream from one bank to the other.

She had seen a mountain ash, the red berry tree. It was big enough for a dream nest along a small river to the east. She crossed the Iron River and headed in that direction. All the omens were good.

Henri Fontenac, waiting by the canoe for Louis Gaudin and *Pere* Baraga, saw that he had a little time before the good Father was ready to depart. The priest was no longer talking to Copper Sky. Henri had seen the chief go into his wigwam. *Pere* Baraga wasn't in sight and Henri suspected he had found an old squaw somewhere willing to listen to him for the attention he paid her.

The priest was so innocent and trusting that he never seemed to realize the Chippewas were full of heathen superstition, and they would never make decent Christians. Henri shrugged. That was the good Father's business, not his. He had seen Crouching Fox with his mide bag and knew there must have been a ceremony. Henri spat. Damn that mide gibberish; he didn't like it one sou's worth. Those mide could change their shape and become bears, wolves, owls or anything. The devil's business, like the *loup-garou*, the werewolf in the old country.

Henri left the canoe and approached Copper Sky's wigwam. When he stood before the open skin flap, he hailed the chief by name, speaking Chippewa.

"Enter," Copper Sky said. He sat on his mat at the far side of the wigwam. His young daughter, Snowberry, stood by and offered him food. He waved her away and told her to leave the wigwam.

Henri studied her as she passed. She was a good-looking squaw with nice big breasts. But she was as far from Birch Leaf in beauty as a squirrelskin is from a sable.

When the two men were alone in the wigwam, Copper Sky stared at Henri in silence.

"I come to talk to you about a maiden," Henri said. "I want her. I'll give extra guns, just for you. Four rifles."

Copper Sky blinked. "Which maiden?"

"Birch Leaf."

"Birch Leaf," the chief echoed. He looked past Henri, through the open flap.

"She's not married," Henri said finally, impatient with waiting. He knew Indians were deliberate, but he often grew tired of playing the waiting game. Besides, *Pere* Baraga might be ready to leave at any moment. Not that the priest would scold him, but he didn't want Father or Louis to know of his movements or plans.

"She's not married," Copper Sky agreed. "But I cannot interfere in her life, married or not. It is dangerous to meddle with the daughter of a mide."

"What do you mean, mide? Birch Leaf has no father."

"Soft Willow is a mide. Her mother."

Henri swore. A woman mide. He didn't know squaws could be mide. He'd never heard of one before. Soft Willow was the squaw he had seen with the mink skin. He'd known it was a mide bag but he hadn't realized she herself was the mide. By damn, he wasn't going to be stopped by any squaw. . . .

Outside the wigwam, Snowberry smiled to herself as she listened to the conversation between Henri and her father. Let this metis take Birch Leaf away beyond the lake to the land where he had come from so many moons before. She liked the idea. If she could think of a way to help Henri, she would tell him. Snowberry straightened and moved from the clump of sumac.

A hand fell on her shoulder, and she gasped in

surprise. The gasp became a whimper of fear when she saw the hand belonged to Crouching Fox.

"A dutiful daughter doesn't listen to conversations behind her father's back," Crouching Fox said mildly. Still, he scowled at her as he spoke.

"I didn't mean. . . ."

"Don't lie and make it worse. Get away from here before I begin to think you might look better as a chipmunk."

Snowberry fled from Crouching Fox, running toward the lake without looking back. Crouching Fox watched until he was certain she was gone, then slipped into the clump of sumac and hid.

Inside the wigwam, Henri shook his head. "I have no more to say this time," he told Copper Sky. "We'll talk again about the rifles."

"It may be so," Copper Sky agreed.

Henri came out into the sunlight and noticed the shadows were growing long. He saw Louis and *Pere* Baraga on the path ahead of him and hurried toward them. The priest intended to go up the river toward Lac Vieux Desert to talk to the Indians there. If they made good time they might camp at Lake Gogebic tonight, fine fishing there.

By damn, Henri thought, he'd have that Birch Leaf sooner or later.

Crouching Fox came around the chief's wigwam but went on toward his own dwelling, disturbed. Was Copper Sky growing too old to remain as chief? Always before, Crouching Fox had been consulted. Now the chief schemed privately with a metis. Why?

The shaman stopped to watch the Black Robe and his paddlers move upriver, standing just out of their sight as they went past the village. How powerful was the Black Robe's god? The whites had plenty of rifles and food, it was true, but for each white man he had met that could be trusted, he had met two that lied and cheated. A white man's god could not be good for the People, no matter what the Black Robe said.

In the woods, Birch Leaf approached the mountain ash in which she intended to sleep that night. Yes, she thought, the branches would hold the dream nest. She found a cedar with low branches growing nearby and, bowing her head, she spoke to the tree.

"Grandmother Cedar, I need your green boughs. I must cut them with my knife. I do not wish to harm you. I thank you for your kindness in giving me your leaves and wood."

When Birch Leaf had cut an armful of cedar branches she climbed high into the ash tree and arranged them to form a bed in a bend formed by two branches and the trunk. The cedar branches became a fragrant, springy cushion. The sun was low in the afternoon sky; dusk would fall shortly.

Birch Leaf bounced on her cedar bed and glanced about.

A gray squirrel peered around the trunk of a pine, chattering, telling her he knew she was there. Below, across Loon River, a mother bear moved down a clay bank to the edge of the water and began to fish for trout. Her hungry cub watched intently.

Birch Leaf could hear something crash through the forest across the river, careless of the noise it made. More than once the she-bear lifted her snout to sniff the air, then went back to her fishing. Her paw raked water and a fat rainbow trout flopped onto the bank, slapped neatly from the river. The cub pounced on the fish. Still, Birch Leaf listened.

Whatever creature was making the noise burst through the bushes at the top of the rise on the opposite bank and slid down the slope, almost colliding with the bear. Birch Leaf saw it was a man with a rifle. Her eyes widened. She tensed. A white man! Was he crazy?

Birch Leaf heard the bear snort a warning. She hastily climbed down the trunk of the ash, expecting momentarily to hear the crack of the man's rifle. But no shot came. The man yelled as the bear roared in rage. Birch Leaf ran onto the log crossing the river.

She saw the man lunge sideways, saw the bear's paw swipe at him, saw blood. Birch Leaf leaped from the log bridging the river and ran toward the cub.

"Forgive me, Great Bear," she breathed as she jabbed her knife into the cub's haunch far enough to make it squeal with pain.

The mother bear wheeled about in answer to her cub's cry. Birch Leaf called, "Run! Get away!"

Before the bear charged, Birch Leaf raced back across the river and climbed into her tree, hoping the cub would distract the bear so it would not come climbing up after her. She heard a splash. Snorting with anger, the bear charged across the log and reared up, clawing the ash, trying to reach her. The cub stayed on the other bank, crying and whimpering.

The bear looked back at her cub, then up at Birch Leaf, then back at the cub. Finally the bear dropped to all fours and returned to minister to the hurt cub.

Birch Leaf saw no sign of the man. His hair had been like fire. She had never seen a white man like him, nor so foolish a white man, to come crashing through the woods so noisily, not knowing what lay ahead of him. He had been injured—she had seen blood.

When the bear found the cub was all right, she nosed it ahead of her and pushed it up the bank. Mother and cub disappeared into the brush. Birch Leaf waited a few minutes, then climbed down cautiously. She crossed on the log once more to the opposite bank and looked for sign of where the man had gone, although she thought the splash she had heard was him diving into the river. He had left a pack and a rifle behind. When she picked up the pack, a Lady's Slipper fell out. Birch Leaf touched the flower. Didn't he know that the plant gave up its spirit and died when its flower was picked?

She hoisted the pack onto her back and carried the rifle as she looked for him. He had run downstream. Here were broken twigs and a splash of blood on a stone. There was the gouge in the muddy bank where he had gone into the water. Birch Leaf went back to the log bridge, recrossed and made her way along the bank. Here he had pulled himself out and crawled along the bank.

Birch Leaf halted, staring at a clump of sumac. He was there. She hesitated. She could call to him, but few white men spoke the People's language. He had run when she told him to, but anyone with sense would have done so. His running didn't mean he had understood her words. Still, he *was* hurt. She must do something.

"*Wabishkize*," she said tentatively. "White man, do you need help?"

"I can't stop the bleeding." His voice came from the stand of sumac. He spoke her language better than most of the metis. She was surprised.

Birch Leaf hesitated. Then she walked up to the

bushes, parted them and looked down at the man. Blood flooded his face and matted his hair. The bear's claws had caught him across the side of his head. She could not tell how severe his wounds were until she cleaned away the blood.

Birch Leaf ran to the nearest birch, asking the tree's spirit for forgiveness as she cut off a strip of bark to fashion into a crude water holder. She brought river water to the man and poured it over his head. He gasped, but she paid no attention, concentrating on cleansing the claw marks. She laid wet sumac leaves over the four raw but shallow wounds.

"I put leaves on your head," she told him, "but I don't have the right medicines here to help more. I'll have to bring you to Soft Willow, my mother. Can you walk?"

"I think so," he grunted. "Is that damn bear gone?"

"She left with her cub."

Birch Leaf helped him to his feet.

"My rifle . . . I threw it across before I dived in," he said. "And there's another gun with my pack."

"I have your pack," she answered. "And one rifle. We'll find the other. Come."

He leaned on her at first, but after a bit he was able to walk unassisted. She carried the pack and, after they had recovered the second gun, both rifles.

"My name is Flann," he told her.

"Flann," she repeated, the word strange to her ears.

"To my father's people, the word means 'red'," he explained.

"Your hair is red."

"Bloody red at the moment."

She noted that he'd given her the gift of his name

41

and that he had known not to ask hers. She decided to tell him. "I'm called Birch Leaf."

"Your eyes are green. Is that why?"

"Yes."

"I was headed for the Meenagha village when I ran into the bear."

It was not her place to tell him how foolish he had been. "We'll come to the village soon," she said.

Blood trickled from under the wet sumac leaves, and he tried to wipe it away with his hand. Dogs began to bark and, when they came running, she shooed them off. Children stared at Flann as she led him between the wigwams. Men and women stopped their work to look.

"Mother," Birch Leaf called as they neared her wigwam.

Soft Willow looked out, saw Birch Leaf and Flann and hurried to them.

"A bear clawed him," Birch Leaf told her. "Will you bring him into your wigwam and treat him?"

Soft Willow lifted the sumac leaves and looked at the wounds. "Bring him inside. I'll care for him."

When they were in the wigwam, Soft Willow looked at her daughter. "Your dream?" she asked.

"I'll go back now. There's time. I couldn't leave him in the woods." Flann was stretched out on a mat. Birch Leaf dropped the rifles and pack onto the floor of the wigwam next to him. "These are his. His name is Flann."

"Be sure to wash all traces of his blood from you before you climb into your nest," Soft Willow cautioned. "And hurry. It grows dark."

Birch Leaf ran from the wigwams into the clustered trees. The long blue twilight lay over the lake, but under the pines it was gloomy with dusk. She hurried across Iron River. When she came to Loon River she washed herself as well as she could without undressing. By the time she climbed into the ash, the stars flickered above her.

She tried to compose herself. Sleep was not necessary for a sacred dream but she had to free *inaindum*, her mind, so *otchichaug*, her soul, could make the journey from her body.

The face of Flann appeared to block the way. His eyes weren't like the Black Robe's, the blue of Kitchigami. They were blue though, the smoky blue of Kaug Wudju, the Porcupine Mountains. She had seen other white men, not just the metis, but Flann was stranger in appearance than any she had seen. Who would imagine hair could be the color of fire?

His wounds would heal, she knew, and she was happy he hadn't shot the bear. Bear was her totem, the spirit brother of her clan. One was never killed without the proper ritual and then only if the need was great.

What was this Flann doing here among the People, she thought? Why was he heading for her village?

Birch Leaf shook herself as if to make all thoughts of Flann fall from her like drops of water. She mustn't let him intrude. She looked up through the branches at the night sky. Remember Namid, the star dancer, she told herself, the foolish one who thought he could whirl among the stars. He fell to earth, but at least he dared the impossible. You'll have your vision tonight, Soft Willow dreamed it so. Like Namid, you can reach for what is beyond you and succeed for the length of the sacred dream.

Birch Leaf heard the night sounds of the woods, the soft hunting call of *kookookuhu,* the owl, *wawaushkashe*, the deer, picking his way through the bushes to the river to drink, the death cry of *wahboos*, the rabbit, as one of the night hunters caught him. The damp smell of the forest penetrated the scent of the cedar boughs that made her nest. Her eyelids drooped.

And into her darkness came a small glow, a rim of light to the east, the door of the sun. Birch Leaf stared at the yellow flare of light. It was not the sun but a bear, walking on his back legs as a man did, coming closer. It was not the Great White Bear, nor the black bear of her totem, but a spirit bear who glowed the red gold of copper. He descended from the sky on a path of flame. Birch Leaf saw he was a bear and yet a man. Fire surrounded him; he was made of fire.

Birch Leaf gazed in awe as the man-bear approached her. He stopped barely a hand's breadth away and she felt the burning heat of his fire. She feared him but willed herself not to shrink away. He thrust out a flaming hand, almost touching her.

What did he offer? She was afraid to take such a fiery gift. Birch Leaf tried to put her hand out to touch his but could not force herself. While she stared at him in desire and terror, a small flame detached itself from his hand and floated toward her, dancing in the air.

Transfixed, Birch Leaf watched the flame come closer and closer until it touched her breast. A sweet, piercing pain shot through her as the bear flame entered her body and penetrated her heart.

The fire about the man-bear flickered out and disappeared.

All was darkness.

Chapter 5

Birch Leaf woke to the squawks of a blue jay perched
in a pine, complaining about her presence in the mountain ash. The sky was pale with dawn. She yawned and
stretched and then she remembered her dream.

It had truly been a vision.

Suddenly she wanted to shout aloud, to run
through the woods crying out that she had had her
vision. Birch Leaf smiled and hugged herself in excitement. She threw the cedar boughs of her bed to the
ground and slid down from the tree. Then she took the
boughs and carried them to the river, throwing them in
one at a time and watching them bob downstream.

She sought a birch. She apologized as she cut off
a section of bark. With her knife she cut a picture of
the man-bear whose flame had entered her heart. She
hid the bark in the wigwam, for no one else could
know exactly what had happened to her in her dream
vision. She knew she must struggle to understand what
was meant by her vision and live her life as her spirit
bear wanted her to.

45

Birch Leaf hurried toward the village. A chipmunk skittered from her path, tail flicking as he ran. A blue heron feeding in the back eddies of the river took flight with a great flapping of wings, ungainly until he was in the air. A porcupine waddled ahead of her and she skirted around him, for he would move for no one.

She could smell the smoke of cooking fires, but now she didn't feel hunger. There were fewer pines near the village. She saw a man waiting. It was Black Rock.

"I've had my dream," she exclaimed. "It was a wonderful one. I still feel it inside me."

"I'm glad," he said, taking her hand to prevent her from going on.

"No, I can't stop now. I want to tell my mother that I had my dream."

"I waited for you."

"I know." She smiled at him as they walked side by side into the village.

"When can we be together?"

"I have to understand my dream first to be sure what it means."

"That white man is in your mother's wigwam."

Birch Leaf drew her hand away. "Yes, he's there," she admitted. "Soft Willow tends his wounds."

Black Rock frowned. "You brought him into the village and into your wigwam?"

"Was I to leave him injured in the woods?"

"Turtle warned us about whites in our villages. And now we've had whites here ever since the warning. First the Black Robe and now this Red Hair."

"His name is Flann."

"I don't care what his name is. He must leave."

She stopped and stared at Black Rock. "You are not my husband. You have no right to order me. You

46

are not the chief of the village to give orders to Soft Willow. Flann will leave when his wounds heal. Turtle did not mean we should turn away a hurt and bleeding man."

"I don't like him being in your wigwam," Black Rock grumbled.

"Do you think I'm in danger?" she asked, her voice mocking him.

He scowled. "I don't trust white men."

Birch Leaf put her hand on his arm. "I feel this man brought me luck with my vision. He'll harm no one."

Black Rock grunted in disbelief.

Birch Leaf continued on to Soft Willow's wigwam, lifted the flap, and entered.

Black Rock scowled still. He stared at the wigwam, controlling his anger, when Crouching Fox spoke behind him.

"Birch Leaf is back," Crouching Fox observed.

"What about this white man in her mother's wigwam?" Black Rock asked.

"He says his name is Flann, that he's a doctor among the whites and he comes to learn how the People cure ills. He speaks our tongue."

"No white is to be trusted," Black Rock muttered.

"I think this Flann is likely to be after the copper boulder which lies above Ontonagon. He first went to your village to speak to Buoy, who was here at the time. All whites who come among us covet the copper rock."

"As long as he stays at Meenagha your village goes against Turtle's warning."

"Soft Willow has said she'll heal him and no good will come of crossing her," Crouching Fox warned. "I

47

saw the bear's claw marks. I say they are not serious. This Flann will be ready to travel by tomorrow's sun or the next day's. What you must do is wait here in Meenagha until Flann is well, then offer to show him the copper boulder. No doubt he'll be eager to go. This village will then be rid of him."

"I'll make sure he doesn't stay in Ontonagon. We won't put up with whites in our village."

"Walk softly," Crouching Fox warned. "You must not shed blood. No good comes of killing whites. The People suffer in the end. Heed me."

"I hear you."

"Then agree."

"I won't shed his blood," Black Rock promised.

By the morning of his second day in the wigwam, Flann was on his feet again, alert and curious. "Will I offend you if I ask questions about the plants you use for curing?" he asked Soft Willow.

"You may ask," she told him. "I'll answer only if I choose."

She voluntarily showed him a sharp bone instrument for pricking medicine into the skin, a wooden spatula for mixing powdered herbs, a sharp-pointed flint lancet, and a birch-bark measure for liquid medicine.

When he asked what a particular hollowed out tube of bone was used for, Soft Willow shook her head.

"This is mide," she told him. "Not of plants or the bark of trees, but of the spirit."

"The leaves your daughter put on my head to stop the bleeding, I call them sumac."

"Those leaves will stop bleeding but not heal," Soft Willow said, "It's best to keep pouring water into

48

a wound—nothing else—so that it heals from the inside."

Flann was amazed that the gouges along his scalp made by the claws of the bear showed no putrefaction.

"Why shouldn't they heal?" Soft Willow questioned. "I've cleansed your wounds often and asked that the Great Bear aid me, for you spared the bear who wounded you."

"My rifle misfired. I got it wet earlier."

He reviewed his journey so far and told her he had been lucky to survive. "Your daughter saved my life," he added.

Birch Leaf, who was outside on the work shelf, heard him and nodded. It was true.

"You don't have to treat me as an invalid any longer," Flann told Soft Willow. "I feel fine."

"You'd best stay with me one more sun," she advised. "Much blood has drained from you and your spirit needs time to put it back."

"All right. But I feel good enough to take a walk about the village."

She hesitated, then nodded. A walk was all right.

Flann left the wigwam, blinked in the sunlight and saw Birch Leaf on the platform. She was sewing beads on a moccasin. The leaf green of her eyes startled him though he vaguely remembered their color. He looked at her skin and observed she was light for an Indian. Who had her parents been? Had the father been a fur trader?

Birch Leaf smiled at him. He realized she was also a very pretty young woman.

"I must thank you again . . ." he began.

"Once is enough," she said. "You brought me luck, for I had my spirit dream when I went back to the woods. It was a very wonderful dream, too, worth waiting years to have."

Flann did not understand. Should he ask her about it? Schoolcraft had advised against asking too many questions. He found it hard not to now.

"Among my people we don't have spirit dreams," he ventured.

She stared at him. "Then how do your young men and women know what course to take?"

"Maybe I don't understand what you mean by dreams. Tell me."

"We fast and go into the woods and stay until we have a vision of the spirit who will guide us in our lives. It might be an animal, a plant, a rock, or even a cloud." Birch Leaf chose several beads and slid them onto her needle. "The time to go is just before becoming a man or a woman. I failed until this year."

"Then I'm happy if you believe I brought you luck. You certainly brought me good fortune." He realized he was staring at her. She was extraordinarily pretty, with lustrous dark hair braided and caught up in back, smooth suntanned skin and those vivid green eyes. Should he tell her so?

Birch Leaf blushed, looking away from him. Flann was captivated by her sudden shyness.

"Among my people," he said boldly, "your beauty would be praised."

Birch Leaf's lips tightened. Was she annoyed? Flann hastened to change the subject.

"Your mother's teaching me Chippewa medicine," he said. "That's what I've come among the Chippewa to learn. Already she's proved herself a good doctor."

"My mother is a mide," Birch Leaf said. "She knows much about healing, and the spirits come when she calls on them to help her."

Mide. That had to do with shamans. Midewiwin was the grand medicine society. So women could belong. Flann had many questions but was afraid of alienating her by firing one after another at her.

"Perhaps you could walk with me through the village," he suggested.

"No, I have this moccasin to finish beading and then other work to do." She tried not to speak too harshly, for Flann might not know that a maiden did not stroll about with a man unless they were courting. His suggestion shocked her. Did the women in his village walk with men so casually?

Flann nodded to her, turned and started toward the beach. Dogs ran up to sniff at him. Children stared curiously.

"Here comes the red-headed woodpecker," one boy said to his friend. Both laughed.

A brave stood by the canoes drawn up near the river mouth, arms folded. He scowled as Flann came toward him.

Flann studied the man. He seemed to be about his age as well as his size. The brave was more than six feet tall and well built. He nodded in greeting.

The brave grunted in response.

Don't push yourself, Schoolcraft had said. Flann hesitated, then started to walk past the man.

"Your injuries are healing," the brave said suddenly.

Flann stopped. "Yes."

"You'll leave soon, then."

"Soft Willow says tomorrow."

The Chippewa seemed to relax a little. "I'm Black Rock, of the Loon Clan. I'll paddle you to Ontonagon tomorrow."

Flann started to smile, then remembered not to.

51

But he must be doing something right if a brave was offering to help him.

"I'd like to talk to Chief Buoy at Ontonagon. It's good of you to take me there."

"You might also like to see the boulder made of copper that lies on the bank of the river, past my village. I'll show you."

There was no way to refuse graciously. Flann didn't want to antagonize the first brave who had tried to be helpful. And besides, why not take a look? "I'd like to see the rock," he answered.

"Good. I'll be here after the morning meal."

Flann nodded again at the brave and went on to the beach. He looked to his left, westward, and saw Kaug Wudju, as the Chippewa called the Porcupine Mountains. Kaug's tail was projecting into the lake. From this view the pines on the mountains resembled bristling quills. He relaxed and smiled. Things were going well, despite his nearly fatal encounter with that bear. Soft Willow had begun to talk to him about Chippewa medicine. Now this Black Rock would take him to Ontonagon. He'd even met a pretty girl.

At this rate, he would soon be able to gain the Chippewas' confidence deeply enough to probe into the gun question. Maybe the best way was to try not to be official, not to expect much from the chiefs. Certainly Copper Sky had done little but grunt when he'd spoken to him the first night, in Soft Willow's wigwam. There had been another man with him, but Flann was not sure who. Offers of friendship might come from lesser men than chiefs. He would have to watch for this and take advantage of it.

The girl, Birch Leaf, interested Flann. He had undoubtedly violated some taboo in asking her to walk with him. Schoolcraft hadn't told him how to behave with maidens. But she had liked talking to him, that was clear. For that matter, he had liked talking to her. A woman might artlessly reveal something a man would not. Flann turned away from the lake and returned to the village.

Birch Leaf wasn't on the platform. Flann found her behind the wigwam, on her knees, a deerskin spread on the ground in front of her. She had kindled a small fire, and over it, on a wooden tripod, hung a birch-bark vessel which Flann recognized as a *makuk*. Steam rose from the evil-smelling contents. He hoped it was not their supper.

The deerskin didn't smell much better. It was a green hide, recently killed. Birch Leaf used a flat bone to scrape off the fat and flesh that still adhered to the skin.

"What do you cook in the makuk?" he asked.

"Deer brains. To rub into the hide later, to make it supple."

"Do you mind if I ask you how you tan the deerskins?"

She tilted her head. Her eyes were like the green shadows in the pine forests to him, cool and mysterious.

"I don't mind. But do you truly not know how it's done? Who cures the hides of the deer you kill?"

How could he explain? "I live in a very large village," he began. "So large that everyone has a different task to do. We tan our hides, cowhides mostly, in large sheds where many men work. I don't even know the man who worked on the leather my boots are made of."

"Men do this work in your village, then. How strange. Don't they know that it's a task for women?"

"Women don't work with skins there. They cook

53

and sew and tend babies and keep the dwellings clean but they also learn many other things like. . . ." He paused. How could he describe playing a piano? Riding a horse? Going to a theater?

Well, maybe he could describe the theater. He picked his words carefully. "Sometimes a woman will dress in her finest clothes and jewels and a man will take her in a carriage, drawn by horses, to a lodge where they watch men and women who pretend to be characters in a story."

Birch Leaf's face brightened. "I know," she exclaimed. "We have celebrations in which men dress like animal spirits and are no longer men but the spirits from a story we all know. We watch them and everyone wears their best beaded tunic and ornaments to go and see the men dance. I watched a horse once in La Pointe. He was like a deer with no horns. Carriage is a word I don't know."

Flann wondered how she really envisioned the things he described. Did she see a barbaric scene of half-naked men dancing about fires? "Men and women also ride on horses' backs where I live," he said, thinking that with no roads and canoes for the streams and lakes, there was no need for horses in this wilderness. "I'll draw you a picture of a carriage," he added, reaching for a stick.

As he sketched the carriage, Flann became aware that Black Rock, the brave he'd met by the river mouth, stood nearby. Flann turned to look at him. Black Rock whirled on his heel and walked away. Flann noticed that Birch Leaf was watching the brave.

"I'm going to Ontonagon tomorrow with Black Rock," Flann told her. "I want to talk to their healers, too."

"Will you then return to your own village?" she asked.

"No. I'm heading for La Pointe after I visit Ontonagon. I want to learn all I can about Chippewa medicine before I go home."

"You should talk to Crouching Fox while you're here. He's the chief mide and knows much medicine."

"Which is his wigwam?"

Birch Leaf pointed, then returned to work on her deerskins.

It was customary to offer a small gift in return for information, Schoolcraft had said. Flann went back inside Soft Willow's wigwam to rummage in his pack. Tobacco, he knew, was always welcome.

Copper Sky could have taken me to meet the shaman, he thought. I told the chief why I was here.

Crouching Fox wasn't in his wigwam. His wife, stirring a stew in her kettle over the outdoor cooking kettle, told Flann her husband was hunting.

Later, alone, Flann wandered through the village, but it was impossible to check closely for new rifles as everyone he met stared at him, watching each move he made. Besides, few braves were in sight. Probably most of the younger men were hunting, rifles in hand.

In the evening, Flann sat on the outside platform next to Soft Willow's wigwam. The sun had set but the northern summer twilight lingered. It was still light enough to make out Birch Leaf's features, though she wasn't sitting close to him. A mosquito sang in his ear and he swatted at it. From the birch grove came a sudden cry, startling him momentarily.

"It's only *wawonaissa*," Birch Leaf said.

As the whippoorwill's cries faded, Flann heard low, mournful notes made by some instrument played nearby.

Birch Leaf said, "We call it a love flute." She spoke so softly he could hardly hear her.

Her voice was pleasing and had a musical lilt. He turned to look at her, disturbed to feel a stab of desire. Good God, desire was the last thing he needed. To involve himself with a Chippewa girl would more than likely ruin his mission.

Besides, there was Lynette waiting in Boston.

But in the soft twilight of this northern wilderness, with the call of a love flute in his ears and a lovely woman beside him, Flann could not keep his mind on either Lynette or his mission.

Chapter 6

Flann awoke in the grayness of early dawn. From his mat on the sleeping platform along one wall, he saw that he was alone in the wigwam. He pushed away the robe of rabbit skins and sat up. The wigwam was as neat as any white home he had ever been in. Soft Willow had her birch-bark makuks stacked on one side of the fire pit. Wooden spoons and ladles hung next to them. On the sleeping platform at the other end of the dwelling, the mats and coverings had been rolled up and stored. Toboggans and snowshoes hung on the walls.

There was no fire in the pit. Flann knew the morning meal would be cooked on an outdoor fire, as was usual in the summer. He swung his legs over the side of the platform and stood. He was fully dressed in shirt, trousers and socks. He ran a hand over his stubbled face, thinking that if he did not shave soon he might as well let his beard grow.

He put on his boots and went outside. Soft Willow was stirring a kettle of rich-smelling stew—rabbit, he decided. He greeted her, looking about for Birch Leaf. But she was nowhere in sight. Soft Willow handed him a makuk filled with stew. He began to eat with his fingers, blowing on the meat to cool it. He knew he would be offered no eating spoon or fork.

When he had finished, he went to the lake to wash. Back at the wigwam, he looked for Birch Leaf again.

"She's in the taboo hut, it's her moon time," Soft Willow reported.

"I'd like to see Birch Leaf before I leave," he said.

Soft Willow's eyes widened. "See a woman in her moon course before beginning a voyage? Bad luck would certainly follow you."

He realized that she meant the menstruation taboo. Schoolcraft had told him the Chippewas believed a menstruating woman was inhabited by a malevolent power and that it was dangerous for a man to even look at her. She had to retire to a small lodge away from the village each month during her period. Flann knew he would not be able to say good-bye to Birch Leaf.

"My daughter wishes you to have these." Soft Willow handed him a pair of moccasins, puckered around the front in the Chippewa style and intricately decorated with beads and dyed porcupine quills.

Flann unlaced his boots and slipped his feet into the moccasins. They fit perfectly. He walked into the wigwam and stood pondering his pack. What could he leave with Soft Willow as a gift for Birch Leaf? He had already given both women metal sewing needles. Jane Schoolcraft had told him Chippewa women prized such needles, so he had stocked up at Mackinac. But Birch Leaf must have a special gift, too.

The tiny mirror in the gold frame he used for shaving caught his eye. Perfect. He took the mirror out and began to repack his gear, then hesitated. No reason he could not return on the way from Ontonagon to La Pointe. Then he could leave the spare rifle and the extra ammunition bag with Soft Willow and have that much less to carry now. He asked Soft Willow if she would store his gear for him until he returned. She agreed.

Black Rock was waiting by the canoes.

"The lake looks calm," Flann said by way of greeting.

Black Rock nodded and pointed to his canoe, watching while Flann stowed his gear carefully in the bottom.

Black Rock said, "You are the *naganid*, the bow man." Flann got in the bow, knelt and took the cedar paddle Black Rock handed him. The brave knelt in the stern. As *wedaged*, or steersman, he would both paddle and steer the canoe.

Lake Superior looked like a gray-blue mirror in the light of the rising sun, the surface unruffled by waves. Flann soon fell into the rhythm of paddling that Black Rock set and the canoe skimmed along rapidly, seeming to barely touch the water. Soon they approached the mouth of the Ontonagon River.

To Flann's surprise, Black Rock paddled past the village, heading upstream. When Flann frowned, the brave said, "We go to see the copper rock first."

Flann shrugged and dug in his paddle again. The going was slower now that they headed upstream against the current. He began to tire. The bruises and lacerations left by the bear on his forehead ached.

After a time he asked, "Where is this boulder? We've come a long way."

Black Rock pointed ahead, and when Flann turned he felt the canoe tip under him. He shouted, grabbing at the gunwales. The next thing he knew he was under water. He kicked his way to the surface, choking as he gulped air. The canoe floated upside down. He could not see Black Rock. He began to tread water, fighting the tug of the current pulling him downstream. Suddenly something grabbed his legs and yanked him under.

He twisted, trying to free himself. He then realized he had not been snagged by an underwater log. Hands held him. He struggled to break away. What the hell? Did Black Rock mean to drown him?

His lungs bursting, Flann curved his body nearly double, reaching for Black Rock's face. He grabbed the Indian's hair, pulled the face toward him and jabbed at Black Rock's open eyes with two stiffened fingers.

The brave jerked back, his hold loosening. Flann kicked free, broke for the surface, sucked in air and immediately started swimming downstream. He stroked rapidly, glancing back over his shoulder. Black Rock's head broke the surface nearly at his heels. That had been too damn close, Flann thought. He tried to increase his speed but the Indian swam close behind.

I can't outlast him, Flann thought. He's a strong swimmer and in better condition than I am. I'll have to make a stand. He turned his head back and forth, scanning the banks. A few yards to his right a sand pit divided the water. In a burst of effort, Flann splashed forward and veered to the right.

Flann pulled himself from the water and pushed himself erect. By the time he had yanked his knife from his belt, Black Rock stood facing him, water dripping from his body.

"All right, you son of a bitch," Flann snarled in English. "I'm ready for you."

Black Rock lifted a knife from his waistband. The two men watched each other warily. The Indian began to circle and Flann kept turning to face him. He had learned hand-to-hand combat at West Point, but he'd never used a knife against a man. He knew he had to kill Black Rock on the first try since he himself was weaker than the Indian. He gauged the exact spot to plunge the knife in so his blade would not be deflected by a rib as he struck for the brave's heart.

Flann crouched slightly, faking a belly thrust, when he heard men shouting. He held. The voices came from downriver. He did not dare look away from Black Rock, and inwardly he despaired. Who else could they be but braves from Ontonagon?

To Flann's amazement, Black Rock stepped back and shoved his knife back into its sheath. He extended his hands, palms up, toward Flann. Still holding his own knife, Flann risked a glance at the river.

Two canoes pointed toward them, coming from downstream. An Indian paddled the first but the second held a priest and a bearded voyageur. Watching Black Rock still, Flann put away his knife, keeping a hand on the hilt.

The canoes scraped onto the sand. The priest and his rowers climbed out. Before anyone spoke, Black Rock said, "We were in mock combat. It was a warrior's contest, nothing more."

Flann opened his mouth to protest, then remained silent, deciding he would get the truth from Black Rock later, one way or another.

"A very dangerous contest, using knives," the

61

priest said to the brave, speaking accurate but clumsy Chippewa. He turned to Flann, speaking then in accented English.

"You must know better than to use knives."

Flann bowed slightly. "I agree knives are deadly, Father," he said in Chippewa.

The priest's eyes widened slightly. He was a small, slight man but there was determination in his stance and in the level look he gave Flann. "I'm Father Baraga," he said. "I don't hear many who aren't of the People using Chippewa language."

"My name is Flann O'Phelan."

Father Baraga looked at Flann, then at Black Rock. "You're wet and I see no canoe. An accident?"

"The canoe overturned and we lost it," Black Rock answered.

"Mock combat is an interesting way to dry off. May I offer help?" the priest asked. "We're headed upriver to see a large copper rock."

"That's where we were going," Flann told him.

Black Rock stepped into the canoe with his clansman from Ontonagon and Flann got into the larger canoe with the priest and the metis. When Flann offered to help paddle, the metis shook his head.

"I, Louis, need no help."

The sun was bright on the river and Flann was glad to rest while its warmth dried his clothes. That damned Black Rock, Flann thought. Why did he try to kill me? He had some explaining to do.

The canoes passed through two stretches of rough water, and Flann estimated that they had come about twenty miles upriver by the time he spotted the copper rock. Flann muttered aloud, "My God." The copper rock was a massive boulder weighing several tons, lying at the edge of the water. After landing, Flann saw a broken axe lying on the ground. The sides of the rock were scarred with axe and chisel marks.

"This is almost all copper," he said, awed.

The priest nodded, studying the mass. Flann heard Black Rock mutter a word he could not catch. He glanced at the two Indians. They were looking skyward. A big bird, an eagle, glided in a spiral far above them. The other Indian took tobacco from a pouch at his waist and sprinkled it at the base of the boulder, chanting softly. Was it an offering to the eagle or the rock?

"Have you plans to move this rock?" Flann asked Father Baraga.

"No, no. I came only to see the copper boulder. It's much better left where it is. Your countrymen, Mr. O'Phelan, are the ones eager for copper."

From the expression on the priest's face, Flann knew he thought copper was the reason Flann was there.

"I have no more interest in copper than you do, Father," he said. "I'm about to finish a course in medicine and I've come to study the plants the Chippewa use to cure illness."

The trip downstream was faster, the current carrying them along, and they used the paddles only to steer the canoes.

"Where is your church, Father?" Flann asked.

The priest waved his hand to take in their entire surroundings. "My mission is with the Chippewa, all I can reach."

"But have you no base?"

"La Pointe, presently."

Flann studied the frail man in the canoe with him. "I'm Episcopalian, not Roman Catholic," he said at last, "and I don't want to offend, but do you think the

Indians can be converted to your faith? The braves back there. Did you see one of them sprinkle tobacco to appease the spirits? How can you overcome such superstitions?"

"I don't think of it as possible or impossible. I only try to save such souls as I can and to help in other ways as much as I can. These Indians have so little. They need God."

"I don't know that they have so little. In Meenagha everyone is well-fed, no one is suffering. Those I met seemed content."

"Have you been here over a winter?"

Flann shook his head. "No."

"The winters are terrible." Father Baraga touched the silver cross that hung at his breast. "Many starve to death. And there's sickness, sometimes smallpox."

Flann had nothing against Father Baraga as a person. Indeed, it was likely that the priest had saved his life, coming when he did. But Flann mistrusted the priest's religion. Flann did not believe in praying to statues and a whole catalog of saints, or claiming all who denied Rome were doomed to be suspended between heaven and hell. To Flann, purgatory was myth. And, confession to a priest in order to win God's forgiveness was rubbish.

As if God needed intermediaries.

Flann ended this line of thinking, disgusted with himself. Would he never overcome his childhood conditioning? His father had hated and mistrusted Catholics and applauded Reverend Lyman Beecher's fiery sermons from the pulpit of Brimstone Corner, as Park Street Church in Boston was called. Flann had grown up believing Catholicism and despotism were allied, and that popishness contradicted American principles.

However, even Flann's father had been horrified when the anti-Catholic sentiment in Boston ran so high that a mob burned the convent of the Ursulines on Mount Benedict three years earlier.

Here I am, Flann thought, still mired in the same prejudices I learned to mistrust in my father. Father Baraga's right about the Indians. They need to be brought to understand that there's only one God for the sake of their souls. If it must be a Catholic priest who teaches them, surely that's better than leaving them heathens.

"I agree the Meenagha village seems to prosper," the priest said. "Unlike the conditions near Sandy Lake when I was there earlier this year."

"That's in the Minnesota Territory, isn't it?" Flann asked.

"Yes, near Leech Lake. Several Pillager bands live in the area." He shook his head. "There is poverty and open depravity." He was silent for a moment. "And yet, do you know, the young men had new rifles."

Flann stared at the priest. "Which band of Pillagers had the new guns? You said more than one lives by those lakes."

"The chief is named Broken Feather. He's old and I was saddened by the way the young men openly scorned him when he said he'd listen to what I might tell him of Jesus."

Louis snorted. "You don't say, *mon Pere*, how they knock you down in the dirt and Alexis try to knife the man who pushed you."

Baraga sighed. "They knew no better, Louis. As I told Alexis when I made him put his knife away, we must forgive the Indian, for he is our brother."

Louis snorted again but said no more.

65

When the canoes landed at Ontonagon, the sun was setting. Father Baraga immediately began walking among the Chippewas gathered to watch them. Flann set off after Black Rock, uneasily aware he was in the brave's own village, but determined to confront him.

"You. Black Rock," he called. "Stop!"

The brave slowed and turned.

Flann came up to him, faced him with a hand on his knife hilt. "Why did you try to drown me?"

"It was wrong," Black Rock said. "I was warned but I paid no heed." He glared into Flann's eyes. "I made a promise not to shed your blood and I broke that promise in spirit. I won't try to harm you again. I give my word." Saying no more, he walked away.

Flann stood watching him.

"You have trouble with that one, eh?" a man's voice asked in accented English.

Flann saw a metis with mustache and beard standing behind him. The man was taller and more lithe than Louis. White teeth gleamed from the curly black beard as he grinned at Flann.

"What you do? Take his woman? I, Henri Fontenac, tell you to choose another squaw. That Black Rock, he is one hothead. What good is any woman if you have a knife between your ribs?"

Flann stared at Henri, remembering Black Rock's scowl at the Meenagha village when the brave had watched him talking to Birch Leaf. Was she the reason?

"I don't see you on the lake before now," Henri went on. "What you do up in the north, eh?"

"I'm studying Chippewa medicine."

Henri frowned. "You mean like the mide, with the dancing and using the sucking tube, like that?"

66

"No, I'm a doctor. I want to learn the plants they use to cure diseases."

Henri shrugged. "Maybe they tell you, maybe they don't. Did they fix up those claw marks on your head, eh?" Henri laughed. "You got away from that bear easy. You come see the chief. Come with me."

Flann followed the metis, since he intended to meet Buoy anyway.

Buoy was an inch or two taller than Flann, a huge man. He stood over Father Baraga, who was talking to him, a giant pine over a seedling. Like all the braves, Buoy was bare to the waist. Flann drew in his breath as he saw the puckered scars that covered his chest and arms.

"You see?" Henri said. "A bear made those. The chief, he kill that bear with his knife."

Father Baraga turned from the chief. "Ah, Henri," he said. "Chief Buoy would rather we didn't camp at the village, so we'll go on up the lake." He looked at Flann. "Perhaps we'll meet again. God be with you, Flann O'Phelan."

"Thank you, Father."

Flann advanced toward the chief and raised his hand in greeting.

Buoy studied him, noting the claw marks across his head. "It is not a good time to talk," he said at last. "It is not a good time for you to be in our village. You go now."

Two braves moved to stand behind the chief. They stared at Flann with no expression.

"You go," the chief repeated. "Now."

Flann walked from the village toward the river mouth. He saw Henri and Louis standing by the canoe. Father Baraga was talking to some children. Flann knew there was no room for him since their canoe held only three.

He had no choice but to hike along the beach toward Meenagha. He had lost his pack and rifle when Black Rock capsized the canoe, but at least he'd left an extra rifle and ammunition with Soft Willow. Black Rock could pick him off now without any trouble. Still, Black Rock had given his word not to harm Flann. Could he, Flann, trust an Indian's word?

Blue twilight stretched over the lake as Flann walked along the beach. He was tired and hungry and knew that soon it would be dark. Schoolcraft had assured him the Lake Superior Chippewas were friendly. Why, then, had Chief Buoy turned both the priest and Flann himself away? Were Canadian rebels influencing the chief?

Flann was armed with only his knife. But he figured his chance of being attacked by animals was slim, as game was plentiful and easy for predators to kill this time of year. He would certainly keep an eye out for bears with cubs. He glanced over his shoulder. It wasn't bears or other animals he feared, but men.

Sand filled his moccasins as he walked. If he had had his boots on when he went in the river he would never have been able to outswim Black Rock, but sand did stay out of boots. He slogged on, trying to ignore the gritty feel, but he finally found each step increasingly uncomfortable.

Flann bent to slip off a moccasin and dump the sand out. As he leaned over something brushed his shoulder lightly. He heard a thud in front of him.

Flann dropped to his belly and rolled behind a driftwood log. Ahead of him the feathered shaft of an arrow still quivered in the trunk of a small pine leaning over the water.

Chapter 7

Flann crouched and ran for the woods, diving into the gloom of the pines. He saw no one and heard nothing but frogs croaking in some nearby marsh. He waited, straining his eyes and listening until it was too dark to see at all.

How the hell had he gotten into this mess? He was alone and unarmed, except for a knife, in a wilderness of woods and water. The Chippewas were unfriendly. Unfriendly? Black Rock was murderous. So much for trusting his word. If I hadn't stopped to dump out sand, Flann thought, I'd be dead with Black Rock's arrow sticking between my shoulders.

Where was Black Rock? Was he waiting? I can't hide here all night, Flann told himself. Black Rock may outclass me as a hunter but he can't see in the dark any better than I can. My only choice is to get away from this Ontonagon village. If I can make it to Meenagha, I've got that extra rifle and ammunition in Soft Willow's wigwam.

He crept to the beach and, staying close to the

edge of the forest, started walking west again. His back muscles tensed in apprehension, yet when he looked back he saw no sign of pursuit. He relaxed after awhile, deciding that if Black Rock had been following him he would have been dead long before now. Boldly, he stepped onto the sand.

The fifteen miles to Meenagha stretched out. Flann hoped he might find Father Baraga and the metis camping along the beach, but he knew they probably had gone up the lake beyond Meenagha before coming ashore for the night. He heard wolves howling and the sound stopped him.

Damn, he admonished himself. You know the wolves are tracking game, probably a deer. They won't come near you.

Still, their wails raised gooseflesh on his arms and he touched the hilt of his knife.

You'd think you had never been in the woods before, he muttered.

But the woods of Massachusetts were not vast acres of pine marching mile after mile from one Great Lake to the other, uninhabited except by Indians. You could not say the few white men who worked among the Indians really lived up here more than temporarily.

A half-moon illuminated the rocks and driftwood along the beach. Nonetheless, he stumbled on unseen obstacles and had to slow his pace. The waves lapped the shore in a monotonous rhythm. He found himself marching in step to the splashes. A breeze flowed from the land toward the lake and brought mosquitoes from the swamps to plague him.

Flann swatted furiously at the insects and cursed them.

Damned mosquito, from Latin, *mosca*. Damned

moustique in French. And in Chippewa, damned *suggema*.

For this I learned three languages, Flann thought. Latin, French, and now, Chippewa. So I can damn the mosquitoes in three languages besides English.

By the time he crossed the log bridging the Iron River, he was dead tired. He had heard shouts from the village earlier, and now, as he walked downstream toward the wigwams, he saw pine torches flaring. Young braves cavorted in the flickering light, shouting and yelling as they staggered between wigwams. Some brandished knobbed clubs and tomahawks. Some held rifles, though he noted that none of the rifles looked new. Three men sprawled on the ground as if dead.

Flann halted in uncertainty. Had there been a fight? He could understand a Chippewa word here and there although most of the yelling was gibberish. Wabishkize, white man, was one he heard often. Flann cautiously retraced his steps to a clump of bushes and hid. He peered at the braves, frowning, seeing them stagger, watching one fall and then struggle to his feet only to fall again.

They were drunk.

Schoolcraft had warned him to stay away from drunken Indians. "Where you and I might be merely befuddled by liquor," he had told Flann, "Indians go mad. They kill their best friends in drunken frenzies. Last year a squaw burned to death while drinking because her husband was too drunk to have sense enough to pull her out of a fire. Whiskey is the Indian's curse."

"I thought there were laws prohibiting giving or selling liquor to the Indians?" Flann had asked.

"Those laws aren't enforced," Schoolcraft answered. "Who's to see they are? It's impossible for me to do alone. Ramsey Crooks is an honorable man in his way. He hates the whiskey trade, too. Yet he dispenses hundreds of barrels of it each year to his traders because he knows he wouldn't get furs from most of the Indians without giving them whiskey."

"You mean he's a goddamned hypocrite," Flann had blurted out.

Now, Flann stared at the drunken Indians in the Meenagha village and knew he wasn't going to chance going among them. He made himself as comfortable as possible in his hiding place. In the morning he would slip into Soft Willow's wigwam and take his rifle. Once he was armed he would determine a route to La Pointe.

As the night dragged on the noise lessened and Flann finally fell into an uneasy sleep. Suddenly he was awake, immediately tense. It was near morning, the sky was graying. Easing his cramped body into better position, careful to make no noise, he looked between the branches of the shrubs that hid him.

A blue jay called raucously from a pine. What had disturbed the bird? Flann turned cautiously. Nothing moved except the bird. It flew to a sapling closer to Flann, perched and cocked its head toward the stand of birch near the edge of the forest. It squawked again, flitting to a higher branch, still looking at the same spot. Flann watched, too. He had almost decided the jay was giving warning of some animal, not a man, when he saw an Indian slip furtively from the birch grove. It did not seem to come as a friend. Flann was puzzled.

The Lake Chippewa were all tribal brothers, or so Schoolcraft had told him. Members of different clans intermarried. Everyone was more or less related by blood. Why would one of them spy on the Meenagha village?

Flann's eyes widened. Could the man be Sioux? He knew the Sioux and Chippewa were sworn enemies. The Chippewa word for them was *Nadouesse*, meaning snake. He glanced to his rear at the quiet village, then ahead at the darkness in the pine trees that lay beyond the clump of birches.

Flann speculated. What if the Sioux were lurking in the woods, planning to raid at dawn? Most of the Meenagha would be snoring in drunken sleep. Who was left to defend the village? What would happen to Birch Leaf if Sioux braves found her?

On the other hand, what if the Indian he had seen wasn't a Sioux? Flann gritted his teeth. He couldn't crouch here and argue with himself until it was too late. He might be called a fool if he roused the village for nothing. But he felt he had no other choice.

He started to stand, then cursed silently. He would have to reach the wigwams without being noticed if there were actually hostiles in the forest. With the bushes and the clump of birches between himself and the woods, he slithered out of cover and inched along the ground like a snake.

Flann felt like an idiot, creeping along as he was. Then, a bone-thin dog trotted past, teeth clamped on a chunk of meat. And when Flann saw what the meat was, he knew his original fear was sound.

Chippewas did not have so much meat that they could leave it about for dogs to steal.

But attackers, hoping to enter a village undetected would have plenty of meat to throw to dogs in order to silence them. A hungry dog chewing meat does not bark.

Damn, the Sioux are really here, Flann thought. And I may be the only one who knows. Somehow, I've got to wake them up without getting myself killed.

On his hands and knees and remaining as low as possible, Flann crawled rapidly toward the wigwams, hoping if he was seen in the uncertain light the Sioux would mistake him for a dog.

When he got to the first dwelling he lifted the flap and hissed, "Sioux!" He hurried on to the next wigwam where he repeated the warning. He did the same at three more, finally coming to Soft Willow's wigwam. He lifted the flap and entered quietly.

Soft Willow immediately sat up on her sleeping mat.

"There are Sioux in the woods," he grunted, reaching under the other sleeping platform for his rifle and ammunition. It wasn't until he had the gun in his hands that he remembered Birch Leaf was in the taboo hut.

"Quickly," he demanded. "How do I get to Birch Leaf?"

Soft Willow told him and he realized with apprehension that the hut was also in the woods, off the trail to conceal it from sight. Flann rammed shot into the rifle, then headed for the door.

"Wait," Soft Willow said. "The Sioux will kill you if you go among them. What good is a dead man to Birch Leaf?"

He turned to look at her. "I'm white. Will they kill a white man?"

"They kill anyone from a Chippewa village. Rouse the men, wait until the fighting starts, then go after Birch Leaf."

He hesitated, then nodded. Whether he liked it or not, Soft Willow's advice was good. He slipped from her wigwam to head for Copper Sky's tent. The chief was on his feet the minute Flann lifted the flap.

"Sioux," Flann told him. "Hiding in the pines."

74

Copper Sky stared at him for a second, then grabbed his rifle. Flann went on to the next wigwam. Some of the braves were hard to rouse. They gazed stupidly at him with dulled eyes. But once they understood, they scrambled to their feet, reaching for weapons. By the time he and Copper Sky had warned everyone, dawn was glowing pink.

"Go into a wigwam," Copper Sky told him. "We'll surprise the snakes when they creep into the village."

Flann hurried back to Soft Willow. She showed him spy holes she had cut in the wigwam. As he peeped through one, he became uncertain of his own obligations when the Sioux attacked.

He was not a Chippewa. And he had no quarrel with the Sioux. He realized that he had been so caught up in warning the village and worrying about rescuing Birch Leaf that he had not considered his own involvement. He held his weapon before him, looked at it, then quickly decided what he must do.

Shoot in self-defense, yes. But otherwise, no. Not unless he was forced. This was not his war. This was not his country.

As the day lightened with no sign of the Sioux, his uncertainty grew. Had he been mistaken in thinking that one furtive Indian and one dog with a chunk of meat added up to a Sioux raid?

Soft Willow shouted and then suddenly Indians erupted from the woods. As they raced toward the village he saw their faces were hideously painted red, yellow and green. There were twenty or more, some carrying clubs, some rifles, and some with bows and arrows and tomahawks. When they were almost to the first wigwam, Flann heard a long ululating screech that chilled him with fear. He whirled and raised the flap of the wigwam, rifle ready.

The screeching Sioux reached the wigwams. And they got no further. Rifles fired. Dogs barked. Clubs thudded on flesh. A woman screamed. The first Sioux warriors fell wounded or dead and the others began to scatter. Yelling Chippewa braves pursued them.

Flann glanced back at Soft Willow. The Sioux were fighting for their lives now. She would be safe in the wigwam. He took off at a run, heading for the taboo hut and Birch Leaf.

A Sioux with a yellow stripe down the center of his face came at him with a war club. Praying the man would halt, Flann raised the rifle. But the Sioux plunged toward him, club aloft. "So be it," Flann said aloud. Flann fired and saw red stain the Sioux's shoulder. The club dropped to the ground as the Sioux clutched his arm. Flann ran past him.

He could hear yells, muted by the trees as the Chippewas chased the Sioux into the forest. Flann turned off the path and approached the hut. As he neared it, he saw the door flap had been torn away.

"Birch Leaf," he called, plunging into the hut. On the floor a woman lay face down. Blood spattered her tunic and her head was a red, raw wound.

She had been scalped.

Flann halted, his saliva bitter in his mouth. He forced himself to grasp one arm and turn the body over. Unseeing brown eyes indicated she was already dead.

He took a deep breath and thanked God she was not Birch Leaf. He backed out of the hut and looked wildly, fear still gripping him. The Sioux had taken Birch Leaf. Where was she?

He rammed another load into his rifle and began to circle toward the spot where he had first seen the Sioux scout creep back into the woods. All the Indian atrocity tales he had ever heard rushed into his mind. He groaned.

Triumphant shouts came from the village, and he knew some of the Chippewa warriors had returned. He felt he couldn't risk the delay of going back and getting help while the Sioux survivors carried Birch Leaf farther and farther away. Yet he wondered how he could expect to locate her by himself in this wilderness.

Flann ranged back and forth among the trees, searching. Surely the Sioux would head west toward their own country. They would have canoes hidden somewhere. A glimmer of light caught his eye. He walked on, paused, turned back and bent down to look for its source. Finally he found it, a sliver of silvered glass among the brown needles.

It was a mirror fragment.

A few yards away he spotted another. Flann walked slowly along, searching the ground. There. Another bit of glass. He followed the trail of mirror shards, frustrated by the snail's pace he had to travel so as not to miss seeing them.

Then there were no more. He stood still, trying to decide which way to go. Someone coughed, then seemed to choke. Flann dashed toward the source of the sound, climbed a rise and halted.

A Sioux warrior faced him, only ten feet away. He held a thong which was tied about Birch Leaf's throat as a leash. Her hands grasped at it to ease the pressure on her throat. She coughed with each breath. The warrior yanked her closer, her body between himself and Flann. His face twisted in a scowl.

77

Flann raised his rifle but dared not shoot because of Birch Leaf.

The Sioux pulled his knife and held the blade to Birch Leaf's throat.

He grinned wolfishly.

Chapter 8

"*Je voudrais celle-la!*" Flann said firmly. He hoped the Sioux understood French. "I want her," he repeated in English. He dared not speak in Chippewa. Even if the Sioux happened to understand the language, Flann was afraid that the fact he spoke the enemy's tongue would doom Birch Leaf.

Blood dripped from a cut on Birch Leaf's neck.

Flann decided to try barter. He pointed to the gun, then to Birch Leaf. He made motions to indicate he would trade the rifle for her. Comprehension brightened the warrior's face. He nodded.

Flann unloaded his rifle and laid it on the ground by his feet. He pointed at Birch Leaf. The Sioux hesitated, then took his knife from her throat. He made kicking motions. Flann understood the Sioux wanted him to kick the rifle toward him. He shook his head, fingering his neck to show the brave he had to untie Birch Leaf's thong first.

The Sioux lifted the knife and Flann tensed, sucking in his breath. But all the brave did was cut the thong. Again he made the kicking motion, holding Birch Leaf by the hair.

Flann shook his head, meaning "no," pushing his hand repeatedly. Finally the Sioux understood. He let go of Birch Leaf and shoved her forward so violently that she sprawled on the ground. Flann kicked the rifle toward the Sioux. Birch Leaf was already on her knees, crawling toward him. He yanked her to her feet, watching the brave.

The Sioux scooped up the rifle and fled.

Flann put his arms around Birch Leaf and held her close, watching until he could no longer see the Sioux. She clung to him. He bent his head and, raising her face, kissed her gently.

"If you hadn't left the broken pieces of mirror for me to follow I wouldn't have found you," he said.

"It was all I had," she whispered. "Your gift."

She stepped back. Her hands went to her neck, and she massaged it gently. "The snake would have made me his slave," she said huskily. "It would kill me to be a Sioux slave."

"He didn't hurt you?"

"Only my throat. It's hard to talk. Morning Wind. . . ." Birch Leaf bit her lip. "He scalped Morning Wind."

"I saw her lying dead in the hut." Flann didn't say he had thanked God the girl wasn't Birch Leaf.

"My mother . . . ?"

"Soft Willow is unhurt. Your people routed the Sioux."

When they returned to the village, jubilant Chippewa braves greeted Flann. They commended his alertness and bravery. Birch Leaf retreated immediately to her mother's wigwam.

An older brave with a scarred cheek approached.

Flann did not know his name, although he thought this was the man who had come to see him in Soft Willow's wigwam after the bear had mauled him. He put his hands on Flann's shoulders. "You will be my blood brother," he said solemnly. "You'll no longer be a white man, but one of the People, a warrior who fights against the Nadouesse, a brave and courageous warrior."

"*Ho, ho!*" other warriors shouted approvingly.

"You'll come to the victory feast," the man went on, still holding Flann. "You'll share in the dance and you'll be one of us. I, Crouching Fox, say this is so."

Flann's eyes widened. Blood brother to the shaman? He had not expected such good fortune. "*Aih!*" he exclaimed. "Yes."

The warriors cheered. Flann saw that one waved a Sioux scalp. And this dismayed him.

"The Sioux have fled. Scouts watch against their return," Crouching Fox shouted. "You'll join us in the sweat lodge."

An auzeum, a breechcloth, was found for Flann. He stripped off his clothes in Crouching Fox's wigwam, feeling he was vulnerable as he ventured forth wearing only the buckskin flap held on by a cord about the waist. The shaman led Flann to a low, domed wigwam and he ducked through an opening, Flann following him. There he discovered he was supposed to remove even the breechcloth.

Steam rose from a pile of hot stones in the center of the floor. It stung the eyes. Flann knew some kind of evergreen concoction had been added to the water that was poured over the stones. He squatted next to Crouching Fox, making room when other warriors pushed their way inside. The air was hot and stifling.

Sweat oozed from Flann's pores and ran down his face and body. Crouching Fox began to sing:

> I have entered
> My bark cloud wigwam.
> Over the Earth
> The manito stone
> Accepts the sacred water
> Grandmother Cedar
> Cleanses me.
> We are cleansed.

The warriors joined him after the first song and repeated the words with Crouching Fox leading the singing. Flann found himself swaying to the rhythm.

The singing ended. The braves put their breechcloths back on and Flann followed suit, trailing after them as they emerged from the sweat lodge and ran toward the beach to fling themselves into Lake Superior.

The cold water made Flann gasp as he dived in, but he swam with the others. When he returned to Crouching Fox's wigwam, he found buckskin leggings ornamented with porcupine quills, a fresh breechcloth with a floral design beaded on and new moccasins. There was no sign of his other clothes.

In for a penny, in for a pound, he told himself, tying the leggings about his thighs and attaching the loin cloth. He was tense with excitement and tried to convince himself he was going along with this adoption by the Chippewa only to speed his mission to a successful conclusion.

Crouching Fox stood beside him. Flann watched while the shaman arranged a roach of stiff animal hair atop his head. The hair piece stood erect like a mane down the center of the shaman's head. An eagle feather rose at the back, and another extended horizontally. The shaman painted his face vermilion with white lines on each cheek and across the forehead. He wore a necklace of bear claws.

Crouching Fox stepped in front of Flann with his paints and began to decorate Flann's face. He used green first, then red. I must be a rare sight, Flann thought, but still his excitement persisted.

Drums began to sound as they left the wigwam. A fire blazed near the long midewigan and most of the village was gathered there. Crouching Fox and Flann took places in the circle of warriors, many of whom wore hair pieces like the shaman's. Others wore headbands of buckskin with one or more eagle feathers. No two faces were painted the same.

A large drum with a beadwork skirt hung from a wood frame. A brave tapped it gently with padded sticks. Copper Sky, dressed as the other warriors and wearing several necklaces of shells and bones and leggings decorated with shiny metal ornaments, stepped from the circle.

Flann stared closely at the metal ornaments. They were copper and silver, he was sure.

Glancing about the circle, he noticed silver circlets on the upper arms of some braves.

"This day we have conquered our enemies," Copper Sky called. "We thank Great Bear for aiding us in war, for making our hearts strong and our arms swift to strike. We thank Thunderbird for sending our shots to their targets."

Everyone shouted in approval as the chief stepped back. A brave sprang into the center of the circle and began to dance, singing of the Sioux he had wounded. Another joined him, chanting his own song of prowess in battle. Another warrior, then another and another began to dance.

A woman stalked among the dancers carrying a pole as tall as herself. Attached to the pole was the Sioux scalp, stretched over a wooden hoop. She planted the pole in the ground by the fire and danced around it, singing about the bravery of her husband. He had brought home the enemy scalp.

Another drum began to pound. Rattles took up the beat. Again Flann found himself swaying, responding to the rhythm. Crouching Fox pulled him forward inside the circle. The few warriors who were not yet dancing gathered around them. The shaman pulled a bone-handled knife from his waistband. He took Flann's left wrist and ran the blade lightly across it. Blood welled up from a thin cut. Crouching Fox then cut his own left wrist and pressed it to Flann's so their blood mingled. He announced: "This day you will be called Ishcoda, Fire, brother to Crouching Fox, brother to Besheu the lynx, my totem, brother to Anishinabe, the People."

Copper Sky put a buckskin band decorated with beads around Flann's head and arranged an eagle feather in the band so that it drooped, indicating he had wounded an enemy.

"Ishcoda, Fire, you are a warrior of the People," Copper Sky said.

The others shouted their approval.

"Now we will feast," the chief announced.

The women brought makuks filled with meat from the kettles and flat trays of wood carrying fish that had been roasted in coals. Flann recognized the fish as lake trout but the taste of the meat was unfamiliar. He asked Crouching Fox what animal it was.

"Dog," the shaman answered. "A dog feast in honor of the warriors."

Flann swallowed and took a deep breath. He wished he had not asked. Damn you, he told himself, you will not vomit and lose face among your new brothers. But even if he had not discovered he was eating dog meat he would have been unable to gorge himself as the braves were doing. Warriors laughed and talked and stuffed meat and fish into their mouths until grease ran down their chins.

Schoolcraft had told him, "The braves must eat all of what's in the kettle. To leave any food is to lose face."

At sunset the drums began to sound again and one by one the warriors stood to begin dancing. Considering all they had devoured, Flann was surprised they could move.

He tried to push his disgust over their gluttony from his mind, reminding himself they were savages and it was their custom. Nonetheless, he couldn't shake his own increasing unease. He had never been able to explain taking sides with one Indian tribe against another. He hadn't actually killed a Sioux but the brave might easily die from his wound.

"How many Sioux were killed?" he asked Crouching Fox.

"*Neesin*," the shaman answered. He raised a finger to signify one. "We have his scalp. Many were wounded but their comrades rescued them from us. If they hadn't, we would have fine sport tonight."

Flann experienced a spreading inner sickness. He knew that when Crouching Fox spoke of sport, he spoke of torture.

Flann contemplated other ways of the Chippewa that disgusted him. They were gluttons in times of plenty without thought of times of little. They dined on dogs. They took scalps in the name of glory. They loved fighting and war.

Somewhere outside the ring of dancers a woman wailed.

Crouching Fox spoke again. "We lost no warrior, no children," he said. "One woman was killed. She was Morning Wind, and her mother grieves her death. We have one warrior wounded, but he will recover. The snakes will fear us and wait in trembling for our next war party to come for them."

"No war party," Copper Sky said from Flann's other side.

"We have our honor to avenge," Crouching Fox exclaimed.

"I speak against war," the chief said. "We have no warriors dead. We routed the enemy. We have killed a Sioux warrior. It is enough."

"The young men won't agree. Their hearts are hot with blood lust. What of Morning Wind's mother? Her daughter is dead."

"I have spoken my mind," the chief maintained.

Crouching Fox gave him a dark look but said no more.

Flann looked everywhere in the crowd without seeing Birch Leaf. Now he got to his feet, determined to seek her out. He had had all the savagery he could take for the moment.

He found Birch Leaf outside her mother's lodge.

"You aren't at the celebration," he said.

"I'm still taboo. The hut was burned in the dance fire because of Morning Wind's death there so I must stay by my mother's wigwam."

He sat next to her.

"You shouldn't stay with me," she warned.

"I don't believe in your taboos." His voice grew harsh. "Damn it, I don't believe in senseless killing either. I shot a Sioux warrior this morning, and I have no quarrel with the Sioux."

"They're bad people. They are snakes in the grass. They are enemies."

"Not mine."

"You wear a headband with a warrior feather, you are now of the People. Our enemies are your enemies."

"No!"

"But that's what it means."

Flann reached to jerk the band from his head, to throw it to the ground, but stopped. Wait. Think. You're here on government business. You'll need the confidence of the Chippewa to succeed. Don't throw away your advantage.

"Soangetah should be your name," she said.

"Which means?"

"Strongheart. This means you have courage. I think you have much courage." Her voice was low.

"They gave me a different name at the feast. Ishcoda."

She laughed. "It might mean your heart is as bright as fire but I think it's because of your hair." She reached toward his stubbled cheek but didn't touch him. "Red hair grows on your face as well. Why is it white men have beards?"

"Why is it men of the People don't?" he countered.

She drew away. "It is not because they're like women. Our warriors are brave fighters."

"I didn't mean to upset you."

The fact is, he had teased her because her nearness disturbed him. Further, he was still troubled by the fighting earlier. Schoolcraft might accept an explanation of shooting the Sioux in self-defense, but how would he react if he heard Flann had seduced a Chippewa maiden instead of tending to business?

"I'm going to La Pointe tomorrow," he told her abruptly.

"I'll wait for your return."

"I'm going on to Leech Lake," he said, realizing as he spoke that he had made up his mind to investigate Father Baraga's Pillager band.

"The Mukundua, the Pillagers at Leech Lake, are treacherous, almost like the Sioux," she warned. "You must be very careful among them. Keep one hand on your knife and the other on your rifle."

"I have no rifle," he reminded her.

He took her hand and kissed her palm. "I don't know if I'll stop in your village again," he said, knowing he wanted to return, wanted to see her again.

"I'll wait," she promised. "Will you come to say good-bye to me before you leave tomorrow?"

"But I'm staying in this wigwam. You said you were, too."

"I am. You cannot. It's taboo now that you're a warrior and no relation to Soft Willow. You'll stay in the wigwam of your blood brother."

"Crouching Fox?"

"Yes. My mother told me he claimed you." Her voice showed a trace of fear.

"I'll say good-bye to you now and tomorrow." He slid from the platform, knowing that if he stayed any longer he would have her in his arms. He must not go off letting her believe he would come back. The odds were he wouldn't.

"Have you a special brave, one you might marry?" he asked.

Birch Leaf hesitated. "No," she said finally.

"Did you once?"

"Once I thought Black Rock and I might marry. Not now."

Black Rock. That metis, Henri, had been right. Flann remembered that Schoolcraft had told him marrying within the clans was taboo. Black Rock was Loon Clan, Birch Leaf was Bear Clan. They could marry. Flann supposed he himself was Lynx Clan, like Crouching Fox. Then he could marry her, too. Good God, what was he thinking?

"I can't promise you anything," he said. "And I don't think I'll see you after tomorrow."

"Be cautious among the Pillagers so you'll live to return if you should so wish," she warned.

Birch Leaf watched Flann, now Ishcoda, walk away from her toward the dancing. She held the hand he had kissed to her lips. At first she had believed her vision dream meant that someday she could become a mide since such a powerful spirit had appeared to her. Now she thought about the tiny flame that had pierced her heart.

Fire.

Ishcoda.

Chapter 9

Flann had a morning meal of stew with Crouching Fox, served by the shaman's wife, a plump woman named Blue Flower.

"We had a feast last night," Flann told the shaman. "A celebration. There was no whiskey. Yet the night before I saw many braves drunk. Do you keep whiskey in the village?"

"No." Crouching Fox spat out the word. "It is an evil drink, a white man's drink. I don't know who brought it to the young men. It was done slyly, a weasel's trick. Copper Sky forbids whiskey in the village. I know the young warriors drink whiskey when we're away in the winter trapping for skins, but we fight against it here." He looked Flann in the eye. "It was well for you the young men didn't see you when they were drunk."

"I hid outside the village. That's how I happened to see the Sioux scout."

Crouching Fox smiled. "Now that you are one of us, you need never fear your brothers." The smile faded.

"However, a man when he drinks whiskey is no longer a man to be trusted."

Flann acknowledged the advice. "Today I go to La Pointe," he said. "Is there a brave who'll lend a canoe?"

"One of us will paddle you to La Pointe."

"Before my journey, will you tell me how you treat diseases common to all men? Ills of the head and stomach and the joints."

"I'll tell you all that's not sacred," the shaman agreed.

Flann bitterly regretted the loss of his paper, pen and ink in the Ontonagon River but was determined to remember every word Crouching Fox uttered.

"First, the sweat lodge is much used for pains in the body. For headaches, the needles of the white pine are boiled and the liquid poured on the rocks. . . ." Crouching Fox began.

Flann couldn't identify some of the plants Crouching Fox spoke of for fever cures and wished he had more time to spend with the shaman. However, he knew his real mission took precedence, and finally he had to leave. "I'll talk to the chief before I leave," he said.

Copper Sky sat outside his wigwam, watching a baby boy toddling about. "A fine boy," Flann said. "Is he your grandson?"

"My sister's daughter's son," Copper Sky replied.

"I leave for La Pointe," Flann told him, then hesitated. He had thought long and hard about how to bring up the subject of guns, finally deciding to be blunt. "I ask if you have a rifle for me, for I traded mine to a Sioux to ransom Birch Leaf. If I visit the Pillagers at Leech Lake I'll need a rifle."

"The Pillagers used to be warriors," said Copper

Sky. "Their name was given in recognition of an honorable deed. Now they live with many who are not Anishinabe in their villages. Some have forgotten what it's like to be a true warrior." He sat without talking for some time, watching the baby. Flann waited him out.

"I have a rifle for you," Copper Sky said at last, rising.

Flann controlled his elation, face impassive. The chief disappeared into his wigwam and came back some minutes later with the weapon.

"A good rifle," the chief nodded. "It is yours."

Flann smiled in thanks and took the gun into his hands. "J. Henry" was stamped onto the brass lockplate of the rifle and it was in fine condition but not new. He had proved nothing.

A warrior named Rift-in-the-Clouds paddled with Flann to La Pointe. He was Flann's age, a talkative young man, eager to go against the Sioux as soon as possible.

"They're cowards," he ventured. "We'll wipe out their village, bring back slaves and many scalps."

"That will take many guns," Flann pointed out. "Do you have enough good rifles?"

"A strong heart wins," the brave said. "We aren't afraid. If we have no guns, we'll use arrows, clubs, tomahawks and knives."

After more probing, Flann had to conclude that this warrior, at least, had no knowledge of any cache of new guns at Meenagha.

The Apostle Islands were at the western end of Lake Superior, off Wisconsin, some seventy miles from Meenagha. The lake was a bit choppy but Rift-in-the-Clouds kept the canoe steady and they made good time. They passed Kaug Wudju. At first the bluff seemed to rise gradually out of the water, then suddenly shoot up to a towering peak. The mountains looked as high to Flann as any in Massachusetts. A blue haze hung over the rounded peaks. The blue mountains, Flann thought. If Jane Schoolcraft's mother was once called Daughter of the Green Mountain, then Birch Leaf is Daughter of the Blue Mountains.

A warm breeze flowed from the southeast. Rift-in-the-Clouds, wearing only a loin cloth, seemed comfortable. However, Flann grew hot and opened his shirt. He tried to banish the image of Birch Leaf. He had no business mooning over a Chippewa girl he would never see again. He thought of the mission ahead.

What did he know of La Pointe? Only what Schoolcraft had told him. The American Fur Company had stores and a fishery there. The factor was a physician from Denmark, Charles Borup. The Indian subagent, Daniel Bushnell, also had an office there along with his Chippewa interpreter. La Pointe itself was the site of a French fort built around 1700.

La Pointe was on the largest of the Apostle Islands, named Madeline. "I don't know why it's called 'Apostle,'" Schoolcraft had said, "since there are twenty-three islands, not twelve.

"The British took over the fur trade at La Pointe after Quebec fell to them in 1759," Schoolcraft had continued. "Our government tried to set up Indian trading posts in the '90s to sell goods at cost but the Chippewa needed credit, and besides, they found British goods of superior quality. So they went right on bringing their furs to British traders working south of the Canadian border."

"Do the Chippewa still sell to the Canadians?" Flann had asked.

"They can't by law. Only American traders can be licensed in this country now. Since the government factory system was abolished in 1822, the American Fur Company has almost exclusive coverage of Chippewa country."

"Mr. Abbott told me the number of beaver trapped every year is dropping," Flann had said.

"But it's still a paying business or the fur company would pull out," Schoolcraft had reminded Flann.

Once I get to La Pointe, Flann asked himself, what's the first thing? See Bushnell, of course. I'll have to talk to him about Father Baraga seeing new guns among the Pillagers and tell him I'm willing to travel to Leech Lake and investigate. I'll meet with Chief Buffalo, too, and see if Dr. Borup will extend me credit for supplies as he does the Chippewas, since most of my money went into the Ontonagon River.

Sweat beaded Flann's face as the sun rose higher and hotter. The sky was cloudless except for a dark smudge to the northwest. It was a fine summer day.

"*Wabun*, the east wind is not to be trusted," Rift-in-the-Clouds said. "And where is the *kayoshk*, the gull? He flies over the land instead. That is not good."

"I'm enjoying the weather. Couldn't be nicer." Flann slid off his shirt as he spoke.

"*Matchi Manito*, the evil spirit who lives in Kitchgami, eats the drowned," Rift-in-the-Clouds said. "He delights in storms."

"There's not a cloud in the sky."

"Look to the north."

Flann saw that the smudge on the horizon had grown. "It'll take a long time for those clouds to get to us," he judged.

"No. We must hurry." Rift-in-the-Clouds increased the tempo of his strokes. Flann took up the new rhythm.

The sun sparkled on the blue-green water. Earlier they had been close enough to shore to see cliffs that had tumbled boulders into the lake and tree-lined pebbled beaches. Now they were farther from land, and Flann couldn't see as clearly. As he watched the clouds build to the northwest, he began to understand the brave's urgency. There was no other boat on the vastness of the lake and the shore seemed very far away.

Sweat slicked his body as he stroked, matching the pace set by Rift-in-the-Clouds. The canoe seemed to flit over the waves. Dark thunderheads formed at the top of the advancing clouds. Lightning flickered.

Flann began to shiver. The southeast breeze had vanished and a chilly wind blew from the north. Thunder rumbled and the sky took on a copper hue, the blue entirely hidden.

"Hear me, mighty Thunderers," Rift-in-the-Clouds chanted, not missing a stroke. "Hear me and hold your strike, that I may live. Mighty Thunderers, hear my prayer." He repeated the words over and over as he and Flann paddled furiously.

The lake grew choppy, then rough. Flann's arms and shoulders ached with the strain of stroking. Drops of rain touched his face. He strained to see land but the rain increased, slapping into his face. Lightning flared across the sky and thunder boomed.

"Stroke harder," Rift-in-the-Clouds cried. "Use all the strength you have."

Flann called up reserves of energy fed by fear. He did not believe in Matchi Manito, but he knew they might very well drown if the canoe swamped.

A yell from Rift-in-the-Clouds startled him. Moments later land seemed to materialize before his eyes. There were trees lashed by the wind, and whitecaps thrusting onto a beach. They headed toward the beach and the waves shoved them onto pebbles and sand.

They hastily moored and climbed out near a dock. Flann saw low gray buildings nearby. Rift-in-the-Clouds pointed at a hill where two other large white buildings showed through the curtain of rain.

"The trader is there."

They hurried up a muddy path, crossed a small plaza where a soggy American flag sagged atop a spruce pole, and came to the first of the white buildings. Flann opened the door and they went inside. A metis stood behind the counter.

"Flann O'Phelan to see Dr. Charles Borup," Flann said in French to the clerk, who nodded and went into a back office.

"I go now to Buffalo's village," Rift-in-the-Clouds said. "You can find me there." He grinned at Flann. "Ishcoda. A good name. Your fire won over Matchi Manito's water." He turned and went out into the rain.

The clerk showed Flann into the back office where Charles Borup stretched out a welcoming hand. "I've heard of you, young man," he said. "Mr. Schoolcraft sent word and then Father Baraga spoke of meeting you a day or two back. What can I do for you? Other than dry clothes, that is. You were lucky to make port here."

"I need supplies. I lost my pack when a canoe capsized on the Ontonagon. I fear I'll need to ask for credit with the Company."

"No problem, no problem at all. We're quite used to supplying goods on credit. In fact almost all of our business is done that way. The Chippewas stock up here in the fall, then bring us furs in the spring and we balance the books. But you don't want to listen to that. You want to dry off. I'll find a shirt and trousers in our stock and you can make use of my office to change."

Borup handed Flann black trousers and a blue calico shirt. Taking them, Flann asked, "Is Mr. Bushnell at La Pointe?"

"No, Dan went up to Grand Portage last week. He should be back any day now."

As Flann put on his new clothes, he noticed the rain was letting up. A bearded man stood near the outer door. Flann recognized Henri Fontenac, the metis who had been with Father Baraga.

"You are one lucky man," Henri told him. "That Lake Superior, she's not one to fool with. As moody as a woman, eh?"

"I'll admit I was scared. Rift-in-the-Clouds knew what he was doing or we wouldn't have made it here."

"I see him go down to the Chippewa village."

Dr. Borup came from the depths of the store. "If you'll give the clerk a list of what you need," he said to Flann, "he'll fix you up." He touched Flann's rifle, which was lying against the counter. "This looks like one of our guns."

"I imagine it is. Copper Sky gave me the rifle to replace one I lost."

Dr. Borup raised his eyebrows and studied Flann for a moment but did not comment.

Flann gathered his supplies together and picked up his rifle. "Thanks for your kindness, Dr. Borup."

Henri followed Flann from the building. The rain had stopped entirely, and sunlight slanted through the clouds.

"This La Pointe, she is a fine village," Henri commented, pointing down a lane lined by white cottages with picket fences. "The Indians have their own village along the beach." Again he pointed.

Flann saw domed bark wigwams like those on the mainland. He started to descend the hill. Henri trailed after him.

"You learn all about Indian medicine now, eh?"

"Not very much yet. How's the priest, Father Baraga?"

Henri shrugged. "He's gone to L'Anse. Always traveling, the good *Pere*."

"I thought you were his canoeman?"

"Sometimes I help. Louis, he goes with *Pere* Baraga always."

Flann glanced sideways at the metis. Why was he staying so close? "Are you from La Pointe, Henri?" he asked.

"For now, yes. One day I go back to Montreal. Ah, *la belle* Montreal."

"You're a Canadian, then?"

"Most of us French, we are. But what difference?" he shrugged. "One side of Lake Superior is much like the other. Montreal, only she is different."

Dogs barked as they approached the wigwams. A crow lifted off from a post and circled over them, cawing. Children ran from between the wigwams to stare at them. Flann saw that cedar bark covered the lodges rather than birch bark.

"You want to talk to Chief Buffalo, his wigwam is there," Henri gestured toward the largest lodge in the village. The crow lit atop this wigwam.

Henry was being almost too helpful, Flann thought. Why?

Flann stood at the open doorway of Buffalo's wigwam. "I come in peace," he said, waiting to be invited in.

Buffalo returned the greeting. "Peace." Flann entered. Henri did not.

The chief sat on a mat near the back of the wigwam. He ordered a young woman to bring another mat for Flann. When he was seated, Buffalo took up a long-stemmed pipe. Flann recognized it as an *opwaugun*. Buffalo began to fill the red bowl with tobacco. Watching him, Flann was reminded of President Jackson and their talk at the White House. Washington seemed as far away as the moon.

The woman brought a flaming twig and Buffalo took a few puffs on the pipe. He pointed the stem north, east, south, west, toward the sky and the earth, and blew smoke in these six directions. Then he handed the pipe to Flann. Flann accepted it, took a puff that left a bitter taste in his mouth and pointed it in six directions as the chief had, then returned the pipe. Now that friendship was established, they could talk.

"You're called Ishcoda by my brother, Copper Sky," Buffalo said. "I've heard about how you saved his village from the Sioux. You are welcome in my wigwam."

Flann acknowledged him with a nod, then said, "I'm a student of medicine among both the white men and the People."

Buffalo waited, looking at him.

Flann knew he couldn't mention the guns Father Baraga had seen to anyone but Bushnell, and the subagent wasn't on the island. Yet he wanted to ask Buffalo about the Pillagers.

"I seek to learn of medicine here and also to the west among the Pillager villages at Sandy and Leech Lakes," Flann said finally.

"You would be better to visit the village at Fond

du Lac and not go farther," Buffalo said. "We have a plant we use for fever, *manito bimakwit.* You would call it 'twisted spirit.' The Pillagers are like this plant."

"Nevertheless, I go tomorrow."

"I don't like to send any of my clan among them," Buffalo mused.

"A canoe, then. Rift-in-the-Clouds, who brought me here, must return to Meenagha."

"Our village medicine men can tell you much. Why travel to those who are twisted?"

"I'll stop here on my way back down the lake. I want to visit all the clans before I return to my own village in the east."

"I'll consider what you ask," Buffalo said. "You'll stay in my wigwam tonight."

Flann left Buffalo and walked along the shore toward the dock as the long afternoon shadows gathered. He thought he might find a voyageur who would be willing to take him to Leech Lake if Buffalo refused. He was standing on the dock, looking out over the now tranquil water, when a man came out of one of the warehouses by the dock with hammer in hand.

"I hear you go to Leech Lake," he said in broken English. "Don't anyone tell you those Indians eat men? The trader, he doesn't buy fur from them. Bad Indians." He spat into the water.

Flann thanked the metis for telling him and left the dock. The Pillagers have a terrible reputation, he thought. But if I wait for Bushnell to return. . . .

He didn't pursue the thought, knowing he meant to go to discover the source of the Pillager guns himself. He heard footsteps behind him. It was Henri again.

"I hear you go to Leech Lake," he said. "You want me to paddle you? I have fine big canoe."

Ah, so that's why Henri was dogging me earlier, Flann thought. He hoped to make money. "I have only one dollar, Henri."

"I accept," Henri said.

"We'll leave in the morning then, weather permitting."

Flann spent the night in Buffalo's wigwam. The next morning he finished his meal and picked up his rifle and pack. When he started to leave, Buffalo held up his hand.

"Dancing Drum will go with you."

"Henri Fontenac is taking me."

"Dancing Drum goes with both you and Henri. He's a mide and you'll need one."

Henri was not pleased to see the middle-aged shaman with Flann, but his canoe was big enough for the three of them and he said nothing. They set off, paddling west.

Late in the afternoon, the mide dropped a fishing line from the canoe. By the time they came to shore to camp for the night, he had hooked a fine lake trout.

"He lured the fish with magic," Henri whispered to Flann, looking at Dancing Drum uneasily. Henri refused to eat any fish, preferring his own mixture of dried peas and lard which he stewed over the fire.

When they stretched out to sleep, Flann was kept awake by the hooting of owls. He had never heard so many in one particular place before. Henri squatted beside him. "You hear those owls?" he whispered.

"Seems to be a lot of them around," Flann answered.

"They don't be real owls. He called them." Henri jerked a thumb toward Dancing Drum, who was sleeping with his back to them. "Spirit owls."

"You believe in such things? I thought you were a good Catholic?"

"I am. But there's more in these woods than the priests know." His eyes shifted to Dancing Drum. "Things he knows . . . things that come when he calls."

Chapter 10

The next day, when they neared the western end of Lake Superior, Flann observed that the bluffs of red sandstone along the shore had been cut out by a multitude of waves into strange and wonderful formations. Evergreens grew from the formations in so orderly a fashion that it was hard to believe no one had planned the display. He could now see the north shore of the lake to their right as well as the south shore to the left.

This was the head of Lake Superior, though the French called this western end Fond du Lac, or "bottom of the lake." Here, Henri steered the canoe into the St. Louis River and paddled upstream. The river was wider here and the edges were swampy, with grass and white and yellow water lilies growing.

Upriver, the land formed rolling hills on either side and soon Flann saw log buildings on the south bank and Indian wigwams on the north.

"The fur company," Henri said, pointing toward the buildings.

"We'll stop at the Chippewa village," Flann told him.

The village chief had already heard of Ishcoda and the Sioux attack at Meenagha. After Flann smoked the pipe, the chief invited Flann and the others to spend the night. Flann saw more Henry rifles and one he identified as a Leman by its dragon sideplate, but none were new.

As they sat about the outdoor cooking fire that evening, Flann noticed Henri flirting with a young woman. Soon she and Henri disappeared. Flann glanced at Dancing Drum but his face was impassive. Finally Flann leaned over and spoke in a low tone to the mide.

"Will Henry get us into trouble?"

"Not here. That woman is no maiden. There is always one like her in a village. Everyone knows this."

In the morning they started upstream again. After paddling about three miles they came to their first portage.

"Nine miles," Henri said, "but easy."

Henri and Flann shouldered their packs and rifles. Dancing Drum carried his small birch-bark sack and a heavily-decorated otter fur pouch. Dancing Drum and Henri flipped the canoe upside down, fitted it over their heads onto their shoulders and set off at a trot.

Flann offered to relieve one of them at the first rest, but both men refused. The pattern for the entire nine-mile stretch was: Trot in short bursts, rest briefly, then trot again.

When they put the canoe back in the water, they went only a short way before reaching still another portage, Knife Portage. Flann realized the name came from the tilted strata in the exposed ridge which had weathered to a sharp edge. This trail was over rough ground and Flann marveled that the traders packed all their trade goods over these portages. After they had put the boat back into quiet water, Flann asked Henri if he had ever trapped in this territory.

"I don't like being a pack horse no more," Henri said. "Once I carry damn big packs, fifty, hundred pounds. I put them on my shoulders, then the tumpline fastens around my forehead, like this." He demonstrated. "Off I go, a damn big fool, seeing if I can carry more than the next fellow. No more." He shook his head. "Let those voyageurs work like horses. Not me."

That night they camped along a stream. They heard wolves crying soon after dark and Henri sidled over to Flann. "He's calling up the spirits again," Henri whispered. "You see that bag he carries? That's a mide bag. He works his magic with that. No good."

Over the next two days they rode portage after portage. Flann tried to talk to Dancing Drum about Chippewa medicine but the mide answered mostly in grunts, either because of reluctance or because Henri was there. That night whippoorwills serenaded them.

Activity melded into a pattern of portage and paddle as the days rolled by. Finally, they entered the East Savan River. And here they encountered still more grievous problems—swamps so thick with growth they could not paddle through them. They had to get out and wade, pushing the canoe through mud and water.

And again, there were the mosquitoes. Flann had never imagined mosquitoes could be such torture.

It was Dancing Drum who finally broke through their siege. From his birch-bark bag he took a wooden container sealed with a plug of clay.

"Bear fat," he said, pulling the plug and smearing himself with grease. Flann saw mosquitoes avoiding the shaman, so he used the bear grease too. Henri refused it.

The bear fat had a rather sweet odor—preferable, Flann thought, to their own body smells after days of travel. He was tired of the portages and of the bog country which Dancing Drum called *muskeg*. By November he would be back east, Flann told himself. He would report to the new president on his mission and then resume his medical studies. He would marry Lynette.

He conjured up her face, her green eyes.

No, damn it, Lynette had blue eyes. Birch Leaf had green eyes. Somehow Lynette's image was not clear in his mind. He could recall her voice—high and somewhat nasal, almost unpleasant, now that he thought about it.

"I declare, I wish those old lawyers would get everything settled for you," Lynette had said before he left on his mission. "I know how you worry, Flann, dear."

Although his father's unsettled estate was an annoyance, he had worried more about how she smiled at the younger of the two lawyers, a widower named Arnold Grant.

And as for his mission, what had he learned? Not much thus far.

The Meenagha villagers did have silver ornaments. If he went back there he might find the source but silver was a sideline. Baraga's remark about the Pillagers had opened up the possibility that he might find out who the supplier of new guns was. The obvious suspect would be a French Canadian like Henri. The Kitchigami country was full of such men. He had seen twenty or more at La Pointe, and he knew others ranged the rivers and woods as voyageurs.

Schoolcraft had already said Borup vouched for his men at La Pointe, but maybe he'd better go over the matter with Daniel Bushnell when the subagent returned. As for Henri, what did he know about him?

Henri thought the voyageur's life was too difficult. He loved Montreal. He paddled around the villages and spoke Chippewa. He liked women. He wanted to take me to Leech Lake—for pay, of course, but is a dollar enough for all of this?

In the afternoon, Dancing Drum picked rushes from the bogs and plaited them into the shape of ducks. He set them out on a swampy lake at sunset. Henri and Flann shot four ducks when they landed among the decoys. Roasted in the coals, the meat was excellent.

Flann studied Henri, seeking more positive intuitions. Outside of having as little to do with Dancing Drum as possible, Henri was friendly and cheerful and, on this trip at least, hard-working. Would Father Baraga let an agent provocateur accompany him to the Indian villages?

Ah, but a priest might not suspect, might take a man's motives for the best, rather than the worst.

Still, why should Flann suspect Henri any more than Louis?

A loon cried, the sad piercing notes of his call lingering in Flann's ears. This was true desolation. The shores of Lake Superior seemed like paradise in comparison to these swamps. If I were alone here I would never find my way out, Flann thought.

Two days later, near evening, Flann saw Dancing Drum sniff the air and wrinkle his nose. He then noticed a smell, growing stronger by the minute, a stink of rancid animal and human hides. They rounded a bend and there Flann saw an Indian village.

"Is this Leech Lake?" he asked Henri.

"Sandy Lake," Henri corrected. "We go no farther tonight."

It was a cheerless and unhappy village with the look of disaster about it. It was not the village of fighters described by Father Baraga.

Bony dogs snarled at them. They appeared hungrier than any he had seen so far and only the babies who still nursed from their mothers were plump. The ground between the wigwams was strewn with broken utensils. Entering the chief's lodge, Flann and Dancing Drum found the inside cluttered and dirty.

Chief Broken Feather was an old man. The chief went through the motions of smoking the pipe with Flann and Dancing Drum, but seemed ill and dispirited. His face was scarred with the healed pits of smallpox. The disfigurement interested Flann. Few Indians survived the disease.

Dancing Drum told the chief about the Sioux raid on Meenagha and for a moment Broken Feather's eyes flared, his face becoming animated.

"We must war against the Nadouesse until no more remain!" he exclaimed. "It's true what Chief Flat Mouth at Leech Lake says. The blood of our ancestors spilled onto the ground calls for vengeance against the Sioux."

Then, sinking back into apathy, he offered them an abandoned wigwam for the night. It was inextricably filthy. As Flann piled refuse outside the door, three young braves with faces painted red sauntered by, glancing slyly at him, then away. One spat. Dancing Drum returned from the woods with cedar branches and used several as a broom. He went back

108

for more to cover the ground inside the wigwam, for there were no mats.

Henri busied himself making a fire outside. Flann ate Henri's pea-and-lard stew for the evening meal. Dancing Drum fasted.

"We'd best take turns standing guard tonight," Flann said. "I didn't like the looks of those braves."

"Yes, you have one good idea. I, Henri, will take the first guard, then you." He pointedly left out Dancing Drum.

Flann turned to the mide. "When I finish my turn, I'll wake you for yours."

Dancing Drum grunted. He seemed preoccupied, gazing into the fire, his lips moving as though in silent invocation.

When it grew dark, Flann settled himself on the boughs inside the wigwam. The clean aroma of cedar was welcome. The Pillagers seemed a poor and miserable group, he thought, but not openly dangerous. He felt the three of them should be safe enough with an armed man on guard. He had noted there were no guns in the chief's wigwam, nor had the swaggering young braves carried rifles. He planned to get into other wigwams the following day on some pretext or other to check further. It was easy enough to believe these desperate villagers might promise anything to a man who gave them new guns.

Dancing Drum came into the wigwam and settled himself. Henri was seated at the door, rifle in hand. Flann relaxed, trying to bring Lynette to mind, her fascinating coquetry, her red pouting lips.

Instead he saw dark green eyes gazing into his, heard in his mind the trill of Birch Leaf's laughter. He fell asleep thinking of her, not Lynette.

* * *

He dreamed he was resting naked in a green sea, a sea of leaves, not water. Someone lay with him in the leaves but was hidden. Flann ran his hands through the green, seeking, seeking, and finally touching a woman's body. She sat up, her breasts round and bare, the leaves covering her loins.

Flann reached for her, but she laughed and ducked under the greenery. He plunged after her, touching her nakedness now and again until he was wild with desire. Still she eluded him.

A wind sprang up from the east and blew the leaves every which way. She lay uncovered before him, smiling, saying the east wind could never be trusted. He ran to her, dropped to his knees, and she held up her arms to him. He reached for her.

Her face, soft and welcoming, changed and grew fearful. Terror clouded her green eyes and her mouth opened. She cried out, pointing at his body.

Flann looked at himself and saw that sores covered his flesh. They were the ugly festering lesions of smallpox. But his desire for the woman was overwhelming and he threw himself upon her, thrusting her legs apart as she screamed and screamed. . . .

Flann woke abruptly, his ears ringing with screams. For a moment he believed he was still dreaming, but then he heard an ululating shriek followed by many more from different directions.

He sprang to his feet and reached for his rifle. Then he reached again and yelled, "Damn!" The rifle was not at his side where he had left it. Neither was his pouch of ammunition.

A nearly full moon lit the wigwam and Flann saw that Dancing Drum crouched in the doorway. There was no sign of Henri. The screeching was almost continuous now. Flann joined the shaman, peering out.

Flames flared into the night from a gigantic fire. Screaming braves pranced and shouted around the flames.

"They're drunk," Dancing Drum said.

Flann glanced at him and noticed that the shaman held the otter skin mide bag in his hands. "My gun is gone," he complained.

"They mean to kill us," Dancing Drum said. "I had a dream that this is so."

"We've got to get out of here, find Henri."

"We won't find Henri," the shaman said.

A chill ran up Flann's back as he stared at the cavorting braves. "You keep watch and I'll cut a hole in the back of the lodge. We'll creep out and make for the canoe."

Flann took his knife and jabbed it through the bark covering at the rear of the lodge, working hastily until a high shrill cry from the shaman froze him. He whirled around. Dancing Drum was standing outside the wigwam, chanting:

> I call on Great Bear,
> I call on White Bear
> Who comes from the center of the earth.
> Our grandfather, Bear,
> Who was black for the first layer of earth.
> Bear, who was red for the next layer of earth,
> Yellow for the next layer,
> White when Cedar pushed him to the top.
> Great White Bear, hear your colleague
> My colleague, hear me!

Flann raced to the door. The Pillager braves

stopped dancing and streamed toward Dancing Drum. Flann glanced back at the opening he had cut and wondered whether the shaman was giving him a chance to escape.

Us, Dancing Drum had said. They mean to kill us. So the shaman did not think the braves' malice was directed at white men alone.

A drunken Indian doesn't care who he kills, Flann recalled.

Was Henri already dead?

I'm damned if I'll run out on Dancing Drum, Flann thought. He stood in the doorway and watched the painted braves race toward them, yelling and brandishing rifles.

Moonlight glinted on the cold iron of the barrels.

As they came closer Flann realized the rifles were new.

Chapter 11

Birch Leaf knelt before the reed mat she was weaving, her fingers holding the reeds but not pushing them in and out as she should have been doing. She faced the unfinished mat hanging from the wood frame but did not see it. After a time, she became aware that her mother stood behind her and hastily began interlacing the reeds.

"You think of Ishcoda," Soft Willow said.

"Yes." Birch Leaf turned to look at her mother. "Of him and of my vision dream."

Soft Willow seated herself on a mat beside her daughter and began to thread beads onto a dress of blue cotton.

"I believe my dream means I can be a mide later, when I'm older, but I think the dream was about Ishcoda, too." Birch Leaf brought the tips of her fingers to her left breast, her eyes dilating as she recalled the dream of the flame entering her heart.

"What of Black Rock?" her mother asked.

Birch Leaf turned to the mat. "What I feel for

him isn't what I feel for Ishcoda. The feeling is as different as watching *shawshaw*, my swallow, dip and swirl, so graceful it touches the spirit. But then *meegeesee*, the eagle, flies high above, so mighty the breath stops as you watch."

Soft Willow's hands lay idle in her lap as she gazed at her daughter. "Ishcoda is our friend, one of the People, but he will not stay with us. What will you do then?"

Birch Leaf frowned. "I think he'll stay."

"No."

"The man who's our messenger from the Great White Father in Washington, the Indian agent . . . this man married one of the People and lives in our country," Birch Leaf pointed out.

"Each man is different. Ishcoda will go back to his own village."

"Perhaps he'll take me there."

"Do you want to leave us?"

Birch Leaf did not look at her mother but stared out at Kitchigami sparkling in the sun of Blueberry Moon. It was the warmest time of the year. Soon the wild rice, *manomin,* would be ready for reaping. This was her world, familiar and beautiful.

"I don't know," she said to her mother.

"If you were married to Black Rock," Soft Willow said, "then you would stop daydreaming. And that metis who wants you would be discouraged from trying again. While you're available he won't give up. I saw the lust in his eyes."

"Him." Birch Leaf's voice was scornful.

"Men such as this Henri are dangerous. Make sure you avoid him."

"Don't worry. I can't stand the man."

"Black Rock will want to see you. What will you tell him?"

Birch Leaf looked around. "Is he here?"

Soft Willow sighed. "Where have you been these last days? You must know Rift-in-the-Clouds has sent tobacco to all the villages to ask the braves to war against the Sioux. Many have accepted the gift and the young warriors arrive for the dance. Certainly Black Rock will be one of them."

"Copper Sky announced we wouldn't send a war party against the snakes," Birch Leaf said.

"The young braves disagreed, as is their right."

"I don't know if I want to see Black Rock. Still, if he goes to war. . . ." She allowed her words to trail off.

Soft Willow picked up her beadwork and walked into the wigwam. Birch Leaf went back to her weaving.

In the chief's wigwam, Crouching Fox sat on a mat next to Copper Sky. "The warriors arrive from the other villages," he said. "I warned you the young braves would not wait."

"I had a dream," Copper Sky told him. "In my dream Thunderbird came to me and cautioned against haste. He held guns in his hand and told me if I waited long enough soon all Chippewa would rise and be armed against our enemy, the Nadouesse, the Sioux. Once and for all we would exterminate those snakes until not even one infant remained. Then if the Great White Father forces us west we survive. That was my dream."

Crouching Fox answered. "Even if you told this dream to the young men you wouldn't quench the blood lust in their hearts. It would be well if they had good weapons now. New ones."

"What do you expect me to do about that? I gave Ishcoda my rifle. Do the young demand my bow, my war club?"

Crouching Fox looked at him in exasperation. He knew Copper Sky understood very well what he meant.

"Are you going on this ill-timed raid?" Copper Sky asked.

"I haven't dreamed your dream," the shaman answered. "Morning Wind's mother hasn't either. She wants vengeance now."

"The agent at Mackinac will be angry."

Crouching Fox snorted. "Think of how much angrier he will be if the day dawns when you feel well enough armed to exterminate all the Nadouesse."

"I had a dream," Copper Sky said stubbornly.

"Not all dreams are visions."

"No, and all braves aren't warriors. Still, most of them turn out to be, given time." Copper Sky turned from him and raised his voice, calling, "Snowberry. Bring food."

As he spoke, dogs outside set up a clamor and the two knew strangers approached.

At the mouth of the Iron River, Black Rock pulled his canoe onto the beach and lifted his bark bag of belongings from the bottom. Sleeping Owl, who had paddled with him, was already on the path to the wigwams. Other canoes from Ontonagon came up behind him.

Black Rock's spirits were high, both at the prospect of the raid and of seeing Birch Leaf. It's well Ishcoda is gone, he thought. She'll forget him. If I'd been here when those snakes took her, not one snake would be alive. Still, Ishcoda showed courage and deserves to be one of us. I'm glad now that I failed to drown him.

Birch Leaf was finishing the reed mat on its frame when he approached and greeted her.

"You come to join the men of the war party," she said.

"All the Ontonagon warriors who were in the village came. With us are men from L'Anse. The party will be large." Black Rock stared at her as she knelt by her weaving frame. When he wasn't with her she filled his mind and thoughts until he had no desire for other women. And yet when he was with her he grew tongue-tied.

Her green eyes looked into his and he felt desire. He almost wished the raid could be postponed so he could take her into the woods this night and show his love for her. He could not. A warrior abstained from women before a fight. The war dance would be tonight. Don't be witless, he thought. Speak your mind to her.

"We'll be together when I return from Sioux country," he said. "If we marry before the Moon of Falling Leaves, you'll be with me for the fur trapping, and we'll have the winter together."

"I've told Ishcoda I'd wait for him," she said. "I can't marry you." Her lips quivered as she spoke.

Black Rock felt pain in his stomach, as though an arrow had pierced him. He looked at her a moment longer, then whirled and strode away.

Crouching Fox emerged from Copper Sky's wigwam scowling. The chief was a stubborn old man. He would not go to war when others wished to. The most he would agree to was to appear at the war dance.

Snowberry was walking just behind him. Crouching Fox glanced back at her.

"I know what you want," she said, bold but

afraid. "I know where my father's cache is. If you will make medicine so Black Rock marries me, I'll show you."

Crouching Fox walked on without answering. She followed.

"I'll grind a love powder for you," the shaman said at last. "It's up to you to find a way to give it to Black Rock."

"Yes, that's what I need. Make me a love powder and I'll show you the hiding place."

Crouching Fox prepared love powder often. There was always a demand for it. He waited until he was certain no one watched him and then secretly slipped into the woods. Where hardwoods mixed with conifers, he pushed through meager underbrush to a small stream gurgling to join the Iron River. He stooped and searched until he found the plant he sought, one that bore small blue flowers in the Moon of Flowering in the spring.

Taking a pinch of tobacco from a pouch, he cast it on the ground by the plant and chanted a quick prayer that the spirit of the plant with the blue flower would forgive what he must do. He dug in damp ground with the shoulder bone from a deer until roots were exposed. Carefully, he cut some of them away, then smoothed the dirt back over the remaining roots. He did the same with the brothers of the plant.

Walking back through the pines, he kept his eyes on the ground until he saw the delicate lavender pouch of the love flower. He dropped another pinch of tobacco, asked for forgiveness and took only a petal of purple flower, for if he picked the entire bloom the plant would die. Each time he found a love flower he took another petal.

When his wife was in the taboo hut and he was

alone in the wigwam, he carefully dried the roots and petals over a sweet fern fire and then pulverized them between stones taken from Kitchigami. This mixture was the love powder. His price for it was high. He received many skins, or ammunition for his rifle.

It was near the time to gather the roots and petals again, but he still had enough left to give to Snowberry. What she had to give in return was high payment, indeed.

That evening Birch Leaf joined the other women near the big fire when the thrum, thrum, thrum of the war drum sounded. Rift-in-the-Clouds brandished a viciously knobbed war club streaked with vermilion. He was the war captain. He had called the warriors together. Part of his hair was gathered atop his head into a half-plaited scalp lock wound with a strip of basswood so the hair stood erect. The part of the lock that was not braided hung loose so the hair plumed over the wrapped portion. His headband bore an eagle feather split down the middle to show he had been wounded in battle.

As he stepped out to lead the dance, his face and body glowed with paint. Warriors circled him. Birch Leaf picked out those she knew. Shining Star from La Pointe and Red Muskrat from Lac Vieux Desert. All the Ontonagon braves were familiar, but there were other warriors she had never seen before. Rift-in-the-Clouds shouted:

> Hear me, warriors.
> Here on my breast I have bled,
> Struck by the enemy.
> See my wound.
> Look, warriors, at the wound.
> No longer does it bleed.

My heart, not the wound, bleeds,
My heart bleeds in anguish.
I am angry that my foe still lives.
Our nation is humiliated by my unavenged
blood.
Who has the courage to follow?
Who among you carries the flame of bravery?
Who will join me against the foe?

The war drum boomed in accompaniment and turtleshell rattles sounded. Rift-in-the-Clouds stamped the ground and uttered a war cry, then began to dance.

The next brave to jump into the circle was Black Rock. He wore the eagle feather erect in his headband to show he had slain an enemy in battle. Birch Leaf saw she was not the only maiden watching him intently. Snowberry stared, mouth slightly open, as Black Rock flung up his arms and chanted.

The war birds fly,
War birds from the south.
They fly overhead.
The fierce birds of the south
Hark to their screams.
Listen to their passing screams.
I will be like the fierce birds.
I will be swift,
I will be cruel,
I will be strong.

Black Rock stamped the ground and circled in the war dance, shouting a war cry.

Now he could not honorably withdraw from the war party. Birch Leaf held one hand to her heart. Black Rock was the bravest, most handsome warrior here. What if he were killed? As if in answer, Snowberry was suddenly beside Birch Leaf, whispering in her ear, "He will be mine."

Birch Leaf moved away. One by one the braves leaped into the circle, chanted their song and started dancing. Soon all the young men were committed. Then Crouching Fox stepped forward, his hair piece bristling. The warriors kept dancing but ceased their cries as he chanted:

> Kitchi Manito is my guide.
> The Great Spirit shows my path,
> He guides me.
> Great will be our courage,
> Great will be our cunning,
> Great will be our victory,
> Guided by Kitchi Manito.

Crouching Fox danced. The rest of the warriors shouted as he joined them. The dancers circled and stomped in the classic patterns of the war dance. Birch Leaf watched until it was time to go to the cooking fires to serve the food with the other women.

The long twilight had become blackness of night. A bright moon shone among the stars. The other women were ahead of her. Birch Leaf felt the sweep of wings as a hunting owl swooshed past her. She speeded her steps. Away from the big fire she could see the faint gleam of the moonstreak on Kitchigami, the pathway of the dead on their way to join the Dance of the Spirits in the northern lights.

Birch Leaf shivered. It was dangerous to think of the dead at night. Unappeased spirits roamed the dark and might sense your thought and try to enter your body. Perhaps the sweeping owl had contained such a spirit. She ran to the cooking fires, glad to be with the others.

Snowberry, after filling a makuk with a cold drink made of raspberries and water, slid the tiny pouch of love powder from under her belt. She stirred the powder into the drink and added a few grains of maple sugar to conceal any possible bitter taste. Hurrying ahead of the other women, she started for the dancers. When she came to the circle, she waited until Black Rock came past her. It was customary for the men to accept drink from the women as they danced. Softly, she called his name.

He looked at her, then moved from the circle, sweat beading his bare torso. Like all the warriors, he wore only moccasins and loin cloth. He held out his hand for the makuk of raspberry drink.

I wish it was Birch Leaf offering me this, he thought as he raised the makuk to his lips. Snowberry was pleasant to look at, she made good garments and cooked good food, but she was not Birch Leaf.

Then he saw Rift-in-the-Clouds was still dancing. As war captain, Rift-in-the-Clouds was entitled to respect. Black Rock motioned to him. Rift-in-the-Clouds dropped out of the dance. Black Rock offered him the makuk of raspberry drink, indicating he would take orders from the war captain as a squaw takes orders from a brave.

Rift-in-the-Clouds drained the makuk. Snowberry put her hand to her mouth to prevent herself from shrieking. The war captain looked past Black Rock at her and she was transfixed by his gleaming eyes. Even if she wanted him—and she didn't—they could never marry. He was of the Bear Clan, as Snowberry was.

What had she done?

Chapter 12

Flann stared at the screeching, painted Pillagers, at the glare of the fire beyond them, at Dancing Drum standing with arms raised before the wigwam.

Dancing Drum pulled a white object from his otter skin bag. Flann squinted in disbelief. It was a large seashell from the Atlantic shore. When the shaman held the white shell in full view of the onrushing Pillagers, to Flann's amazement, they stopped short. The drunker among them staggered and fell.

"You see my shell," Dancing Drum intoned. Then, after a long silence, he chanted:

> Here is my shell.
> You will feel its sting,
> You will feel the bite of the shell,
> The shell that I shoot.
> The megis, the sacred shell,
> The spirit of the shell,
> The spirit of the shell kills.
> The megis kills.

Be warned,
Here is my shell.

Muttering, they fell back before the shaman. As Dancing Drum brought his arms down, one of the Pillagers rushed forward, brandishing a war club. The shaman thrust the seashell toward the attacker, shouting, "I shoot."

The Pillager faltered. He dropped his club. He clutched at his stomach, doubling up. Slowly he sank to the ground and lay motionless. The others cried out in alarm, shoving at one another in their hurry to move back.

Dancing Drum waved the shell from one side to the other and the Pillagers panicked, fleeing toward the fire, running away from the menacing shaman. Flann was bewildered. Why did they so fear this seashell? How did Dancing Drum acquire a shell from the Atlantic? What had happened to the brave on the ground?

Dancing Drum thrust the shell back into his mide bag and grabbed Flann's arm. He pulled him from the wigwam toward the shore where they had left the canoe.

"Henri?" Flann asked.

"Too late."

In the light of a waning moon, the two men trotted along a path until they came to the canoes on the bank of the river. Dancing Drum shoved one into the water. Flann climbed into the bow, taking up a paddle. Together they stroked from the bank.

Suddenly the canoe seemed to wobble and lose stability. Flann could not hold a true course. He glanced about. He saw Dancing Drum was standing. He seemed to be clawing at something between his shoulders. Then the shaman stiffened and toppled into the water.

Flann reached for Dancing Drum's leg. The canoe tipped and threatened to swamp. Flann saw the feathered shaft of an arrow protruding from the shaman's back. He lost his hold on Dancing Drum's leg in his effort to keep the canoe afloat.

The body slid into the dark river and disappeared.

Desperately, Flann paddled off, heading east, expecting pursuit at any moment. Much later, he slackened his pace, listening. The only sounds were the frogs in the swamp and the buzz of mosquitoes in his ears.

Flann paddled through the night. At dawn he came to a portage through muddy swamp. As he lifted the canoe, he noticed a pouch in the bottom. It was Dancing Drum's otter skin mide bag. He hooked the bag under his belt and put the canoe on his shoulders.

All morning Flann slogged along in mire up to his knees. He was both hungry and thirsty, but green bog water did not tempt him and he carried nothing to eat. All he had was the mide bag and his knife. The bag held the seashell and various packets of pulverized and powdered roots and leaves in twists of buckskin. He was afraid to sample these. If the shell was believed to be deathdealing, the potions might be poisonous.

He struggled onto dry land sometime after midday. Here he tried to fashion rushes into the shapes of fowl as Dancing Drum had done, thinking he might somehow snare a duck. His decoys did not even faintly resemble birds and after a time he gave up. He stretched out and rested but did not sleep, fearing pursuers.

Soon he was back pushing and pulling the canoe across the mud, heading east. The reeds and cattails of the swamp towered all about him. Scraggly cedar clumps poked up here and there. By sunset he was to a point where he no longer felt hungry, but he was desperately thirsty. The scummy water seemed less foul than before as he cupped his hand and drank, grimacing at the taste but swallowing anyway. He could not find dry ground, so he cut rushes with his knife and piled them up to make a floating bed on the mud. He knew Chippewas preferred not to travel at night and he hoped the Pillagers shared their distaste. He had to sleep. Even the swarming mosquitoes could no longer keep him awake.

When he woke near dawn he found his rush bed had sunk into the mud. His face was filthy with muck. He stumbled to his feet. His stomach hurt from hunger. He drank more of the swamp water and pressed on eastward. He realized that where the mud stuck to his face the mosquitoes had not bitten. He then covered his exposed skin with mud.

Late in the day he came to deep water. He was able to canoe again. So grateful was he for the relief that the shadows grew long before he realized the stream had twisted and he was heading southwest, the wrong direction. He had to go east. Never mind for now, he thought. Correct direction tomorrow. He found a patch of small shrubs growing among a few cedars. He paddled the canoe among them for the night.

Flann fell asleep immediately but suddenly woke some time later. Something had roused him and he lay very still, listening. Darkness had fallen. For a long time he heard nothing but the steady piping of frogs. Suddenly a howl sounded to his rear. He lurched erect, heart pounding. The cry sounded again and Flann sucked in a deep breath. Let it be a wildcat, a lynx, he prayed. But not Pillagers, oh Lord, not Pillagers.

126

He tipped the canoe onto its side and crawled under the lean-to it formed. He kept his hand on the hilt of his knife. Did a lynx attack a human, unprovoked?

There was another cry, then nothing. As time passed, Flann relaxed. He found himself thinking of his father and the man's determination to force him to return to West Point. He thought, I love my father even when defying him. And in thinking of his father, Flann vowed, I will not finish my life here in this desolation. I'll make it back to Boston, I'll finish my medical studies, I'll straighten out the old man's estate. And I'll marry Lynette. She's there waiting for me.

What would father have thought of Lynette? Surely he would have been captivated by her, but not for long. Father admires openness in women, not coquettishness. And Lynette *is* a flirt.

Not to say that Lynette isn't honest. Of course she is. But open? No. Birch Leaf is open, Lynette is not.

Birch Leaf is waiting for me, too. She said she would. Lord, two women waiting for a fool lost in an endless swamp.

Flann laughed humorlessly. He experienced a physical sensation which troubled him, a growing euphoria. Then he began shaking, not violently, yet he was unable to stop.

He recognized what was happening to him. Fever, this ague is fever. I need quinine. Quinine. And I have none, dear Lord. My quinine is at the bottom of Kitchigami by now, carried there by the Ontonagon.

But wait, O'Phelan. Wait.

What was it that Crouching Fox showed you once? The bark of some bush he used to treat fever. It looked like dogwood, all right.

I haven't seen any dogwood.

I haven't heard the lynx, either. Is it creeping toward me, waiting to spring?

Eventually Flann dozed. Apparitions stalked his dreams. Lynette with the face of a lynx, springing at him, tearing his flesh with her sharp claws. Dancing Drum, arrow embedded in his back, hovering above him on owl wings, whispering about spirits that killed. Pillagers crouching around him their arrows thudding into the canoe.

Flann awoke to grayness and rain splashing on the birch-bark of the canoe covering him. He no longer shook with fever, but when he crawled out of the shelter and tried to stand, his legs buckled. He rested a few minutes and tried again. His head swam when he came upright. He forced himself to walk.

He staggered through the shrubs and saw small berries growing on plants near the ground. The plants stretched away into the rainy distance, seemingly for acres. He smiled. Here was breakfast. He had found a blueberry marsh.

Flann fell to his knees and grabbed at the berries, shoving them into his mouth as fast as he could pick them. Many were old and withered. It was late in the season for blueberries, but they tasted as good as any food he had ever eaten.

Flann vomited long before his hunger was appeased.

After he was no longer sick he waited, then drank a little water from the stream, and when that settled he cautiously ate a few more blueberries. His nausea passed.

The rain was gentle but steady and the sky was uniformly gray. He had to move on. Flann returned to the canoe and launched it into the stream. He placed blueberries into the bottom before paddling away. His clothes were soaked and before he had gone far he began to shiver again. He tried to recall what he had planned to accomplish. It was something important, but his thoughts were blurred and scattered. Mechanically he dipped the paddle in and out, in and out. When his shaking hands could no longer hold the paddle, he stowed it and drifted with the current until the canoe became stuck among reeds.

Flann bowed his head and shut his eyes. He was lost in the swamps of some damned wilderness of scrubby cedars and reeds. He had no idea how long it was before he realized his feet were in water. When he opened his eyes he saw blueberries floating in front of him. The canoe slowly settled as water rose inside it.

Goddamnit. He scooped berries into his mouth so all of them would not be lost. Then he left the canoe. The swamp water was hip-deep. Inside the canoe was a rip where a seam had given way. He yelled in rage. Couldn't those bastard Pillagers even build a decent canoe?

He abandoned the canoe and slogged downstream for some time before he felt the tremble in his legs that meant the fever was returning. He had to find high ground or collapse and drown ignominiously in a foot of water.

Flann began to mumble. "He turneth the wilderness into standing water . . . He poureth contempt upon princes and causeth them to wander in the wilderness. . . ."

He knew the words were from Psalms and set his mind trying to remember which one. When he was a child he had learned Psalms by heart to please his father. More words came to him. "He turneth rivers into a wilderness. . . ." He knew it was the same Psalm that told of going down to the sea in ships. He could not remember.

"I shall remember!" he shouted. "I shall!"

It seemed that a voice answered him, but he couldn't understand its words. Stumbling and falling and rising again, Flann kept moving. The voice spoke once more. Was it his father? He called him by name. "Father."

"Ishcoda!" a man exclaimed.

Flann stared at the apparition in front of him. It was a brave dressed in buckskin loin cloth. He fumbled for his knife.

"Ishcoda!" the brave cried again.

Flann tried to focus on him, but his knees buckled and he fell forward. He never hit the earth. He was aware of many hands catching him. He was being lifted and carried.

The Pillagers had captured him, he thought. He would be taken to their squalid village and there be tortured slowly to death. He groaned angrily and cursed himself for a fool.

"You're not torturing me, you're not," he mumbled, struggling to free himself. He twisted, he kicked, he punched. It won nothing for him. He was weak. The hands that held him were strong.

In delirium, his mind continued to wander.

Why have you come in to this country? The sin of pride, that's why. Believing you can succeed no matter how great the task. Oh, yes. So superior, you are, compared to the simple savages. You are convinced they will trust an honest man and that you are that man. Children of nature, you believe. How wrong you have been from the beginning. You've found the guns you came to find, all right. The Pillagers have them. And you'll die knowing this. Shoot? No, roasted. Eaten, if you die bravely enough before these cannibals.

He drifted into unconsciousness.

Psalms again. "Give thanks unto the Lord for He is good. . . . For His mercy endureth forever. . . ." That was the beginning of Psalm 107. I remembered after all. . . . "Let the redeemed of the Lord say so, whom he hath redeemed from the hand of the enemy . . . The Lord is good. . . ."

I have fallen among savages who know not the Lord . . . I won't die, I say. Damn you, you won't eat me. . . .

"Ishcoda," one Indian said.

The word echoed in his mind. He understood its meaning. He was fire. He was Ishcoda.

"Ahab was roasted in the fire by the King of Babylon," Flann muttered. I am not Ahab. I am fire itself. Ishcoda. I cannot be roasted. You cannot roast what is already fire.

I'll explode into flame and sear these savages . . . I speak the words. Words. The Bible has no words to strike men dead. . . .

Then he bellowed aloud. He remembered.

Those words belonged to Dancing Drum, who knew the arrow-sharp words for killing.

A void opened before Flann and he fell headlong into it.

131

Chapter 13

"Drink," a man's voice ordered, speaking Chippewa.

Flann swallowed bitter liquid, feeling he had swallowed it before. He gagged, but kept the potion down. He opened his eyes and saw the scarred face of Crouching Fox.

"Good. Your spirit returns," the shaman said.

Flann raised himself on an elbow and looked around. He was surrounded by Chippewa warriors, some still sleeping, some sitting up. Though the early dawn light was faint, he recognized Black Rock and Rift-in-the-Clouds. He sighed happily. He had not been taken by Pillagers after all.

"I've been dosing you with a broth of dogwood bark and other sacred roots," Crouching Fox said.

Flann eased to a sitting position. He felt lightheaded, but otherwise surprisingly good.

"How did you find me?" he asked.

"Thunderbird, who flies with us, directed you to cross our path," the shaman told him.

Flann glanced about at the men. "You've brought many braves."

"These warriors all lust for Sioux blood."

Flann blinked and understood with sadness. This hadn't been a rescue mission for him. The Chippewas were on a raiding party, heading for Sioux country.

"By nightfall we'll be within striking distance," the shaman said.

Rift-in-the-Clouds squatted beside Flann. "Ho," he said. "Ishcoda again joins us against the snakes. Here. Food to give you strength."

Flann took the stick with a duck skewered on it from the brave, nodding in thanks. He tore at the meat with his teeth, forcing himself to chew slowly so he would not eat too much at once and be sick. Rift-in-the-Clouds watched with approval.

When he had gnawed the last of the meat from the bones, Flann stood. His feet were bare.

"Brother, here are moccasins," Crouching Fox offered. "I have the auzeum—you call it the breech-cloth—for you after you wash."

Flann stripped and washed himself in a stream. He put on the breechcloth and the new moccasins. He was bent over rinsing out his filthy clothes when he raised his head and saw Black Rock beside him. Hastily Flann stood up to face him, hand going to his knife hilt.

"You do not trust me," Black Rock said.

"Why should I? You first try to drown me, then send an arrow after me."

Black Rock frowned. "I don't understand your talk of arrows."

"You know you tried to put an arrow in my back at Ontonagon right after you promised you wouldn't harm me. Why should I trust you?"

"I did not shoot at you."

"Someone did."

"Am I a dog? Would I lie?" Black Rock demanded.

The two stood glaring at each other. Finally, Black Rock spoke. "When I use my bow, the arrow flies true. I said I wouldn't harm you and I won't, although I'll shed no tears if a Sioux bullet finishes you." He strode off.

Flann watched him go. Was it possible Black Rock hadn't shot at him? No. Flann shook his head. The brave hated him because of Birch Leaf. No one else at Ontonagon had any reason to wish him dead.

Flann returned to the camp. He would have to go with the war party. He knew the Chippewas would never turn back from their raid. It would be useless to ask Crouching Fox to send a brave to guide Flann east to La Pointe. No warrior wanted to miss the glory of war.

He could not find his way alone. He said softly, "Like it or not, I'm headed for Sioux country.

"But I will not take part in the fighting," he told himself. "Not this time. The Sioux aren't my enemies."

Crouching Fox muttered something about mad white men talking to themselves as if they themselves were the Great Spirit and gave Flann a blanket for his shoulders. He put Flann in the bow of his canoe. Flann placed his soggy clothing on the canoe bottom and noticed two rifles there. They were new. He looked back at the shaman.

"New guns," Flann said.

Crouching Fox pushed the canoe away from the bank. "Many rifles are needed to kill Sioux," he said. "One is yours."

"It must have cost many skins for new rifles."

"Copper Sky tends to such matters. Paddle, brother."

The stream grew larger farther on and spilled into a wide river. "Mississippi," the shaman said, anticipating Flann's question. After a time the canoes edged into the mouth of a stream feeding from the west side of the Mississippi River and paddled upstream.

The day was cloudy, but the rain held off. They portaged four times, leaving the canoes hidden in the underbrush at the last stream. After walking about five miles, Rift-in-the-Clouds chose the night camp.

No fires were built. Crouching Fox offered Flann a dried meat and berry mixture that, taken with water, tasted good and was filling.

As the warriors settled down, Flann moved casually among them. All the rifles he saw were new.

"Thunderbird told me in a dream that you'd come with us," the shaman said as they sat together. "I knew we'd cross your trail."

Flann realized he hadn't yet given any explanation of what had happened to him on the Leech Lake expedition. Nor was he anxious to do so even now. He nonetheless felt he owed an accounting.

"The Pillagers got drunk and attacked us," he recalled. "They were a band on Sandy Lake. Broken Feather's their chief, but I don't think he had much to do with the attack. Henri disappeared. I think they killed him. They came after Dancing Drum and me. He took out a white seashell—you'll know about that because you're mide, too—and 'shot' one of them with it. He scared the rest. We got to the canoes, but someone put an arrow in Dancing Drum's back and he fell into the river. All that was left in the canoe was his otter skin bag." Flann hesitated. "I no longer have it."

Crouching Fox reached into the buckskin sack he

carried and pulled out the otter skin bag. "You keep the wayan if he left it for you," he said.

"I don't know that Dancing Drum meant for me to have this," Flann said, feeling the softness of the otter fur under his fingers.

"If he left his bag behind, it's yours."

"But he was dying."

"A mide knows even at the moment of death what must be done," the shaman responded.

Flann secured the otter bag under his waistband. "Can you tell me about the shell. Or is that too sacred?"

"Mide spirit power is in the megis, the seashell. The spirit of the shell is deadly and can kill if a powerful shaman directs the force. Dancing Drum was such a shaman." Crouching Fox touched the mink-skin wayan at his waist. "I, too, can kill with the megis."

"Could you kill me?"

The shaman looked into Flann's face. In the twilight, his eyes were hidden in pools of shadow. "Even though you are my brother, you're still a white man. No, the power is useless against whites. I would not use it against you anyway. The spirits would punish me for trying."

"Because I'm white?"

"No. Because you're my blood brother."

"Could I become a mide?"

"No. Still, as I've promised, I'll teach you all that's not sacred."

"Henri Fontenac was afraid of Dancing Drum. When we camped at night, Henri thought the shaman called up spirits to haunt the camp. Owls and wolves."

Crouching Fox nodded. "Henri was right. He is metis and belongs to the People as well as to the whites. He knew that a mide can call spirits to protect the men in the camp. Dancing Drum could have killed Henri with the shell, had he wished."

"I owe you my life," Flann realized. "I was lost and would have died in the swamps except for you."

"Thunderbird meant it to be so. And Thunderbird prophesies you will aid us with the Sioux."

"I don't intend to use the rifle."

"Thunderbird is never wrong."

Flann shrugged. There was no point in arguing.

"You were chanting in the language of the white man when we found you," Crouching Fox said after a time. "Were you talking to your own spirits?"

Flann dimly remembered himself mumbling verses from the Bible. "Yes, I was, in a way," he said. "My fever brought dreams into my mind."

"And will your gods also help against the enemy?"

"I have but one god, like the Black Robe."

Exactly the same god as the priest's, Flann thought. Even though mine is Protestant and his is Catholic, and sometimes we are at each other's throat over true possession. Does God really care how He is worshipped?

"That god is a powerful one," Crouching Fox said. "If he helps you, all will be well."

"My god could be yours, too," Flann said. "He loves all men."

"Your god is right for you but not for me," Crouching Fox replied. "I've listened to the Black Robe. He says I must give up all the spirits of the People for his one god. How can I do this? The spirits have protected and helped me all my life. I am theirs and they are mine."

I don't know how to answer this, Flann thought. I'd best leave theology to ministers and priests.

137

"The Great Spirit, Kitchi Manito, made the People to be different from the whites. This is what I told the Black Robe," Crouching Fox said. "We live differently and we go to a different place when we die. No doubt your god and Kitchi Manito are friends and brothers as you and I are friends and brothers, although different."

Rift-in-the-Clouds approached and sat down. "What do you see for tomorrow?" he asked the shaman. "Are the omens good?"

Crouching Fox did not speak. At last he looked at the war captain. "I'll need a jizikun."

Rift-in-the-Clouds rose and called to several braves, telling them to cut poles and to bring their blankets. They built a tepee of saplings and used their blankets for a cover. Just before dark the shaman crawled into the jizikun. Flann had not seen him bring a drum in with him, but now a drumbeat sounded softly from inside.

The drum stopped. The warriors surrounded the jizikun, standing quietly. Flann heard frogs calling in the ponds and the cry of a bird settling in for the night.

Suddenly the frogs stopped. Silence blanketed the camp. The jizikun shook so violently that Flann was surprised the structure didn't collapse. The shaking stopped. When a howl rose from inside, Flann shook with fear. An eagle screamed, a lynx caterwauled, a bear grunted, all seemingly in unison. And all the sounds seemed to originate from inside the jizikun.

A tiny, shrill voice spoke in a tongue Flann did not understand. The sound inside the jizikun was like the piping of a bird. The warriors all clapped softly when they heard the voice.

"The Great Turtle Spirit," Rift-in-the-Clouds whispered.

Crouching Fox spoke. "Colleague, we go against

138

the enemy, the Sioux snakes, Nadouesse. When the sun rises on the new day, we attack. I ask, colleague, that you tell me how it will go for us."

The shrill voice answered in gibberish. Flann shared the tension of the warriors around him and was sure they could not understand what was said any more than he could.

At last the voice stopped. Moments later the frogs began croaking again.

"Turtle has answered," the shaman said. He al-allowed the tension to build before going on. "The People will triumph in the light, was his message. In the light will the warriors fall upon the enemy as victors."

"Ho!" The yell of approval came from all sides.

After dismantling the jizikun, the braves dispersed, taking their blankets and stretching out on the ground to sleep.

Flann was roused before dawn by Crouching Fox's low voice in his ear. "Ishcoda."

He found everyone else awake and prepared to move on.

"Our scouts say the enemy village is quiet, that the Sioux sleep without worry."

"How near are we?"

"A fast march will get us there before dawn. You'll be the last to arrive, for you make much noise when you walk. I'll stay behind with you."

This suited Flann. He carried a rifle and pack. He hiked along with the shaman until the sky grayed. Then they stopped in a grove of elms. Crouching Fox took paint from his pouch and carefully streaked his own face with red stripes, painting half-circles on each cheek with lines radiating from them. He approached Flann. Flann shook his head.

139

"It's necessary," the shaman insisted, smearing vermilion on Flann's forehead.

Flann gave in and let Crouching Fox paint his face. Next they placed all their belongings, except knives, rifles and ammunition, on Flann's blanket. Flann started to undo the otter skin bag at his waist, but Crouching Fox shook his head and rolled up the blanket. Flann noticed the shaman kept his mink skin wayan, too.

Clad in nothing but a breechcloth and moccasins, Flann stood beside Crouching Fox, shivering slightly in the predawn breeze. My God, I must be a sight, he thought. I'm dressed like an Indian with my face painted as red as my hair and beard.

The shaman hid the blanket containing their belongings. Warning Flann he must do his best to move quietly, he motioned him to follow. They crept toward a rise but did not crest it. Then they turned aside to enter a clump of oak saplings. Ahead, Flann now saw a village of conical tepees beside a creek. They were the lodges of the Sioux.

A penetrating shriek made Flann jump. Rift-in-the-Clouds leaped from cover a few yards away and raced into the village, bellowing war cries as he ran. Other Chippewa warriors catapulted from behind rocks and bushes, also yelling and running after their war captain.

"Now," Crouching Fox ordered, dashing from cover toward the tepees.

Flann stayed where he was. The shaman glanced back, hesitated, then ran on.

Flann tightened his grip on the rifle as he heard shots, then Sioux women screaming and hoarse shouts of pain. Dogs barked frantically. Chippewa warriors brandished clubs and tomahawks and Sioux warriors leaped out of the tepees. From his distant observation point, Flann couldn't tell one from the other as they grappled together. However, as the fighting continued, other men and women ran from the tepees toward the cover of the trees. He saw the Sioux braves had no paint on their faces.

A succession of events occurred almost simultaneously. A Chippewa warrior, whose name Flann did not know, overtook a woman and swung his knobbed war club. The sound of her skull shattering sickened Flann. The Chippewa turned to intercept another woman. Flann suddenly ran from concealment to stop him. At that moment, three Sioux braves carrying clubs and lances ran toward them from the village.

The Chippewa warrior whirled to face them. Two Sioux went for him. Another headed for Flann, lance extended. Flann stared at the advancing Sioux and realized desperately he could do but one thing. He leveled his rifle and shot him.

The Sioux fell, blood welling from his chest. Flann reloaded, his eye on the two Sioux attacking the Chippewa. One of them came for Flann, his tomahawk raised.

Flann rammed the shot home, brought the rifle up and fired again, dropping the Sioux with a bullet in his belly.

The Chippewa smashed in the third Sioux warrior's head but then fell himself. The Sioux woman behind him plunged a knife into his back. He fell forward and lay still. The woman turned to face Flann, her teeth bared.

"I won't hurt you," he said in Chippewa. She glared at him, not understanding. However, when she realized he did not mean to shoot her, she edged away and ran through the trees.

His mind churning with many emotions—conflict, excitement and disgust—Flann returned to the shelter of the young oaks. He knew that if he attempted to help anyone in any way, he would have to defend himself against Sioux warriors and would have to kill to save his own life.

From hiding, Flann saw the woman he had saved creep from cover to the second man Flann had shot. The brave writhed with pain when she urged him to stand. Finally she lifted him to his feet and, blood running down his legs, he staggered with her into the brush. The other Sioux, with a bullet in his chest, did not move. Flann was sure he was dead.

The Chippewa warrior knifed by the woman struggled to rise. He coughed and vomited blood. She got his lung, Flann told himself. He's losing too much blood to live and there's nothing I can do to help him. It was not pleasant to watch him die, Flann thought.

Why do they fight one another? He asked this of himself in anguish, again and again.

Chippewa warriors began returning from the village. Flann saw that Rift-in-the-Clouds was driving a Sioux brave bound as prisoner before him. Black Rock and another warrior stopped to pick up the dead Chippewa and carry him with them.

Another Chippewa knelt by the dead Sioux and Flann watched in horrified fascination as the brave took his knife in one hand, the dead man's hair in the other, then delicately slit the scalp skin in a circle so the top of the scalp with its attached hair came away from the dead Sioux's head. The Chippewa waved the scalp aloft, cried out triumphantly, then turned to the dead Sioux woman with his knife. Flann looked away nauseous.

They were all savages, bloody savages.

Chapter 14

The Chippewas hurried back to their canoes. Flann saw they had two Sioux braves with them, bound with one cord circling both their necks so they could easily be choked. Both men also had their hands tied behind their backs. They walked defiantly erect, glaring at everyone who caught their eye. Despite their show of courage, Flann thought the younger Sioux was fighting to conceal his terror. He was about fourteen.

The dead Chippewa had been tied to a hastily contrived travois of poles and bark. The braves took turns pulling it. Flann saw three wounded Chippewas. One was limping with a leg injury, but all three kept up with the raiding party as they headed back to their canoes. Flann doubted they would reach the canoes before nightfall.

"A great victory," Rift-in-the-Clouds exclaimed. "We lost one warrior but we have his body. He was not left for the Sioux to scalp and throw to the wolves. We killed many snakes and took many scalps." His eyes gleamed as he glanced at the captives. "And we bring sport home for the women."

Flann did not ask for an explanation. He knew what sport the women took with prisoners. He made up his mind to talk to Crouching Fox later about the welfare of the prisoners. For the moment, he was determined not to allow any mistreatment of them on the journey back to Meenagha.

Rift-in-the-Clouds announced a night camp when darkness fell. They had not reached the canoes. As soon as they stopped, Flann changed into his own clothes and scrubbed the paint from his face. He picked up the otter skin bag Dancing Drum had left him and shoved it under his shirt.

The Chippewas set guards around the camp. Though they had been contemptuous of danger on the way to the Sioux village, now the warriors were edgy and slow to settle into sleep.

"Spirits stalk the woods," Crouching Fox told Flann. "Unfriendly spirits of the Sioux dead who seek revenge. Only the mide power keeps them from us." He touched his mink wayan.

The guards stayed close to the camp, evidently fearing the spirits mentioned by the shaman. There was no night fire, and even Flann felt uneasy. He risked raising his head and exposing it now and then to peer into the darkness.

Flann wondered, as he often did. What would his circle of friends and relatives back home in Boston think if they could have seen him at that moment? Flann pictured a platoon of sour faces. There was no one back home he could freely tell of his life among the Chippewa.

Certainly he could not tell Lynette.

Lynette would not willingly listen without protest

to his tales of violent killing raids by night, of scalpings, of dining on dogs, of near-drowning. He could not tell her of a Chippewa woman with green eyes beautiful enough to stop a man's heart.

Stop at once, Flann, Lynette would say. It all makes me ill. I am faint. How disgusting and crude and rough it all must be.

He had an insight. Andrew Jackson would listen to him and understand.

But he would probably never tell Old Hickory. Martin Van Buren had taken over the White House in March. It was President Van Buren he would report to this November. And Van Buren struck him as smaller than Jackson, not only in stature but in spirit.

An owl hooted. The sound jerked Flann out of a doze, his pulse racing. It's just an owl, damn it, he admonished himself. What would you believe? Spirits, as Henri Fontenac does?

Laying back and closing his eyes, he mulled over the guns. He planned to confront Copper Sky when they got back. He wanted to know the name of the Canadian agent who supplied the weapons. I'm one of the People now, Flann thought. Copper Sky might well trust me. If Henri had not disappeared at Leech Lake, I might have named him to the subagent as a suspect. But the Pillagers must have murdered Henri. God knows the Pillagers would never reveal the name of their gun supplier. More than likely they would kill the man who asked for it. Perhaps I should go to La Pointe first, Flann thought, report what I do know to Daniel Bushnell, then tackle Copper Sky....

"Ishcoda." Crouching Fox breathed the name into his ear, placing a hand on his wrist at the same time. "Quickly. Reach for your gun. Sioux." Flann had not even heard him come.

145

A high-pitched war cry split the night. Torches sputtered and flared into life. A horde of screaming Sioux warriors fell on the Chippewa camp. Flann shot at the closest attacker, but the man plunged on toward him. Flann ducked away to reload. Crouching Fox shot the Sioux in the face. The man fell backward, his face smashed and bloody.

In the flickering torch light, Flann could not distinguish Chippewa from Sioux. Therefore, he fired at every Indian who charged, assuming he was Sioux.

Flann reasoned the Chippewas would know him by his red hair and white man's clothes. He prayed his reasoning would prove correct.

He finally found himself at the edge of the fighting. Before him, an injured Indian struggled to stand. Was he friend or foe?

It did not matter. Before Flann could decide, another Indian rushed at the injured man and opened his head with a war club. Then the victor sawed at the fallen man's head with his knife. A few moments later, he leaped away with a whoop, a scalp dripping blood held high.

The dead man sprawled face up. "No, no, no!" Flann roared.

The dead man was Rift-in-the-Clouds. Flann felt he might weep. Had he fired, he might have saved his friend. As he cursed for not shooting the Sioux, Flann sensed motion behind him. He turned. Something slammed his head. He stumbled forward, dropping his rifle and falling to his knees. Hands grabbed his shoulders and spun him about. He saw a grimacing face. Then he was pulled to his feet. Dazed, Flann realized someone was binding his hands with leather thongs. Next, a cord was pulled down around his head and tightened on his neck.

For a long time events blurred in his mind. There were bodies to be stepped over or around, voices yelling words he didn't understand, the cord around his neck jerking him forward and choking him when he didn't move fast enough.

When Flann returned to his senses, he found himself trotting along beside a Sioux warrior who held the thong about his neck. Flann tried to move his hands. They were tied firmly behind him. Ahead he saw the conical shapes of tepees.

I'm back at the Sioux village. My God, I'm a prisoner, Flann thought, slowing. His captor pulled on the lead, and the thong cut into his neck. He increased his pace. A fire in the center of the village sent sparks into the night. Dark figures clustered about the flames. As he neared the fire, Flann saw these were old men, old women and children. They stared at him with eager, burning eyes.

Fear cut through his confusion as he remembered Henry Schoolcraft telling him the Chippewa sometimes called the Sioux by the name *aboinug,* meaning roasters, their custom of torturing foes by fire.

A tall man, impressive in a feathered crest, approached Flann and pointed his finger at Flann's breast. He spoke impassioned words. Flann did not understand one.

He tried to organize, think logically. The Sioux can see I'm white, he thought. I must give them another reason for letting me go. How was it best to speak? Certainly not in Chippewa. In English? No. He decided to try French first. The Sioux who had captured Birch Leaf had not understood French but perhaps this chief did. Many did, Flann had been told.

"I am a messenger from the Great White Father in Washington," he said, hoping the words sounded

147

bold and threatening. "Why do you treat me this way?"

The tall man, obviously the chief, stared at him. Another man came forward and spoke to the chief. The chief answered. The man turned to Flann.

Flann had guessed correctly about choice of language.

"White Coyote asks why you fight us?" he said in accented French. "Why would the Great White Father send his man against us?"

There was no use lying, Flann knew. Many surviving Sioux must have seen him fire at them. He took a deep breath and said, "I shot to keep from being killed."

White Coyote received this from the interpreter, staring at Flann as he listened. Then he spoke.

"He wants to know why you came with a Chippewa war party into our country," the interpreter said.

Why indeed? The truth was complicated and unbelievable. Flann never had a chance to reply.

"*Ecoutez,*" a voice said from behind. Flann turned his head to see who had demanded in French that they listen. He stared in surprise, for the man who had spoken was Black Rock. He was also a prisoner. A wound on his shoulder bled freely.

"The man with red hair lies," Black Rock shouted in fair French. He lunged toward Flann, but was brought up short when the cord about his neck choked him. Black Rock fell back, clawing at his neck. "Red Hair is a thief of wives," he gasped. "Don't believe what he says. He's just a fur trader. I forced him to come on the war party so that he might die by your hand instead of mine, for I have promised not to harm him. You have made no pledge. Roast him. Cut out his heart. I'll rejoice in the sight."

As White Coyote listened, he studied Black Rock.

He flung out his hand, spoke orders, and Black Rock was dragged away and tied to a post near the fire. He gave another order, and Flann's captor struck off his bonds.

Flann rubbed his wrists as the circulation came back into his hands.

"He says you have the freedom of the village, but you'll be killed if you try to escape," the interpreter told Flann. "He welcomes you into his tepee."

"I am grateful to Chief White Coyote," Flann said, thinking of how truly grateful he was. He heard drums. And then wailing began, the mourning of women. The mourning sounds rose and fell with the drumbeats.

Five women with hair shorn close to their heads and bearing bleeding gashes on their cheeks filed past Flann. They stood by the fire, staring at Black Rock. They began to dance in a circle about him, shrieking and screaming at him, telling him of their hate.

A Sioux warrior offered a Chippewa scalp attached to a short pole to one of the women. She refused, but the next took the scalp and dropped from the circle around Black Rock to start another dance. She waved the scalp over her head as she chanted in rhythm to the drums. One by one, the women accepted Chippewa scalps and joined the first woman, also leaving Black Rock alone.

Blood clotted the wound on Black Rock's shoulder. Despite his bonds he stood straight and defiant, looking at no one.

Flann turned to the interpreter to ask what would happen to Black Rock, but changed his mind. He decided it was best not to show any interest.

White Coyote motioned Flann nearer. Flann went to the chief who stared intently at his hair and beard, then at his eyes. He spoke. The interpreter again translated.

"He says you are as strange a white man as he's ever seen. He invites you to smoke."

"I accept."

White Coyote sat on a mat and gestured to Flann to sit beside him. The sky was beginning to lighten. The chief took up a pipe of red stone decorated with dyed braids, porcupine quill and downy feathers. He lit it and took a puff, then pointed the pipe in the traditional six directions exactly as the Chippewa did. He handed the pipe to Flann.

Flann drew on the pipe. The tobacco was cut with other herbs, he noticed. It was strong and bitter. He removed it from his mouth and pointed it six ways as the chief had done.

The chief regarded Flann approvingly, speaking in Sioux.

The interpreter again translated. "He says he's a friend of the Great White Father, and if you are his messenger, he's sorry to keep you from traveling but you must stay here until the Chippewas are back in their own land."

Some Chippewas had survived the Sioux night raid then, Flann thought.

"I wish to leave," he stated firmly.

White Coyote frowned when he heard this. He answered at length.

"He says no," the interpreter finally said. "He says you'll enjoy seeing your enemy of the Chippewa nation roasted after we feast. There'll be much sport, for he seems to be a courageous warrior and will survive a long time."

Flann fought to keep his apprehension and disgust

from showing on his face. "We don't treat enemies in this manner," he said.

White Coyote nodded and spoke again.

"He says he's heard the white men also shut their foes in a lodge with an iron door," the interpreter said. "What honor is there for a warrior in that?"

Flann did not answer. Trying to persuade White Coyote to spare Black Rock seemed futile. He clenched his fists, then forced himself to relax.

Frenzied yells came from the dancers, and Flann saw some Sioux warriors had joined the women dancing with the scalps. They formed a larger circle about them.

"The Great White Father does not like to hear of Sioux warring with Chippewa," Flann said, trying another approach to White Coyote's logic. "He wouldn't approve of killing a prisoner by burning him alive."

"White Coyote says we fight the Chippewa only because they make war on us. White Coyote has heard the white men put ropes around the necks of foes and hang them from trees until they die. He doesn't tell the whites not to do this thing although he wouldn't kill even a dog in such a miserable way."

Flann had no immediate response. White Coyote was speaking as other Indians had spoken before concerning the ways of the white man. Flann despaired. They'd stripped him of his knife, and he had no other weapon. Was he to sit here and watch Black Rock roast?

Flann leaped to his feet. The interpreter got up, too, saying, "He says I'm to go with you wherever you go."

A watchdog, Flann realized. What the hell does White Coyote think I'll be able to do? He stared into the interpreter's face, and knowing he was being discourteous, bluntly asked, "What's your name?"

"Day Ending."

"I wish to bathe. Must you watch me wash myself?" Flann's tone was deliberately mocking. He had no notion of how he could free Black Rock, but he couldn't remain passive any longer.

Day Ending showed no expression. "I'll take you to the chief's tepee and ask the women to bring water."

"I prefer a stream."

"You can't go out of the village."

Flann shrugged. He had had a faint hope he might somehow get away and find the trail of the surviving Chippewas. But even if he did, the Sioux must have guards posted. It would be impossible for the Chippewas to rescue Black Rock. An attack could only mean more losses.

The chief's tepee was made of buffalo hides over a conical framework of poles. Geometric figures were painted in red on the hides. Inside, the ground was covered with rawhide rugs. Buckskin pillows lay atop a bed platform. The tepee was clean. With the painted bags and gaily decorated clothes-holders hanging on the walls, it was also colorful and attractive. Except for the conical shape, Flann thought the inside was much like a Chippewa wigwam.

An older woman brought him water in a clay bowl. Then she withdrew. Day Ending remained inside the tepee while Flann washed. He called in Sioux to the woman when Flann was finished. She returned with a pair of intricately decorated moccasins for Flann. He knew he must take them or offend her. He thanked her in French and slipped out of his worn moccasins.

She took the old moccasins and the water away. When she had left the tepee, Day Ending gave Flann a

152

wary look, as if to speak. He shifted from one foot to the other.

Flann watched him. The brave seemed almost afraid of him. Why? He hadn't acted this way earlier.

"You carry an otter skin pouch," the Sioux said at last.

Flann remembered the wayan tucked into his shirt. The Sioux must have seen it while he was washing. And that was what intimidated Day Ending. Could Flann take advantage of this? The problem was, even if he should convince the Sioux he was a Medicine Man, he didn't have the slightest idea what to do with the contents of the mide bag. Therefore, it might be best to make light of the pouch.

"Just an empty bag I found on the trail," he said.

"A medicine sack?"

Flann shrugged. "I don't practice your medicine. I thought I might use this to carry tobacco."

Day Ending seemed to relax. He was preoccupied. "We feast soon," he announced.

Flann realized Day Ending clearly wished to celebrate victory far more than he wished to watch over a prisoner. On this night, chaperoning a strange visitor was a bore to Day Ending. Flann smiled. A bored and angry man was a man who might be manipulated and deceived.

"And may your need for feasting and play be turned against you," Flann said softly in English.

"What did you just say?" Day Ending demanded crossly.

"Nothing," Flann answered. "Just feast and play well."

Chapter 15

"Will all the warriors dance and talk of their exploits?" Flann asked Day Ending.

"Yes," the Sioux said. "Much dancing."

"And feasting to come."

"A dog feast."

"I saw the women dancing with the scalps. Who tends the kettles?"

"Only those who lost warriors dance," Day Ending told him. "Most of the women are busy cooking."

Flann nodded. Women always prepared the food. The cooking fires were outdoors, exactly as they were in Chippewa villages. In fact, the more Flann saw of the Sioux, the more he found them like the Chippewa. The language was different, but both Chippewa and Sioux were tall, handsome people with similar customs and beliefs. Why were they enemies?

The meat was deer as well as dog, Day Ending told Flann. There were blueberries and raspberries, but no rice. Last year's supply was gone, and this year's harvest was still to come. They would also eat boiled fish. The kettles were simmering over the fires, copper ones obtained from the traders in exchange for furs.

Flann hoped to distract Day Ending's attention somehow. The Sioux brave was young, so a pretty girl might do the trick.

"I find the Chippewa women attractive," he said to Day Ending. "I have not noticed that the Sioux girls are as pretty."

Day Ending drew himself up. "We have the fairest women of any," he exclaimed.

"Where? All I saw were those dancing with scalps. They had their hair all cut off. They certainly weren't agreeable to look at."

"In their grief they cut their hair," Day Ending said.

"All right. I can understand that. But where are these beautiful women you speak of?"

"I'll show you."

Flann followed Day Ending to a group of women tending a cooking fire. All the women turned to stare at Flann, and he realized he was such an oddity to them he might have trouble with his plans. He turned to Day Ending and said something very softly.

"This way," the Sioux said, leading him to a small clump of saplings close to a tepee. Rose streaks along the horizon hinted of dawn.

Flann ducked into the trees and turned his back on Day Ending. He quickly yanked the mide bag from his shirt. He dumped the small buckskin packets into his hands, then stuffed the otter skin back inside his shirt. He relieved himself as he had told the Sioux he must. Flann turned and started back to the cooking fires with Day Ending at his side.

Some of the Sioux women were quite attractive.

One reminded him of Snowberry at Meenagha. "She's pretty," he said to Day Ending, indicating the girl. "Why don't you tell her why you brought me over to meet them?"

While Day Ending told the women, Flann managed to slip a buckskin packet of powdered roots into the two kettles over the fire without being seen.

"Show me all the women," he demanded. "I know one Chippewa girl who shines like a star. Do you boast of any such as her?"

Birch Leaf, you do shine, he thought as he trailed the Sioux from one kettle to another. Yes, you are a star, shining and untouchable.

At another cooking fire he asked what was stewing and dropped the powder undetected as he bent over the kettle. At still another he pretended to stumble against the kettle. He burned his hand, but the powder fell into the stewing meat unseen.

At last he had dropped a packet into every kettle in the village. What if the pulverized roots and plants from the mide bag of Dancing Drum were totally harmless? He didn't believe they were, but still he had no idea what he had put into the food. He suddenly realized that if the powders were deadly poison, he would be murdering women and children as well as the braves, for although the men ate first, everyone would get a portion of the food except Black Rock.

He groaned. Good God. He, Flann O'Phelan, responsible for wiping out an entire Sioux village?

On the other hand, he rationalized, the mide were medicine men and women. Wasn't the mide bag more apt to hold plants used for purging and the like? He prayed this was so.

The women at the kettles began to ladle the food into wooden plates. One walked toward the woods.

156

"She serves the scouts," Day Ending advised him. "It's time for us to take our place with the warriors."

Flann sat next to White Coyote. Moments later he stared at the steaming contents of a plate being offered to him by one of the women. He had to take the plate from her. In fascination, he watched White Coyote lift chunks of meat to his mouth and eat them with gusto. On his other side, Day Ending smacked his lips as he enjoyed the food.

The sky grew lighter. White Coyote glanced at him and spoke.

"He wonders why you don't eat," Day Ending interpreted.

"I . . . my stomach. . . ."

White Coyote frowned and spoke again before Flann finished his halting explanation.

"He says maybe you find the food of the Sioux not good enough for you."

"No." Flann took a deep breath and picked up a chunk of meat. His stomach contracted as he raised it to his lips. Both White Coyote and Day Ending watched as he opened his mouth to take the meat. They watched until he began to chew.

"Good, good," he mumbled, fighting the nausea that threatened to make him spew out the food. The meat tasted like meat, nothing else. Still, he feared he was poisoning himself. If he vomited, White Coyote might begin to suspect something was wrong.

The chief continued to stare at Flann until he had swallowed the chunk of meat, then waited until he took another. Satisfied, White Coyote turned his attention to his own food. The women came with large bone spoons full of the stew and kept refilling the plates. Flann ate only when he saw White Coyote glance at him. The

157

chief and the other warriors took four and five platefuls of the meat stew. Grease dripped from their chins as they chewed and swallowed with obvious pleasure.

Flann saw that the women had begun to eat. He winced as he watched mothers offering food to their children, but he knew it was too late to undo what he had begun.

A warrior across from Flann suddenly rose, groaning. He clutched at his stomach and doubled over, nearly falling. He recovered and staggered away toward the trees. Others rolled over laughing at him.

The sun rose, promising a fair day. For a few minutes more everyone ate gluttonously as before. Then another man tried to get up and fell back, retching. This time no one had a chance to laugh. All at once the entire group of braves began gagging and vomiting. Flann felt sickness in his own throat as he got up and eased away from the men. White Coyote was on his knees, retching, and Day Ending lay on his face, moaning.

By the tepees, children screamed, groveling in the dirt with their mothers. Flann clenched his jaws, sickened by the sight. Pain twisted his guts. When he doubled over, he realized the mide powder was affecting him, too. He staggered toward Black Rock, who was still bound to the post. Taking a knife from a warrior too sick to resist, Flann sliced through the thongs binding him. Then he himself dropped to his knees, gagging and retching.

Black Rock tried to lift him. Flann tried to walk. A hideous shrieking commenced, grew in volume, and warriors with painted faces leaped from the concealment of the trees and rushed into the village.

Chippewas, Flann realized. The survivors who

had lain in wait. Black Rock eased Flann down beside a young elm at the edge of the village and returned to join his tribesmen.

Pain cramped Flann so badly he could not sit straight. His guts felt fiery as he vomited again and again. He staggered to his feet and looked at a ghastly scene of carnage in which the Chippewa warriors struck at the downed Sioux easily and mercilessly. To his horror, women and children were butchered as well as the men. He stumbled toward the tepees, fighting nausea and pain so severe they made his eyes water.

A woman ran toward him carrying a child. Behind her a Chippewa raised his hatchet. Flann rushed forward and put his arms about the woman.

"No," he cried.

The warrior hesitated, then lowered the tomahawk and turned toward other victims. Flann started after him, but the woman clutched at him and the child began to cry.

Flann doubled over in a spasm. When he could walk again, the woman helped him toward the trees. He sank to the ground. She huddled beside him. Through a haze of pain, he saw her face was wrinkled with age. The small boy she cuddled stared at him with frightened eyes.

He tried to get up, to go back to the tepees and stop the killing, but he could not stand. He drifted in and out of consciousness.

"Ishcoda."

Flann opened his eyes. Crouching Fox stood over him.

"You must travel with us. I'll help you."

With the shaman's aid, Flann got to his feet, his head whirling. "Mide bag," he mumbled. "I used Dancing Drum's medicines. In the food. Ate some."

"You'll recover, but the Sioux won't. We've killed them. Every one. Are these your captives?"

Captives? Flann looked about, confused. The old woman stood next to him, still holding the little boy. He glanced at the bloody remains of the Sioux among the tepees. The woman pointed at herself, then to Flann, and nodded vigorously.

"She wants to come with you," Crouching Fox said. "She'll probably starve here." His voice was casual. "She is old and not much use to you. Do you want her along?"

Flann shuddered. "Yes. Bring them both."

It wasn't until sundown that Flann recovered from his own illness. Somehow, he stumbled along until they reached the hidden canoes. Soon they portaged to the next stream and went on until they had crossed the Mississippi. There was no night camp, but near dawn the Chippewas halted to rest.

Flann stared around him. Fifteen braves were left out of twenty. Two of the warriors had Sioux captives—men—on thong leads. The old woman and the child huddled next to him.

Flann recalled Crouching Fox's words.

Back at the Sioux village, no one was alive. My fault, Flann told himself. My fault. A deep gloom settled over him. What was the Hippocratic oath? To administer no harmful drugs, to abstain from every evil use of the art of medicine. A hollow oath for me, he thought.

The Chippewas slept, then resumed the journey at midday. That night they did camp, and after eating they grew lively, boasting of their war deeds. They felt safe from pursuit.

"I bring a captive with me," Crazy Crane said. "The women will be pleased."

160

"I bring six scalps," Shining Eye bragged.

"Ishcoda brings an old woman to warm his bed," Little Cedar put in, laughing.

The braves roared with laughter and even Crouching Fox chuckled. Flann forced himself to smile. He didn't hate the warriors. They had only taken terrible advantage of what he himself had started.

"And Ishcoda has a son, too, without any of the effort," Little Cedar added, grinning. The braves laughed again, but with approval now, for a son was of value.

Looking at the captive Sioux warriors, Flann saw that they were the same two originally taken from the village. He asked Crouching Fox about this.

"When we crept back to the village after being surprised in the woods, we tied these prisoners to trees with buckskin across their mouths so they couldn't warn the Sioux."

"They aren't helpless like the old woman. Why not let them go?"

"To follow and try to kill us? Or to run to the nearest Sioux village to muster a war party? Besides, our women will expect captives to ease the loss of our dead warriors."

There were five Chippewa dead, including the war captain, Rift-in-the-Clouds. Crouching Fox told Flann the bodies were hidden where animals could not reach them. Men would return later to retrieve the bodies for proper burial beside Kitchigami.

Black Rock said nothing at all to Flann, but Flann knew Black Rock was watching him. I saved your damned life, Flann thought, and wiped out a Sioux tribe to do it. Just as Black Rock had saved his life by his outburst in front of White Coyote. He had

161

owed Black Rock. And he had paid; at a terrible price in Sioux lives.

Flann tried to forget his feelings of guilt as the group journeyed east. He was among these people for a reason. He must get to La Pointe as soon as possible and forget everything but his mission.

Days passed. Flann saw no sign of Lake Superior, and he was troubled by this.

"We go by the inland route," Crouching Fox said. He drew a map in the dirt. "See? Here is the village of Lac Vieux Desert where two of the warriors live. We go there first. Then we come to Lake Gogebic. Ontonagon is this way. Here some of us separate. The Ontonagon braves travel northwest from Lake Gogebic and we travel north."

Flann saw from the map that Kitchigami was miles to the north. "I must go to La Pointe as soon as possible."

"You'll be taken there after the dances, after the mourning for the dead."

By the fire that night, Crouching Fox told Flann the Sioux woman's name was Fire Grass. "I know something of how the Sioux speak," he said. "The boy is called Squirrel."

Flann looked down at the bright eyes of the child squatting by his side. The boy came to sit near him every chance he got and had grown bold enough to tug at Flann's beard.

"She has told the boy you are his father," Crouching Fox said, smiling as Flann dodged Squirrel's attempt to get at his beard.

My God, what next? Flann wondered. He hoped Soft Willow would be willing to take Fire Grass and

Squirrel into her wigwam. He certainly couldn't be responsible for them. If she wouldn't, perhaps a family who had lost a warrior would adopt the child. Then perhaps he would bring Fire Grass to La Pointe and let the subagent solve the problem.

The two captive Sioux warriors were another matter. They had been fed on the journey and Flann saw this as an indication that they might be meant for adoption, too. He had asked Crouching Fox.

"They're for the women. The women decide," was the answer he got.

Did that mean adoption for husbands. Sons? What?

Squirrel succeeded in scrambling onto his lap and now yanked at Flann's beard.

"Ouch! You little imp." Flann seized the boy and, rising, threw him into the air and caught him. Squirrel chortled and squealed with glee.

An image of Birch Leaf holding Squirrel flashed through Flann's mind. He saw himself with them in a wigwam around a fire. It was a pleasing image. He caught the boy for the last time, then set him on the ground. As he looked up he saw Black Rock staring at him.

Damn it, I've had enough of this, he told himself. "We've settled our debt to one another," Flann said, "yet you watch me like an enemy."

"I seek to understand you," Black Rock replied. "I know only traders among the whites, and you are not like them."

I seek to understand myself, Flann thought.

"If not for you I'd have been burned by the Sioux and my heart would have been eaten. I would have died well, I think." Black Rock spoke quietly but with assurance. He nodded at the larger of the Sioux warriors. "He'll die well, but the other trembles already at what he faces. I think there'll be but one courageous heart to feast on in Meenagha."

Chapter 16

They arrived at Meenagha late one morning. The women, who had been hauling rice makuks and flails toward the village canoes, dropped everything and ran along the river bank, crying out. Dogs barked. The children and the older men hurried to the river as the war party canoes came downstream.

The women scanned the canoes, looking for husbands and sons. Wails sounded for the missing. The canoes were moored and the captive Sioux warriors were led through the crowd of screaming women and taken to posts set in the ground by the midewigan. There they were tied.

Flann looked for Birch Leaf and when her green eyes met his, he felt momentarily unnerved by the leap of excitement inside him. The warriors, led by Crouching Fox, approached Copper Sky. Crouching Fox spoke.

"Rift-in-the-Clouds fought bravely and died well. Ten Geese took three scalps before he died fighting. Night Rain captured one of the Sioux warriors we have brought with us, but then was killed. Dead Meenagha warriors, all courageous, their hearts brave and true."

The women of the dead warriors increased their mourning shrieks and, to Flann's horror, began tearing at their own faces and arms with their fingernails, producing deep, bleeding gashes.

"I, Crouching Fox, tell you Night Rain's captive belongs to the women."

"I, Crazy Crane, give my captive to the women, also."

The bereaved women left the others, hurried toward the Sioux tied to the posts and began to circle them. They were screaming, as the Sioux women had when they harried Black Rock.

One by one the six Meenagha warriors told of their war deeds. Finally, it was Flann's turn to report. He shook his head, indicating he wouldn't speak. Gently he took the arm of Fire Grass, who was carrying Squirrel, and led her to where Birch Leaf stood beside Soft Willow.

"Except for the captive warriors, she and the boy are all who are left of the Sioux village," Flann said, giving their names.

"Squirrel's a fine, healthy boy," Soft Willow said.

"Will you take these two into your wigwam?" Flann asked. "I have no place for them."

Fire Grass, who had been staring intently at Birch Leaf, suddenly began shouting in Sioux, pointing to Birch Leaf again and again. Birch Leaf shrank from her. Heads turned to the Sioux woman.

"I make them welcome," Soft Willow said hastily, taking Fire Grass by the arm. The old woman quieted and walked with her.

Birch Leaf stared after Fire Grass. "What did she say?"

166

"I don't know," Flann replied.

"She frightens me."

"I'm sure she's harmless, an old woman."

Birch Leaf turned to him. "I'm glad you've returned." She smiled. "Even though you said you wouldn't."

Flann wanted very much to take her into his arms. Instead he looked away. "Black Rock is all right. He left us at Lake Gogebic to paddle down the Ontonagon River. He saved my life in the Sioux village."

"He's always been a courageous warrior, afraid of no one. I didn't know you had joined the war party."

Flann shook his head. "That's a long story."

"Will you come to the wigwam? I've made new clothes for you while you were away." She touched the sleeve of his shirt and wrinkled her nose. "You need them, I see."

Flann was suddenly conscious of his travel-stained, worn clothes. "You're right, I do need a change of clothes. And a bath, I'm afraid. But I must leave for La Pointe as soon as possible."

Her eyes widened. "Before the dancing? You can't leave before the celebration if you were with the war party. The spirits of the dead enemy must be soothed and laid to rest, or they'll follow you the rest of your life. And that's a terrible fate."

He took her hand. "Birch Leaf, my beliefs are not yours. No spirits will follow me." Just my own conscience, he thought.

Holding him by the hand, she brought him to Soft Willow's wigwam. She ducked inside and came out with buckskin moccasins, leggings, breechcloth and a blue tunic. All were beaded with intricate and colorful designs of leaves and flowers and birds.

"Will you tell of your bravery at the dancing?"

167

she asked. "I haven't yet heard how many warriors you. . . ."

"I don't want to think about that," he snapped.

Startled, Birch Leaf stepped back. She retreated into the wigwam. Flann swore, hesitated, then turned away to Crouching Fox's wigwam.

Later, in the sweat lodge with the shaman and the other warriors, Flann asked Crouching Fox again about La Pointe.

"After sunrise. No one will go now before the celebration. Why are you in such a hurry? The journey is not safe for you alone. Kitchigami has a restless spirit."

Flann started to object, then thought of the storm he and Rift-in-the-Clouds had experienced together and decided the shaman was right.

A boy entered and poured water over the hot stones. Clouds of steam thickened the air. Flann found himself relaxing in the heat and thinking of days past. Life was short. He had thought his was over at least three times in past weeks. He had lived, but Rift-in-the-Clouds was dead and so was the proud Sioux chief, White Coyote. Henri Fontenac and Dancing Drum had died among the Pillagers. So why should he risk his life alone in a canoe when one day more wouldn't make any difference? He could not count on good luck forever. Or on God's intervention. Or on whatever it was that kept him breathing while other men died.

Besides, he could use the extra hours for approaching Copper Sky about the new guns he had seen in Indian hands.

"Soft Willow takes the Sioux woman and the boy?" Crouching Fox asked.

"Yes. The old woman seemed excited about something. Did you hear her?"

"I heard."

Flann waited, but Crouching Fox did not elaborate. "Did you understand her words?" he asked finally.

"She spoke of Birch Leaf."

"I saw Fire Grass staring at her. What did she say?"

Crouching Fox did not answer for a time and Flann grew uneasy. What was wrong? At last the shaman spoke.

"The Sioux woman recognized Birch Leaf as one she had known as a child living in the Sioux village."

"Are you saying Birch Leaf is, was a Sioux?"

"No. She was never adopted by them. I remember the raid, when Birch Leaf was brought to Meenagha, although I didn't live here then. It was my first war party. We crept up to the Sioux village and discovered their warriors had just returned from a raid against the Sauk. There they had seized the child, Birch Leaf, who'd been taken by the Sauk from whites. We took the child as a captive when we fell on the village."

Flann half rose, staring through the steam at the shaman. "You mean Birch Leaf is a white woman?"

"No. She's Anishinabe. She's Soft Willow's daughter."

Flann sank back down. After a moment, he said, "What I hear you say is that Soft Willow adopted Birch Leaf. The girl did have white parents and was stolen from them by the Sauk."

"It's as you say."

Flann sat still for a long time before speaking. More hot stones were added to the pile with wooden tongs, and an evergreen-and-water mixture was poured over them.

"I never would have heard this if Fire Grass hadn't recognized Birch Leaf. Do you deny it?"

"There is no reason to speak of the matter."

"No reason? What of the girl's parents? They lost a daughter. They may still search for her. And Birch Leaf herself. . . ."

"I tell you she is one of the People. As you are. I talk no more of this." Crouching Fox's tone was harsh. He rose and, grabbing his loin-cloth, put it on and left the sweat lodge.

Flann followed, plunging into the lake with the shaman, then went back to his wigwam to dress. Birch Leaf had done a fine job with the clothes. They fit him well. He still preferred trousers to the breechcloth and leggings, but had to admit he found moccasins more comfortable than any boot he had ever worn.

Outside, the drums were throbbing, bringing to his mind the plight of the Sioux warriors.

"You and Crazy Crane gave the captives to the women," he said to Crouching Fox. "Yet Black Rock spoke of eating their hearts."

"The women who have lost men in the battle decide the fate of each captive," the shaman said.

"Then the Sioux might be adopted to replace sons or brothers?"

"Yes."

"Will this happen?"

"The women are angry. The Sioux attacked us first and killed Morning Wind. They'll want blood."

Flann left the wigwam. He heard the wails of the grieving women sounding above the drumbeats. He saw they were still dancing around the Sioux. Fresh blood ran down some of the women's arms from self-inflicted wounds. An older brave stood watching them. He was a man whose name Flann didn't know. As Flann came abreast of him, he saw his face was painted black. He had lost a son.

Flann stood quietly beside the older man. He let time pass before he said, "I, Ishcoda, tell you your son fought bravely." Even though he didn't know which warrior had been the man's dead son, all the Chippewa warriors had shown courage, so he told no lie.

The man looked at him, nodded, but did not speak.

"The Sioux fought fiercely," Flann said after a time. "Both those captive warriors are courageous."

The man still did not reply. Flann was determined to go on. The frenzied women might not even hear if he tried to talk to them. This man might be his only hope to save the captives.

"One Sioux is a man much as I am in years," Flann said. "The other is still a boy, hardly old enough to be a warrior. I, Ishcoda, who killed Sioux myself, ask you to consider this. I ask you to think about these two captives, both brave, though one is very young."

He waited beside the black-painted man. He grunted to indicate he had heard Flann, but gave no other reaction. Flann had not learned the Chippewa speech for mercy. He realized that perhaps there wasn't a word for it in their language.

The drumbeat quickened. Rattles sounded above the wailing of the women. Flann had given up any hope of the bereaved father taking action when the man unfolded his arms and started toward the circling women. Flann held his breath as he stopped and stared first at one Sioux prisoner, then the other. Both captives gazed over his head, as if not seeing the older man.

Then the Chippewa spoke to one of the women, taking her arm and pulling her from the circle. Flann

171

let out his breath. For a moment she fought to get away, then stood limply beside him. He talked in so low a tone that Flann couldn't hear. The woman's head drooped. She seemed resigned to what was happening. The man spoke, the woman stood mute at his side, the other women wailed and danced and the two Sioux looked at no one. Tension grew in Flann. He had to struggle to stay where he was, to remain still.

At last the woman raised her head. She turned and looked at the younger Sioux. Her hand went to the knife at her belt. She slipped between two of the women so she was inside their circle. Flann saw her hand come up with the knife blade glistening silver in the sun.

"Know this," she cried. "I, the mother of Night Rain, claim this warrior as my son." The knife slashed downward through the bonds of the captive. She took the young Sioux's hand and led him to her husband. "Here, my husband, is your son."

As she spoke, clouds cut off the sunlight. Everyone looked up. "An omen," the woman said. "He shall be called Cloud-across-the-Sun."

With his new mother and father each holding one of his hands, the Sioux was brought toward the wigwams. As they passed, Flann saw the boy's face showed fatigue and a guarded relief. He understood what had happened. He realized he would live.

Flann hurried to the remaining women. He tried to talk to them, to persuade them that one of them should choose the other captive as a replacement for a lost loved one. They ignored him. They wailed and shrieked until his words were lost in the noise. Finally, he gave up.

As Flann walked away from the women he saw that Crouching Fox waited, and watched.

"Good," the shaman said. "The young warrior might have proven weak, and we all would have been sorry then to kill him. Now he can grow and learn more courage and be a true warrior of the People."

"You still have the other." Flann's words were bitter.

"Ishcoda. Listen carefully. You will not interfere with what must be done."

"I won't be a party to torture."

"I tell you that you will not interfere."

They stood face to face, measuring one another. At last the shaman said, "Come to the dance, brother." He motioned toward the captive. "He stays as he is until dark. The warriors who fought with you against the Sioux will want you at the celebration. Do you hate them so much that you won't see them now?"

What could he do? Skulk in a wigwam while the celebration went on? Flann knew there would be a scalp dance and each warrior would tell of his exploits in detail. The warriors would feel slighted if he did not stand with them. He decided he had no intention of saying a word, but that he could be there. Later he would find a way to get a rifle, for even if he had to stand off every Chippewa in the village, he was not going to let them burn the Sioux brave alive.

Copper Sky invited Flann to sit at his right. Some of the warriors had begun to dance with scalps already stretched and attached to poles. He knew the women would be given these poles later to dance with, and then to place on the graves of their dead warriors.

Flann became fascinated while watching the dancers. He had never seen such adroit suppleness in men, and since he had grown more accustomed to the grotesque painting of face and body, he paid more attention to the movements. The leaps were always ex-

actly after a certain number of one, one-two steps, all
in rhythm with the drumbeats.

A makuk of drink was thrust into his hands, and
he lifted it to his lips, then paused. Crouching Fox had
handed him the makuk. Unobtrusively he smelled the
red liquid. Raspberry.

He glanced at Crouching Fox. His blood brother
was just as crafty as his name. True, other men were
drinking but how did he know there was not something
extra in his? Not to kill him, but to put him out of the
way for awhile. The shaman was certainly capable of it.

Flann set the bowl down, then knocked it over
carelessly so the drink spilled onto the ground.
Crouching Fox paid no attention. Flann frowned.
Could I be wrong, seeing deviousness where none was
intended? Even if I am mistaken, it does not hurt to be
wary.

Women, Birch Leaf among them, carried fresh
containers of drink toward the seated men. He watched
Birch Leaf approach. Her beaded blue dress fell below
the calves of her legs. She had belted it at her waist
with a beaded thong, a fringe at each end. Her shoulders were bare, except for the straps of her dress. She
wore neither cape nor leggings since it was warm. The
other women were dressed in similar fashion, but none
had the slim, graceful loveliness of Birch Leaf.

When she handed Flann a wooden container of
raspberry drink, he raised it to his lips, still looking at
her.

"To the most beautiful girl in the world," he said
very softly in English, and drank.

She poured him more of the drink from a clay
pot. Aware of her closeness, his breathing quickened.
He swallowed.

"Stay near me for I'm very thirsty," he whispered, smiling at her.

Birch Leaf did not smile in return. In fact her face appeared to show strain. He found it difficult to focus as he blinked to clear his vision.

It was getting dark. Strange, when the sunlight still warmed him. Flann started to glance skyward. His head was heavy, much too heavy, he realized.

As he slid into blackness, the last thing Flann saw was Birch Leaf's frightened face.

It was the face of guilt.

Chapter 17

Flann floated in darkness. His feet were warm, but the rest of his body had no feeling. A plaintive melody circled in his head, the words nonsense syllables.

"*Koo koo ku hoo,*" a soprano voice sang.

If my feet weren't so hot I'd be able to think more clearly, he thought. The high, sweet voice sang on. There was something familiar about the words.

Flann tried to jerk his feet from the heat but his body refused to obey him. His feet were on fire.

Fire. The fear flared red and hot in his mind.

They are burning me! I'm tied to a post, flames at my feet, flames that will soon rise to sear my body. The Sioux have captured me. The torture is beginning.

Flann tried to cry out that he was white, not Chippewa, but he had no voice.

Wait. I've left Sioux country, I'm safe in Meenagha.

Then why do my feet burn? Crouching Fox. Treachery. My Chippewa brother has tied me to burn with the Sioux captive.

Flann strove wildly to burst through the darkness.

"No!" He thought he had yelled, but his voice came in a feeble groan.

"Ishcoda," a soft voice said. "Do you wake?"

Flann struggled to lift heavy eyelids. A woman's face swam before him. Her hand touched his cheek. Gradually his vision cleared and he saw Birch Leaf kneeling beside him.

His bed was sand, he could feel the grains in his fingers. Above his head, stars twinkled. The steady swish he heard was caused by Kitchigami's waves licking the shore near him. The smell of burning wood filled his nostrils. He saw the flicker of a tiny fire near his feet. With great effort he bent his knees and drew his feet away from the flames. He sighed with relief.

Flann's mind whirled with confusion. "You were singing," he said to Birch Leaf, his tongue and jaw feeling so heavy he could barely push words from his mouth.

"I sang about an owl looking down into a wigwam through the smoke hole, and how he frightens the little boy who then sings to conquer his fear."

"Not an owl," Flann managed to say. "A fox. Crouching Fox. He. . . ." His words trailed off as he remembered.

Birch Leaf had handed him the drink.

"Why?" he asked.

Her expression told him she knew what he meant. She looked away. "My mother gave me the drink," she said. "She told me I must see that you swallowed it or you'd be shamed before the warriors." She looked at him again. He could see the flames reflected in her eyes. "I sang the song about the owl because I was afraid. You lay so still that I feared your spirit would not find its way back."

Flann tried to sit up but could not.

"If you wait," Birch Leaf said, "soon you'll be the same as before you drank. Soft Willow told me this."

You won't interfere, Crouching Fox had warned him. Well, the shaman had made certain Flann wouldn't, and couldn't.

"What was in the raspberry drink?" he asked.

"A sacred plant. Only the mide know such plants."

Flann moved his arms, noticing the heaviness was lessening. With Birch Leaf's help, he propped himself into a sitting position with his back braced against driftwood. When he looked about he saw the glow of the village fires to the east and knew he had been carried west along the beach. He felt, rather than heard, the steady beat of the drum.

Flann looked at Birch Leaf. Even she had betrayed him. "You're missing all the excitement back at the village," he said sarcastically. "Don't let me keep you from the pleasure of watching a fellow man roasted alive."

"Sioux are the enemy. If they capture our warriors they do the same."

Flann thought of Black Rock tied to the post in the Sioux village. "But that doesn't make torturing a man right, because the enemy does it."

"This is the way of the People. Each warrior understands. Bravery is tested. If I was married and the Sioux killed my husband, I'd want revenge." Birch Leaf showed her teeth. "Never would I adopt a Sioux!"

Flann stared at her, remembering what Fire Grass had said of Birch Leaf's origins. Didn't she herself know? "Birch Leaf," he said, "you're adopted. Soft Willow adopted you as her daughter when the warriors brought you home from a raid on the Sioux."

"I am not a Sioux!"

"No, that's right. You're not a Sioux. They captured you from the Sauk who had stolen you from your white parents. You're white, Birch Leaf, not Indian at all."

She sank back on her heels, bringing a hand to her heart. Her lips moved but no words came out.

"Birch Leaf?" Flann asked, reaching toward her. He was able to move and bend forward quite easily now, and he touched her shoulder.

"Car-o-line," she whispered. "Car-o-line."

"Caroline? Was that your name? Have you remembered something?"

She brushed off his hand and jumped to her feet. "No. I remember nothing. I'm Birch Leaf. Soft Willow is my mother. I belong to the People! I am Anishinabe!" She shouted the words.

Flann struggled to stand. He planted his feet wide apart for support. "Soft Willow is your mother," he said. "She raised you. But you had another mother who bore you, a white mother. Did she name you Caroline?"

Birch Leaf covered her face with her hands. "Don't call me by that name," she begged. "Please don't."

"I won't if you don't want me to." He tried to touch her, but she moved away and his balance was too unsteady for him to follow. "You have to face the truth, though. You're a white woman who's been raised as a Chippewa. What's going on back there at the village, the torture . . . you're not a part of such things, Birch Leaf. Burning men, eating their hearts . . . that's not the way of civilized men and women."

She wiped tears from her cheeks. "You speak nonsense. I am Anishinabe. And I shall always be of the People. What they do is what I understand. Who are you to call it wrong? What do you know? Crouching Fox made you his blood brother, but you won't try to understand and be a part of us."

"Birch Leaf, torture is cruel. Can't I make you see?"

"I wish I had never seen you," she cried. "I hate you!" She turned and ran along the beach toward the village.

Flann started after her, finding he could walk if he did not move too quickly. Suddenly Birch Leaf stopped, turned to watch him, then slowly made her way back to him as he staggered toward her.

"Soft Willow said I must stay with you until you were as before," she said in a low tone. "You walk like an old man. That means you haven't recovered."

"I feel fine," he said stiffly. "Don't trouble yourself about me. You didn't worry about me when you gave me the drink."

"I, I felt bad when I saw what was happening to you."

"But you'd do it again to stop me from interfering with your bloody customs, wouldn't you?"

"It's unthinkable for a warrior to demean himself by trying to take a captive from the women. The Sioux belongs to the women. Don't you understand?"

They glared at each other.

Flann sat on the sand again. Birch Leaf dropped down beside him. "Do you feel weak?" she asked.

"No, I'm all right. How long have I been on the beach?"

"So long that the ceremonies will soon be over."

"Maybe they'll save you a bite of Sioux heart," he said, knowing with bitter resentment that it was too late to try to save the captive.

180

"You wish you'd never met me," Birch Leaf said. "But even Nanabozho can't turn back time, no matter how many different shapes he changes into. We've seen each other. We can do nothing about it."

Flann did not speak for awhile. Finally he turned to her. "I've blamed you and it's not your fault. I'm sorry. Who is this Nanabozho you're comparing me to?"

She smiled. "He's the great-grandson of the moon and the son of the west wind. Nanabozho can accomplish great deeds and also make many very stupid and funny mistakes. In the winter you can hear all about him."

"I won't be here in the winter. I'm leaving tomorrow for La Pointe and then next month for my own village in the east."

Birch Leaf drew in her breath.

"Will you be sorry to see me go?" he asked gently.

She raised her eyes to his, and desire stirred in him. He touched her bare shoulder. "I'm glad we met, Birch Leaf."

She came to him and he gathered her into his arms. Desire flooded through him as he kissed her hair, her neck and finally bent to her mouth. She clung to him, her lips parting under the pressure of his. His hand stroked the smooth skin of her arm.

"Birch Leaf," he murmured. "You're so lovely. Like a star. You shine like a star."

She moaned as his hand caressed her breast, slipping under the strap of her dress. He felt the warm softness of each breast, the nipples stiffening to his touch. He slid the straps from her shoulders and put his mouth to her bared breasts. His body throbbed with his need for her.

181

"Beautiful, my beautiful Birch Leaf," he whispered.

He pulled away and unbelted her dress. She smiled shyly and slipped it over her head. He caught his breath as he saw the outline of her naked body in the dim light of a quarter moon. When he tried to take her into his arms again she drew back and shook her head.

"Why are you dressed while I am not?" she murmured.

Flann flung off his own clothes. He pressed her gently backward onto the sand, then lay on his side next to her. Curbing his desire, he began to stroke her inner thighs, tracing her delicate womanhood with the tips of his fingers. Soon she turned her body to his, putting her arms around him and pressing close.

He groaned and, unable to wait any longer, eased her onto her back, moved her legs apart and covered her body with his, guiding himself into her welcoming and smooth softness.

Although she was indeed ready for him, he had to force entry to bring himself all the way inside her. Birch Leaf cried out once, then her arms tightened, holding him, rising and falling with him until his desire peaked into climax.

Afterward, he held her in his arms, her head on his shoulder. Suddenly she pulled away and looked at him. "Since you are recovered," she said, smiling mischievously, "bathe with me." She stood and ran down into the lake.

Flann rose and followed her, noting that he moved freely now. He grunted when the water of Kitchigami chilled him. Did the lake never warm? he wondered.

Hearing him, Birch Leaf laughed and splashed

water at him. He dove beneath the water and caught her ankles, pulling her under. She kicked and squirmed from his grasp and began to swim away. Flann swam after her, but as hard as he tried, he couldn't catch up to her.

Birch Leaf changed direction, stroking for shore. She waited for him at the edge of the water and took his hand, pulling him toward the embers of the fire. They leaned over the hot coals to warm themselves. He took her in his arms again, pressing her to him, feeling the length of her soft body against his.

He licked drops of water from her lips, then kissed her.

Birch Leaf felt the strange new warmth rise in her again as Ishcoda's hands slid down her back to cup her buttocks, holding her close to his hardness. His lips pressed to hers, his tongue flicking against her tongue in a way that made her quiver with excitement.

She eased from his grasp finally and clamping her hand on his arm, dropped onto the sand. He dropped with her, but when he rose to move his body over hers, she pushed at him until he lay on his back. She raised herself on one elbow so she could see and wonder at his maleness. She reached out tentatively, closing her hand about its throbbing hardness.

He groaned with pleasure as she moved her fingers, feeling him respond. He pulled at her until she fell over on top of him. Her breasts pushed against his chest. As she felt her nipples draw up, little stabs of warmth ran through her.

Ishcoda's hands came around her body and held her buttocks again, raising her until he could put himself inside her again. He moved himself beneath her slowly, and her breath quickened.

There was no pain this time, nothing but arrows of pleasure shooting into her loins. He took her nipple into his mouth.

"Oh," she murmured. "Oh, oh, oh. . . ."

Now he grasped her firmly, locking himself to her, and he rolled over so that she was beneath him. Still he moved slowly inside her, making her writhe and twist and arch up to meet him.

He moved faster, stronger now, and she was lifted high until she left herself and was a star dancer, shining across the sky, exploding in fiery fragments as she fell, fell, fell. . . .

"Birch Leaf," he said after they had rested. "I know this was your first time with a man. Were you afraid?"

"Not of you," she said. "Besides, I knew what to do, for Soft Willow told me about men and women. What men like, how to please them. However, I didn't know about how I'd feel, how good it would be with you, Ishcoda, with the man I love."

He sat up. "Your mother told you how to please a man?"

Birch Leaf sat up, too, staring at him. "How would I know what to expect if my mother did not tell me?" Then she understood. "Now you're going to say women in your village are different. Why is it you always want to tell me that?"

"They are different. If Lynette. . . ." He broke off and stood up, brushing sand from his body.

Birch Leaf got to her feet. "Is this Lyn-ette a white woman's name?"

"Yes. I think we'd better get dressed."

A terrible fear struck Birch Leaf like a lance through her heart. "Is Lyn-ette your wife?"

"I'm not married." Flann put on his breechcloth and picked up his shirt.

"You must know Lyn-ette or you wouldn't have said her name. Have you been with her as we were tonight?"

"Birch Leaf, you don't ask questions like that."

She took her dress from the sand to hide her body. "You think I'm not as good as your white woman. Is that what you won't say?"

"Don't be ridiculous. You *are* a white woman."

"I am not. You can tell me I am as many times as there are grains of sand along Kitchigami, and I'll still be Anishinabe." Tears glittered in her eyes. She yanked her dress over her head and ran from him toward the village.

"Birch Leaf," he called after her.

"I won't hear you," she cried. "Man from the east who will not understand."

Left alone, Flann slumped by the dead fire. What the hell had he done? What had happened to make him lose his head over Birch Leaf? What poor timing, for in a few hours he would be heading for La Pointe, and he would never see Birch Leaf again. Why hadn't he left well enough alone?

His only reason for being among the Chippewa was to discover the source of the new rifles the Chippewa men had carried raiding the Sioux. He had come as a professional, or so he fancied himself. Now, having slept with a Meenagha woman, he saw himself as an amateur and a betrayer of the woman and her Bear Clan, which had embraced him as a blood brother and saved his life.

How could he have compromised himself so easily?

Damn it, he reasoned, he would go to Copper Sky

right now, he would demand to be told about the guns. He should have stuck to business from the first. Damn trying to save that Sioux warrior. Look where it got him. Nowhere.

Damn Birch Leaf, too.

His allegiance was not to her.

It was to the President of the United States.

Chapter 18

The warriors had returned. The celebrating was over. The Meenagha villagers prepared to paddle to their rice camp.

Birch Leaf rode Soft Willow's rice canoe and knelt in the bow. The canoe was made with a birch-bark box in the middle and used only for the wild rice harvests. The flails lay in the bottom of the box, along with the larger copper kettle and other household equipment. Soft Willow was steersman.

The lake where the rice grew was inland, two streams away with one portage between. As Birch Leaf pushed away from the bank, she saw canoes already traveling up the Iron River. Behind them, other villagers loaded their canoes for the trip. All of Meenagha was headed for the wild rice harvest.

No. Not all.

Ishcoda was on his way to La Pointe, paddling with Crazy Crane. He had not come to say good-bye to her. Birch Leaf sighed. In Crouching Fox's canoe, just ahead, she could see Fire Grass hanging onto the squirming Squirrel. Now that she knew why Fire Grass had stared at her, she was no longer afraid of the old woman.

Car-o-line. No, that's not my name. I am Birch Leaf. And I'm not white, no matter what Ishcoda says.

A white woman may have borne me. A white man may have been my father. I am still a child of the People. If they are alive, if we met today, we would be strangers. And those are the truths. The facts of birth do not alter them.

Birch Leaf's paddle dipped smoothly into the water as she tried to imagine this strange white mother. Their canoe traveled upstream between tree-lined banks. Leaves had begun to turn color—yellow and red and orange—but most were still green like the pine needles.

Does my white mother still mourn a lost daughter? Birch Leaf wondered. Are her eyes green, like mine?

She would never know. Ishcoda had said that if her parents were not killed in the Sauk raid, when she had been captured, it might be possible to locate them. He promised he would try when he returned to his village. Birch Leaf shook her head. Ishcoda must not. He might hurt everyone, for she could not imagine living anywhere but by Kitchigami.

Ishcoda had not asked her to leave with him as his wife. If he did. . . ?

Birch Leaf glanced about at the other canoes moving swiftly upriver. A kingfisher swooped from the high bank to her left and hovered above the river. Then he dove into the water, appearing a moment later with a fish struggling in his long black bill. She watched the bird until it perched on a maple limb overhanging the river.

She enjoyed watching the jaunty blue-gray king-fishers that lived along the rivers, nesting in the banks. They were favorites of Nanabozho, too. When she was small, the story of how Kingfisher got his crest had been her favorite and she often begged Soft Willow to tell it over and over.

Birch Leaf smiled. She imagined she could actu-ally hear Soft Willow speaking.

"It is true that Wolf came to live with Nana-bozho, to be his adopted brother," Soft Willow always began:

"This made the other animals jealous because Wolf got all the glory of hunting and killing the meat and they had only the work of hanging it up, drying, smoking, and cooking it.

"So the animals went to Kitchigami and offered tobacco to the evil spirits under the lake, to Mishibe-sheu and his evil friends, asking them to kill Wolf. They heard the animals and sent a white deer to lure Wolf onto the icy lake and the ice broke and they dragged him under water and drowned him.

"Nanabozho, looking for Wolf, found the hole and asked Thunderbird to bring summer so the ice would melt and the evil serpents would come up from the water caves to bask in the sun. In four days the ice melted.

"Kingfisher was sitting on a cliff. Nanabozho watched him fly down to the beach every so often and eat a scrap of something. He asked Kingfisher what he found there to eat.

" 'Wolf,' Kingfisher said brashly. 'I'm eating Wolf. Those who killed him live nearby.'

"Now Nanabozho was glad Wolf had been found, so he gave Kingfisher a necklace of shells to wear around his neck as a reward. And that's why Kingfisher has a white band around his neck today.

"But Nanabozho was angry too, because Kingfisher was eating Wolf. And, as he put the necklace around Kingfisher's neck, he tried to seize him, intending to kill Kingfisher.

"Kingfisher flew very fast, and he darted away. But not before Nanabozho seized the feathers on Kingfisher's head and pulled them.

"And so today Kingfisher sports a tufted crest on his head and the back of his neck where Nanabozho's grip pulled feathers loose as Kingfisher flew away."

The story went on to tell about how Nanabozho revenged himself on the evil spirits who had killed Wolf, but the first part was the one Birch Leaf liked most. Kingfisher was bold and daring and not even Nanabozho could get the best of him. Soft Willow had told her all the stories of the People, as she one day would tell them to her child.

She wondered if the stories would have meaning for a child born in Ishcoda's village.

Ishcoda, she cried silently. Come back. Don't leave me alone.

"Black Rock will be at the rice camp," Soft Willow said. "Do you intend to let Snowberry have him?"

Birch Leaf sighed. "Black Rock will make his own choice. He knows how I feel."

"Ishcoda will leave you."

"Maybe not. Last night. . . ." Her words trailed off, and she smiled as she thought of Ishcoda holding her.

"Lovemaking doesn't bring trader's kettles for the

190

fire nor meat into the wigwam in winter. Husbands do that. We eat because I'm mide and am paid for my powers. You are not. You must put Ishcoda from your mind."

"My dream vision was partly of him," Birch Leaf said defensively.

"You'll do as you must, whatever I say." Soft Willow's voice was tart. She did not speak of Ishcoda again.

As they neared the wild rice marshes, flocks of ducks flew past, preparing to land on the water beyond. Soon Birch Leaf spotted the slender stems of the rice with their broad leaves. The rice grew in the lake shallows, and during the previous moon they had come here with other women in canoes to tie the standing stalks in bundles. This kept the ripening kernels from the birds and made the harvest easier.

Birch Leaf found their wigwam from the previous year was still dry inside, despite several holes in the bark covering. As Soft Willow gathered stones and wood for the fire, Birch Leaf covered the holes with rush mats from Meenagha. Then she found a cedar and cut boughs to cover the wigwam floor.

When they had stowed their belongings inside, both women stood by the canoe. Soft Willow raised her arms and said, "We give thanks to Kitchi Manito for the manomin, the good rice berry we gather here. May the Thunderers keep from the skies while we harvest and the Winds hide in their homes."

Birch Leaf paddled at the stern while Soft Willow, in the bow, reached out with the hooked flail to pull in the rice plants they had tied in bundles during the previous moon. Other canoes floated among the rice plants as theirs did. The Ontonagon village shared this rice camp with Meenagha. Men or grown boys paddled many of the canoes, but only women and girls gathered the rice.

Taking the curved rice stick, Soft Willow pulled down the stalks so the heads of the plants hung over the birch-bark box in the center of the rice canoe. With the flat flail in her other hand, she beat the heads until the long needlelike grains spilled into the box. As soon as the box was full, Birch Leaf paddled to shore.

Birch Leaf and Soft Willow emptied their box of grain onto large mats near their wigwam so the rice would dry in the sun while they gathered more. As Birch Leaf paddled the canoe to keep it from drifting while her mother harvested, she began to sing about shawshaw, the swallow, who swirls and dips for its food.

The air was crisp, the sky a deep blue and the sun warm on her bare shoulders. Were there rice fields near Ishcoda's village? she wondered. Although he could paddle a canoe, he did not do so in the People's way. She was certain he had never helped women gather rice.

Many of the men had hunted during the harvesting. That evening Black Rock brought them four ducks for roasting. He handed the birds to Soft Willow while he looked at Birch Leaf.

"I heard you brought many scalps back from the Sioux raid," she said.

"I was taken captive by those snakes," he said harshly. "Ishcoda set me free. Now he is gone from your village." His eyes asked the question he was too proud to utter.

Birch Leaf forced herself to look directly at Black Rock's face. She refused to glance away like a coy maiden flirting. She admired Black Rock. He was everything a brave should be. She had to admit that she

192

did not want Snowberry to have him for a husband. But she must be honest with Black Rock, she decided.

"I believe Ishcoda will come back," she said.

Black Rock turned away without another word.

After the rice had dried in the sun for three days, Birch Leaf and Soft Willow put it into a large kettle to parch so the tough hulls would split open. They took turns tending the fire and stirring the grain so it would parch evenly. When they finished, Soft Willow went to the hole she had dug many seasons before and, after lining it with newly tanned buckskin, she dumped in a basketful of the parched rice.

Next, they needed a man to be trampler, for women never trampled the rice.

Soft Willow glanced about the rice camp. "I see Black Rock is trampling for Snowberry," she noted. "I'll find someone else."

A youth called Dog Nose put on loose-fitting new moccasins with high tops Birch Leaf had specially sewn for the rice harvest and stepped down into the rice pit. He was careful not to touch the ground with the moccasins, for if he got them dirty, the next year's harvest would be poor. The spirits would see to it. As he trod the grain to loosen the husks from the kernels, he supported himself on two sticks so only a part of his weight came down on the kernels. Dog Nose grinned happily as he trampled the rice. He was obviously proud to have been chosen by a mide.

Birch Leaf and Soft Willow spread threshed rice on birch-bark trays for winnowing. As they slowly poured the rice from one tray to another, the wind blew away the hulls, leaving the heavier green kernels. The pouring was done with a special twist of the wrist. The women shook the tray and poured at the same time so that the kernels fell to one side. The chaff was carried away by the wind. Many days passed before all the rice was winnowed.

Not all the rice was parched, trampled and winnowed. Some of the harvest was saved, as always, to be resown in the lake shallows for the next year's crop. The women went out in the canoes and scattered these grains over the water.

Manomin, good berry, they chanted,

> Hide for the winter, manomin.
> Under the water, in the frozen mud,
> Stay safe, manomin, until the ice is gone.
> When the ice melts
> Push your green shoot through the water.
> Wave your head in the sun.
> We ask this of you, manomin.

Although most of the rice was packed into makuks to take back to Meenagha, some was boiled to eat. Soft Willow put dried raspberries in their kettle for sweetening. The fragrant grassy smell of green rice cooking made Birch Leaf's mouth water. It seemed forever since she had eaten rice, although she knew it had been only last spring when Soft Willow cooked the last of their rice supplies.

Birch Leaf watched Black Rock as he got ready to leave the rice fields. Snowberry stood next to him. Birch Leaf wondered if they would marry before the men left for winter trapping. The rice harvest had taken half of this moon and the next was Falling Leaves Moon. White men called it October. This was the time the braves went west and north to find beaver. If a brave went without a wife, he had no one to make his moccasins and cook his meat and keep his wigwam warm.

Birch Leaf knew that Snowberry was eager to go. Why did the thought of their marriage put heaviness into her spirit? If she did not wish to marry Black Rock herself, she should wish him happiness with another.

With Snowberry.

Flann did not manage to talk to Copper Sky before he left for La Pointe. The chief adroitly avoided him. Flann fought down the urge to seek out Birch Leaf, knowing it was better for both of them if he didn't see her again. But as he and Crazy Crane paddled along Kitchigami, he could not put her from his mind.

The Porcupine Mountains crouched to his left, smoky blue. Daughter of the Blue Mountains, he had named Birch Leaf. The maples along the shore had begun to turn color, their leaves red and orange among the evergreens. The sky was as blue as cobalt, and the blue was reflected in the lake waters. Birch Leaf lived in beauty.

Suddenly the narrow cobbled streets of Boston, the brick buildings with their second-story balconies, seemed dingy and stifling to Flann. When he returned and married Lynette, perhaps he would not live near Beacon Hill on one of the better streets such as Chestnut, as planned. Lynette wanted to live on the Hill. Flann thought now that he might prefer to build in the country, where he would have space.

First he reasoned, the lawyers must find a way to settle his father's estate in his favor. Without money, he could not plan to either buy or build a house. But if things were straightened out, he would talk to Lynette about his new idea. In his mind, he could imagine her raised eyebrows. He shook his head. Her heart was set on living in one of those tall brick houses in the Back Bay area. He imagined the clatter of carriages and horses' hooves on the cobblestones, the clamor of a busy city, the multitudes of people. Flann was not pleased.

He took a deep breath. Good God, he had come to like this damned wilderness.

In Boston, he reminded himself, were his friends and relatives, culture, people who lived as he did and a society he could understand. His home was there. Lynette was there. He belonged in Boston.

A strange, wild calling brought him out of his reverie, and he stared about, trying to locate its source.

"*Wawa*," Crazy Crane said, pointing to the sky. "He travels early."

Wild geese. Flann saw the vee, flying south across the lake. Their honking was unlike any bird sound he had ever heard.

Black Rock would be at the wild rice fields where Birch Leaf was going, Flann thought. It wasn't really rice, this good berry of the Chippewa, but a variety of wild oats that grew unaccountably in water as rice does, causing the French to name it "crazy oats."

Suddenly Flann snorted and shook his head. He should have been thinking about his meeting with the Indian subagent, Daniel Bushnell, not about Birch Leaf and rice. The news he had to report about the Pillagers was straightforward enough. They had new guns and were obviously going to use them. The Meenagha braves were a different matter. He could not believe Copper Sky intended to use his new guns to help the Canadian rebels. Yet he had them. And he had avoided talking to Flann about them.

Who was the Canadian agent who had given the Indians of the two villages their guns? What had the Chippewa chiefs promised the agent in exchange? That was what he needed to know, what he wanted to be able to report. He had an excuse for not doing more at Leech Lake, but not at Meenagha.

Damn it, he had been distracted by trying to save the Sioux captive and by Birch Leaf. He should have been prying information from Copper Sky, insisting that the chief tell him where the guns came from and why.

Was it possible to learn anything more at La Pointe? He could question Charles Borup. Maybe the fur factor was so used to the comings and goings of the voyageurs and metis that he paid them too little attention. The Canadian agent must be one of them. It might be that the Chippewas in Buffalo's village had observed some suspicious behavior by the metis. Even if Buffalo wasn't back from the treaty signing, Flann could stay in the Indian village.

Henry Schoolcraft claimed Buffalo knew nothing about the guns. If Buffalo wouldn't talk to the Indian agent, either he was not aware of any plotting or he had no intention of telling anyone what he knew. Nevertheless, Flann was now Ishcoda, and as an Indian brother, might learn something from Buffalo.

Flann's sympathies lay with the Canadian rebels who yearned to throw off England's yoke, but he knew Jackson was right in saying that another war with England must be avoided. As for the Indians, they had been used by the French, by the English and by the Americans to fight white men's battles. War had profited the Indians little.

Flann decided he would let the subagent worry about the Pillagers. As for Meenagha . . . Flann shook his head. He had failed dismally. Good God, they had accepted him as one of them. Why hadn't he demanded to know where those guns came from?

There was also the matter of the silver. He had seen silver ornaments and had done nothing about locating the source of the metal. What was the matter with him?

He smiled.

What he had done was leave himself excellent reasons to return to Meenagha. In fact, he must return.

He had let his infatuation with Birch Leaf overwhelm his common sense, that's what he had done. He could almost taste the sweetness of her lips, feel the softness of her body next to his. Savagely he dug the paddle into the water.

"Gently, brother," Crazy Crane said. "There's no need to hurry. Already I see the islands."

Flann looked up and saw the dark dots of land ahead. Let Birch Leaf go, he told himself. Lynette is waiting for you. You're promised to her. You can try to find Birch Leaf's parents once you're back in civilization, but don't see her again.

His hands tightened on the paddle. He did not want Lynette with her affected, posturing ways. Why hadn't he seen through her before? She had none of Birch Leaf's honesty or openness in loving. And she never would have, not even as a wife. He wanted Birch Leaf.

Damn it, no!

"Ishcoda."

Flann glanced at Crazy Crane.

"Don't you see the nets? I've been trying to turn the canoe but you resist."

Flann realized he had been fighting Crazy Crane's steering. He saw the fish nets of the fur company straight ahead and helped the brave paddle to the left. They skirted the island and glided up to shore near the dock.

Flann walked up the hill toward the stores, marshaling his facts for the subagent. He would have to tell him about the deaths of Henri Fontenac and Dancing Drum. He knew he couldn't leave out the Sioux raid, as every Chippewa along Kitchigami undoubtedly knew every detail by now. And he feared that no explanation of his own part in the raid would sound plausible, no matter how desperate his situation had actually been at the time.

Flann climbed the steps, opened the door and walked into the store. Dr. Charles Borup was in front of the counter, talking to a metis. They both turned when Flann entered.

Flann scarcely heard Dr. Borup's greeting as he stared into the dark eyes of the metis.

It was Henri Fontenac.

Chapter 19

"I thought you were dead," Flann exclaimed.

Henri Fontenac smiled. "I fool those Pillagers. Me, I'm not dead. They think so, like you, eh? So I get away."

Flann grasped Henri's hand. "Thank God you're alive."

"I think them one bad tribe, those Pillagers. Kill you, kill the mide, I think. Then I hear Red Hair fights the Sioux. I be damn big surprised."

"What *did* happen at the lake, Henri?" Flann asked.

Henri hung his head. "I fell asleep on watch," he frowned. "First thing I know, they drag me off with a hand over my mouth so I can't yell to warn you. What I did, I put your rifle next to me, outside, so I could get off two quick shots, and they took both rifles. They tie me, toss me inside a wigwam, and start to dance." Henri gesticulated and began hopping up and down.

"I say to myself, 'Henri, it don't look good.' But then I remember a little squaw who likes me. I call to her, and after awhile she comes with her knife and I'm free. All those braves outside have their war paint on, and they are hollering and drinking, and the squaw wants her reward. You know how Indian women are." Henri chuckled.

Flann was not amused.

"They like a little loving," Henri said hastily. "So I had to." He shrugged. "She was sweet as honey afterwards, fixed me up like a squaw. Even chopped off my beard with her knife. By that time the braves had attacked your wigwam and I say to myself, 'Henri, you're a dead man if you stop now.' I go to the canoes. Never have I paddled so fast." He beamed at Flann.

Was Henri telling the truth? Even though he was pleased that the metis lived, Flann still suspected he might be the Canadian agent he sought.

"Then I pull the canoe onto the bank and say, 'Henri, are you a man? Go back for your friends.' So I turn around and then. . . ." He paused and shuddered. "A dead body hits the canoe. I see the arrow in his back and then I look at his face and see the mide. I say, 'Henry, if the mide is killed, the Red Hair has no chance. Go while you can, that you don't float dead like this one.' "

Henri's story was plausible. He could be telling the truth. Or lying. Flann could not decide.

"I'm certainly happy to see you're all right," Dr. Borup said to Flann. "Mr. Bushnell has been inquiring about you since Henri made it back to La Pointe. We heard rumors of the Sioux raid and thought the red-haired man with the Chippewa might be you."

Flann met Dr. Borup's inquiring gaze. "Where is Mr. Bushnell?" he asked.

"I believe he's talking to Chief Buffalo at the moment." Dr. Borup's glance swept across Flann, noting the Indian clothes, but he said nothing more.

"I tell him Red Hair has come," Henri offered.

"No," Flann insisted. "I'll walk down to the Chippewa village myself."

Again the crow circled above Flann's head. Borup chuckled. "Meet Buffalo's pet and warning signal. The damned bird seems to sense it whenever anyone is visiting Buffalo. Few arrive unannounced with this devil about."

The crow escorted Flann to the chief's wigwam. Bushnell was not there, but Buffalo was. He invited Flann to smoke. When he had finished the ritual pipe ceremony, Flann reached inside his tunic and took out Dancing Drum's otter skin bag.

"Dancing Drum left this in the canoe when he was killed," Flann told the chief. "I used the medicine inside against the Sioux."

Buffalo smiled. "Good."

"I didn't touch the shell. I'm no mide." He handed the wayan to Buffalo. "Dancing Drum saved my life. Twice. He was a true warrior. If I could have brought his body to you, I would have, but this is all of his that is left."

Buffalo turned the otter bag over in his hands. "We'll bury this in his place. Because of the megis, the shell, his spirit is in it."

"If you hadn't sent him with me, I'd be dead," Flann said.

"I didn't send him. Dancing Drum came and told me of a dream that meant he must go with you. Thus he went. Stay with us, Ishcoda, for the dog feast and the death dance."

"I'll stay. First I must talk to others."

202

"You're welcome in my wigwam for as long as you wish. Perhaps you'll tell of the Sioux raid."

"Crazy Crane can tell the tale better than I can," Flann said.

"I'd like to hear you tell *your* story," Buffalo said. "Tonight, maybe."

Flann found Daniel Bushnell on the dock with another man watching the nets full of fish that were being unloaded from large canoes.

"A good catch," he observed, turning to Flann. "The fur company prospers." He held out his hand. "I'm Dan Bushnell. You can only be Red Hair, Flann O'Phelan."

Flann tried to ignore the frantic fish flopping in the nets as he shook hands with the subagent. "This is St. Ivan, my interpreter with the Chippewas," Bushnell said.

Flann shook hands with St. Ivan, surprised that Bushnell did not speak Chippewa.

"Shall we walk along the beach while we talk?" Bushnell asked. He turned to the interpreter. "I won't be needing you."

As they made their way along the pebbled sand, Flann began his tale of attack and death among the Pillagers.

"How many new guns would you estimate they have?" Bushnell asked when he finished.

"Thirty," Flann guessed. "As to the supplier, what do you know of Henri Fontenac? I'm not accusing him," he added hastily. "It's just that he seemed eager to take me to Leech Lake. And then he miraculously escaped from the Pillagers."

"I've had an eye on Henri and one or two others," Bushnell confessed. "He's done nothing wrong that I know of, but he's a restless type. I've learned to watch that kind of man."

They reached a sandstone ridge extending into the water, and stopped. "How about the other Chippewas you visited?" Bushnell asked.

"I saw new guns on the Sioux raid," Flann said reluctantly. "They came from the Meenagha village."

"What's Copper Sky say?"

"I couldn't get him to talk. I thought I'd go back to Meenagha after I met with you and try again."

"We'll check out his guns," Bushnell said. "No need for you to be involved any further. You've done your job. Under stress, too, I'd say. We'd have had a lot of explaining to do in Washington if the Pillagers had killed you. And a lot of work trying to round up the actual murderer to bring him to trial."

"Well, actually, Schoolcraft told me to stay away from the Pillagers. If I hadn't heard this rumor about new guns at Leech Lake I'd never have tried to make the journey there."

Bushnell frowned. "Look, O'Phelan. There's not a more competent agent than Henry Schoolcraft anywhere. He knows the Chippewa better than any white man. You were a damn fool not to listen to him."

"Yes, of course," Flann said. "I was impressed by his knowledge. But about the Meenagha village. . . ."

"We could have handled this matter of the guns ourselves," Bushnell said. "My advice to you now is to stay out of it, to stay here at La Pointe until the *Astor* arrives. She's due any time, and this is her last trip until spring. You wouldn't want to miss her. And, as I've told you, *I'll* talk to Copper Sky."

Flann realized he was being dismissed. He tensed with rising anger. Daniel Bushnell might be an extremely capable subagent, with interpreter or without, but Flann resented being given orders barely disguised as advice. What the subagent said was logical and practical but the whiff of patronage in Bushnell's words infuriated him.

Damn it, President Jackson appointed me, Flann thought. Am I to report back to the new President, saying I've done what I could, but. . . ?

No.

"I imagine the *Astor* can be requested to anchor off Meenagha on her way back down the lake," Flann drawled in his haughtiest Boston manner. "I'll come aboard from the village. O'Phelans don't like to leave a job unfinished." He smiled thinly, then added, "If you don't mind."

"I can't stop you," Bushnell said stiffly, "but I advise against it. If you go ahead regardless, make sure you board the *Astor* when she comes by Meenagha. I doubt you'd enjoy spending a Lake Superior winter holed up in a wigwam."

"Mr. Schoolcraft expects me to report to him at Mackinac by November," Flann said. "I need no reminding."

Bushnell eyed him, again noting the beaded tunic, buckskin leggings and moccasins. "There's more to being an Indian than dressing the part, O'Phelan. Men who live in cities don't understand. The wilderness is against you. You must always be on your guard. This country has finished more than one man who forgot that."

Flann said nothing.

"Consider the copper," Bushnell went on. "You've seen the Ontonagon boulder. At least five attemps have been made to remove it in the last hundred years. The country defeated every one, like it defeated the English copper miners in 1770. They got out with their lives, but nothing else. You've been lucky so far, O'Phelan."

"The Irish are famous for their luck," Flann said, dismissing the warning. "I'll be staying with Buffalo for the next few days, Mr. Bushnell, should you have additional advice for me." Flann turned and walked rapidly along the beach.

When he neared the Chippewa wigwams, Flann smelled the stench of burning hair and knew the women had killed a dog and were singeing off its hair over a cooking fire. He grimaced, thinking of the feast to come.

Buffalo ordered his wife to put down a mat for Flann next to his own outside his wigwam. The pet crow perched on his shoulder and cocked its head to stare at Flann.

"We must talk," Flann said after he had seated himself and accepted a drink made with wintergreen berries. "You're the Great Chief of the Kitchigami clans."

Buffalo inclined his head in acknowledgment.

"You must know, then that Copper Sky has new guns. The Pillagers near Sandy Lake also have many new guns. Their warriors tried to kill me with them."

"You've said Dancing Drum died from an arrow," Buffalo reminded him. "Henri, the metis, also told me of the arrow."

"I want to talk about Henri as well. Could he be the one handing out new British guns in return for a promise to help the Canadian rebels?"

Buffalo considered. "Help them? How?"

"In a revolt against England."

Buffalo shook his head. "I have heard no talk of this. I know Returning Cloud killed traders many years past at Lake Pepin, but the People consider traders as little fathers and wouldn't hurt them. Even the Pillagers leave traders alone. As for *shogonos,* the Canadian white men, our loyalty is to the Great White Father in Washington. Why should we help shogonos?"

"How about Henri?"

"He's not a man to trust, but if he has new guns to give, he hasn't approached me. Copper Sky is a man who keeps his own counsel. The young warriors worry that he's too old to be a proper chief but will do nothing in fear of Crouching Fox. He is married to a sister of Copper Sky." Buffalo eyed Flann slyly. "What is all this talk of guns, Ishcoda? Where now is your interest in the plants that heal?"

Flann smiled. No doubt Buffalo had suspected from the first that he was interested in more than plants.

"It is true that I'm learning to be a healer in my own village," he said. "I want to learn what I can of your medicine. But I seek knowledge of the guns, too."

"What I know, I have told you," Buffalo said. "I don't understand why Dancing Drum was shot with an arrow. It's easier to kill with a gun. Did the Pillagers at Sandy Lake lack bullets?"

"I heard guns fired while they were dancing," Flann said.

"Dancing Drum died honorably," Buffalo said. "He'll have a warrior's burial now that you've brought his megis. It's a good death for a shaman. A mide can die in terrible ways because of evil spirits."

The sun moved lower in the sky as they talked. Village women began to wail in mourning. Two of them, one old and one young, brought a trader's blanket to Buffalo. Other villagers gathered nearby.

Somehow, they knew I told Buffalo of Dancing Drum's death, Flann thought. The blanket was spread in front of the chief by the older woman, who then left. She returned in a few moments carrying new clothes, a pipe, various ornaments and feathers. These were all placed in the center of the blanket. Flann noticed silver and copper armbands among the ornaments.

When the woman was finished, Buffalo rose, came forward and, taking the otter skin wayan belonging to Dancing Drum, laid it carefully among the other articles. Then he closed his eyes and spoke:

> You, who go before us,
> You who take the long journey,
> You, who have finished your journey with us,
> We say to you that we shall follow.
> In our time, when our time comes,
> We shall rejoin you and the happy ones.
> We shall meet you and the happy ones
> In the land where our forefathers have gone,
> In the land of the hereafter.

A drum began to beat and the women folded the blanket around Dancing Drum's belongings. They placed the bundle on an open roll of birch bark. When they had wrapped the bark tightly about the blanket and tied it with thongs, two men with painted faces lifted the roll of bark as though they carried an actual body. Flann saw mide bags at their waists.

The villagers followed, the two women wailing, as the bark roll was carried to a shallow grave dug in an east-to-west direction. The roll was laid in the grave. The mide priests took up their wayans. Opening the bags, they chanted and sprinkled powder onto the bark.

The grave was covered with earth, and notched sapling trunks were fitted together to form a rectangle over the low mound of dirt. A bark roof was added. Similar structures covered nearby graves. The older woman placed an unlit pine torch at the head of Dancing Drum's grave.

The drumbeat quickened as the sun moved below the horizon. The smell of cooking meat drifted through the village. Flann hoped there would be other food besides dog, for he knew he must eat to show respect for the dead. Flann felt so tired that he wondered whether he could stay awake through the feasting. The past few days had been hard.

By the time the wooden bowls of food were handed around, Flann knew something other than exhaustion ailed him. After a token tasting of the meat, he told Buffalo he had to be excused. The twilight was shorter each day and the nights colder as the year waned. Flann walked away from the circle of Chippewas into the dark, feeling the chill of the coming winter settle into him.

He went to where the waves of Kitchigami washed up onto the pebbles, then stared east toward Meenagha. Was he fooling himself about his reason for wanting to return to the village? A damp breeze blew in his face and he shivered. Of course he was.

A city man in the wilderness? That was a joke.

Behind him men shouted, and he knew the dancing had started. He turned from the lake and headed for the chief's wigwam. If he slept, maybe he would feel better tomorrow.

A flicker of light caught his eye. The light grew into a small flame. He changed direction to pass it, realizing he was nearing the Chippewa graveyard.

A woman crouched by the flame. Her head was bowed, but he recognized her as the older woman who had mourned for Dancing Drum. Was she his wife?

She had a small pile of pine torches beside her. Did she mean to keep a light at the grave all night?

He remembered the Chippewa belief that the spirit takes four days and four nights to make the journey to the land of shadows. He stood staring at the woman beside the grave, the flickering torch shadowing her face. Did she really believe Dancing Drum's spirit had been brought back in the mide bag?

Flann's legs began to tremble. He staggered when he moved on. He was suddenly afraid. The damned ague had come back and he was getting worse by the minute. He concentrated on walking, heading now for the shouting dancers. He wasn't sure he could make it to the wigwam. He was no longer certain whether the throbbing in his head came from drums or his pulse.

With a last burst of effort, he stumbled into the circle around the dancers. When the villagers made way for him, he staggered into the midst of the dancing braves.

His last clear memory was that of blackened faces staring down at him.

Chapter 20

Flann opened his eyes. He was in Buffalo's wigwam. Two men with painted faces stood over him. These faces were not black. One had a green line across his forehead and a yellow line down each cheek. The older man's face divided vertically, half red and half blue.

"He'll need to have the evil sucked out of him," the older man said.

"At least his spirit has returned," the other replied.

Flann tried to stand. He found himself very weak. He saw mide bags at the waists of the two men. They are shamans, he thought, now recognizing them as the men at the grave. "Dogwood bark?" Flann asked, remembering how Crouching Fox had dosed him.

"No good," the older man said. He turned from Flann, motioning to someone near the door of the wigwam. A young brave with one red line painted below each eye came in carrying a drum and rattles.

The young man handed the rattles to the younger mide, then sank onto his haunches and began a slow pounding of the drum. The mide began to dance, shaking the rattles as a counterpoint to the drumbeats.

"Buffalo?" Flann managed to say. "Where's Buffalo?"

"Don't talk," the older shaman ordered. He too started dancing.

Both dancers circled Flann, slowly at first, then faster and faster.

The mide voiced shouts and chants Flann could not understand. They must be speaking their spirit language, he thought. He closed his eyes.

The older mide pulled a long bone from his wayan. He flourished it over Flann, turning the bone end over end. Flann noticed it was hollow. The shaman began a chant, this time in Chippewa:

> Colleagues, see this man before you.
> I speak in his behalf.
> Spirits have entered him,
> Evil grips him.
> Colleagues, I will heal him.
> Help me to heal him.
> Colleagues, hear me.

The shaman shrieked, startling Flann so that his heart raced. Then the mide knelt beside him and pressed the hollow bone to Flann's bare chest. He put his mouth to the other end and began sucking.

The other mide continued to dance, shaking the rattles and leaping high in the air at measured intervals.

After a few moments, the shaman removed the bone from his mouth and spit out a small green snake. Flann gaped in bewilderment.

"The spirits of dead Nadouesse sent evil to you,"

the shaman said. "Now it is gone. I've sucked out the evil within you. You'll soon recover."

He waved his hand. The drums stilled. The other mide stopped dancing. The three men quietly left the wigwam.

In the silence and solitude, Flann fell into a deep sleep. When he awoke again, he saw Buffalo regarding him.

"The mide tells me you are cured," Buffalo said.

"Ask for some dogwood bark," Flann said. "I've got a fever. Crouching Fox used it to help me before."

Sometime later, another man came with a bitter drink. After downing it, Flann slept again. When he awoke the next morning, he felt better but found himself surprisingly weak. He thought of Dr. Borup, wondering whether he should ask Buffalo to fetch the Dane. He was a physician, after all. But Borup will want to bleed me, Flann thought. I've not seen that bleeding helps a fever. Better leave well enough alone. He drited back into a slumber.

"The Black Robe waits to see you," Buffalo told Flann the following day.

"I'll talk to Father Baraga," Flann said.

Buffalo called to the priest to enter the wigwam.

Flann managed to raise himself to a sitting position as Father Baraga approached. The priest knelt beside him, his blue eyes studying him.

"My son, may I be of help?"

"I think it's intermittent fever," Flann told him. "I've had it before. I'll be all right in a day or two."

"I thank God it's not smallpox," the priest said.

"No, I've been vaccinated. I won't catch smallpox."

"I wish my poor Indians could say the same. It's a deadly scourge for them." Father Baraga touched his silver cross. "My quarters aren't much of an improvement, I'm afraid, but you're welcome to share them with me if you like."

"Thank you, Father. I'm fine here." Flann managed a smile. "Buffalo had his shamas treat me."

The priest shook his head sorrowfully.

"They didn't hurt me," Flann assured.

"'No. They will not harm you. But they do harm among their own people." The priest got to his feet. "I despair sometimes of eradicating heathen beliefs and practices. Still, if they accept the true God, all will be forgiven."

Flann studied the priest's small, slender frame. I make at least two of him, Flann thought, yet Father Baraga manages to survive in this wilderness year after year.

"Dr. Borup and Mr. Bushnell ask for you," the priest said.

"Tell them I'm recovering and that I'll stay with Buffalo. Thank you for coming to see me, Father."

"I'll pray for your recovery," Father Baraga told him. "May God speed it."

Flann fell back. I've had the Chippewas intervene with their gods in my behalf, he thought. Now a Roman priest prays for me. If I don't get well quickly, the devil must truly have me in his talons.

Slowly, Flann's strength returned. At times he cursed Crouching Fox for using a drug which paralyzed him temporarily and blamed it for the return of the fever. Yet he knew the intermittent fever recurred spontaneously, as its name indicated. He chafed at the delay in paddling to Meenagha, fearing the *Astor* might dock at La Pointe before he was well enough to get into a canoe.

"That metis, Henri, is gone," Buffalo said one morning as Flann returned from a short walk.

"Where?"

"He returned to Montreal," Buffalo said.

Did Henri's departure mean guilt? Well, it would be Schoolcraft's worry if Henri came back in the spring, Flann thought. If no new guns turned up this winter it might well mean that Henri was the Canadian rebel agent.

"The little chief is gone also," Buffalo added. "He travels with many voyageurs to speak to the Pillagers at Sandy Lake."

Little chief? Buffalo referred to the subagent, of course. Schoolcraft would be the chief.

Flann nodded. "I too am ready to go. To Meenagha."

Crazy Crane had paddled on from La Pointe to visit relatives at Fond du Lac. Buffalo found a Lac Vieux Desert brave who, while returning to his village, agreed to take Flann as far as Meenagha in his canoe. Before he left, Flann visited Dr. Charles Borup. He asked the fur factor to tell Captain Tobias Stannard to stop at Meenagha when he piloted the *Astor* back down the lake.

"Mr. Bushnell has already instructed me about this," Dr. Borup said, showing no trace of his former friendliness.

Flann realized he had probably offended the doctor by not asking to see him when he was ill.

"I have a word of advice for you, Mr. O'Phelan," Dr. Borup said. "It doesn't do to become too familiar with Indians. We learn this very early in the fur business. Friendliness only encourages arrogance in the young bucks. They become unmanageable. There's an impassable gulf between a savage Indian and a civilized white man. Take care you remember this." He gazed sternly at Flann. "I would assume you'd have better sense than to involve yourself with the squaws."

Squaw. The doctor pronounced the word without emotion, but somehow he made it sound belittling. Yet *ekwai* simply meant "woman" in Chippewa. White men not only distorted the pronunciation of ekwai, but also the meaning, Flann thought.

He got into the canoe shaken by Dr. Borup's comments. Borup had spoken of white men as though Flann O'Phelan was no longer one.

Flann's Chippewa traveling companion kept a taciturn silence. Flann found it took all his newly recovered energy to keep up his share of the paddling, so he said nothing either as the canoe skimmed along the lake. He had been at La Pointe for almost two weeks. Had Birch Leaf believed him when he told her he would not return? Memory of her in Black Rock's embrace made Flann clench his teeth.

No, he wouldn't think about her. He intended to go straight to Copper Sky. Copper Sky would not be expecting him back. There would be no time for the chief to avoid the confrontation.

"Walk-in-the-Water," the brave said.

The sun, sparkling on the water, blurred Flann's vision at first. Finally he saw a tiny smudge of smoke in the distance. The *John Jacob Astor* was on her way to La Pointe. He had two days at most to get his job done at Meenagha.

The wind blew from the northwest, speeding their journey. Even so, Flann knew it would be nearly sunset before they reached the village. *Kewadinoong,* the home-blowing wind, the Chippewa called it. Well, it would blow him home, too, down the lake aboard the *Astor.*

Clouds trailed along the horizon when they reached Iron River. The setting sun colored the clouds red and salmon pink and cast a fiery glow over the wigwams as Flann stepped ashore. He saw many canoes, and as he pushed snarling dogs aside, he wondered why no children had run to stare at them.

Flann and the brave walked toward the fire, hearing voices and men's laughter. A sweet, pleasant smell drifted from the cooking kettles. The brave sniffed the air and smiled for the first time since Flann had met him.

"Manomin," he said.

A boy spotted the two men and ran back to the village, shouting, "Ishcoda!"

A woman left a group by the kettles and started walking toward them. Flann's heart quickened. Then he saw that she moved without the lightness of Birch Leaf. It was the old Sioux woman, Fire Grass. She carried Squirrel on her hip. As she neared the men, she set the boy down on the path.

Squirrel stared at Flann, then ran toward him, laughing and holding out his hands. Flann, amused and touched, knelt and picked up Squirrel, settling him on his shoulders. The boy clutched his hair, chuckling.

The brave glanced at Flann. "Ishcoda's son?" he asked, his voice betraying surprise.

Flann hesitated, then decided it was simpler to say yes than to tell the entire story.

"Wigwam," Fire Grass said proudly, pronouncing the Chippewa word with care. She pointed to herself, to Squirrel, and then to Flann.

He smiled at her, unsure of what she meant.

"Ishcoda."

Flann looked up to see Crouching Fox.

217

"You're in time for the wild rice feast," Crouching Fox said. "We've just begun to eat."

Flann handed the boy to Fire Grass and followed the shaman to the men's circle. The first man he saw was Black Rock. Then he recognized the Ontonagon chief and realized the Loon Clan had been invited to the feast. All the braves wore ornaments, and many of the armbands and discs attached to their leggings were silver.

Room was made for Flann and his traveling companion next to Copper Sky. Before Flann had a chance to do more than greet the chief, a woman handed him a bowl of food. Another proffered a stick with roast duck impaled on it. The aroma made Flann's mouth water. He began to eat.

The wild rice had a flavor unlike either rice or oats. Eaten with the duck, it was delicious. When he had finished, Flann turned with determination to the chief.

"Very good," he said, fixing his gaze on the silver band Copper Sky wore around his left arm. "*Shonaiu,* the metal we call silver," he said. "I like the shine. Where does the silver come from?"

"Near," the chief said. "A secret place."

Flann leaned close and spoke in a low tone. "Secret, like the guns your braves used against the Sioux?"

"There's no wrong in having guns to use against our enemies."

"No. The wrong lies in what was agreed when the guns were given to you," Flann said.

"The man lied to me, why shouldn't I lie to him?"

"What man?" Flann asked.

"I cannot give his name," Copper Sky said. "He wanted me to tell the warriors to fight at the side of

218

certain Canadian white shogonos against other shogonos. Why should we help white men fight their battles? I took the guns to use against the Sioux because we needed powerful weapons."

"How did the man lie?"

"He said the Great White Father in Washington didn't care about us, but the shogonos thought of us as brothers. I'd be stupid to believe this. Each year money and goods come from Washington. What comes from Canada? Nothing. Not unless we trade skins. So I knew he lied."

"I must know who this man is," Flann insisted.

"I am not going to tell you. It's none of your affair."

"The White Father in Washington wishes to know," Flann said.

"It's not his affair either. He tells me not to fight the Sioux." Copper Sky paused, staring at Flann. "Is this a reasonable request? How can you not fight an enemy? White men go to war. Are we different?"

Flann finally gave up his attempt to persuade Copper Sky to name the gun supplier. The chief obviously would not. Even when he had mentioned Henri Fontenac's name the chief had not changed expression.

Perhaps Crouching Fox would be more forthcoming. Flann suspected the shaman missed nothing that went on in the village. He rose to confront him.

"Brother, you mustn't ask me about matters pertaining to the chief," Crouching Fox told him. "I can't and won't answer your questions. Why not enjoy the feasting?"

"Don't call me brother," Flann exclaimed. "You drugged me when I was last here."

"To save you from foolishness. Are you the worse for it?"

"I had fever in La Pointe. It could have been your medicine," Flann said.

"No. What I gave you has no lasting harm. It's more likely you offended against spirits, since you don't know the ways of the People. You're my brother, Ishcoda. I would never hurt you."

Flann stared at him. Schoolcraft told him the Chippewas were generally truthful. Yet he found it difficult to trust the shaman.

A hand touched his sleeve. He whirled and saw Fire Grass behind him, carrying a torch. She spoke in Sioux.

"She says she'd like to show you to your wigwam, where you may change into new moccasins," Crouching Fox told him.

Flann took a deep breath and let it out, realizing he was fatigued. "I don't understand," he said. "Your wigwam is where I stay."

"Go with her," the shaman said.

Flann walked with Fire Grass. They came to a wigwam behind Soft Willow's. He didn't remember seeing one here before. The Sioux woman gestured indicating he should enter. Then a voice spoke to him.

"Do you like your wigwam?" Birch Leaf asked.

He turned. It had grown so dark he could not make out her features, but the sound of her voice speeded his pulse.

"I helped Fire Grass make it for you," Birch Leaf said. "Now you can live in your own home."

Flann took the torch from Fire Grass, holding it high so he could see Birch Leaf. Her green eyes reflected in the flames as she smiled up at him.

He had the feeling he had come home at last.

Chapter 21

Flann, who had had no trouble adjusting to being a guest in other wigwams, now found himself uneasy in his own. Although Fire Grass was more than old enough to be his mother, he felt uncomfortable with her sleeping only a few feet away from him. He didn't know whether she expected to act as his mother or his wife. He tossed fitfully, then fell into a deep sleep near dawn.

He woke suddenly, aware of a weight on his chest. Squirrel was sitting astride him. The boy smiled and grabbed Flann's beard, pulling it.

"Ouch! You little. . . ." Flann searched for a Chippewa word equivalent to monkey, found none, and sat up.

Fire Grass cooked rice over the outside cooking fire. The morning was crisp, with white clouds drifting across the bright blue sky. Flann ate his meal of boiled rice and blueberries while Squirrel watched him.

"*Adjidaumo,*" Flann said to the boy, repeating the Chippewa word for squirrel until the child tried to say it. Flann scooped him up and tossed him into the air, making Squirrel laugh with glee.

After playing with the boy for a time, Flann handed him to Fire Grass and went to look for Birch Leaf. When he found neither she nor Soft Willow at their wigwam, he walked to the river mouth and saw that the Ontonagon canoes were gone. As he made his way back to the village, he was intercepted by Crouching Fox.

"Tonight we hunt deer. Why not join us?" the shaman asked.

"A night hunt?"

"We use a canoe and torches."

Flann thought this might be the shaman's way of trying to compensate for drugging him. "I'd like to come along," he said. "I don't think the ship will come past until tomorrow."

"You are returning to your own village, then," Crouching Fox said. "I'll be sorry to see you leave."

If the shaman was feeling penitent, maybe he would talk about his methods of healing, too. "I'd like another lesson in plants that cure," Flann said. "And I want to ask you about what two of your mide colleagues did to me while I was at La Pointe."

"*Nanandawi iwe winini,* curing by sucking," Crouching Fox told him. "I heard they sucked out a snake. It's bad to leave warriors unburied such as the Sioux we killed. With their village destroyed, there was no one to say the proper words to show their spirits where to go. One of those evil spirits entered your body and made you sick."

"I think the dogwood bark I insisted on helped cure me," Flann said dryly. "Evil spirit or not."

"We journeyed back for our own dead. They're safely buried now. Their spirits don't wander."

222

"What do you believe causes sickness besides evil spirits?" Flann asked.

"A man may lose his own spirit while still alive if it can't find the way back into his body. He'll die if no one can show the spirit where it belongs. If he doesn't stay asleep while the spirit roams outside the body, he gets sick."

"This is the spirit that leaves the body for good when a man dies?"

"No. Each man has two spirits. One stays with the body always, until death. The other departs on trips when he sleeps. If there was only one spirit the body would die when a man dreamed. How could we know how to live in the right way without dreams?"

"The whites believe in only one spirit, one soul."

Crouching Fox shrugged. "There are two," he repeated. "Another way a man can sicken is by violating a taboo. That's why we keep the women away during their moon blood. Should a bleeding woman fix food, all who ate it would become ill." Crouching Fox paused. "Also a man can become ill when the vision animal lodged in his body becomes ill. He can be anywhere, be very small, so he can't be seen. Ordinarily he causes no trouble. But if a man eats food or commits an act that sickens the animal, the man will be sick as well."

"I've been taught disease comes from bad air, or crowded and dirty living quarters," Flann said. "And some disease is contagious, like smallpox."

"Smallpox is a white man's disease. Our forefathers knew nothing of it long ago when they lived beside the great sea of salt. No medicine works for us against smallpox."

"Have any of the Meenagha villagers been vaccinated?" Flann, knowing no Chippewa word for "vaccinate," used the English word.

"I don't understand your meaning," Crouching Fox told him.

"A doctor takes a knife or needle and scratches the skin of a man who has not yet been sick with smallpox, then rubs in a bit of matter taken from a smallpox sore of another. The man will then grow a sore in that spot, but after the sore heals he'll never be sick with smallpox though he lives to be old. Women, children and babies can be vaccinated, too."

"I've heard of this being done at Fond du Lac, but not here in Meenagha."

"It works well."

Crouching Fox nodded. "If a white doctor should be sent to vaccinate the People, I shall remember what you've told me."

Flann spent the rest of the morning with the shaman, roaming the woods about the village. Crouching Fox identified trees and plants he used for treating different illnesses. Flann discovered the water in which the inner bark of black ash was soaked to cure sore eyes. Boiled cattail roots healed suppurating wounds. Sphagnum moss was used for wound dressing because of its absorbency.

After leaving the shaman, Flann went again to Soft Willow's wigwam. Birch Leaf sat on the outdoor platform making cord from basswood bark.

"I see you're wearing Sioux moccasins," she said.

Flann looked down at his feet and saw they were different from Chippewa moccasins. Chippewa moccasins were puckered in front. Sioux moccasins were not.

"I preferred yours," he said, "but they wore out."

"You have a woman to make your clothes now."

He put his hand over hers, stilling her busy fingers. "Fire Grass isn't the woman I'd choose."

Birch Leaf flashed her eyes to him, then away. "Too old?" she asked mockingly.

"She could be my mother."

Birch Leaf broke into laughter. "I was teasing you. I know Fire Grass doesn't act as a wife."

"If I stayed here," Flann said, "I'd want you."

Her laughter died. "If . . . ?"

"The Walk-in-the-Water will be coming past Meenagha tomorrow and will stop for me."

She pulled her hands from his. "I thought you might stay," she said softly.

"I can't."

"Why?"

Flann started to speak, then stopped. He had been about to say, "Because I must report to President Van Buren."

But he had already told Daniel Bushnell everything he had discovered about the Canadian guns. As for the silver, all he knew was that it came from some secret place. He knew that Bushnell would surely report on the weapons to Henry Schoolcraft, and Schoolcraft in turn would report to Charles Madden in Washington. Van Buren would hear a full report from Madden's superior, C. A. Harris, commissioner of Indian Affairs, and probably would not miss Flann O'Phelan's personal report at all.

So there was actually no critical need for his return east at all.

Of course, there *was* Lynette and his promise to her that they would marry on his return. However, he had already conceded that the promise was not really worth a Continental dollar to him.

What if he did stay over the winter? President

Jackson had instructed him to report to Van Buren *when* he returned, just as Flann had promised to marry Lynette *when* he returned. But the only person who had told him to report anywhere at a specified time was Henry Schoolcraft. By November, he had said.

In fact, he might actually be of more value to Van Buren by staying here rather than going. By staying, he would learn whether Henri Fontenac returned to the village in the spring. And Flann might also learn the location of the silver lode by then.

And if he stayed the winter, he would be with Birch Leaf.

Birch Leaf spoke again. "You do not want to tell me why you're going," she said quietly. "I think it is because you have a woman in your village to marry. You hurry back to her. To Lyn-ette." Birch Leaf wrinkled her lips and nose in distaste.

He looked at Birch Leaf. She was gathering strips of bark again and would not meet his gaze. Her dark hair was gathered into a braid that was tucked over and attached in back with a carved piece of wood. Strands escaped to curl about her face. Her skin glowed golden in the sun. The blue cloth of her dress gently outlined the shape of her breasts. Flann caught his breath, remembering the feel of her softness against him.

"There *is* a woman," he said. "She's not like you, not as lovely, not as honest, not as desirable."

"Still, you prefer Lyn-ette," Birch Leaf said.

"No," he implored. "No, I don't."

She turned her head and stared at him, puzzled. Her eyes glistened with tears. He had never wanted a woman as he wanted her.

Suddenly Birch Leaf dropped the bark, slid off the platform and ran into the wigwam, yanking the skin

226

flap shut behind her. He stood. A hand pushed the flap open. Soft Willow shook her head and dropped the skin to close the wigwam again.

Flann strode away. When he reached the lake he turned and walked along the beach toward the mountains. He looked for the ashes of the fire Birch Leaf had built the night they had made love on the sand. Had it been here? Or farther along? He didn't know. Thinking about that night aroused desire with every heartbeat.

What did Bushnell really know about him, Flann O'Phelan? Dismissing him as a city man. It was damned cold in Boston during the winter. Could Michigan be colder? Did they think he came from the tropics? Run along home, sonny, the real men'll take care of things. That's what Bushnell had implied with his dismissal. And Borup had been saying the same with his offensive advice about squaws.

Flann walked faster and faster until he was running. His anger blinded him to his surroundings until he splashed into a creek emptying into the lake.

He turned around, returning slowly to the village, conscious now that the wind had a bite and the massing clouds had turned a dirty gray. He fancied he could feel winter's frosty promise in the air. In the east they called the last few warm days of autumn Indian summer.

His Indian summer was over.

Shortly before dusk, Crouching Fox sought Flann out and reminded him of the hunting trip.

He followed the shaman to the river. Four braves were attaching poles to their canoes. Flann watched as Crouching Fox himself picked up two long slender poles and fastened them, one to each side under the

227

forward spreader of his canoe so they rested on the gunwales and extended well out in front. Between the ends of the poles he suspended a birch-bark box filled with sand on a wooden frame. Then, across the poles, closer to the canoe, he fitted on a broad piece of birch bark.

"What are they for?" Flann asked.

"To shield the hunter's eyes," Crouching Fox explained as he took a dried pine knot and placed it in the sand-filled box. "When I light the torch I hope to blind the deer, not myself."

Jacklighting, Flann thought, and all the preparations suddenly made sense to him.

When he was satisfied, Crouching Fox waved Flann into the stern of the canoe. He himself took the bow. "We'll go up the lake to Wintergreen Creek," he said. "A good place to find deer."

Flann saw that the other canoes were heading into the lake, one turning east, the other west, as Flann and Crouching Fox were. The shaman had no rifle, only a bow and a quiver of short arrows. All the shafts were feathered. He reached to touch them but the shaman stopped him.

"Not until the deer is shot," he warned.

It was dark by the time they neared Wintergreen Creek. The other canoe had turned up an earlier stream. The wind from the lake was cutting, so Flann was happy to turn into the creek. Crouching Fox pulled the canoe to the bank and lit the pine torch with his flint and firesteel.

"You must not lift your paddle from the water when we go upstream or the drops of water falling from it will frighten the deer," he said. "We'll go slowly and silently. No need to hurry."

Flann found it difficult to keep the paddle in the

water and still propel the boat forward, but he struggled along stubbornly. As steersman, he was responsible for keeping the canoe steady. They moved slowly upstream, the pine knot flaring ahead, the dark closing in behind them. At the stern, Flann was not totally shielded from the torch. The light partially blinded him. His first realization that they had come on a deer drinking from the stream was the touch of Crouching Fox's hand. Flann backpaddled, holding the canoe in place and, peering into the darkness, he saw the gleam of two golden spots—the deer's eyes.

He heard the soft twang of the bow. The golden eyes moved upward, then disappeared.

"To the bank," Crouching Fox ordered.

The shaman lifted the torch from the box of sand. Flann secured the canoe by taking hold of a sapling. The body of the deer lay several feet away on the bank.

"Good shot," Flann said.

"This time of year is best for taking deer at night," Crouching Fox told him, "for it doesn't matter if they're does or bucks. In the spring and summer, the does are nursing fawns and it's against Kitchi Manito's wishes to kill them."

They moored the canoe and carefully loaded the deer so that the sharp hooves wouldn't pierce the bark.

"We'll feast well tomorrow back at the village," Crouching Fox said.

It rained the next morning. As he gathered his belongings for departure, Flann had to discourage the curious Squirrel from carrying things off. In spite of the gloomy weather and his own melancholy, Flann smiled when the boy peered up at him and said, "Adjidaumo," then stumbled and fell as he tried to walk with his feet in Flann's moccasins.

"You go?" Fire Grass asked in clumsy but careful Chippewa, and he realized she too was learning more of the new language.

"Yes."

He knew Soft Willow would take charge of Fire Grass and Squirrel as she had promised when he brought them into the village from the Sioux raid.

The cooking fires were inside the wigwams now because of the cold weather and the rain. Flann had barely finished his venison stew when he heard the steamboat's whistle. The *Astor* was waiting for him. He rose from his mat and picked up his gear. As he walked to the door, Squirrel fastened onto one of his legs. Flann plucked the boy loose, hugged him, and handed him to Fire Grass.

"He's a good boy," he said in English, knowing she didn't understand. "A fine boy."

He felt the prick of tears as he left the wigwam, bending his head into the rain. He glanced at Soft Willow's wigwam but the door flap was closed. He hesitated, then went on toward the canoes. As he approached the river mouth, he saw a huddled figure in the stern of a canoe. Crouching Fox had promised to paddle him to the *Astor*.

Flann looked through the gray curtain of rain to where the side-wheeler lay offshore. The whistle sounded again. He headed for the canoe. He drew up short as he recognized the paddler.

"Birch Leaf."

"You need someone to take you to the ship. I offered," she said.

He spread his gear carefully in the bottom of the canoe and climbed into the bow. Birch Leaf immediately pushed off. He tried to look back at her, but in paddling he found it difficult. Soon the ship loomed above him. He saw a rope ladder hanging over the side.

"Is it Mr. O'Phelan?" Captain Tobias Stannard's voice called across the water. The misty rain blurred Flann's sight of him.

"Flann O'Phelan," he answered.

The canoe gently nosed against the ship.

"Birch Leaf," he said.

"Ishcoda, I love you," she said. "Remember."

Flann reached for his gear.

He dropped it again. He had made a decision.

"Captain Stannard?" he called.

"I hear you," the captain's voice said from above.

"I'm not sailing with you."

Silence. Then, "It's the *Astor*'s last trip this year," the captain called.

"I know. I'm staying over the winter. Please tell Mr. Schoolcraft for me."

"I'll do that. But sir, you have a letter here that I've carried up from The Soo. If you'll kindly climb the ladder I'll hand it to you."

"Wait, Birch Leaf," Flann said, then pulled himself up the rope ladder. When he was within arm's reach of the deck, Captain Stannard leaned over with the letter. "Sure you know what you're doing?" he asked.

"Quite sure," Flann said briskly. "Thank you for delivering my letter."

He clambered back down the ladder and into the canoe.

Birch Leaf pushed off, and they paddled quickly back to Meenagha. As soon as the canoe was safely moored, he reached for her and held her while the rain beat down on them. He kissed her, tasting the rain on her lips.

Finally he let her go and reached for his belongings. Thrust among them was the letter gleaming white. Flann picked it up and saw Lynette's careful penmanship. The ink was running in the rain. He tore open the envelope and pulled out a single sheet of paper. "My dearest Flann," Lynette wrote:

> I know you'll understand when I tell you I release you from your promise. By the time you receive this letter, I'll be Mrs. Arnold Grant. Please forgive me, dear, dear Flann and always remember me kindly.

Lynette's writing was blurred by raindrops even as Flann read. He held the letter for a moment, then threw it into the air and boomed with laughter.

Chapter 22

The leaves of the hardwoods had scarcely turned to red, orange and gold before they were swept off the trees by Old Cold Maker, *Kabibonokka,* the North Wind. The birds had flocked and flown south except for a few winter ones like the chickadee, blue jay and downy woodpecker. Ice Moon or Lake Freezing Moon, November, had begun.

When the snow stayed on the ground without melting, the Meenagha villagers packed to move to their winter wigwams. The *nobugidabans,* the toboggans, came down from the walls. So did the snowshoes, made of ash branches bent into rounded frames and strung with nettings of moosehide strips or basswood cord.

Flann tried to help Soft Willow and Birch Leaf as they harnessed their two dogs in tandem to the larger toboggan with collars and side straps. They turned him away, saying this was women's work. Their smaller toboggan had straps attached so it could be pulled by a man. He made up his mind to pull it, whether it was women's work or not.

Some toboggans had seat frames for the old people and toddlers. Everyone who could walk strapped snowshoes onto their feet, from the oldest grandmother to the youngest child. Two women with small babies strapped them onto their backs in *tikinagens*. They wrapped trader's blankets loosely about these backpack cradle boards to keep their babies warm on the march.

Fire Grass had made Flann a wolf fur jacket with extra-long sleeves to cover his hands. She had also fashioned bearskin coats for herself and Squirrel. All wore winter moccasins lined with rabbit fur.

The women had removed the bark coverings from their wigwams, rolled them into bundles tied with cord and placed them and all their other household goods on the toboggans. All that was left of the village were the stripped frames of the wigwams and the sticks showing where the canoes had been buried for the winter to prevent the bark from freezing and cracking.

"It will be good to have a man in our winter wigwam," Soft Willow told Flann. "You are welcome, with Fire Grass and Squirrel."

Flann knew she meant he was welcome as a hunter. All of the young braves had left before the first snow, with their wives if they were married, to go west and north to trap. They would be gone until spring.

He saw that the birch-bark bundles from Fire Grass's wigwam had been added to Soft Willow's on the large toboggan. Birch Leaf nodded.

"We'll use all the bark," she said. "The more covering the better on a winter wigwam. Old Cold Maker is hard to keep out."

Fire Grass had learned enough Chippewa to follow the exchange. She nodded in agreement, quite ready to share Soft Willow's wigwam for the winter.

Many toboggans had already left the village by the time they headed into the woods along Iron River. The water was choked with ice, and only a thin stream of water flowed. As soon as they were well into the pines, Flann felt the wind's bite ease. He shuffled awkwardly on his snowshoes, hardly any nimbler than Squirrel. Soft Willow's two dogs pulled one toboggan and Birch Leaf the other. When Flann tried to take the thong from her she had insisted men did not pull toboggans, and she wasn't willing to have both of them become objects of ridicule. At that moment he did not argue. He was having trouble learning to use his snowshoes.

When Squirrel lagged farther and farther behind, Flann finally picked up the boy and carried him. He considered taking off his clumsy snowshoes to walk but decided he would make poor time in the snow without them. I'll have to get used to the damn things anyway, he thought.

Each family normally placed its winter wigwam in a sheltered spot miles away from any other family so there would be game enough for each to hunt. Late in the afternoon, Flann and the women came to a small clearing among the pines. Bare skeletons of deciduous trees dotted the clearing. In the middle was a framework of poles. Soft Willow and Birch Leaf immediately began unrolling the birch bark, and Fire Grass hurried to help them. Flann felt useless watching them, but knew they would resent any help from him. Women of the People performed certain tasks. Men performed others. Interference was not welcomed.

He unharnessed the dogs, then watched Squirrel. The boy had slept for several hours wedged among the household goods on one of the toboggans. He was now wide awake and climbing over the tired dogs in the snow.

Soft Willow and Birch Leaf quickly placed the bark on the framework. Fire Grass walked into the woods and came back with a cedar bough and began to sweep snow out of the wigwam.

Flann saw they would need firewood badly. He hauled the small toboggan into the woods. Squirrel followed. Flann found he could not load the toboggan with windfall logs and keep track of the boy at the same time. So he left Squirrel with the women when he hauled in the first load and told them to tie him up with the dogs, if necessary, to keep him home. He piled his wood near the wigwam and returned to the forest for more.

He had a large pile of logs and branches stacked up before dark. The women started a fire in the deep pit in the center of the wigwam. Flann stuck his head inside the opening and saw the fire was set like a star, with five long and solid logs fanned out from it, one end of each resting in the fire. He realized that as the logs burned they would be pushed farther into the flames.

Fire Grass and Soft Willow were busy hanging mats on the inner walls as a lining. Birch Leaf came toward him, holding Squirrel by the hand.

"We need cedar boughs for the floor," she said. "Squirrel and I will help you cut them."

Instead of continually running after the boy, Birch Leaf showed him how to drag a bough to the toboggan and load it on. This task kept Squirrel busy while she and Flann gathered enough boughs to strew across the earthen floor of the wigwam. When they returned, Squirrel proudly dragged a branch inside and handed it to Fire Grass. She praised him, careful to use Chippewa words.

The woman spread mats atop the cedar, being careful not to place them too close to the fire. Soft Willow threw makuks of snow into a kettle hanging over the fire. When the snow melted she added wild rice and dried raspberries. Fire Grass arranged the sleeping robes about the fire while Birch Leaf finished hanging a mooseskin over the door opening.

Flann saw that he was to sleep closest to the door. Fire Grass spread her own robe on the opposite side of the fire, taking the grandmother's place. Next to her was Squirrel. Flann wasn't certain which of the other two coverings was Birch Leaf's and which was Soft Willow's. In any case, neither was close to him.

He had known there would be definite disadvantages associated with communal living in one wigwam. However, he didn't plan to spend a winter with Birch Leaf on one side of the fire and himself on the other.

The rice in the kettle began to boil, filling the wigwam with a mouth-watering smell. Squirrel ran to Flann and clutched at his leg, begging to be picked up. It was warm enough inside now to remove the fur jackets. Flann took his off, sat down and took the boy onto his lap.

After they had eaten, Soft Willow settled herself by the fire and said, "Mishibesheu, the water monster, and his attendants, the water serpents, now sleep beneath the icy water of Kitchigami. Soon the lake will freeze and keep them underneath for the winter. It will then be safe to tell the stories."

Fire Grass turned to her expectantly. Birch Leaf's gaze was fixed on her mother.

"I'll tell about when Nanabozho was born," Soft

Willow said. "It's true that Nokomis fell from her home with Moon and it's true she bore a daughter, beautiful Winona, who was stolen by West Wind. Winona wasn't happy with West Wind, who neglected her, and she made the long journey back to her mother. When she arrived she was very sick. Before she died, Winona gave birth to twin boys. One of the babies went away with his mother to the land of spirits, but the other lived. Nokomis put him under a bowl to keep him safe while she grieved for her daughter. When she came back and lifted the bowl, there was no baby underneath. Instead she found a little white rabbit nibbling grass, for the baby had gotten hungry and since grass was all he could find he had to change to a rabbit.

" 'Your name is Nanabozho,' Nokomis told him. 'My little rabbit.'

"You see, even though just born, already Nanabozho could be whatever he liked. He could become an animal, a tree or a rock, for he was a great-grandson of Moon and the son of West Wind and had many powers."

Soft Willow glanced at Squirrel's drooping eyelids. She motioned to Flann to put him under the sleeping robe of rabbit skins. When Squirrel was tucked in, Soft Willow leaned over him.

"Nokomis sang to the baby Nanabozho," she said to Squirrel, "a song I'll sing to you if you close your eyes." She gently touched each of his eyelids, then began to croon:

> Sleep, go to sleep,
> The owl with his big eyes
> Keeps watch.
> Close your eyes, go to sleep.

You're not an owlet.
Sleep, go to sleep.

The next day was cloudy, but the snow held off. Flann took his rifle and snowshoes and, with Birch Leaf accompanying him, went into the forest to hunt. She carried a bow and quiver with the same kind of short arrows Crouching Fox had used.

"Why are they so short?" he asked.

"Long arrows would catch in the trees," she said.

He examined one of her arrows, touching the flint head, the wood shaft and hawk feathers at the tail. He thrust it back into the quiver she carried across her right shoulder and asked to see the bow. He pulled the string, testing its flexibility.

"Deer sinew?" he asked.

"Yes. The men who make the bows say the skin from a snapping turtle's neck is the best bowstring because it won't stretch or shrink no matter what the weather. But turtle skin is for a brave's bow only. This is a woman's bow, made especially for me." The bow's length was the same as the distance from her right shoulder to the tips of her fingers on her outstretched left arm.

"Bows are always made to fit the hunter."

He reached for it again and took an arrow. When she saw he intended to try the bow, she stopped him.

"You must kneel first," she said. "Why would you shoot standing if it wasn't necessary?"

Flann knelt and aimed at a pine trunk about seventy-five yards away. He pulled the string back, surprised that the pull required considerable strength, and shot. His arrow missed the pine completely. Birch Leaf hurried to retrieve the arrow.

"You try," he said.

She knelt, fitted the arrow, drew and released. The arrow thudded into the center of the pine trunk. Birch Leaf went to pull it out and returned it back into the quiver.

"You're a good shot," Flann acknowledged, trying to ignore his injured pride.

"Soft Willow taught me when I was a child. We had no men in the family so we needed to hunt for ourselves in the winter. Other seasons my mother earns food by healing with her mide power."

"How about a rifle?" he asked. "Have you ever shot a rifle?"

"No. We've never had a gun."

"This winter I'll teach you."

Flann ached with the need to hold Birch Leaf, but knew they could still be seen from the wigwam. When they were deeper into the woods and he was certain they were completely hidden, he took Birch Leaf into his arms and kissed her. Her face was cold but her lips were warm and responsive. Their snowshoes clattered.

"Are we never going to be alone except in the cold?" he whispered.

She looked up at him with mischief in her eyes. "Are you so certain I want to be alone in a wigwam with you?" Before he could grab her, she ran off. He pursued her but she was much faster on snowshoes than he was. He caught up with her only when she stopped beside a small conical lodge.

"A tepee," he said. "Whose?"

"I found this last year just before we left for maple sugar camp," she said. "I don't know who built it, but no one has used it for a long time."

Flann looked at the tepee, seeing that the bark and deer hides covering it were cracked and torn. Nevertheless, it was sound. Birch Leaf glanced at him, then

240

turned away. She took off her snowshoes, pulled away the stick that held the doorflap closed and lifted it back.

Flann stepped out of his snowshoes, following her inside. Dead cedar branches covered the floor. It seemed even colder inside. The tepee was very small, barely large enough for two people.

"We'll make a fire," he said.

"I'll cut new boughs," she told him.

The fire caught quickly with the dry cedar to fuel the blaze. Flann took off his bulky fur jacket and helped Birch Leaf off with hers. He touched her cheek. "You're so beautiful," he told her as he bent to her mouth. "I never tire of looking at you."

They undressed before the fire. He caressed her bared breasts, murmuring, "I can't get enough of touching you." He took her breast hungrily into his mouth, running his tongue over her nipple.

She moaned and arched to him. Firelight licked over her body. Excitement fueled his desire. He eased her back among the cedar boughs and lay beside her.

Birch Leaf reached for his manliness, touching and caressing him until he was ready. He positioned himself above her, and she guided him inside her. He groaned with pleasure as he penetrated her welcoming softness, but he forced himself to move slowly and once again put his mouth to her breasts, first one, then the other. Her arms tightened around him, and she brought up her legs to pull him even closer.

He kissed her, their tongues intertwining, and he began to thrust deeply inside her. When she gasped and cried out, trembling, he unleashed his passion and thrust faster and harder until he throbbed in climax.

"My Ishcoda," she whispered. "I love you."

Flann pushed the log farther into the fire. He held

Birch Leaf in his arms and thought he had never been more content. After a time, she began to run her fingers over his chest.

"So much hair," she said. "Here as well as on your face. Men of the People have no hair on their chests or faces. Why is it white men do?"

"The People have brown or black eyes," he replied. "Yet, whites have blue eyes, green eyes, gray eyes and hazel eyes as well as brown and black." He touched her eyelids. "My little green eyes," he said. "I don't know why any of this is so. It might be that our forefathers were given eyes and skin and hair suited to the land where they lived in the beginning."

Her fingers traced patterns on his stomach. He felt himself began to harden again in anticipation of her touch.

"Your hair is red even down here," she said. As she felt his hardness her eyes lifted shyly to his. "You like me to touch you here," she whispered.

"Everywhere," he agreed. He explored her inner thighs until he reached her beautiful femininity. He caressed her until she sighed and pressed herself to him.

Flann entered Birch Leaf once more, slowly pulling all the way out with each lazy thrust, teasing her until she clasped him firmly to her. She began to move in a rhythm that matched his, increasing his excitement until he plunged into her, gasping with passion.

Birch Leaf made wordless sounds, panting as she clung to him, trembling, shuddering with her climax. He felt his own burst of pleasure matching hers.

"We must leave," she said moments later. "This puts no food in the kettle."

"Who cares?"

"You will when your stomach goes empty." She sat up and began to dress.

Flann reluctantly dressed, too. As he helped Birch Leaf pile snow on the fire, she said, "I'll have to come here at my moon blood time, now that you're in the wigwam."

He glanced around the tepee. "You're not going to come here alone," he said. "That's crazy. Moon bleeding won't hurt me. I've told you I don't believe in such taboos."

"There's the boy, Squirrel, too," she said.

"He's a baby yet. When you have your courses you can hang a few mats in the wigwam and hide behind them if that'll make you feel better about the taboo. I tell you you're not coming alone to this tepee. What if there's a blizzard?"

"Misfortune will come to you and Squirrel, if I stay. It's always been this way, even if you don't believe."

He took her hand. "I'm the most fortunate man in the world because you love me. Nothing's going to spoil it." He pulled her to him, then held her away and shook her gently. "We'll come here again. Together. This is our place of love, not a place of taboo. I, Ishcoda, say this is so."

Her green eyes stared into his lovingly, yet with apprehension. Flann felt a twinge of irritation because of her Indian superstitions.

After all, she wasn't even an Indian.

Chapter 23

On the way back to the wigwam, Birch Leaf shot a porcupine. She used a long stick to flip the dead animal onto its back and slit the underside, where there were no quills, then skinned it. She was careful not to stab herself on the hooked ends of the sharp quills.

"You'll have no luck today," she told Flann. "A hunter doesn't make love before he goes into the woods for game."

"It seems to me it took two of us to make love. What about you?"

Birch Leaf laughed. "I'm a woman. The taboo only affects warriors." She hooked the quilled skin onto the stick to carry it. "To decorate moccasins," she explained. "Beads are prettier and easier to use, but we have few left."

The porcupine was the only animal they saw before reaching the wigwam, although Birch Leaf pointed out the tracks of rabbits, a fisher and a fox. When they entered the wigwam, Birch Leaf immediately removed her moccasins and shook the snow from them. She told Flann to do the same.

They smelled the rich aroma of cooking meat.

"*Koshkoewasoo*," Soft Willow said, nodding at the kettle.

Flann repeated the word, puzzled. "He who startles?" He peered into the kettle as Soft Willow raised pieces of meat he recognized as bird. She pointed to a small box of feathers she had saved.

"Grouse," Flann exclaimed.

Soft Willow smiled and nodded.

The ruffed grouse drums in the spring to attract a mate and the sudden noise can be a surprise, Flann thought. Also the bird often waits until a hunter is almost stepping on it before flying up from his feet, and that can be quite startling.

"Nanabozho named him," Soft Willow said. "It was Fire Grass who caught two today by finding where they had taken shelter under the snow."

The old woman grinned in pleasure.

"Father," Squirrel cried happily, rushing at Flann from his mat where he had been napping. All three women laughed at the expression on Flann's face when he heard Squirrel's new word.

The next day it snowed, light flurries blown by the wind. Soft Willow went out with Flann to show him where she had seen many rabbit tracks the day before.

"A rabbit run," she said. "If we set snares we'll have rabbits without the effort of hunting."

She showed him how to make a simple snare, a young sapling bent across the run and set into a notch cut into another sapling. She fashioned a loop from deer sinew and suspended it from the tip of the bent sapling. The loop rested partly on the ground. When

245

the rabbit hopped into the loop, its weight would release the bent sapling from the notch. It would spring upright with the rabbit hanging from the loop.

They walked along beside the rabbit run and he set two more snares before they headed back to the wigwam. At the edge of the clearing Fire Grass was preparing bird snares. Flann stopped to watch. She pulled a long hair from her head, looped one end and fastened the other to a small stick set in the ground. She dropped a pinch of wild rice beside the loop.

"Hair?" he asked Soft Willow.

"Hair is very strong. When the bird gets his feet entangled, he falls over, helpless, unable to walk or fly."

The next day the snow increased, but they snared two rabbits for stew. Fire Grass caught three small birds.

The following day dawned clear. Flann told Birch Leaf they would go into the woods and he would teach her to fire the rifle. He found it difficult to keep from touching her when they were confined in the wigwam. Even outdoors, he knew a casual brushing of arms would cause his smoldering desire to flare.

They snowshoed across the new fall of snow toward the pines. "If there are others in the winter wigwam of a married man and woman," Flann asked, "how does the couple have any privacy?"

"A blanket is hung. Or mats," she said. "If only children are there, and they are little, often nothing is necessary. How else would the child learn?"

"But even with a blanket, the others in the wigwam would know."

"Yes."

Flann raised his eyebrows.

"The grandmother or grandfather has made love in their time. Why should they care what the younger couple do?"

"I was thinking of the man and woman, how they feel," Flann said. "I couldn't make love to you with others in the wigwam."

She slanted her eyes at him. "Couldn't?"

"I'd better say I wouldn't want to."

She laughed.

Flann showed her the rifle mechanism, how to load, aim and fire, interrupting himself often to kiss her. Their embraces grew more and more passionate.

"How do you expect me to remember what you tell me about the gun?" she asked, freeing herself from his arms. "I can't concentrate."

"I'm going to topple you into a snowdrift in a moment," he said, reaching for her.

She backed away. "I think we'd be warmer in the tepee. But first let me shoot the rifle once by myself."

The recoil staggered her. "I like my bow better," she told him.

"You did well for the first time. We'll make a warrior out of you yet."

The next day, Birch Leaf told him she could not hunt with him and retired behind a hastily hung curtain of mats.

Flann went out alone, saw deer tracks, followed them for miles, but never found the deer.

By the bank of a frozen stream, he found animal tracks he didn't recognize and followed them. This time he trailed a muskrat to its hole in a bank under the roots of a tree. One shot killed the sluggish animal, who had been preparing to hibernate. Flann brought the muskrat back triumphantly.

Lake-Freezing Moon, November, passed with few storms. However, the weather stayed cold and the snow on the ground did not melt. When a storm ushered in the Snow Moon, December, no one could hunt. Although they were not going hungry, Flann felt he never had quite enough to eat. The snow kept them from checking the distant snares due to the risk of getting lost. Flann realized he must try harder to find large game so the meat could be dried and set aside for the depths of winter.

"The deer have gone to their secret place in the woods," Soft Willow told him, "for the snow is too deep for them now. Hunters look for their hiding place, but never in my lifetime has anyone found it. You'll do better to search for a bear in his winter sleep. Since you're Crouching Fox's brother, you're Lynx Clan and can kill Bear without fear of its angry spirit.

"Bear likes to dig his hole beneath a log or in an earth hill. When the snow comes, his warm breath makes a hole in the snow and you can see the rising cloud of his breath."

Flann and Birch Leaf went hunting as soon as the weather cleared. They were both hungry, and neither suggested going to the tepee. Flann knew much of the pressing need for food was his responsibility, for Soft Willow had only expected to have two mouths to feed this winter, not five. Her cache of wild rice was almost gone. They searched all morning. They had turned back toward the wigwam when Flann noticed claw marks on the trunk of a huge pine.

He showed them to Birch Leaf and she nodded excitedly. She circled the tree and called to him. Steam rose from a hole in the snow at the base of the trunk and Flann realized a bear must have dug his den among the roots.

They both began scooping snow away and soon uncovered the den opening. The pungent odor of bear was strong. The den seemed scarcely large enough for a man, much less a bear, but he could see dark fur. The bear didn't move. Flann aimed his rifle, reconsidered, and glanced at Birch Leaf.

"He'll weigh four or five hundred pounds," he said. "How are we going to drag a dead bear out of that small hole?"

"I'll shoot an arrow into him, just to wake him," she said. "He'll come out if he's hurt."

"That's all we need, a wounded bear charging us."

"I doubt if he'll attack. He'll be too sleepy. You'll have time to kill him with the rifle."

He looked at her skeptically.

Without waiting for his agreement, she shot an arrow into the dark mass curled in the hole.

There was a grunt, followed by a thrashing. Birch Leaf shot another arrow. The bear moaned, and his head appeared in the opening. His eyes appeared dazed as he crawled laboriously from his den.

"Get back," Flann warned.

The bear staggered to his feet and looked around, then saw Flann and growled. As he fired, Flann noticed both arrows protruding from the animal's left side. He aimed for the eye. His bullet sped true. The bear snorted, shaking its head. Blood spattered the snow.

Flann poured new gunpowder into his rifle, backing up as the bear charged.

"Run," he implored to Birch Leaf.

The bear loomed over him. He sidestepped to its blind side. The animal turned its head to search for him with the good eye. Flann was ramrodding bullet and patch down the barrel when the bear lunged at him. He tripped on his snowshoes as he stepped backward. He sprawled in the snow, staring up at the bear's teeth.

An arrow pierced the bear's remaining eye. The beast snorted and, as it tried to charge blindly, fell heavily onto its side. It made one feeble attempt to get to its feet, then shuddered and lay still.

Flann struggled to his feet.

"I'll go for the toboggan," Birch Leaf said.

Flann knew this had to be. He had to stand guard in case a wolf pack got wind of the kill. After Birch Leaf was out of sight, he leaned against the pine and stared at the massive beast they had killed.

It weighed six hundred pounds or more, he decided. He had never seen such a fat bear. Blood from the animal's wounds melted the snow. He pushed himself from the tree and approached cautiously. Once, a friend of his father had been fatally injured when he started to skin a supposedly dead deer. The animal's hooves had flailed out suddenly in a final death spasm. This bear showed no sign of life. Flann took out his knife.

He had the bear gutted and partially skinned when Birch Leaf returned. She was riding the toboggan, pulled by the dogs, and was dragging the second toboggan behind her.

Flann quickly threw the offal to the dogs. They fell on the meat, growling at one another. With Birch Leaf helping, Flann butchered the bear and loaded both toboggans. Birch Leaf insisted on taking the bear's head with them.

"We must do honor to the spirit of the bear," she said. Birch Leaf caressed the bloody and eyeless head. "I'm sorry you had to die. You die that we may live. It's hard to kill one's friend but at times it's necessary. Forgive me. I ask you, Bear. Forgive me, dear honored guest."

Flann's clothes were smeared with the blood of the dead animal.

With Birch Leaf driving the dogs and Flann pulling the other toboggan, they arrived at the wigwam late in the day, the time when long blue shadows fall on the snow. Squirrel tumbled out to greet them, inspecting the meat and managing to get himself covered with blood.

Soft Willow immediately dropped chunks of meat into the steaming water in the kettle, then showed Flann the scaffold she and Fire Grass had erected outside to keep the rest of the meat from the wolves. Flann heaved the rapidly freezing flesh atop the wooden frame.

Birch Leaf handed him a bowl of warm water. "Wash," she said. She laid out a new buckskin shirt and leggings she had made for him. They were decorated with the flattened and dyed quills of the porcupine she had killed on their first hunt.

When Flann had finished eating, he reclined on his mat, full and tired and content. When Squirrel tried to play with the bear head, Birch Leaf snatched it from him. Squirrel stamped his foot and scowled. The howling of wolves from the woods near the wigwam distracted him and he looked about, his eyes wide, as though expecting to see the wolves clawing at the door flap.

"Ah, little Squirrel, the wolves won't get you," Soft Willow said, "but I'll tell you the story of a little boy who wasn't as fortunate as you are, the story of Sheem."

251

Fire Grass, who had been standing near the kettle, sat on her mat. Squirrel came to cuddle up to Flann. Everyone looked expectantly at Soft Willow. She began:

"A man and his wife lived in a wigwam on a lonely island, far away from everyone. They lived there all the time, not just in the winter. They had three children, Older Brother, Older Sister, and Sheem the Younger Brother. The father got sick and before he died he told his children that he'd built his wigwam for the mother on this island to keep them all from the evil that lives in the world of men.

" 'After I'm gone you must obey your mother,' he told them, 'and if anything happens to her, you, Older Brother and you, Older Sister, must take care of Younger Brother.'

"When four moons had gone by and the fifth was near its full, the mother sickened and, dying, made the two older children again promise to care for Younger Brother. All through the winter Older Brother hunted, and Older Sister cooked the meat he brought to the wigwam and made clothes from the skins and Sheem was well cared for.

"In the spring, Older Brother decided he needed a wife, and so he went off in his canoe, promising to come back when he found one. He never returned. For a time Older Sister watched over her little brother, but when fall came she thought she'd like to be near other people and have the braves court her. So off she went, promising Younger Brother she'd come back before winter.

"Older Sister did not return, and soon the food began to run out. Every day Sheem went to the shore of the lake and looked for the returning canoe, but nei-

252

ther his brother nor his sister came back. By winter he grew very hungry and left the wigwam to wander in the woods where he could feed off the scraps the wolves left. He found a cave in which to sleep.

"The wolves saw so much of Sheem they grew accustomed to him and didn't bother him. Sometimes they even left scraps on purpose for him to eat. Ice covered the lake and thickened with the cold until the wolves could cross on it to the mainland. When Younger Brother saw them leaving the island, he followed them across the ice.

"On the other shore he saw a brave hunting in the woods and he recognized Older Brother. '*Neesia, neesia!* My brother, my brother!' he cried.

"Older Brother turned and saw a strange creature who stood on four legs staring at him. This creature looked familiar. Younger Brother called again to him:

> Neesia, neesia,
> *Ne maheengun iew!*
> My brother, my brother,
> I am turning into a wolf!

"Now Older Brother recognized him. '*Nee sheema, nee sheema!* My little brother, my little brother!' he cried, starting to run to him.

"Before he reached Younger Brother, the boy howled, '*Heo hwooh,*' and fur grew all over him. 'I am a wolf,' Sheem cried and ran off to join the other wolves."

Flann noticed Squirrel did not seem frightened by this tale. "Heo hwooh," Squirrel called, trying to imitate Soft Willow's wolf howl. "Heo hwooh."

"Time for sleep, my little wolf cub," she said, smiling.

The following day, Birch Leaf cut the tongue ligament from the bear's head and cooked it for Flann to eat, taking but a bit for herself. She scraped the skull clean of hair and meat and washed it, all the while crooning that Bear was an honored guest in the wigwam. When she had finished, she painted the skull red and blue in a striped and sunburst design and hung it high on the wall of the wigwam over the door flap.

Soft Willow took a skin pouch and approached Flann, asking him to hold out his hand. She poured a small amount of tobacco into his palm.

"Burn this for Bear," she said. "He prefers the offering from a brave."

Flann did as she asked, tossing the tobacco into the fire. The smell of it mingled in the air with the odor of bear fat being rendered in the kettle. When Flann asked Birch Leaf to go outside, she shook her head, holding up the moccasin she was making.

He knew this was an excuse. She was refusing him because she had had a part in killing the bear and thought she had to appease its spirit. Her offering consisted of denying herself pleasure.

Flann got up and pulled on his furs, irritated at her superstitions and unable to stand being inside any longer. Squirrel came running, holding out his fur so Flann could help him dress for the cold outside. Flann was ready to shove him aside and go alone, but the eager face of the boy made him hesitate.

Finally he dressed Squirrel and took him out into the snow. He taught the boy to make a snowman. When they went back inside, Flann's mood had lightened.

Every day after that, when the weather was clear,

Squirrel waited for Flann to take him out and play in the snow. If Flann went checking snares or hunting, he watched for Flann's return, then ran to meet him, sometimes before Soft Willow or Fire Grass could put his fur on.

Flann loved it when Squirrel rushed to greet him.

But he would live to regret it bitterly.

Chapter 24

Flann realized one morning that Christmas was either near or just past. In his preoccupation with Birch Leaf and his struggle to keep meat in the kettle, he had set aside his God.

I'll have my own celebration, he decided. Tonight I'll tell the story of His birth in the manger. They'll hear of the Christ child instead of yet another story about Nanabozho.

I'd like to give Squirrel a present, he thought, remembering how he, as a child, had enjoyed Christmas. And Birch Leaf. I'd give her the moon if I could, and the stars so that she could dance among them. Soft Willow and Fire Grass were his family too. He loved them all. He wanted to give something to everyone.

Flann listened to the sweep of the wind around the wigwam and smiled. Slim chance of anyone getting a present, he thought. He didn't have the skill to even make Squirrel a small bow and arrow like those he had seen young boys carrying at Meenagha. Whittling had never been a talent of his. Any attempt to carve a recognizable animal from wood was futile. If it had been spring he could have made a willow whistle, but there were at least two more months before Old Man *Peboan*, Winter, departed.

If I could find where the deer have yarded for the winter, he reflected, I'd be giving a present worth more than anything else—a supply of food to last until the snow was gone. It was a superstition that the deer could not be found, and he did not believe in superstitions. But he would have to go alone.

The sun glittering from the snow blinded him until he pulled down the buckskin mask Birch Leaf had made for him. "Sometimes a hunter is blinded by the *wendigo* in the snow," she had told him. "You must take care because wendigos are evil spirits, ice skeleton cannibals who try to catch and eat men."

Flann knew of snow blindness. This was why he wore the mask with its small eye slits, not for fear of the wendigo.

He snowshoed through the woods briskly, as fast on the *raquettes* now as a Chippewa. Although the sky was clear, he memorized landmarks as he passed. Carelessness killed quickly in the wilderness, and a man could not count on being able to follow his own trail home. A black-capped chickadee flew past him to perch on the naked branch of a birch.

"Chicka-dee-dee-dee," it sang, cocking its head to look down at him. He marveled again that such a tiny bird could survive the cold and snow.

He read the tracks in the snow. Here a fox had stopped and dug through the snow, hunting mice in their hidden snow tunnels. There a rabbit had plunged across the trail, obviously frightened and trying to outrun something. What? No tracks followed the rabbit's. Perhaps it had been an owl, hunting at dawn or dusk.

I've never felt so alive, Flann thought. I never realized before how hard it is to stay alive when meat isn't simply something I can buy from the butcher. Everything around me has a meaning. If I read and understand the meaning, I'll survive. This is the way of life every winter for the Chippewa, a hard and dangerous way to exist. Does living close to the edge of death account for the exhilaration I feel? Does it explain the closeness I feel for those sharing my wigwam?

There was Fire Grass, no longer young, uprooted from her home and family. Everything she had known had been destroyed. Now she was valiantly struggling to learn the Chippewa language and adjust her ways to those of her traditional enemies. Yet she retained her spark, enjoying life.

"Among my people there's a spirit man who can be an animal if he chooses, much like Nanabozho," Fire Grass had said one night after listening to one of Soft Willow's tales. "He's called Iktoma, the spider, and he has many foolish and funny adventures. Maybe someday I'll tell one."

"Perhaps someday we'll be ready to listen," Soft Willow had replied.

Flann had smiled at this polite exchange between the two matriarchs, one who had authority and one whose own authority was now only a memory. Actually, he knew Soft Willow accepted Fire Grass and suspected they would hear a tale about spider before the winter was over, with Soft Willow's full approval.

Flann believed Soft Willow would be a force anywhere. He found her an extraordinary woman. She was intelligent, compassionate and strong enough to insist on her place in what was essentially a man's group, the Midewiwin. And, while instructing Birch Leaf in all that a Chippewa woman must know, she had also encouraged Birch Leaf's independent spirit.

Flann grinned as he thought of Squirrel. By God, he hoped a son of his seed would be as bright and active and loving as this boy was. Squirrel's small, healthy body showed the promise of the handsome, strong man he would become. I'm proud that he calls me father.

Birch Leaf filled his thoughts. How could he live without her? He had no intention of ever giving her up. She was the loveliest woman he had ever seen, and her equally beautiful spirit showed in all she did. When she made love with him. . . .

Flann halted suddenly, looking through the slits in his buckskin mask. Had something moved to his left? He lifted the mask from his eyes to see better, blinking in the increased light. Yes, an animal floundered in the snow among the trees, a large animal. Flann reached for his rifle, then paused.

No, it wasn't an animal.

It was a man—stumbling, falling, sometimes crawling. Flann moved toward him cautiously, keeping his rifle ready. Birch Leaf's story of the wendigo flashed across his mind, and he shook his head impatiently.

"I come," he called in warning as he neared the man.

The man, struggling to get to his feet, collapsed into the snow, then pushed himself up to a sitting position and peered at Flann. He was a Chippewa, but Flann did not recognize him.

"I am sick," the man mumbled.

Flann slung his rifle onto his shoulder and knelt beside him. The brave appeared to be young, but his

259

face was gaunt as though he had not eaten for a long time. When Flann touched his forehead he found the skin hot.

"I'll help you," Flann said.

Grasping the Indian under the armpits, he lifted him to his feet and, supporting him, tried to walk with him through the snow. It was difficult. The Chippewa had no snowshoes. He stepped onto Flann's as he staggered forward, causing Flann to stumble. Flann realized he would have to sling him across his shoulders and carry him back to the wigwam.

He trudged along with the man on his back. By the time Flann came to the edge of the woods near the clearing where the wigwam stood, he could not take another step. He eased the sick man into the snow and bent over him.

"Almost there," he said. "Have to rest."

The Chippewa opened his eyes. "All dead," he said.

Flann, who had been reaching out to touch the man's forehead again, held back. A horrible suspicion jolted him. He opened the man's fur at the neck, then jerked back in horror at what he saw on the man's skin.

"Smallpox!"

"White man's pox," the man muttered, "Wife dead. Son dead. No food. Sick."

Flann stared at the telltale signs on the man's skin. The red macules visible on the neck and hairline. All too soon the sores would spread over the man's entire body, then blister and become fat with pus. Afterward they would crust over, if he lived that long. Indians as well as whites almost always died from smallpox.

"Thank God I stopped before we got to the wigwam," Flann said aloud. He could not leave the man here to die in the snow. He would take him to the old tepee, build a fire, and do what little he could for him. At least the brave would have warmth and shelter and another human being with him when he died. He took a deep breath and shifted, turning so he could once again lift the man.

Flann, facing the wigwam now, stared in dismay as he saw a small figure stumbling through the snow.

"No, no, go back," he yelled, jumping to his feet.

Before he could take a step, Squirrel had flung himself at Flann. He grabbed for Flann's leg but fell short, rolling over and tumbling against the stricken brave.

Flann snatched Squirrel away from the sick man. He carried him several yards away.

"Stay here," he ordred sternly. "Don't move."

Squirrel was startled, but he obeyed. Flann walked back to the brave. Sightless eyes were turned to the sun. Flann checked his pulse, but there was no beat. He was dead. Flann bowed his head briefly. "God," he whispered, "let me do the right thing."

He got up, pointed a finger at Squirrel and repeated, "Don't move. I'll be back." Then he grasped the dead man's legs and pulled him into the woods. He scooped a deep hole in the biggest drift he could find and dropped the brave into it. He tossed snow atop him, cut spruce boughs and piled them over the spot.

Squirrel was squatting in the snow when Flann returned. The boy smiled uncertainly.

What can I do? What am I going to do? He looked toward the wigwam, then down at the boy. Both had touched the brave. Both had made contact with smallpox. He knew he could not take Squirrel back to the wigwam or go there himself. He knelt down and forced a smile.

"We're going to have an adventure like Nana-bozho," he said. "You and I are going to stay by our-selves for awhile, just the two of us in a little tepee like you used to live in many moons ago."

Squirrel reached for Flann's hand.

Onset of disease occurs within two weeks of ex-posure to smallpox. If nothing happens in two weeks, we'll come back, Flann thought. I'm safe enough with my vaccination, but Squirrel. . . .

Flann's throat tightened. He swallowed. Take things as they come, he warned himself. Maybe the ex-posure wasn't enough to infect the boy.

Holding Squirrel's hand, he walked into the clear-ing, but stopped ten yards from the wigwam. "Soft Willow," he called, repeating her name until he saw the door flap stir. A figure appeared.

"Ishcoda?" Soft Willow called back. She started toward them.

"No."

She stopped.

"A man died of smallpox," Flann said tersely. "Squirrel and I have touched him. We've got to stay in the tepee in the woods on the other side of the clearing for a half-moon. If Squirrel's all right then, I'll bring him back."

Flann saw Birch Leaf come out and stand beside her mother. Soft Willow restrained her daughter as she started forward.

"No one is to come to the tepee," Flann called to them. "You risk dying. Understand me, Soft Willow, for I know the white man's disease."

"Ishcoda, I'll come with you, I'm not afraid," Birch Leaf called.

262

"You don't know enough about smallpox to be afraid," Flann told her. "I do. Soft Willow, you will see that no one visits the tepee."

"I hear you," Soft Willow said. "You'll need food. Robes."

"Yes. Leave food at the edge of the woods. Two robes. Squirrel and I will only hunt near the tepee. Stay away from us."

"Ishcoda," Birch Leaf cried.

"I won't get smallpox," he assured her. "It's Squirrel I'm worried about. If I bring him to the wigwam now and later he proves to have smallpox, you'll all be sick. If he doesn't get it in a half-moon, then I'll come back with him, for I'll know he wasn't exposed. Heed what I say. Stay safe for me."

Flann went back to the woods with Squirrel, circling around the edge of the clearing. He saw Soft Willow come out and place robes and food on the snow, then return to the wigwam. He retrieved the supplies and they headed for the tepee.

The first week with Squirrel went quickly. Every day Flann took the boy with him to hunt. Twice he was lucky enough to catch a rabbit in a snare he had fashioned near a rabbit run. They broiled the meat on sticks cut from a birch sapling. Squirrel's enthusiasm kept Flann amused and interested.

In the evenings he told the boy tales he remembered from his childhood. He recounted Bible stories. Squirrel liked the one of the birth of the Christ child best and demanded that Flann repeat it nightly.

When Squirrel fell asleep, Flann would look at the boy and tell himself he had taken needless precautions. Squirrel was obviously healthy. With such minimal exposure to the dead man, he surely would not contract smallpox.

During the second week Flann grew apprehensive. Their food supply was almost gone, and he hadn't shot or snared a single animal in days. Squirrel now missed Fire Grass and the others. He often looked at Flann when they set off to hunt each morning, saying, "Go?" while pointing toward Soft Willow's wigwam.

Flann was proud of him for remembering the direction of the wigwam. At the same time he was irritated by constantly having to care for and amuse the boy. He loved Squirrel, but he longed for the second week to be over. He felt that perhaps he had been overcautious in insisting on this isolation.

One day near the end of the second week, as Flann and Squirrel walked back to the tepee from a futile trip to the snare, Flann saw the aurora borealis, the northern lights, flickering blue and white.

"What?" Squirrel pointed.

Flann remembered something Birch Leaf had told him. "The spirits are dancing," he said. They stood for a few moments watching the sky until the cold drove them inside.

Two nights before they were due to return, their food ran out. When he woke the next morning, Flann pondered taking the risk of going back early. He looked at Squirrel, curled asleep next to him. Usually the boy woke before he did.

"Ho, sleepyhead," he said.

Squirrel opened his eyes and Flann drew in his breath. The boy's eyes were glazed. He touched Squirrel's forehead and found him burning with fever.

"Oh, God," Flann said under his breath. "Oh, God."

Squirrel whimpered and tried to raise his head, then vomited. For two days Flann tried to keep him comfortable while the child shook with chills and cried weakly, complaining of pains in his head and back.

On the third day, red macules appeared on his face and spread to his neck, arms and chest. But the fever lessened and Squirrel felt better. He was thirsty. Flann melted snow for him. Flann himself was weak from hunger, so when the boy fell asleep, he went out to check his snare. A pine marten hung in the noose.

The marten was not as tasty as rabbit, but to Flann, hungry as he was, it did not matter. Squirrel was persuaded to eat some of the meat. He did not get sick. Flann grew hopeful that the boy would be one of the few who survived smallpox. He knew the fever was certain to rise again in a day or two when the lesions filled with pus.

That night Flann woke from a horrid dream of skeletons in the snow and found Squirrel thrashing in convulsion next to him. The child's flesh was burning hot when Flann touched his forehead.

He lifted Squirrel into his arms and carried him outside, then laid him in the snow for a few moments to cool his fever. When Flann brought him back to the tepee, Squirrel had calmed down, but his mouth hung open and his breath came in short, rasping gasps.

Flann cradled the boy in his arms. His eyes rolled until Flann saw only the whites.

"Please, God," Flann whispered. "Don't take him."

Squirrel's breath rattled in his chest and then ceased. Flann bent over him, agonized. The boy shuddered and took one more breath. That was the last.

When Flann was positive Squirrel's heart no longer beat, he wrapped the small body in the sleeping robe of rabbit fur which Fire Grass had made. Flann wept as he huddled over the boy, his tears dropping onto the sores that had marred Squirrel's face.

At last Flann forced himself to move. He did not know how long he had knelt next to the dead boy. The fire had burned low and Squirrel's flesh was growing cold. I have things to do, many tasks I must perform, Flann told himself numbly.

He took his knife and cut into one of the pustules on Squirrel's face and carefully squeezed some pus into a small makuk Soft Willow had given them. He incised lesion after lesion until he had a tiny pool of pus on the bark bottom of the makuk. He brought the makuk outside, dropped snow onto the pus and left the makuk there so that the contents would freeze.

Back inside, he took his bearskin robe and cut it into strips. He wrapped Squirrel in the rabbit skin robe, fastening it around the body with one of the bearhide strips. Then he tied the rest of the strips together to make a long cord. He weighed one end with a stone from the fire pit. Picking up the wrapped body, the bearhide rope and his rifle, Flann plunged out into the night.

A full moon silvered the snow as he walked under the trees, staring up at the branches.

It took three tosses before Flann managed to throw the weighted end of the cord over a thick branch fifteen feet or more up the trunk of a large white pine. Flann tied the small fur bundle to the bearskin cord and hauled Squirrel's body up until it rested in the crotched part of the tree between the trunk and the branch. He flung the weighted end over the branch again and again until the cord was wrapped many times around both bundle and branch. He reached up and cut off the stone.

Flann stood at the foot of the pine. "Squirrel," he

said silently. "God loves children. Be with God." He turned away, then stopped and faced the tree again.

"May you join your forefathers in your hereafter," he said aloud in Chippewa, "wherever it may be."

A fire, he remembered. Squirrel needs a fire to light his way. He's only a little boy, and it's dark. Yes. A big fire. And throw everything in it. Fire burned away all contamination.

Flann rushed back to the tepee and threw all the wood he had gathered for the past two weeks onto the glowing coals inside. The fire flared up, flames licking greedily at the wood. He tossed the empty makuks into it, then stripped off his moccasins and threw them onto the fire. He grabbed a burning brand and touched it to the dry and cracked hides and bark that covered the tepee frame. The flames caught, climbing yellow and red to the top of the tepee. He laughed and took off his fur and threw it into the blaze, backing out into the snow as the fire raged. He stripped off his shirt, leggings and breechcloth, adding them to the flames.

Naked, he stood in front of the flaming tepee and raised his arms to the blue lights of the aurora borealis.

"Dance, spirits!" he shouted.

He turned toward the pine that was Squirrel's burial scaffold. "I lit a fire for you," he yelled hoarsely, "so you can see the way. Don't be afraid, little Squirrel. Don't be afraid."

Chapter 25

"Hark! The herald angels sing
Glory to the newborn King. . . ."

Flann's voice rang out in the cold night as he ploughed naked through the snow, heading for the wigwam, rifle slung on his shoulder and a small makuk, gripped in his right hand.

He shoved his way through the door flap, still singing. The three women huddled together at the far end of the wigwam, puzzled and apprehensive. He dropped the rifle and reached for a trader's blanket to cover himself. As he did, he hefted the makuk in his hand.

"Bring me a knife," he ordered.

For a long moment, no one moved. Finally Birch Leaf said quaveringly, "Ishcoda? Why do you behave so?"

"A knife," he said. "I need a knife. Mine's gone."

She edged away from the others and walked toward the fire, watching him.

"Hurry," he commanded.

Birch Leaf skirted the fire to come to him. She pulled her knife from its sheath, reluctant to pass it to him.

"I won't hurt you," he said, "but what I now do to all of you must be done. Trust me."

Tears glinting in her eyes, she offered him the knife. Flann took it and thrust the blade into the makuk, stirring the mixture of melted snow and pus.

"Bare your upper arm," he ordered. When she frowned, puzzled, he yelled. "Bare your arm!"

Birch Leaf unfastened the top of her dress and slid it from her shoulder. Firelight flickered on her arm and shoulder. Flann took the knife and scratched her upper arm with its point. He dipped his finger into the makuk and rubbed more pus into the scratch.

"That's all," he told her. He saw a container of sphagnum moss, picked out a bit and laid it over the scratch. He looked at the other women. "Soft Willow, come. You're next."

"What is it you do, Ishcoda?" she asked. Her face no longer wore the expression of fear, and her voice was steady.

"I'm vaccinating all of you so you won't die of smallpox. If I'd had the sense to earlier, if I'd dared to. . . ." He shook his head, his voice breaking. "Squirrel is dead," he said hoarsely.

When he had scratched the arms of Soft Willow and Fire Grass, Flann threw the makuk into the fire. Fire Grass wailed in mourning and his heart seemed to beat in accompaniment to her keening. He knew he was feverish again.

He knew he had put the women at high risk by vaccinating them. But the alternative, smallpox itself, was worse. He saw the smallpox as a ghastly, unstoppable adversary which would have killed them all if he hadn't taken the risk.

"I thought you were a wendigo coming for us, singing a death song," Birch Leaf said. "We all thought so."

"Maybe I am." Flann's legs would not hold him up any longer and he sank down onto a mat.

"Mother, he's sick," he heard Birch Leaf say as he closed his eyes.

Sick, yes, he was sick. The fever came first. Would the red circles that heralded smallpox come next? Had his vaccination long ago lost its effectiveness?

"Wendigo," he muttered. "Bringing death."

They forced bitter liquids down his throat and helped him swallow meat broth. Reality and dream united in his mind. Was the dancing skeleton real? Was the sight of Birch Leaf's green eyes above him a dream?

"Hungry Moon, January," Soft Willow's voice said.

Flann brought her face into focus. She sat nearby, not looking at him, saying, "Hungry Moon and a storm are near. I feel Old Cold Maker hovering nearby, waiting."

The other women nodded. They knew she was right.

A fresh storm was burying them alive as they sat in the wigwam. Time was a blur. Days and nights were one. Flann's fever worsened.

"It is I who must hunt, Mother," Birch Leaf said finally. "There is no food. If I do not go now, I'll lack strength to go at all."

At this moment, Flann came to for the first time

in days. With a painful effort, he turned his head and saw Birch Leaf standing near the door flap, holding his rifle. He tried to call to her. No voice came. Birch Leaf pushed the door flap aside and was engulfed by flying snow. Flann tried to call again.

Soft Willow comforted him. "Today your spirit is with you again," she said. Flann remembered being sick. He raised his head to look at his hands. He saw no crusted sores. "Smallpox?" he croaked.

"No," Soft Willow told him. "You didn't have sores." She touched her chest. "The sickness was here."

Flann shifted position and began to cough, a loose productive whoop, raising phlegm. Soft Willow nodded approvingly.

"You bring out the evil by coughing. I gave you medicine for this."

Pneumonia, he decided, observing the rusty blood streaks in what he had coughed up. He had passed the crisis. He would improve now. "How long have I been sick?" he asked.

"Over a half-moon."

"Your vaccination. Did anything happen?"

Soft Willow raised her left arm and carefully uncovered a large yellow pustule. Flann nodded with satisfaction.

"You used your power to place the white man's pox into my arm only. I understand now," Soft Willow said.

"When that heals you'll be safe from smallpox. What of Birch Leaf?"

"The sore she has is smaller. Fire Grass sickened with fever at first. She grew two sores. Today she hunts wood for the fire. I'll go out for wood, too, for you can

271

be left alone now that your spirit is with you again."
Soft Willow rose and put on her fur.

Alone, Flann lapsed back into sleep. When he
woke, he felt stronger still, even hungry, but recalled
Birch Leaf saying there was no food. He raised himself
on his elbow and looked about. Soft Willow and Fire
Grass huddled beneath their robes on the other side of
the fire, sleeping. Birch Leaf was not there. The wind
whipped around the wigwam. He tried to stand, but his
head whirled and he fell back. Soft Willow roused.

"Where's Birch Leaf?" Flann asked.

"Hunting."

"But it's night, it's. . . ." His words died away.
Soft Willow knew the danger as well as he did. In the
firelight he saw tension in her face.

A log spit sparks. The snap was the only sound in
the wigwam. Outside the pitch of the wind increased.
Fire Grass sat up too and glanced overhead as smoke
swirled back from the smokehole, thrust inside by the
wind.

"Another storm comes," she said. "A blizzard.
Very bad."

Birch Leaf was well into the forest when a thin
snowfall began. As she moved on, the pines overhead
soughed in a strange pitch. She knew the wind had increased and was thankful that the big trees protected
her from most of its force. When she reached a stand
of hardwoods, the wind whistled through their stripped
branches and hurled stinging pellets of snow at her.

She considered turning back, but even though the
wind blew strong it was only carrying loose snow from
the ground. Very little fell from the sky. In this
weather she would be able to find her way back even if

her tracks drifted over because she could still see landmarks. She was safe enough.

Birch Leaf pulled her fur hood farther forward to protect her face and snowshoed on. It was necessary to keep hunting. They had no food and she had left Ishcoda laying on the mat, coughing, his body burning with fever. Soft Willow said his spirit wandered, lost in the snow. She must find meat for him, for them all, or they would die.

The sore Ishcoda had made on her arm wasn't painful now. Her heart ached for Squirrel. If Ishcoda also died, she did not want to live.

She thought of her spirit dream, the great fiery bear who came to her from the sky. "Dream bear," she said aloud, "I, Birch Leaf, call to you. Lead me, that I may find food." She looked very hard for an omen to indicate her plea had been heard but saw nothing significant.

She came to a small clearing. Here the wind blasted full force across the drifts, forcing her to put her back to it as she crossed, changing direction. Then she hurried toward a stand of leafless trees. As she plunged among them she caught a glimpse of red, stopped, and stared overhead. On a bough high above her hung a frozen twig bearing a tiny clump of withered berries which the birds and squirrels had missed. Mountain ash berries.

Birch Leaf's heart leaped in delight. The dream bear had shown her the berries to remind her of the mountain ash where she had had her spirit dream. He had heard her plea and would surely help her. She walked on with renewed strength.

But eventually her pace lagged once more. She knew she was far from the wigwam and the weather was worsening. The snow now fell thickly from the sky, obscuring the trees around her. The wind covered her tracks with snow almost as fast as she made them.

Birch Leaf paused and huddled in her fur. If the dream bear meant for her to go on, she must. Otherwise she would find no food. If he had brought her to food once, then he would continue to help her. She could turn back, but then she would have rejected what she had asked for and ill luck would surely follow. For a moment she thought she saw movement to one side, but when she whirled there was nothing but the blowing snow.

A wendigo is white, she thought. His bones are ice as he creeps toward you, his teeth grinning hungrily from the skull with no eyes. You don't know he stalks you until his icy arms seize you and you feel the agony of his teeth ripping your flesh.

Birch Leaf clenched her teeth to stifle a scream. She fought an impulse to run wildly, forcing herself to continue on at a steady, even pace.

There was no sound in this white world of blinding snow, no sound except the triumphant cry of Kabibonokka, the north wind, as he hurled white death at the earth, as he tried to snatch her breath. She must find shelter or the north wind would claim her as his victim.

Birch Leaf searched for an evergreen with branches sweeping the earth. She stumbled into a small clearing and at its center found a tall cedar growing alone. Desperately she dug through the snow until she had made a tunnel under the bottom branches. She crawled through the tunnel and reached bare ground near the trunk.

Birch Leaf could tell by the smell that *shi kaug*, skunk, had once lived there but was now gone. There was room for her to curl up in the space between the ground and the lowest branches of the cedar. Protected from the wind by the branches and the thick cover of snow, she grew warmer and soon became drowsy.

Birch Leaf woke to threshing sounds above her. For a terrible moment she imagined the wendigo had tracked her but then she smelled the urine of wawaushkaste. A panicked deer had released urine. The threshing sounds meant the animal was in some struggle. She cautiously raised herself to her hands and knees, peering upward. Were wolves attacking a deer? She heard no snarling, but perhaps the snow muffled the noise. She touched the hilt of her knife and, grasping the rifle and her snowshoes, pushed upward until her head was above the snow.

Windlashed snow stung her eyes. In the grayness of early morning, she saw a deer struggling immediately before her, hooves slashing against the cedar as it tried to stand. Shielding her eyes, Birch Leaf saw that the right front leg of the deer was broken. Bone was protruding through the skin. She nodded. Deer, with their long slender legs, usually did not try to venture from their hidden places when the snow was deep because they fell through the drifts and became helpless, often breaking a leg as this doe had done.

Briefly she wondered what had driven the deer to brave the storm. Had the dream bear beckoned to the doe to follow him to be food for Birch Leaf? She managed to fasten the snowshoes to her feet, then stood. The deer stared in fright at her and jostled about frantically. Avoiding the sharp hooves, she circled behind the doe; grasped an ear and jerked its head up.

"Forgive me, I am hungry," she said to the doe.

Then she slit its throat.

Blood gushed onto the snow. Birch Leaf felt the

warmth of it flowing across her hands as the deer gave a convulsive shudder and died.

She recalled instructions Soft Willow had repeated often. "If the place is wrong for cooking meat, and you are hungry, you must drink the blood of your kill for strength, then cut out the heart and eat it raw."

Birch Leaf placed her lips to the knife wound on the doe's neck and began sucking. The hair was rough to her lips. Blood ran down her chin. The taste was rich and salty and the warmth felt good. Birch Leaf realized that she liked it.

Then she cut into the doe's chest and reached for its heart.

When Birch Leaf had finished eating the deer's heart, she wiped her face with snow to remove the blood. Her stomach was full and she could feel the blood of the deer strengthening her. The doe was young, one of last year's fawns and not too large.

"Thank you, dream bear," she said, "for sending me a small deer that I can carry."

Quickly she gutted the doe, then lifted the animal to her shoulders. Its weight staggered her for a moment, but she stayed on her feet. Ignoring the swirling snow she started back to the wigwam.

There were no old tracks to follow and the blizzard blurred all landmarks. Birch Leaf trudged on, the deer's weight slowing her. She trusted to her instinct and to the dream bear, for she was unsure of the exact location of the wigwam. Old Cold Maker blew from the north but the wind eddied in gusts and it was hard to tell which direction it came from.

The blood and heart she had eaten sustained her. Twice she heard wolves howling behind her but did not increase her pace. She could walk no faster.

"I'm coming, Ishcoda," she muttered as she

slogged along. "Don't die, my love, wait for me. Ishcoda, Ishcoda."

She thought of his arms around her, his lips pressed to hers, the warmth of his body, the pleasure when they were one.

She knew the wolves were close behind. She turned and counted five dark forms moving through the snow.

It was true that *maheengun*, wolf, did not molest the People, did not kill them for food. Wasn't the wolf Nanabozho's dearly beloved brother?

But she carried a deer on her back. If the pack brought her down, she and the deer would be good for only one thing—food. If she didn't outwit the wolf pack she would never see Ishcoda again.

Birch Leaf stopped, backed up to the trunk of a huge pine and raised the rifle.

Flann was jolted from an uneasy sleep.

The night had passed into day and the blizzard still raged outside the wigwam. Neither of the women worked at sewing or their other usual tasks. Like Flann, they stayed in their sleeping robes, rising only to feed the fire. He had dozed on and off throughout the morning. Now he felt like someone was calling him.

He sat up. The faint howling of wolves sounded over the keening of the wind. Soft Willow sat up too, looking across the fire at him.

"Did you call me?" he asked.

"No."

"I thought I heard my name." He turned to the door flap. Suddenly he got to his feet. He swayed but stayed erect.

"She's out there," he said. "Birch Leaf needs me."

Soft Willow got up immediately. She brought him

a fur and helped him into it. "Wait," she said, going to her mide bag. She took out a fragment of dried root. "Chew this," she ordered. "It will give you strength."

Flann put it in his mouth and swallowed the resulting bitterness. "What is it?" he asked, grimacing.

"*Zhigowau.* Warriors chew it before battle."

He nodded and looked around for his rifle, then remembered Birch Leaf had taken it. Soft Willow gave him Birch Leaf's hunting bow, quiver of arrows and snowshoes.

"Hurry," she urged him.

Flann thrust open the door flap. The wolves howled again, closer now. He turned toward the sound, coughing when the wind filled his lungs. Snow swirled into his eyes. He set off, unsteady on his snowshoes at first, but improving after a few moments.

He gasped with relief when he reached the shelter of the trees. As he slogged between the pines, a rifle shot cracked. Flann broke into a run, stumbling forward as fast as the snowshoes permitted.

"Birch Leaf!" he called. "Birch Leaf!"

Chapter 26

As the five wolves closed in around her, Birch Leaf
fired at the nearest. The recoil of the rifle slammed her
against the pine trunk. The wounded wolf yelped and
whirled in a circle, snapping at his own flank before
collapsing onto the snow, writhing and snarling.

The remaining four wolves divided their attention
between their fallen mate and Birch Leaf, as if unde-
cided which prey to attack. She reloaded the rifle. She
knew that if they all came at her at once she would not
have a chance to load a third time.

Her name was carried in the wind. The wolves
heard it too, turning their heads. She understood then
that a human voice called her.

"Ishcoda," she cried.

As Flann loomed through the blizzard, the wolves
snarled and drew back. He came to her and took the
rifle, motioning for her to go on ahead of him. As they
retreated to the wigwam, the wolves did not pursue.
They fell on the wounded wolf instead.

The venison from the deer lasted well into

Snowcrust Moon, February. After that their snares netted them enough rabbits to feed them.

One morning Soft Willow tested the air and smiled broadly. "It's warmer," she said. "Time to go to the maple camp. Boiling Moon comes and the sap is rising."

"Everyone will be at the maple sugar camp," Birch Leaf said happily. "We'll see all our friends from Meenagha and Ontonagon and there will be games. It is a good time."

Boiling Moon. That would be March by my calendar, Flann thought. He found himself eager to go and yet was reluctant. As much as he loved the women, he longed for men's company. At the same time he feared his closeness with Birch Leaf would suffer if he did go. Theirs was more than a physical intimacy, or so it seemed. Ever since her flight from the wolves, Flann often felt they shared one another's thoughts, almost as though their minds were linked.

Snow was still thick on the ground and the streams had not thawed but the sun had begun to stay a fraction longer each day, hinting of warmth to come. They loaded the toboggans with household goods and the bark covering of the winter wigwam. Before they left, Flann made a special trip to the pine where Squirrel rested. There he had his final farewell.

As they journeyed with the toboggans, Flann enjoyed the white beauty of the wilderness and the dark green of the pines and spruces etched against a blue sky. Even the gaunt forms of the leafless hardwoods pleased his eye. He was elated. He had survived the worst of the winter, and so had the women.

The maple grove was to the east, between Meenagha and Ontonagon, less than a day's travel. Even before they came in sight of the maples, they heard dogs barking and smelled the smoke of fires. When they emerged from the white pine forest, Flann blinked at the activity ahead.

About twenty wigwams were scattered under the bare branches of the maples. Some were already covered with birch bark, smoke drifting from their smokeholes. Women worked busily, placing bark around the framework of others. Bare poles of the remaining wigwams showed that their owners had not yet arrived. Soft Willow directed the dogs toward one of these.

After the toboggans halted outside Soft Willow's wigwam frame, she rummaged among her belongings, lifted out a hatchet and handed it to Flann.

"Man's work," she said, picking out several carved wooden pegs. Each had one pointed end and a small groove down the center. She gave these to Flann also. She then piled birch-bark containers into his arms and gestured toward the trees. He saw men clustered about the trunks of the maples.

Flann smiled. We Bay Staters make maple syrup back home every spring, too. Flann knew the rudiments. You drive a spile into a maple trunk and collect the sap, cook it and, *voila*, syrup.

He walked over to the men. As he approached, he observed they were all older braves. Copper Sky turned to him, smiling.

"Ho. Ishcoda has returned."

As he greeted the chief, Flann saw that the men's faces looked thinner. When he had acknowledged all present, he gave his attention to the maple trunk in front of him.

Copper Sky had just tapped a wooden peg, a spile like the ones Flann carried, into the lowest of three slashes in the bark of the tree. He hung a birch-bark basket onto it. Drops of sap oozed down the groove in the spile and dripped into the basket.

Flann nodded and advanced to an untapped tree where he repeated what he had seen Copper Sky do. As the first drops of maple sap fell into his container he felt a jolt of accomplishment almost as great as when he had hit his first bull's eye target shooting with his father. The actual killing of an animal had never measured up to that first bull's eye. He licked his finger after putting it in the sap. He was surprised to find it only faintly sweet.

He set all the spiles and containers, then rejoined the men, knowing Soft Willow would not let him help with the wigwam. In her eyes it was disgraceful for a man to do women's work, and she was shocked and upset if he persisted in trying to help. He had given up the effort.

Large fires burned outside to cook the sap. Sturdy wooden frames were made to hold the heavy iron kettles. The men then erected a bark windbreak to shield the fires from the worst of the weather. Everyone then retired to their wigwams for the evening meal.

Early the next morning, Soft Willow sent Flann to collect the baskets of sap. He saw that the outdoor fires had been stoked and when he brought the nearly full buckets back to Soft Willow, she pointed to her kettle. He emptied his buckets into it, then replaced them on the spiles.

Flann watched the women make the syrup. They boiled the water from the sap, stirring the liquid often so it would not burn at the bottom. When they were satisfied with its thickness, they called the men to tip the kettles and let the syrup run into large wooden troughs.

Most of the syrup stayed in the troughs, where women and girls stirred it gently and constantly until it was transformed into fine grains of sugar. However, some of the syrup was poured into small makuks where it hardened into maple cakes. Sometimes dabs of hot syrup were poured onto the snow to cool so that the children could pull it into soft chewy candy.

Flann watched as Copper Sky's grandnephew ate his chunk of candy and thoroughly licked each sticky finger. The boy was about the size of Squirrel. Flann felt tears sting his eyes.

He was distracted by dogs rushing past him, barking. A few minutes later he saw braves approaching the sugar camp. The fur trappers and their families had returned.

The entire camp turned out to greet them, children racing and shouting, women laughing, men talking. Bark was quickly fastened to the remaining wigwam frames and that afternoon the feasting began, a meal of maple sugar and fresh fish the trappers had speared through holes cut in the lake ice.

Both Meenagha and Ontonagon braves were in the group. Flann noticed these younger men looked well-fed. He also noticed that Black Rock soon found his way to Birch Leaf. She stood talking to one of the Meenagha wives.

Birch Leaf turned when she heard her name and saw Black Rock looking at her. She smiled and greeted him, glad he had survived the winter in the lands of hostile tribes.

"Was the trapping good?" she asked.

"The animals grow fewer every year, and we must go farther to find them," he said. "But we did well enough. We met the Sioux once only."

She clasped her hands together, her face alight with interest. "What happened with the Sioux?"

"We saw them first. When they discovered us we had our rifles ready. We knew they were closer to home than we were, and they knew we could kill many of them." Black Rock grinned. "So nothing happened. We used sign language to tell them we were passing through to trap farther north. In return they signed back an agreement not to attack us. Winter is no time to be making war."

"Birch Leaf is happy to see Black Rock," a voice said in Flann's ear. He looked around to find Snowberry at his side, watching the pair as he had been.

"We're all glad to see the trappers return," Flann said stiffly.

She gave him a look which said quite plainly he didn't fool her. Flann remembered then that Birch Leaf had once told him Black Rock might marry Snowberry. He looked at her with new interest.

Snowberry's plump cheeks were thinner than they had been when he last saw her. She wore a beautifully decorated dress under an open jacket fashioned from a white trader's blanket. She wore silver circles among the blue and red and yellow beads to create an unusual and lovely design.

"Your dress is attractive," he said. "And you have silver pieces on it."

She glanced down at her dress, then speculatively at him. "Would you like the dress for Birch Leaf?" she asked after a moment. "When you take her away with you to your own village, I'll be pleased to give her this dress."

"I'm really more interested in where you got the silver," he told her.

"My father fashions it for me."

"Where does he get it?"

Snowberry smiled secretively. "I know, although he believes I don't. I might show you, but only when I'm sure Birch Leaf is leaving with you."

"I'm not certain when we'll be going."

"Tell me when you do know. Then I'll take you to the silver."

Flann nodded. He could not imagine leaving without Birch Leaf but, of course, he *was* going to leave. He had to report to the President of the United States. He could not justify staying away from Boston much longer. He would have to go back and resume his interrupted medical studies, reassure his relatives he was still alive and see how far the lawyers had gotten in unsnarling his father's will. Lynette had chosen to marry one of the law firm's junior partners. And that was all right. But perhaps she had done so because she had learned Flann O'Phelan was to be left without a penny. He saw Lynette very clearly after long absence as a woman with her eye on the main chance.

"The sooner you take Birch Leaf away, the better it will be," Snowberry told him.

He caught himself nodding as Birch Leaf smiled at Black Rock in a way that sent rage flaring through him. He strode toward them.

Black Rock looked at him without expression. Flann greeted him with clipped words. Birch Leaf's face showed animated interest, then puzzlement, then incomprehension. She turned to a nearby syrup trough and reached for another woman's paddle. She felt it best to separate herself from the two men.

"I'll stir for awhile," she said.

Flann eyed Black Rock, who met his gaze calmly.

"Stay away from her," Flann said between his teeth.

"Is she your wife?"

"She will be."

"When she is, I'll stay away," Black Rock told him. He walked from Flann toward a group of braves near the boiling kettles.

Flann marched over to Birch Leaf. "You seemed very friendly with Black Rock."

"Yes. Friendly. Is that wrong?" She did not look at him.

Flann felt no trace of closeness to her. He controlled his impulse to take her by the shoulders and shake her. He knew he was being unreasonably jealous. At the same time a wild anger tensed his muscles and speeded his pulse.

"Ho, Ishcoda," Crouching Fox clasped Flann by both arms. "I hear miracles of this medicine you call vaccination. Soft Willow says you gave her smallpox in one place on her arm and now she will never have it again."

Flann took a deep breath and smiled at the shaman. "She's right. I wish I could have done the same for all Meenagha and Ontonagon, too. When I return to Washington I intend to tell the Great White Father of the need for vaccination here."

Crouching Fox nodded his head toward a wigwam. "Come, we play the moccasin game inside."

Flann glanced at Birch Leaf. He wished to re-establish peace with her, but she seemed engrossed in stirring the maple syrup and didn't look his way. He shrugged and followed the shaman into the wigwam.

"Here is Ishcoda," Crouching Fox said. "Who'll play against him?"

"Wait. Play what? I don't know the rules," Flann objected.

Crouching Fox pointed down to four moccasins lined up on a mat. Next to them were four small bones. The shaman picked these up, holding them on his palm. "You see, one has a notch. The other three are smooth. One man hides the bones in the moccasins. The other must guess which holds the notched bone. He must find the notched bone on his third pick to win. Otherwise he is penalized. The men take turns hiding and picking. Simple."

The game sounded easy. It reminded Flann of something he had played as a child called *"Who's Got the Button?"*

"I'll play against Ishcoda if he's not afraid," Black Rock challenged.

Flann stiffened. When Crouching Fox raised his eyebrows in speculation, Flann nodded, indicating he would play. He sat down on the mat beside the moccasins. Black Rock sat down on the other side of the mat, facing him. A drum began to beat softly. The drummer was seated near the mat.

Crouching Fox tossed a knife into the center of the mat and spun it. When it stopped turning, the point faced Black Rock. The Ontonagon brave nodded. The shaman handed him the four bones.

Black Rock took the bones in his left hand, rubbing them together slightly, then closed his hand completely. He began to sway to the drumbeat, moving his right hand over his left as he slid a bone into each moccasin. He stopped moving, took his hands away from the moccasins and sat back. Everyone now looked expectantly at Flann. He realized a large crowd had gathered, drawn by the competition. The wigwam was jammed with men.

Flann reached for a moccasin, touched the second to his right, picked it up and took out the bone. It was the notched one. He knew he would be penalized. The object was to find it on the third guess. He looked around to see how the score was kept.

Crouching Fox took four blue sticks from a pile of twenty beside him and passed them across to an Ontonagon brave Flann recognized as their shaman, Star-in-Cedar. Star-in-Cedar had twenty red sticks by his right knee. He put the blue sticks to his left.

Black Rock dumped the remaining bones from the moccasins and handed the bones to Flann.

Flann did what Black Rock had done, swaying to the drum rhythm as he slipped a bone into each of the four moccasins. It was harder to do than it looked, but he managed well enough. He sat back.

Black Rock stared at the moccasins. He chose the first to his left and dumped out a smooth bone. On his second try he picked the notched bone. Star-in-Cedar took three red sticks from his pile and passed them to Crouching Fox. Black Rock had done better than Flann.

You must gather all twenty of the opponent's sticks to win, Flann realized. But what if he has some of yours?

Flann asked Crouching Fox about this fine distinction in scoring.

"You must regain all of yours as well, then, to win," the shaman answered.

On his next attempt, Flann found the bone on his third try. Crouching Fox smiled as Star-in-Cedar handed him four red sticks.

Black Rock lost several sticks on his next turn. He won the following time. The luck shifted back and forth. Neither man was ever far ahead of the other.

As the game progressed, the tension among the men watching told Flann that this was a gambling game, and they had all wagered heavily. God only knew how much each village had riding on the outcome.

He grew more adept at hiding the notched bone in the moccasins as the afternoon faded. He also grew more tense. He had few belongings to lose, and they weren't important. He also knew that he would not personally be blamed if the Meenagha village lost to Ontonagon.

But he had a gut feeling that he and Black Rock alone knew what they really played for, what the luck of the game would win or lose for each. It was probably a foolish notion. But he couldn't shake the idea that somehow Birch Leaf's love rode on the outcome.

Sway to the drum. Drop the bones. Watch your opponent win or lose. Then it was your turn to choose. Which moccasin held the magic bone? Decide. Win or lose.

It grew dark. The gaming mat was dragged closer to the center fire. Flann had finally won all of Ontonagon's red sticks but Star-in-Cedar still held three of Meenagha's blue sticks.

It was again Black Rock's turn to put the bones in the shoes. Flann watched carefully as Black Rock's hand passed over the moccasins. Then it was time again to choose.

Slowly Flann reached out, touched the last moccasin to his left. He picked it up and dumped out a smooth bone. Men exhaled pent-up breath.

Flann next chose the moccasin on the right end and dumped out the bone. Smooth. Again the men sighed.

Two moccasins were left. This was the chance to

win. He touched the toe of the one on the left. He picked it up. The notched bone fell out.

The Meenagha men shouted and laughed. Flann stared across the mat at Black Rock.

"We will play again, sometime soon," Black Rock said. "The loser has the right to challenge."

Chapter 27

When the new moon showed its ghost, Soft Willow announced that the maple sap was turning bitter. She called it Putting Away Snowshoes Moon and said it was time to go back to Meenagha. Flann knew it must be April. The weather was warmer and the trees were budding.

Snow still lay in heavy patches in the woods when they loaded the toboggans, so the dogs had no trouble pulling them until they neared Kitchigami. Here dried needles and earth poked through the scant snow.

"The ice is breaking up in the rivers," Crouching Fox told Flann the next week. "*Nahma*, the sturgeon, will soon swim upstream to spawn. His air bladder I use in medicine and the fish and the eggs are good to eat."

Flann helped the braves build a weir several miles up Iron River. They used saplings and extended the weir from one bank to the other, paddling about in canoes dug up from winter burial. The icy river water numbed Flann's hands as he held the poles while

Crouching Fox worked them into place. A small opening was left near the west bank to allow big fish to pass upstream. It was constructed so that it could be closed off easily when the sturgeon had spawned and were returning to the lake.

"When they come back, we spear them," the shaman told Flann.

While they waited for the fish, the men built new canoes to replace those damaged by frost over the winter. Crouching Fox showed Flann how to choose a birch with smooth bark, how to slide the knife underneath the layers so the bark came off the trunk in large, complete sheets, and how to roll the sheets without splitting them.

"Easy work," the shaman said. "Women do it sometimes."

Birch Leaf cleared a level space near the lake shore and sprinkled clean sand over it. Blue Flower, Crouching Fox's wife, readied split spruce roots to be used as cord to sew the birch-bark sheets together.

Crouching Fox unrolled the bark on the clean sand to form the bottom of the canoe, weighing it in place with stones. On each side of the spread of bark he placed long poles bent in a shallow curve so that they joined at either end. He drove stakes into the ground to brace these bottom poles in the shape of a frame, twelve to each side.

Blue Flower knifed the bottom sheets of bark, shaping them to fit at the bow and stern. While she sewed them together with the spruce cord and a bone awl, Crouching Fox cut and fitted bark to the outer sides of the canoe. Then she placed strips of cedar along the top for gunwales. Birch Leaf sewed the cedar to the side bark.

The crosspieces which held the sides apart went in

next. When they were fitted to Crouching Fox's satisfaction, he left the women to finish sewing the bark and went back to the fish weir.

"Tomorrow we'll put the floor and ribs and sheathing in," he said to Flann. "The cedar is soaking in water now."

Although the river ran high and fast with the run-off from the melting snow, the sturgeon coming up from the lake were so big that they were easily seen. Flann stared in amazement as an immense dark fish passed close to the bank.

"It's as big as a man," he exclaimed, watching the sturgeon make its way through the hole in the weir to continue upstream.

"Tastes better," Crouching Fox said.

Flann shifted his gaze hastily to the shaman and saw he was grinning. Was the shaman joking?

"You could spear enough of these fish to have food all winter if you smoked the meat," Flann said after a few moments.

"The traders give us smoked fish if we're hungry," Crouching Fox noted.

"You have to pay the trader in furs," Flann said. "If you smoked your own fish for the winter, you would pay nothing."

Crouching Fox shrugged. "This is how we wish to live."

"But your furs could be used for kettles and hatchets and rifles, things you can't make for yourselves, instead of for smoked fish, which you can."

"We do it our way." Crouching Fox's tone held finality, and Flann knew the shaman was finished with the discussion.

It would do no good to remind Crouching Fox

that starvation stalked the People every winter. They now had plenty.

The next day, Flann helped Crouching Fox place the ribs of bent cedar and the cedar strips in the canoes for sheathing. The shaman put in the inner gunwales and wooden pieces for the bow and stern and the thwarts. Birch Leaf and Blue Flower sewed the bark to the frame at the bow and stern and along the gunwales.

"We leave the waterproofing to the women," Crouching Fox explained. He nodded toward a fire where a mixture of aromatic spruce resin and bear fat and charcoal bubbled.

Flann had often seen women pouring the resin mixture over the leaky seams of old canoes. He stayed behind when the shaman went back to the weir, saying he would help. He was lonesome for Birch Leaf. Now that he and Fire Grass were in their own wigwam again, he saw little of her.

Flann pulled up the outer stakes and piled them while the women finished their sewing. Birch Leaf was among them.

"I miss you," he said softly.

"I miss you, too," she said.

He ached to hold her. "Go up the beach just before the sun lowers," he said urgently, whispering so Blue Flower couldn't overhear.

Birch Leaf smiled and nodded quickly.

When they met in the late afternoon, the wind off Lake Superior made it too cold for them to stay on the beach, even though the sun warmed the sand. Flann and Birch Leaf entered the woods and found a sheltered spot underneath the low branches of a cedar.

Flann took her in his arms and they made love hungrily.

"We'll get married before we reach Boston," he

said to her afterwards as they lay naked, holding one another. "You'll come home with me as my wife. I believe there's a minister at The Soo."

Birch Leaf interrupted, pressing her fingers to his lips to quiet him. "Go home with you? You assume this? You have not even spoken to me of going with you. You have not even spoken of leaving yourself."

"You know I can't stay here forever." He hugged her. "I stayed as long as I have only because of you."

"I want to marry you," she said. "I want to be with you."

"We can board the *Astor* on one of her downlake runs. But first I must go to La Pointe and see if I can locate Henri Fontenac. We have unfinished business."

"Him."

"You know Henri?"

"He wanted to buy me from Soft Willow. I do not like him. I think of him as a weasel. The other animals kill to eat. The weasel often kills just to kill. You can never trust him."

"I don't. Nevertheless, I must meet with him if he's returned from Montreal. You stay here in Meenagha and wait."

"We could marry here," she suggested. "I could go to La Pointe with you then."

Flann shook his head. "We'll wait for the minister at The Soo. You'll like Boston, Birch Leaf." He hesitated. "Maybe you'd better get used to thinking of yourself as Caroline ahead of time. My relatives. . . ."

"Car-o-line is not my name. It's a name with no meaning, not mine." Birch Leaf wrenched away from him and began to dress.

"All names have meaning. Caroline is the feminine for Charles. Charles means . . . Never mind. The name isn't that important."

"What does the name mean?"

"Charles means man."

"You want, then, to give me a man's name."

"No, let's forget it. I didn't name you Caroline in the first place. Your white parents did."

She turned from him.

He reached for her hand. "Don't be upset. I love you by any name. My relatives will say it's unusual, but they'll get used to it."

When they were dressed, they walked back toward the village through the woods, skirting patches of snow.

"Is Boston a large village?"

Flann thought for a moment, deciding how to explain the city's size. Schoolcraft had said there were about 30,000 Chippewa in Michigan and Wisconsin and the upper Minnesota Territory. "Boston has more people than all the Anishinabe clans put together," he said finally.

"All those people in one place? With so many wigwams together, how can the men find game to hunt?"

"You'll see. We don't hunt for wild animals but buy meat from men who raise animals for food. The lodge I live in is made of wood like the store in La Pointe."

"But then you can't move it for the winter."

"We don't move our houses from place to place." He glanced at her, amused. "You won't have hard work to do in Boston, no helping to make canoes or gathering firewood. Women don't do such things. Men build the houses. It's difficult to explain. Everything is so different from here. You'll soon get used to the change."

"Will I?" She gripped his hand. "It sounds very strange."

"Everyone will love you as I love you."

"I must be certain I know all the stories so I can teach our children."

"Our children will go to school and learn many things the People's children don't know," Flann said. "You can tell them your stories, too." He imagined Birch Leaf holding a boy with bright, inquiring eyes, a boy who would call him father as Squirrel had done.

"There's a school at La Pointe," Birch Leaf said, "where the children hear stories about the white man's god."

"That, too. God is for everyone, Birch Leaf."

"Like the Great Spirit."

"Like the Great Spirit," Flann agreed.

The following morning two braves Flann had never seen before paddled in from the lake to speak to Copper Sky. Crouching Fox joined the chief at the meeting. The braves ate, then moved on up the river, heading for Lac Vieux Desert.

Later, Crouching Fox came to the weir where Flann waited with other men for the sturgeon to come back downstream. The shaman stared solemnly at the river, not speaking. Finally, Flann decided to risk angering him with a direct question.

"What did the braves want?" he asked.

"Ishcoda." Crouching Fox placed a hand on each of Flann's shoulders and looked into his face. "We're brothers. The People feel you're one of us. Yet you also have pale skin and your mind knows the way of white thinking. Can you tell me why the Great White Father in Washington wants us to move from our lands, thus delivering us to our enemies?" Crouching Fox dropped his hands, waiting.

"Have the Chippewa signed a new treaty?" Flann asked. "I know the People have agreed to give up land along the east part of Kitchigami. That treaty was signed the year before I came. That doesn't affect you. I know Chief Buffalo met with agents of the Great White Father last summer, but he told me that treaty had nothing to do with Kitchigami."

"It is true Buffalo put his mark on an agreement last summer as the other chiefs did. Buffalo was told the Great White Father wanted land south and west of Kitchigami, but he only wished to take the large pine trees and the minerals in the rocks. Indians could keep the maples and the cedars and the birches. They could harvest the rice, hunt and fish and live there, as always."

"How does such a treaty affect you?" Flann asked.

"Now we know white men have lied again, for white families have moved among the People that live in that country. They plough the land and say it belongs to them and threaten to shoot the brave who tries to hunt there. The Indian agent says soon the People will be moved west, that they signed away the land entirely when they agreed to give up the pine and the rocks." Crouching Fox sighed.

"We'll be next," he said. "The Indian agent at Mackinac has already warned us about a move to the west. West, where the Nadouesse have their tepees. West, where we'll die."

Flann thought of President Andrew Jackson moving the Creeks west from their southern lands to Indian Territory in 1836. The Cherokees had been scheduled to make the same move. Perhaps they were gone too, by now.

"I hear from the braves that furs here become harder to find," he told Crouching Fox. "You travel farther each winter and find fewer."

"It is true."

"When you find none, what will you do? The Great White Father sees far ahead and worries about this."

"Does he think if he moves us among the Sioux that we will fall on one another in war until both the Nadouesse and the Anishinabe are no more? He would have no need to worry then about either of us."

"I don't have answers."

"We chose not to follow Black Hawk seven years ago when he called on us to war against the whites. We call his people *odugameeg*, Those Who Live on the Other Side. Though they are not our allies, they aren't our enemies either. He warned us that the whites, who came to live beside his villages, were worse than Indians. Instead of scalping the head they poison the heart and turn Indians into white men, turn them into hypocrites and liars. He said this.

"We did not follow Black Hawk, and he fought without us. He lost. But he lost honorably. Copper Sky and Buffalo know as I do that it's too late to go to war with white men. But it is hard to be defeated without honor." Crouching Fox had finished speaking.

Flann felt a sadness so intense it hurt as he looked into the shaman's black eyes. What was he to say? How could he sincerely repeat what he had been told about the Indian having to change?

He was no longer the same man who had come into Meenagha almost a year ago.

"My voice is small," Flann said at last, "but when

I speak again to the Great White Father, I shall tell him what you say." And then there was no time to say more.

Crazy Crane was shouting from his position above the weir, warning that spawners were returning. Crouching Fox lifted his spear and hurried upriver. Flann followed.

The sturgeon slammed against the poles of the weir, fighting to get back to the lake. The huge fish lunged from the water and braves with spears aimed their thrusts at the gills. Others used large iron hooks that had been fashioned to jab through the tough plated skin of the sturgeon.

Water foamed and splashed. Men shouted. Flann took a spear and tried to impale a fish, finally getting the point through a gill after it repeatedly slid off the bonelike plates covering the sturgeon's back.

"Ram it in farther and twist," Crazy Crane shouted. Flann did as he was told and secured his fish. Crazy Crane helped him lift the writhing fish from the river. Flann estimated it weighed more than he himself.

The mottled brown fish was ugly as well as strange to Flann, with a long, pointed head, thick lips and large, bony plates running along the back and sides. A peculiar set of hairlike appendages dangled in front of the lips much like a drooping mustache.

"Good to eat," Crazy Crane assured Flann, seeing the look on his face. The brave turned to the dying fish and spoke.

"Nahma, forgive us for taking you from the water. We are hungry and you will feed us. We are grateful that you chose to swim to our spears. Forgive us, Sturgeon, for killing you."

Watching Crazy Crane, Flann thought of all the labels he had heard for the Indian. Simple child of nature. Noble Savage. Worthless degenerate. Red Devil. They were none of those.

Methods proposed for dealing with the Indians also came to Flann's mind, and he was saddened.

"The only way to civilize them is to dilute the race with white blood," one man in Washington had said. "Make Christians of them whether they like it or not," another had proposed. "Make farmers of them. If they stop roaming, they'll forget killing," still another had advised. "Build schools and educate them," said one man, and that seemed to Flann to be the only reasonable suggestion of the bunch.

Charles Madden had handed him a pamphlet issued by the House Committee on Indian Affairs in 1818. It said: "Put into the hands of their children the primer and the hoe, and they will naturally, in time, take hold of the plough, and as their minds become enlightened and expand, the Bible will be their book, and they will grow up in habits of morality and industry, leave the chase to those whose minds are less cultivated, and become useful members of society."

Flann doubted this would happen. Many of his countrymen had good intentions. Why couldn't they deal with the Indians as one man to another?

With respect.

Chapter 28

Before Flann could make arrangements to travel to La Pointe, Father Baraga arrived at Meenagha. After the priest had visited among the villagers, he approached Flann.

"I have a message," Father Baraga said. "Mr. Bushnell asked me to pass word to you that Mr. Schoolcraft will be at La Pointe in August and will expect to meet with you."

"August? I'd hoped to be on my way east by then."

"That was Mr. Bushnell's message."

"Thank you for passing it along," Flann told the priest. "I'd like to ask you a question. Have you seen Henri Fontenac at La Pointe?"

"No. Henri left for Montreal last fall, as you may know. He hasn't returned."

"You're sure?"

"He hasn't been at La Pointe, nor have I heard talk of anyone seeing him." The priest appraised Flann. "How have you been, Mr. O'Phelan? I fancy you're thinner."

302

Flann looked at the priest's gaunt face. "I believe we're both happy to have the winter behind us," he said.

"Lake Superior winters are cruel and merciless," Father Baraga agreed, "but my poor Indians have survived such winters for many generations. What I fear they *won't* survive is the coming of droves of copper seekers. I know many such men will be here soon, men who hope to mine copper and silver. They'll care nothing for Indians, I'm afraid. Indian land, yes, they'll want the Indian land because of the copper and silver underneath."

"If I could stop more white people from coming to Kitchigami country, I would," Flann said fiercely. "I would keep the Chippewa safe, keep white men away from them."

The priest shook his head. "I know that to be impossible. I'll continue to do what I can to try to prepare my poor Indians for what will come as surely as winter follows fall."

Later, Flann considered, then rejected the notion of going to La Pointe to talk to Bushnell. They would inevitably argue. The subagent didn't like him. He didn't much care for Bushnell, either. If Schoolcraft wanted to see him at La Pointe in August then that's when he would go.

May, the Flower Moon, was rainy. The snow gradually disappeared from the woods. The trees burst into leaf. Meat was hard to come by, but fish were plentiful in both lake and stream. The wild strawberries ripened in June, the Strawberry Moon, and the women tilled a patch of cleared ground near the village to plant corn.

"Corn must not be planted so close that the plants

smell each other or the ears won't be plump," Birch Leaf told Flann. "*Mondamin* is shy and slow to ripen. If the frost comes early, we must pick the ears too young, but still they are good. Corn is always gathered before the Moon of Turning Leaves and we have a feast."

They are always having feasts, Flann thought. The first sturgeon, the first rice, the first berries, always with dancing and games and everyone eating until they could hold no more.

"If the village saved food, dried and stored more of it, there would be enough to eat each winter," he pointed out.

"Would you have us give up the feasts?" Birch Leaf was surprised and somewhat indignant.

He tried to explain. "I don't care if you hold feasts. I enjoy them. But it would be wiser to think of the winter to come."

"We do. We save rice, we dry meat."

"Not enough. If the men caught fish all summer instead of just in the spring. . . ."

"The warriors seek coups in the summer, not fish!"

"Fighting with the Sioux is. . . ." Flann broke off. He had planned to say "self-defeating." He couldn't, for she would not understand. At least one young warrior was killed every time a war party went out. Crouching Fox had told him of one small village on the mainland near La Pointe that had no warriors left. And to them, to her, this was proper.

To say, send these young men to trap, to hunt, to fish, not to war, *that* would be self-defeating to them.

In July the raspberries turned red on prickly canes that grew in clearings. After the women and children gathered them, the village was fragrant with the sweet smell of raspberries being boiled for keeping. Birch Leaf and Flann wandered in the summer woods and along the warm sand of the beach.

"You speak to me of many lodges and people in your Boston. Are there woods and beaches, too?" she asked.

"The ocean is near, the salt sea. And although the woods aren't like these, there are forests nearby."

"We'll go there, to the forests and to the beaches?"

Flann hesitated. "Not often. You'll find there's much to do in the city. Perhaps in a year or two we can make the journey back here to see Soft Willow."

"She will not be with me when I bear a child." Birch Leaf sighed and looked at Flann. "You'll have to learn to fashion a tikinagen. A man makes his children's cradle boards."

"Birch Leaf," Flann said gently, "you'll see when we live in Boston that there are other ways to do things. Babies aren't carried on their mothers' backs. They sleep in little rocking beds. You'll learn these ways and find them good."

"From what you say, nothing is the same as here in Meenagha. Only white faces will look at me. I must learn white words."

"You're learning English very quickly, Birch Leaf." He knew better than to tell her she was white, for that always provoked her.

"Flann." She said the word flatly. "To me you're my Ishcoda."

He stopped and hugged her. "I love you. We'll be happy together."

The blueberries ripened and it was August. Before he left for La Pointe, Flann went to see Copper Sky.

"I'll soon be going to my home in the east," he told the chief. "I ask you again about the man who gave you the guns. Will you tell me his name?"

Copper Sky looked at Flann. "I'll make an agreement," he said finally. "If I see this man in Kitchigami land, then I'll tell you his name."

Damn, it *was* Henri, I know it, Flann thought.

"We'll be paddling to La Pointe in a few suns," Copper Sky went on. "The Great White Father sends our payments there soon. Why not wait and go then, go with us?"

Henry Schoolcraft was probably traveling to La Pointe with the government men for the annuity payments. But Flann could not take the chance that Schoolcraft wasn't already there. "I can't wait," he said.

As he came out of the chief's wigwam, Snowberry was waiting. "I heard what you said to my father," she confessed. "Are you taking Birch Leaf?"

"She'll come aboard the Walk-in-the-Water with me when it leaves La Pointe."

"Then I'll show you the secret of the silver. Come."

Flann remembered Snowberry's boast that she knew where the silver was mined. He followed her into the woods. She led him about a mile into the midst of a muskeg, a cedar swamp. Mosquitoes rose from stagnant water and plagued him as Snowberry climbed onto a rocky outcropping. Flann scrambled up after her.

She slid down into a shallow pit. He followed.

"See?" She pointed. *"Shuniah."*

Veins of silver shone in the rocks all around him. Flann knew little of mining, but he thought this much silver showing must mean that much more waited in the rock that rose from the muskeg. Perhaps tons of silver were under the ground nearby. Flann's eyes gleamed for a moment. Then he sobered. He thought of how close the site was to Meenagha. Any mining venture here would destroy the village.

The next morning he paddled off to La Pointe where he found Bushnell with his interpreter, St. Ivan. Schoolcraft had not yet arrived. Flann did no more than make his presence known to the subagent before going to the Chippewa village.

Once more, Buffalo's tame crow flew from the top of a pine and followed him as he approached the chief's wigwam. It turned out to be empty. Nearby was an old man dozing in the sun.

"They're all fishing for the trader," he told Flann.

Flann sat down by the old man. "I'll stay with you, Grandfather, and wait for them."

The old man straightened. "I know you," he said. "You are Red Hair who fights the Sioux. I welcome you."

"In your young days, no doubt you warred against the Sioux," Flann said politely.

The old man looked up at the crow perched atop a wigwam, watching them. "I was a great warrior," he declared. "The young braves today only play at war. They have courage but we were more cunning, more resourceful. I remember one war party against the Sioux. We were outnumbered ten to one by the wily Nadouesse, who knew of our coming and tried to ambush us.

"By my own hand I slew five and helped to kill others." Proudly he showed Flann a large puckered scar on his back. "A Sioux arrow," he explained. "I fought with that arrow in my back. Only after we routed them did I even know it was there.

"Where are our warriors now, they who should be fighting?" The old man waved toward the water. "Fishing. Pah. Women can fish. Men were born to fight."

"Kak, kak," the crow called, flapping his wings. He rose into the air and began to circle.

"Someone comes," the old man said. "A stranger."

Flann got to his feet. He caught a glimpse of a bare shoulder vanishing around a wigwam. It was a man, darkskinned, wearing a breechcloth, heading for a stand of pines.

"He's gone, whoever he was." Flann shrugged. The man had been an Indian, not a white man or a metis, perhaps someone from another village, looking for Buffalo.

When Chief Buffalo himself finally did return, Flann asked him if anyone had seen Henri Fontenac.

"Not on our island, not here. I haven't heard of his return," Buffalo told him.

Several days later, canoes began to arrive and by the end of the week the island was dotted with wigwams and tepees. Some families slept in the open around their fires. This was the gathering of the clans at the annuity payments.

The Meenagha villagers settled in at the far end of the island and Flann left Buffalo's lodge to join them. He estimated more than three thousand Chippewas were on Madeline Island by the time the government men and Henry Schoolcraft arrived. Dogs fought and children played underfoot as Flann went to visit Schoolcraft. He found him in the plaza in front of the company stores. The United States flag whipped in the breeze from atop the settlement pole. There stood Schoolcraft. Tables were being set up for the payments.

"Well, you seem to flourish in our lake country," the agent said, greeting Flann.

Flann smiled slightly, relieved at Schoolcraft's mild tone. "I know you can't be particularly pleased with me," he said. "But I must tell you this. I did what I felt I must."

"With a girl on the side, I understand."

"I plan to make her my wife. To take her to Boston as my wife," Flann said stiffly.

"Does she want to go?"

"We love each other."

Schoolcraft smiled, then stiffened. "We have little time to talk now. What I need to know is, have you discovered the name of the man handing out guns?"

"I have Copper Sky's promise to give me his name if the man returns. I'm all but positive he's a metis named Henri Fontenac who went back to Montreal for the winter. No one's seen him since."

"Bushnell talked to me of your suspicions. He's inclined to agree. Your wintering here may have scared Fontenac off. I hope the Canadian rebels don't try to sneak in another agent, thinking we're on to Fontenac."

"There's been no talk or sign of new guns," Flann said, "except those accounted for by furs being traded."

Schoolcraft nodded. "It could be the alarm's over. Bushnell put the fear of God into the Sandy Lake Pillagers after your disastrous trip into the Minnesota Territory."

Flann smiled. "I'd say he tried to put the fear of God into me, too, for traveling there in the first place."

"Good for him. I take it you *are* going back to Boston now? You and your bride-to-be?"

"As soon as the *Astor* sails down the lake."

"I wish you and the woman every happiness." Schoolcraft shook Flann's hand. "In spite of your unpredictability and rashness, I like you. My wife, by the way, sends her greetings."

Flann bowed slightly. "Please tell Mrs. Schoolcraft I'll never forget meeting her."

A man emerged from one of the store buildings. "Henry," he shouted to Schoolcraft, "where's the blasted interpreter gotten to?"

Schoolcraft waved to him, then said to Flann, "I'm heading for Fond du Lac after the payments, so I'll say Godspeed now." He turned and walked toward the store.

The speeches began that afternoon. Schoolcraft spoke at length to the assembled chiefs and the Chippewas around them, assuring everyone there were no plans for a western move that year. He reminded them that the Great White Father in Washington was their great chief and that the King-Across-the-Waters did not care about their welfare.

Buffalo responded with a speech stressing his loyalty and describing how hard the winter had been on his people. When he finished, Chief Buoy from Ontonagon delivered a similar, even longer oration. It was nearly dark when he was done. The crowd dispersed to eat.

The next day was devoted to more speechmaking. All the chiefs had their say.

"I am not an ungrateful dog to turn and bite the hand that gives me gifts," Copper Sky proclaimed when it was his turn. "Never would I take up arms against white men. Did the Meenagha Bear Clan fight alongside Black Hawk? No. Did we listen to the great prophet when he begged us to fight many years ago?

Did we stand with Tecumseh against the whites? No. I
say we can be trusted, and I do not lie."

He went on like this for some time, eventually
coming to the same conclusion as Buffalo and Buoy by
asking that this year's provisions be generous. Another
chief began as soon as Copper Sky finished.

That night every clan held a dance. The warriors
painted their bodies and faces, the drums sounded and
each man had his chance to tell of enemies killed and
scalps counted.

The next day the payments started. Dr. Charles
Borup of the American Fur Company sat alongside the
government men at the payment table. Flann watched
as Buffalo stepped to the table to receive the first payment of money and goods.

Dr. Borup consulted his records and spoke to
Buffalo. The chief nodded. The government agent then
handed Buffalo the quill. The chief made his mark of
receipt on the payment paper. He gave the quill back
and was handed four silver dollars. Buffalo was also
given a blue coat with brass buttons, a blue cap and a
length of cloth.

Flann saw that only the chiefs were asked to
make their marks. The other Chippewas merely
touched the quill in token of receipt. No one got more
than four dollars, and many got no money at all. Ac-
cording to Dr. Borup, these Indians owed the Company as much as or more than he was owed by the
government. No Indian disputed the factor's figures.

Flann shook his head in disbelief at the exploita-
tion. The coats were given only to the chiefs. Also,
other Indians had a choice of cloth or a cap, not both.
For this pittance they had signed away their lands?

Flann resented Dr. Borup's presence at the payment table. He knew the Company let the Chippewas

charge goods against furs or their annuity payment. He knew that an Indian often desperately needed what he received from the trader, but to have the U.S. government collaborate in making sure the American Fur Company made a profit! "Criminal," Flann muttered. "Criminal."

When Flann took a close look at Buffalo's brass-buttoned coat, he found it poorly made, the cloth cheap and sleazy. The United States government was a party to this? He imagined himself describing the fraud to Andrew Jackson. "Outrageous and reprehensible, sir."

The Chippewas seemed to feel satisfied, however. Buffalo wore his coat proudly.

"Like a Washington man," he bragged to Flann, jamming the cap over his braids. "Like the army officers who shoot cannons in the forts."

Looking at him, tears burned in Flann's eyes. At the same time a dark anger rose to choke him.

Chapter 29

Birch Leaf slipped into a thicket of maple saplings. She knew there was a danger she might be seen. Someone had sold whiskey to the braves. Many of them were drunk already and liable to assault her or any other woman.

How she hated the white man's drink. Men she had known since childhood became frightening strangers. Respected older men changed to lecherous enemies who had to be fought off. It was like some evil magic. If a woman drank, she forgot all modesty.

Birch Leaf remained in the shadow and shelter of the thicket, looking carefully about. Earlier, a man was following her, a brave she didn't know, but now she saw no sign of him. Good. She would have stayed with Soft Willow and Fire Grass if she had not promised Ishcoda to meet him at dusk. It was better to stay out of sight when the braves were drinking.

Not all the men in Meenagha drank when whiskey was brought to the village. Always a few kept order and tried to see that the women weren't insulted.

But here there was no order. The shouts she heard were garbled and senseless. Some warriors danced drunkenly, stumbling through the steps, their dance a mockery. Others lay wherever they had fallen, sprawled in a stupor.

Quickly she moved from among the saplings and darted to the next clump of trees, waiting there until she felt it was safe to go on. Slowly she made her way toward the giant cedar she and Flann had agreed on for a rendezvous. She wondered if men drank whiskey and behaved this way in Boston.

Payment time was always exciting. Relatives from far away met. Warriors who had raided the Sioux villages together in past years had joyful reunions. Dances were held and dog feasts given. But always, this was before the money and goods were paid out.

After payment, someone always came among the People with whiskey to sell, even though she had heard Copper Sky say the government men would punish anyone caught selling whiskey.

She and Soft Willow had both chosen the blue cloth. Also, since they owed the trader no money, they planned to buy another kettle and more beads with their dollars before going back to Meenagha. There had been some trouble earlier with the government man over Fire Grass, but she had finally been listed as a Chippewa and received her payment also. She, too, had chosen cloth. Now both wigwams would be well-furnished with trade goods.

But I won't be there, Birch-Leaf thought, remembering she would sail on Walk-in-the-Water with Ishcoda. She would be going to Boston, not back to Meenagha.

She feared leaving everyone and everything she knew.

As she neared the cedar, Birch Leaf saw some-one. She stopped, waiting to be certain it was Ishcoda before she showed herself. He wouldn't stay silent for long, she knew, because he still hadn't mastered all the ways of the People. She smiled, remembering how she had met him, how he had crashed through the woods like a moose in rut and blundered into a bear with her cub. He had learned stealth since then.

The dark figure near the cedar shifted position and she was reassured. It was Ishcoda. She spoke his name softly.

"Birch Leaf," he answered.

She saw he carried his rifle. "Why didn't you tell me how wild things became after payments?" he de-manded. "I wouldn't have had you come out alone. It isn't safe."

"I took care. I know what whiskey does to braves."

He held her close. The shouting was muted by the trees but seemed to come from all sides. He touched her face. "This is no time to take any risks. I'll go back with you to Soft Willow's wigwam and stay with all of you until morning."

Birch Leaf was pleased. "It's good," she said.

They returned to the wigwam without trouble, but as they came to the door flap a brave rose from a crouch in the shadows and intercepted them.

"I've come to challenge you," Black Rock said to Ishcoda.

Birch Leaf drew in her breath. Black Rock's knife was drawn, and she smelled the reek of whiskey.

Ishcoda thrust her behind him. "Go into the wig-wam," he ordered. But she stayed with him, edging to one side.

315

"*Pagessan*," Black Rock said, "I challenge you to pagessan."

She sighed in relief. A game, that was all. Black Rock wanted to gamble with Ishcoda. Still, he had been drinking whiskey and so couldn't be trusted. She was alarmed. Black Rock was known as a brave who habitually scorned the white man's drink. Yet tonight he had taken it.

"Tomorrow," Flann said. "We'll play the game tomorrow."

"Now."

"I told you, tomorrow."

Black Rock glared. "What kind of man are you? At the feast when any honorable warrior would eat all put in front of him, you left food. When we danced and showed scalps, you did not dance. You did not open your mouth to tell of your coups. Tonight you refuse my challenge. Where is your warrior's courage? Are you a dog?"

Birch Leaf gasped at the insult.

"I don't play with drunken braves," Flann retorted.

Birch Leaf lifted the flap of the wigwam, ready to ask Soft Willow to try to defuse the fight she feared was coming. Coals glowed in a small center fire, but neither Soft Willow nor Fire Grass was in the wigwam. Fear gripped Birch Leaf. Tonight anything might have happened. She stepped out beside the men.

"Black Rock," she exclaimed, "listen to me. Soft Willow and Fire Grass are gone. Have you seen them?"

Black Rock blinked and shifted his gaze from Ishcoda. "I know nothing of them," he muttered.

"My mother isn't in her wigwam."

"She wasn't inside when I came here," Black

Rock said. "Stop interfering in men's business. Go into the wigwam and keep quiet."

She did not move. Flann caught her shoulder and pushed her toward the door flap, handing her his rifle and ammunition pack. "You know how to use it if you have to," he said. "Get inside. This is between Black Rock and me. It's unfinished business." He smiled grimly at Black Rock.

"Listen to me, warrior," Flann said. "I'm blood brother to Crouching Fox and I honor the People's ways. But I'm a white man, too, with ways of my own. I don't ask you to live up to mine, but I will not be criticized for not conforming to yours. I don't deal with a white man who's been drinking, and I don't deal with a Chippewa brave who's been drinking, either. I'll accept your challenge when you're sober. Do you understand?"

Black Rock had no chance to answer.

The crack of a rifle startled both men. Before they could react, more shots sounded. A woman screamed, and the savage ululations of a war party rang out.

"Nadouesse," Birch Leaf gasped.

"No," Black Rock said. "Not Sioux. Chippewa."

He turned, ran and was lost to sight as other braves ran by.

My mission has failed, Flann thought in despair. The Chippewas planned all along to attack the American whites and none of us realized it. Why didn't I see it coming?

"Stay in the wigwam," he shouted to Birch Leaf. "I think you're safe enough. They're not after you." He took his rifle from her and raced toward the white settlement.

Flann heard sporadic firing as he shouldered past confused Chippewa women and shouting braves.

Darkness had fallen, and the glow of fires guided him. His fear gave way to confusion. Nowhere did he see evidence of an organized attack. Confused braves, many without rifles, milled about. The ones with rifles seemed uncertain as to what to do with them.

"What is it?" he heard one after another ask. "What's happened?"

Flann ran up the hill toward the plaza, seeing that torches flared above him. A crowd of Indians and whites eddied haphazardly in front of the stores. As he shoved his way among the men, he recognized Buffalo, still wearing the brass-buttoned coat.

"Who fired the guns?" Flann asked.

"Pillagers from Sandy Lake," Buffalo answered. "They're drunk."

Flann took a deep breath. "Anyone hurt?"

"One brave shot himself in the foot." Buffalo snorted in disgust. "We took their guns and tied the men to posts until morning."

So it wasn't an attack on the whites, Flann sighed with relief. He spotted Bushnell in the crowd.

"Chief Buffalo says it was Pillagers," he told Bushnell. "Everything all right now?"

"Over almost before it started," Bushnell said. "I kept my eyes on those Sandy Lake troublemakers from the minute they got here. When I saw someone had slipped them whiskey, I alerted Buffalo. The Pillagers got off a few shots but did no damage. They were so drunk it's a wonder they didn't shoot each other."

"Definitely not an attack on the whites, then."

Bushnell smiled sourly. "They just had to fire their shiny new guns, that's all. I'll give them hell in the morning and send them off home."

Flann left the plaza and trotted back to the Meenagha encampment. He hurried into Soft Willow's wig-

wam but saw only Soft Willow, alone, adding sticks to
the coals of the fire.

"Where's Birch Leaf?" he asked.

Soft Willow put her hand to her lips in alarm. "I
thought she was with you."

"How long have you been in the wigwam?"

"A few moments. I came from treating a sick
woman. I left Fire Grass with her."

"Have you seen Black Rock since the shooting
started?"

"No," Soft Willow said.

"Damn him, damn him, damn him," Flann
grunted. He rushed out of the wigwam. Black Rock
could have taken Birch Leaf anywhere on the island,
or even off to the mainland in a canoe. He himself had
little chance of locating them in the dark. By God, he'd
try anyway.

"Ishcoda."

Flann turned to see Crouching Fox hurrying to
catch up to him.

"Have you seen Black Rock?" he asked the
shaman.

"No. Copper Sky is looking for you."

"I haven't time," Flann answered. "I've got to
find Birch Leaf. That snake, Black Rock. . . ."

"Come with me and listen to the chief. It's about
Birch Leaf."

Copper Sky stood outside his wigwam. "I told you
I'd tell you the man's name if I saw him," he said to
Flann. "I've seen him. He brought whiskey. His name
is Henri Fontenac."

Fontenac.

Flann grunted. It was as he had suspected.

But at that moment, Flann was not concerned
about the weapons.

319

"Birch Leaf," he yelled at Copper Sky. "Where is Birch Leaf?"

"I fear he took her," the chief said.

"Who? Black Rock?"

"Henri. He took her because of the guns, I think. He came tonight dressed as a Chippewa with no hair on his face so that it was hard to see he was Henri. He brought whiskey to sell to the warriors, and he told me I must go east to use the guns against the Canadian whites. I said I fight the Sioux with the guns. That's what they were for. I said I had no quarrel with white men."

"What about Birch Leaf?"

"He said he'd take payment in his own way. I know he lusted for Birch Leaf."

With sick horror, Flann remembered Birch Leaf telling him once how Henri had tried to buy her from Soft Willow.

"I have the notion he caches guns on the big island were spirits guard the mines of the Old Ones," Copper Sky went on. "The island is to the northeast. He may head there with Birch Leaf. He's not fool enough to stay at La Pointe after this."

Flann stared at Copper Sky.

"The island is on the way to Montreal," the chief added.

Flann turned from him and ran toward the lake. As he neared the water, he saw by the faint light of the stars that someone was trying to launch a canoe. Let it be Henri, he hoped as he flung himself forward, thudding into the man. They both rolled onto the sand.

"Damn you, Henri!" he swore as he dug his thumbs into the neck of the struggling man.

"Ishcoda," the man managed to gasp as Flann's grip tightened.

Flann loosened his hold. Henri had never used his Chippewa name. He peered closely at the man he was strangling and realized it was Black Rock, not Henri Fontenac. Flann released his grip on him and got to his feet.

Black Rock sat up, gagging, rubbing his throat. "Henri's gone," he said. "He took her, took Birch Leaf."

"I know. I'm going after them." Flann put his rifle into the canoe beside them.

"We'll go together." Black Rock struggled to his feet, swaying.

"You're no use to anyone drunk."

"I'm not drunk. That snake hit me with a rock when I came after him. I moved too slow. Whiskey. Pah! If I had been sober, Henri Fontenac would never have seen me before I killed him. I am sober now. And you do not go without me. In this we are not enemies. We are brothers." Black Rock leaned over and sloshed cold lake water over his head and face.

"Copper Sky says Henri has gone to some island where spirits stand guard over mines. Do you know where it is?"

"Yes." Black Rock picked up a paddle and helped Flann lift the boat into the water.

Flann stopped talking and took the bow of the canoe, leaving the stern for Black Rock as steersman. He cursed silently. He would have wished for any other brave but Black Rock. Yet he had no choice but to ally himself with his enemy. As they were united in their hate for Henri Fontenac, perhaps he could trust Black Rock, this once.

Flann knew he had to trust him. God knows he had no idea of how to find the spirit island which Copper Sky had described.

Black Rock's rhythm with the paddle was steady.
Flann matched him stroke for stroke and they drove
steadily out into the dark lake. Flann's tension eased
somewhat as he fell into the pattern of paddling. Dawn
was painting the morning sky rose pink when Black
Rock lifted his paddle to point to a smudge of land
ahead.

"We'll beach the canoe and rest," he said.

"I don't want to stop," Flann protested, staring at
the land. He knew it must be the north shore of Lake
Superior, in the Minnesota Territory.

"It is too far to go without resting," Black Rock
maintained. "It'll take all day to paddle there."

Flann knew Black Rock was right but he chafed
at the delay as they lifted the canoe onto the sand and
stretched themselves out. He settled himself to rest,
and immediately his eyelids drooped.

The sun was a quarter of the way up the sky
when Black Rock woke Flann, offering blackberries he
had gathered. As soon as they ate, they launched the
canoe and set off again.

"I know of a copper island called Isle Royale,"
Flann said as Black Rock set a course to skirt the
north shore of the lake. "I think it might be the spirit
island we seek."

"I don't know what name whites give the island.
It's near the rocks where Thunderbird lives. On the
north side of the island, the traders smoke fish. But no
one will be there now, for everyone came to the payment."

I've guessed correctly, Flann told himself. It *is*
Isle Royale. He recalled that the island was far down
the lake. He had first heard of it that day aboard the
Astor. Captain Tobias Stannard had pointed off to

322

starboard, to the north. It was way out there, he had said, but it was too distant to be seen.

"That's a long way," he said. "Will we get there before dark?"

Black Rock glanced up at the sky. "I hope so."

Flann looked up. A few fluffy cumulus clouds drifted in the blue. The lake was still relatively smooth.

"There are many little islands near the spirit island," Black Rock said. "We'll put in at one and creep across to the big island at night."

"I pray Henri is still there," Flann said.

"He'll be there. The weather's changing. He won't risk going on."

Neither of them mentioned Birch Leaf's name.

Flann looked again at the clouds. Now he saw they were clumping together in towering masses. He remembered the lake storm the year before. He twisted around to look at Black Rock.

Black Rock raised his paddle to his mouth, drinking water from the blade. "We'll outrun the Thunderers," he said confidently.

Flann noticed the brave's stroke rhythm increased after this. Soon the water grew choppy and slowed their progress. The cloud cover thickened, and the day darkened.

When lightning flickered near the horizon, Black Rock started to chant. "Take pity on me, oh mighty Thunderbird. You, who have power over the storm winds and the rain, Thunderbird, see me here and take pity."

The wind shifted to the north and cold blasts swept across the lake. Thunder boomed. Waves lifted the canoe, tossing it wildly. Water poured over the gunwales.

God, Flann prayed silently. Black Rock has Thunderbird, but I'll need *Your* help to survive.

A bolt of lightning stitched sky to water. A great clap of thunder followed at once. Rain pelted down, then icy pellets of hail battered the canoe and slammed onto the unprotected men.

Suddenly water swirled about Flann's legs.

"Sinking," Black Rock shouted, his voice barely audible.

The canoe swamped and Flann sank. He pushed to the surface to gasp in air. A wave crashed over him, sending him under again.

Chapter 30

Water was everywhere. There was no land, no canoe, no other human. Flann fought to gulp enough air before the next wave swept over him. He could not swim in such turbulence. He could scarcely manage to stay afloat.

When his foot struck something solid, he did not understand for a moment that he was among rocks. The next wave threw him against a boulder slick with algae. Desperately he pushed himself between this rock and another. Then he felt smaller rocks under his feet, and he waded onto land. He staggered into the shelter of pines and supported himself against the trunk of one. He looked back at the lake.

Thunder still crashed and rain beat through the canopy of needles above him. Kitchigami flung white-capped waves at massive brown rocks. Lightning lit the sky and lake with eerie brilliance. He had no idea whether he was on the Canadian mainland or an off-shore island.

He had little hope that Black Rock was alive, but

pushed away from the pine, deciding he must search the water's edge in case the brave had been washed ashore and needed help. Flann climbed over rocks and the decayed trunks of downed trees calling Black Rock's name.

"Ishcoda."

Flan whirled and saw Black Rock behind him at the tree line.

"Come into the woods. I'll make a fire," the brave called.

By the time Black Rock had coaxed a small twig blaze to life in the shelter of overhanging rocks, the worst of the storm was over. Rain fell steadily, but the wind had lessened, and there was only an occasional rumble of distant thunder.

"Do you know where we are?" Flann asked. He had lost both moccasins and his leggings in the water. He now wore, as Black Rock did, only a loin cloth. He still had his knife.

"We're on a small island near the copper island where we wish to go. Where that snake, Henri, is."

Black Rock left the shelter of the rocks to cut pine boughs. Flann knew these were for sleeping and got up to cut his own. If they spread the boughs near the fire to dry, they'd have good beds. Nothing could be done until the storm was over.

At dawn the sky was overcast, and a drizzle oozed from its grayness. The seas were still heavy, but the waves had receded considerably. Flann could see land to the east, several small islands and one large one that could have been Isle Royale.

"It's too far to swim in water like this," Flann said. He knew that under the best conditions the distance would try his endurance. With the lake as choppy as it was, and the unforgiving coldness of the water, he knew he'd be a fool to even try it. He looked at Black Rock, who nodded in agreement. "We could make a raft of logs," he suggested.

Black Rock agreed. "We'll find ones that float well."

The first log they launched sank. As they searched for another driftwood log, their appearance frightened off a sandpiper that teetered along the sandy strip by the water. Black Rock stopped.

"We'll eat," he said, plucking a hair from his head.

Flann knew what the brave intended and decided he would try to make a bird snare using his own hair. Black Rock disappeared into the woods and came back with a piece of bark swarming with white grubs on the inner side. He crushed some and baited the hair loop with them. Flann did the same using his own strand of hair.

Black Rock's snare caught the sandpiper when it returned to investigate the grubs. He took the bird off to roast over the coals of their night fire. Flann sat watching his own trap. It was empty. He was about ready to give up when a small brown bird flew out of the pines, landed and approached the bait. It pecked at the grubs, hopping forward until its feet were so entangled in the hair loop that it couldn't move.

Flann roasted his prize among the coals. He was pleased, even though the bird was little more than a mouthful.

He and Black Rock finally found two buoyant logs. Using pieces of wide driftwood for paddles, they set off, each astride a log. Flann estimated Isle Royale was at least a mile away. Black Rock soon pulled ahead. Trying to maneuver a log, Flann discovered, was nothing like skimming over the water in a birch-bark canoe. About all the paddle accomplished was to keep the log headed in the right direction. After a time he realized he was sitting lower in the water and knew the dead wood he perched on was becoming water-logged. In a few more minutes water rose to his waist as the log continued to sink beneath him.

"Black Rock," he managed to yell just before he found himself floundering in the swells.

Flann swam toward Black Rock, pushing through the icy water. After several yards, an agonizing pain suddenly gripped his calf muscles. He went under, swallowing water.

Flann rose to the surface, choking and sputtering. The pain in his legs brought tears to his eyes as he fought to keep from going under again. Frantically he looked around but saw no sign of Black Rock.

He'll let me drown, Flann thought bitterly, gasping in air, then bending his body, his face under water, to massage his calves. Black Rock began by trying to drown me in the river and now he'll succeed. But Flann found he was mistaken again.

He turned up his head for more air, then felt hands grip his arm. He saw Black Rock next to him. "Grab hold of the log," he ordered Flann.

The weight of two of them clinging to one log threatened to submerge it. As soon as the cramps in his legs would permit, Flann joined Black Rock in kicking as they rested their upper bodies on the log. He judged they were about halfway to the big island. Their progress was slow and erratic. They finally came close enough to risk swimming for shore, and Flann found himself putting his utmost effort into beating Black Rock to land. He failed. They reached shore neck and neck just as the sun broke through for the first time that day.

As they crawled to a rock shelf, Black Rock stood, water dripping from his brown skin, his back to the lake. Flann watched him without speaking, knowing the brave would hear sounds he himself might miss, and read significance into sights he might ignore. In strength, he might be able to match Black Rock. In wilderness knowledge, he probably never would.

"Someone has had a fire on the island today," Black Rock said finally, speaking softly. "Not close. North wind blows on us yet so we go in that direction. We're downwind from Henri, which is good for us, bad for him."

As they started out, Flann tried to recall what he knew of Isle Royale. It was forty-five miles long, narrow and rocky. Back in Washington, Madden had told him about Isle Royale and Benjamin Franklin in France, negotiating the Treaty of Paris with England in 1783.

"Old Ben listened to three Chippewas," Madden had told him, "telling of the wondrous copper deposits on their spirit-haunted island in Kitchigami. An inspired American businessman interested in this copper brought the three Indians, along with an interpreter, all the way from Kitchigami to Paris to see Franklin. Ben always had a patriotic eye for our natural resources, and so he fought to have Isle Royale included on the American side of the boundary line. You know, there's a story about a conversation Ben had after the treaty was signed and Isle Royale was safely ours. He was at a party with Lord Rockingham, who was Prime Minister of England at the time. 'I knew all along Isle Royale was inlaid with copper,' Franklin boasted. 'I don't give a damn if that island is solid copper,' the Prime Minister answered. 'If the treaty conference had lasted another week you Yankees would have insisted on running your infernal boundary line around Ireland.' "

Flann saw Black Rock had gotten the lead and hurried to catch up. Black Rock stopped and turned to him.

"You make too much noise walking," he said. "Henri will hear us before we're close enough to surprise him."

Flann nodded. "What do you want me to do?"

"Stay behind. Walk slow. When I spot his camp, if I can't jump him right away, I'll come back and tell you."

Flann watched Black Rock glide ahead until he could hardly make out his figure among the trees, then started to follow. After passing through a pine grove, he crossed a stream on fallen logs, forming a bridge, then discovered when he emerged into a rocky clearing that he had lost sight of Black Rock. He stopped. Now what? He looked around and decided to walk ahead to the trees on the other side of the clearing and wait there. He believed Black Rock would probably back-track as soon as he realized Flann wasn't following. As he made his way toward the trees, Flann noticed a circular depression in the ground to his left. Could this be one of the ancient copper pits?

Large chunks of broken granite lay near the depression. Looking at the granite, Flann realized that the chunks, if fitted together, would form a crude stone hammer. Had it been used to knock copper free? He lowered himself into the shallow pit and knelt, poking into the layer of old leaves and pine needles with a sharp fragment of the broken hammer. He struck hard rock under the leaves. Quickly, he shoved the debris aside and saw the green oxidation of copper. He picked up a loose fragment, a shard shaped almost like an arrow point, and scraped at it with his fingernail. It was copper, without a doubt.

A strangled cry startled him. Cautiously, he inched up until he could see above the edge of the pit, hoping his red hair would not be spotted. Five yards away, at the edge of the clearing, he saw Black Rock on the ground. Standing over him was Henri Fontenac, rifle in hand. Flann eased his knife out and dropped the copper fragment into the empty sheath.

Henri's back was to him. Flann saw only one thing to do. If he could climb out without alerting him, he had a chance to disarm Henri. Flann came up from the pit as quickly and quietly as he could. Black Rock was not moving, but Flann had heard no shot. Had Henri bashed his head with the rifle butt and stunned him?

There was no sign of Birch Leaf.

Flann had little doubt Henri would kill him if he attacked. But Henri would also kill him if he did not. He took a deep breath and charged. He had covered half the ground between them when Henri whirled, rifle pointed at Flann. Flann held.

"Ah, I knew if this one on the ground had another with him, my little tableau would flush that one from cover. But it's you. How fortunate, *mon ami*."

Flann glared at the metis who looked him up and down insolently.

"I think you will put your knife on the ground and kick it to me, my white Indian friend."

Flann gauged his chances of throwing the knife, knowing he lacked the skill to be sure of a killing toss. Merely wounding him would not be enough. Henri would blow a hole in his guts and then reload and shoot Black Rock. He dropped his knife and, with his bare toes, pushed it toward Henri.

"Walk to your right, away from the knife," Henri ordered. "A little farther, if you please."

Flann watched him pick up the knife and toss it into the trees.

"I don't hear you ask how your little squaw is, Red Hair. She is most sweet, I find."

Flann clenched his fists.

"She don't come to me easy, but in time she will. A Frenchman knows how to deal with squaws. In *la belle* Montreal, she'll beg for me to love her."

"You son of a bitch," Flann said.

Henri smiled. "But a smart one," he said. He motioned Flann forward with the rifle barrel until Flann stood beside Black Rock. "Sit down next to him," Henri ordered. He tossed a rope to Flann. "Tie him."

Although Flann tried to keep the rope loose around Black Rock's wrists and ankles, Henri saw to it that he tied him tightly. The brave gave no sign that he was conscious while Flann bound him. Black Rock's knife was missing.

"Come with me," Henri barked.

Henri forced Flann to walk ahead, carrying the helpless Black Rock, until they reached a small lake ringed by birches. There, near a fire burning in a clearing, Birch Leaf sat bound to a tree trunk.

"Birch Leaf," Flann yelled.

She looked away from him, tears streaming down her face. She was naked. Bruises darkened her thighs and breasts.

"Take water from the lake," Henri told Flann. "Pour it on the Indian to wake him."

Flann obeyed.

Black Rock grunted and coughed as the water sluiced over him. He opened his eyes.

332

"Where did you beach your canoe?" Henri asked Flann.

"At the bottom of Kitchigami."

Henri shrugged. "The storm wrecked my canoe, too. Smashed it on the rocks." He prodded Black Rock with his foot. "You, Black Rock," he said in Chippewa. "What do you say now, eh?"

Black Rock did not speak, his eyes fixed on Henri's. Henri raised the rifle, aiming it at the brave.

"Black Rock, you will build me a birch-bark canoe. You and Red Hair here. I, Henri, order you to do this."

Black Rock spat.

"You don't do what I say, I'll hurt her." Henry jerked his head toward Birch Leaf. "I know you wanted her until Red Hair took her. Now she is mine."

Black Rock glanced at the naked Birch Leaf, then looked at Henri. "I'll build a canoe," he muttered.

"Good." Henri turned to Flann. "Untie him."

Flann worked at the knots binding Black Rock, trying to plan how to spring at Henri and somehow disarm him. But the metis moved away from the two men to crouch beside Birch Leaf. He put the muzzle of the rifle to her temple.

"You work hard for Henri, eh?" he said. "You make a poor canoe, she'll drown with me. You understand? You try to rush me, she dies first."

Flann kept his eyes from Birch Leaf, unable to look at her without rage. He knew Henri would kill her, just as he threatened, if he made any attempt to jump him.

"Am I a beaver to gnaw bark with my teeth?" Black Rock asked. "My knife is gone."

Henri tossed a knife to him, the blade biting into the ground at the brave's feet. He watched, keeping the rifle at Birch Leaf's head while Black Rock grabbed the quivering hilt.

When Black Rock headed for a large birch, Henri ordered Flann to go with him. "You keep together all the time," he commanded. "You stay close as brothers, eh?" He laughed as though he found this amusing.

Black Rock sliced bark from the birch and spread it on level ground. Flann gathered rocks for weights to keep the bark flat. "I need cedar for the ribs," Black Rock said. "Spruce roots for sewing."

"We go find these things," Henri said. "You give the knife back first." He looped a noose over Birch Leaf's head with one hand, his eyes on the men. He untied her from the tree, keeping the end of the rope that went around her neck pulled tight.

"Walk ahead," Henri told Black Rock and Flann. "You try to do anything and I kill her."

They slogged across a blueberry marsh to a clump of spruces. Flann and Black Rock dug at the roots with stones. Henri watched closely, rifle muzzle pressed to Birch Leaf's back.

"Soon men will work for me in Montreal, too," he boasted. "I, Henri, say that I am more clever than Indians, than Americans. Soon Canada will be free from England and will take all the fur country. Henri Fontenac will be a rich man." He prodded Birch Leaf with the rifle, making her wince.

"This one here will lick my feet like a dog, wanting me then. You'll see. I might keep her, I might not. Henri Fontenac will have any woman he wants then."

Don't listen, Flann told himself. Keep calm. Wait. He'll make a mistake. He's too confident.

"Red Hair, you are one hard man to kill, but now Henri has you, eh? You think Black Rock shot the ar-

334

row at Ontonagon. No. Me, Henri. By damn, I miss. You are one lucky bastard. Why you come here to Lake Superior to bother me, eh? The guns I must now conceal here, because you sniff at my heels like a white dog. And you talk to Copper Sky and scare him off. Very bad.

"I think the Pillagers finish you but that mide he scare hell out them. I got him, at least, killed that devil."

Despite himself, Flann looked up at Henri. So, Black Rock hadn't shot the arrow. It had been Henri all along, in Ontonagon, at Sandy Lake. Flann closed his eyes, thinking, forgive me, Black Rock. Henri grinned. Flann held his face stiff, forcing himself to look casually back at the ground. Then Flann saw what he was looking for.

Behind Henri, a black bear ambling among the blueberry bushes raised his head, scenting the men.

The bear was their only hope of distracting Henri. Flann dug at a root a moment more before he looked up again. He widened his eyes in mock alarm.

"A bear," he shouted at Henri. "There's a bear behind you!"

Chapter 31

Black Rock heard Henri speak with Ishcoda in the white man's tongue. His head throbbed with each move. He was filled with anger and shame at letting a snake such as Henri outwit him. He was shaken by self-doubt. What sort of warrior was he? What sort of brave did nothing while Henri Fontenac shamed and violated Birch Leaf before him?

He gritted his teeth, knowing he had to wait or Birch Leaf would die. He felt Ishcoda grow tense, heard his shout of *"Mukwah*, bear."

Black Rock looked up. Beyond Birch Leaf and Henri a bear reared on his back legs to sniff the air. The sun striking through clouds cast light over the bear's dark brown coat. There were no cubs with the bear. Judging by size and hair color, it appeared to be an old male.

Henri started to turn, held, then turned back to face Ishcoda. "You think to fool me, eh? I don't like tricks, Red Hair."

"A bear stands behind you," Black Rock affirmed. "He's deciding what to do."

Birch Leaf managed to turn her head despite the noose about her neck. Henri turned sideways and glanced quickly toward the marsh.

Henri leveled the rifle at the bear. Before Black Rock or Ishcoda could move, he aimed it at Birch Leaf again. In that short time, Black Rock saw Ishcoda had taken something from the sheath at his waist.

Black Rock knew Henri's thinking as though it was his own. No cubs. If I don't bother mukwah, he won't bother me. If I shoot I might not kill with the first bullet. Then there will be trouble. A wounded bear wars to the death.

Birch Leaf began to chant:

> Bear of copper, Vision Bear,
> I am she you came to.
> Help me, oh Bear,
> Help me, my colleague.
> Bear of my dream,
> Come to my aid.
> Strike with fire, burn with flame,
> Copper Bear.

Her words choked off as Henri tightened the rope around her neck. She coughed and clawed at her throat. Henri hit her in the face. Black Rock tensed to spring at him, but was distracted by Ishcoda who flung what he concealed in his hand at the bear.

The bear squalled with pain, pawed at his nose, then dropped to all fours and charged. "Good throw," Black Rock yelled, eyes fixed on the bear.

Henri snapped off a quick shot. The bullet did not

even slow the bear. Henri turned to run. He pushed Birch Leaf into the bear's path. Black Rock caught his breath and sprang forward, Flann following.

The bear did not even seem to see Birch Leaf. He stepped over her and continued his rush toward Henri, as though she was not even there before him. Black Rock knelt beside her, loosening the rope about her neck. She lay motionless, but the color slowly returned to her face again.

Flann touched her jaw in the angle under the ear to see if blood pulsed there.

"She'll be all right," Ishcoda said. Black Rock said nothing. He already knew she would recover.

He turned, looking for Henri.

"Henri is going for that tree," Flann said. "Doesn't he know bears climb?"

"A frightened man forgets all he knows," Black Rock said.

Henri scrambled up a small birch, dropping his rifle as he climbed. The bear tried to follow, but he was too large for the tree. Enraged, he clawed at the trunk until the bark was in ribbons. He lunged at the birch, shaking it furiously. Henri screamed in terror, clinging desperately to a branch.

Birch Leaf sat up, hands going to her throat. She stared toward the bear and Henri.

"Kill him," she cried hoarsely, getting to her feet. "Bear, kill him."

Flann tried to take her in his arms, but she pushed him away. "Kill him," she repeated. Before either of the men could stop her she ran toward the bear. "Colleague," she cried. "Colleague."

"No," Flann called, starting after her.

Birch Leaf grabbed the gun from under the bear's

feet. The animal again ignored her. Black Rock caught Ishcoda's arm and held him back.

"Don't interfere," he warned, struggling with Flann. "She won't be harmed. You would be."

Birch Leaf calmly retrieved Henri's ammunition pouch and began to reload the rifle, standing unharmed within a paw swipe of the bear. The animal now sat on his haunches, staring up the tree, growling.

"Shoot him, Birch Leaf," Henri called down to her. "Shoot that damn big bear. I give you much money. I give you anything you want."

Birch Leaf did not look up as she rammed the rod into the muzzle of the rifle. She finished and aimed the gun carefully, upward, at Henri.

"No, wait," he begged.

"Birch Leaf," Flann called, trying to wrench himself loose from Black Rock.

She paid no attention. Black Rock smiled as he saw her finger tighten on the trigger. A true warrior gave no quarter to an enemy.

The rifle cracked. The heavy lead slug lifted Henri backwards out of the tree. He twisted in midair and crashed to the ground. The bear walked to him, sniffed, flipped him over with a massive paw, sniffed again, then turned his back and ambled into the woods.

Birch Leaf stood, rifle in hand, staring at Henri's body. Black Rock let Flann go. Birch Leaf dropped the gun and darted to Henri. She knelt beside him and fumbled at his clothes.

"Birch Leaf," Flann said, touching her shoulder.

She looked up at him, then at Black Rock. She had Henri's knife in one hand. She grasped his hair with the other.

"I want to scalp him," she told Black Rock. "Show me how to do it properly."

Three days later, the men who ran the fishery for the American Fur Company on Isle Royale returned from La Pointe. Black Rock had insisted they wait for them, saying he could not build a good canoe with bark taken in August, that the returning men would have boats.

They borrowed a canoe and set off, Birch Leaf wearing a skirt and cape she had fashioned from reeds. She wore Henri's scalp fastened at her waist. They had buried his body in a shallow grave and piled stones atop it to discourage the wolves. Black Rock persuaded her to conceal the scalp from the fishery men. They did not speak of Henri at all.

"What of the guns he cached?" Flann asked.

Flann and Birch Leaf had discussed Henri Fontenac's storing of the guns before, always to Flann's frustration.

Birch Leaf said again and again that she did not know where the guns were hidden. The denial disturbed Flann, because for the first time, he did not know whether or not to believe her.

"I don't know where he hid them," Birch Leaf said.

Black Rock felt he himself knew where the guns must be, but he said nothing. Ishcoda thought like a white man, warrior though he had proven himself to be. Later something could be done about finding the rifles, after Ishcoda returned to his village in the east.

From the stern of the canoe, Black Rock looked at Birch Leaf sitting just before him. He wanted her. He would always want her. What a marvel she was, beautiful in her face and body. Here was a woman who tended to wigwam duties with care and skill, yet was brave as a warrior and able to deal with spirits like a mide. No doubt she would qualify for the Midewiwin

340

when she was old enough. If she was his wife he would never glance at another woman.

He knew Ishcoda had asked her to go with him, to be his wife, to leave Kitchigami land. And he knew she loved Ishcoda.

Black Rock himself no longer hated Ishcoda. Indeed, he respected him. But never would he truly like him. The two were not meant to be friends.

Flann glanced back from the bow at Birch Leaf. He had tried to persuade her to discard the grisly ornament she wore at her waist. The scalp, along with her costume of rushes, made her look like a primitive savage in a woodcut sent back to Europe by the early explorers of America.

He realized it would be harder than he had thought at first for her to adjust to living in Boston. His aunt would faint outright if she ever heard that her nephew's wife had once scalped a man. Not that he cared what anyone thought. He loved Birch Leaf. He had been taken aback at first when she shot Henri from the tree. Then he had thought, why should men be the only ones to exact vengeance?

Flann looked forward to returning home to Boston, to taking Birch Leaf to her first concert. He had not realized how much he missed those musical evenings until he was deprived of all music except the Chippewa drums and rattles and the mournful notes of a love flute.

Birch Leaf had a beautiful voice. If she took lessons and learned to sing the kind of music he liked, he suspected she would be marvelous. He would see that she was kept busy, he vowed. He would see that she was happy.

* * *

Birch Leaf watched the distant horizon for the first sign of land. She wanted to be by herself, away from Black Rock and Ishcoda. One or the other or both of them had hovered over her ever since Henri's death. Before that she had had to endure Henri's brutality.

Something had happened to her on the island. She had become aware of her spirit power, and she wanted to be alone to think about it. She decided she might make a tree nest and stay in the woods for a few days, away from everyone. She knew it was important that she understand what she was to do with this power, and what the Vision Bear wished of her.

The land of Ishcoda seemed like a dream country to her, where nothing would be familiar. The more questions she asked, the more she realized she would have to learn to be a woman all over again, for the People's ways would not be proper there. Ah, but she loved him so. She would never love another man as she loved Ishcoda.

Yet she had seen the strength and bravery of Black Rock and admired him greatly. He understood about the Vision Bear and the scalp. He approved. Black Rock was truly a friend.

Much as she loved Ishcoda, she did not want to be alone with any man for awhile. Henri had shown her how evil men could be with women, and she needed to cleanse herself of the memory.

Yes, she would go alone into the woods as soon as she was back at Meenagha, to fast and wait for enlightenment.

And when she emerged, she would know exactly what she had to do with her life.

Dogs and children raced to the river when Flann

and Black Rock lifted the canoe onto the bank. The morning was warm, the sun moving through a cloudless sky. Behind the children came the rest of the villagers, hurrying to greet them.

Black Rock had stopped at the Ontonagon village to get a proper dress for Birch Leaf as well as moccasins for all three of them. They stood waiting by the canoe.

Soft Willow hugged her daughter. Crouching Fox clasped Flann's arms, then Black Rock's. "A feast," Copper Sky proclaimed when he saw the scalp. "We'll have a warrior's feast."

After the dancing and the songs of bravery and coups, Flann searched for Birch Leaf and found her outside her mother's wigwam.

"Crouching Fox tells me the *Astor* went uplake two days ago," he informed her. "I'll put up the signal so she'll stop for us on her way back. Most likely it'll be tomorrow." He put his arms around her.

Birch Leaf allowed him to hold her, but when she felt him stir with desire she stepped back. It was time to be honest with him.

"I can't be with you in love," she confessed.

"I understand. But you'll forget what happened after awhile. I'll try to be patient."

"That is not all, Ishcoda." She paused. "I can't go with you on the Walk-in-the-Water, either. I don't want to live in Boston."

He saw tears glinting in her eyes.

"Birch Leaf, you're upset. You. . . ."

"I tell you, I can't go."

Flann gripped her shoulders. "You must come. I love you."

"Then stay with me," she said softly. "Stay with me. Here I'll be your wife forever."

343

He dropped his hands. "I can't stay. You know I can't stay."

She nodded.

"Yet you ask me to."

"Here I'll be a good wife. In Boston I won't." She clenched her fist and pounded it between her breasts. "My spirit tells me I belong here. You could belong too, Ishcoda."

"No." His throat ached with grief. "Why won't you sail with me?"

Birch Leaf stood tall. "I had a vision the night after I met you. Someday I'll be a mide because of that vision dream. Am I to turn aside from the power granted me by Kitchi Manito, the power to help others?"

"There'll be ways for you to help in Boston. The women. . . ."

She brushed his words aside. "You speak of ways any woman might use. I speak of mystic power. I know you don't even understand what I speak of, though you try."

"You can't become a mide until you're older. Now you're young. I know you love me, Birch Leaf. How can you throw love away?"

Tears ran down her cheeks. "It's wrong to leave the People. Bear thrust the flame of power into my heart. If I betray my vision, misfortune will follow me. I'll become as nothing. All who know me will sicken and wither. I could not wish such a fate for you."

"But you're a white woman," he cried.

"No," she shook her head. "And if I ever was, I am no longer."

They stared at one another. She reached out at last to touch his face.

"I'll come back," he promised. "I must leave now.

I have obligations to meet, but I'll come back. Wait for me."

"And when you come back, will you stay here and not leave again?"

Flann blinked back tears.

He could not make this promise.

He would never be able to live his life with the Chippewa. He could not. Not for Birch Leaf, not for anyone.

As she could not live her life in Boston. Not the life she chose to live. Birch Leaf was right. She was Anishinabe, not white, whatever her parents may have been.

"By your silence, I know your answer. I understand." She paused. "Remember me," she said and leaned to kiss him softly on the lips.

Before he could grasp her, she eluded him and slipped into the wigwam.

Flann stood on the beach at dawn, waiting for the *Astor*. He had not slept at all. He had paced the sand, grieving, remembering, realizing he had always known in his heart that Birch Leaf would not sail with him.

Words from a song one of Henry Schoolcraft's daughters had composed for him at Mackinac persisted in his memory:

> *Wah yaw burn maud e*
> *Chippewa quainee un e*
> *We maw jaw need e.*

The daughter had explained the song, called "Chippewa Maid": "The young American weeps for his love, a Chippewa girl, for he's leaving and he'll never see her again. Ah, but he'll not sigh long, the girl thinks as she, too, sobs. As soon as he's far across the waters and no longer sees her, he'll find a new love and forget his Chippewa maid."

The *Astor* lay offshore, waiting for him. The villagers crowded around to say good-bye. Crouching Fox waited to paddle him to the boat. Soft Willow was there and so was Fire Grass. He did not see Birch Leaf.

He looked back when the canoe was halfway to the ship.

On the beach away from the village, standing at the lake's edge, a slim figure stood, waving.

As he watched, a tall brave emerged from the woods and came to stand beside her.

Tears dimmed his vision, but Flann knew the man was Black Rock.

Chapter 32

Flann tried not to stare too obviously at the man who faced him. Almost a head shorter than Flann, his curly gray hair had receded far up his head, and he had let it grow in front of his ears and part-way across his cheeks, as if in compensation. His dark eyes smiled in friendly greeting.

"So you're Flann O'Phelan," President Martin Van Buren said. "When your note came last week, I recalled General Jackson telling me about you. The notes he left confirm what I remembered. I know your uncle, Whitney McNeil. A fine man. Do have a seat, Mr. O'Phelan."

"Thank you, Mr. President."

President Van Buren seated himself behind a polished cherry wood desk and picked up a paper before him. Flann settled himself in a straight-backed gilt chair. He wore new clothes. They were still uncomfortable, especially the shoes. They pinched his feet after the comfort of moccasins.

"It looks to me as though you're approximately a

year late in reporting to me, give or take a month or two," Van Buren said.

"Yes, sir. My fault, sir."

"Still, the mission you were sent on must have been successful. The only trouble we got into with those Canadian rebels happened in New York. No doubt you heard about last December's countretemps."

"News travels slowly to the Lake Superior country," Flann said. "There were rumors about Canadians attacking an American boat. I've heard since from Mr. Madden that the boat was in the Niagara River and had been carrying arms to the Canadian rebels."

Van Buren nodded. "I had to send General Winfield Scott to the border to try to prevent any further incidents which could lead to another war with England." He shook his head. "Too many Americans sympathize with the rebels. There are possibly as many Americans as Canadian rebels keeping the issue hot."

"The Indians of the Lake Superior region aren't interested in what they call 'white men's wars,' " Flann said. "They did accept some guns, as I reported to the Indian agent, Mr. Schoolcraft, and also to Mr. Madden here in Washington. The Chippewas wanted the guns for their own war with the Sioux and had no intention of using them the way the rebel agent wanted them to."

Van Buren became thoughtful. "I suppose we can be thankful the guns won't be used for worse purposes, although what you describe is bad enough. I see no sense in the tribes warring with each other. You were there with them, Mr. O'Phelan, and I understand you speak the Chippewa tongue. What reason do the chiefs give?"

"For fighting against the Sioux? Why, sir, Chief Flat Mouth of the Pillagers told Mr. Schoolcraft that the Great Spirit had decreed that hatred and war should exist between the Sioux and the Chippewa forever, and this decree could never be changed. He insisted that, since the country was strewn with the bones of his fathers and enriched with their blood, the very ground called to him for vengeance."

"Savages. We must see to their enlightenment."

"The land is important to them, Mr. President. The Chippewas fear being moved west into Sioux territory. I sympathize. I sincerely hope the move won't be necessary. The land's not at all suitable for farming."

"The Army had to move the Cherokees earlier this year," President Van Buren said. "Why can't the Indians see it's for their own good, these moves?"

"Is it always?"

Van Buren stared at him. "Mr. O'Phelan, those Cherokees had given up their land legally in return for lands across the Mississippi. In Florida, the Seminoles resisted all negotiations and fought us bitterly. We lost far too many soldiers before their chief, Osceola, was captured last October." He stretched out his hands, palms up. "All I wish for the Indian nations is that they may prosper far in the west. New land is there for them, set aside as Indian territory. I don't want to send the Army to fight against them."

"No, of course not, sir."

"The Indians. Slavery. When will we see the end of these problems?" Van Buren picked up the papers on his desk and glanced at them. "Is what you say here true? Copper? Silver?"

"I could tell you about the copper boulder at Ontonagon and the copper mines on Isle Royale, but I believe you're well aware of those. As to silver. . . ." Flann hesitated. "Yes, there's silver. The Chippewas wear ornaments made of silver, ornaments they fashion themselves. The source is another matter. They wouldn't reveal the source. I thought perhaps if I went back. . . ." Flann leaned forward.

"Smallpox is a terrible scourge among the Chippewa, Mr. President. And among the Sioux, for that matter. If I could be sent back to the Lake Superior country with enough vaccine to inoculate every Chippewa man, woman, and child against smallpox, it would be a magnificent present from the Great White Father in Washington, and one they could understand. After all, smallpox came with white men. White men should prevent it if they can. Meanwhile, of course, I might be able to locate the silver deposits you're interested in."

"Yes, I've been told smallpox is a problem," Van Buren nodded. "I'll refer the matter to our new commissioner of Indian Affairs. Money isn't easily available right now, as you may be aware." He smiled without amusement.

Flann had discovered since his return that many banks had failed, prices were up and an alarming number of men were out of work in the cities. He nodded.

"I'm interested in the silver," Van Buren went on, "and intend to take steps to see something is done. I believe the young governor of Michigan is attempting to set up an office of state geologist. There's some young doctor who's done explorations in the Lake Superior area. Houghton, I think his name is, and Governor Mason feels this man is an excellent geologist. If Mason's plan falls through, I'll have to see what I can do about funding for Dr. Houghton."

Flann sat in silence a few moments. "You've no need to send me, then," he said at last, preparing to rise.

"Come, Mr. O'Phelan, don't look so downcast.

350

You've accomplished what you were sent to do. I'm grateful, and the country's grateful."

Flann got to his feet. President Van Buren rose also, coming around the desk. "Now, sir, I have a favor to ask of you," he said. "My daughter-in-law has a small dinner dance planned for this evening. She whispered to me as I came downstairs to meet with you that an extra man is always welcome and, if you were at all presentable, I should invite you."

Van Buren grinned. "Angelica is a great tease and I believe I'll call her on this one. Although, Mr. O'Phelan, she will be delighted to meet you. Will you be so kind as to join us tonight? Dancing will be first, dinner later in the evening."

"If you think I fit the particulars, Mr. President, I'd be honored."

Flann returned to his hotel, Fuller's, on Pennsylvania Avenue at Fourteenth Street, then hurried out to purchase dancing slippers.

When Flann was ushered into the East Room of the White House, he found a group of young men and women so richly dressed and bejeweled, it was hard for him to believe that men walked hungry in the streets of Washington and Boston.

The Royal Wilton carpet had been lifted from the floor. A group of musicians had been installed at one end of the room, playing violins, flutes and a large gilt harp. The young Mrs. Abraham Van Buren, the president's daughter-in-law, introduced Flann to several women. He politely asked the last to dance. She was blonde, with brown eyes, and was lively and talkative. Her first name, he soon discovered, was Caroline.

Flann realized she must have thought him a terrible boor when he left her suddenly after one dance, but all he could see in his mind was Birch Leaf's face once he heard the name Caroline.

What was Birch Leaf doing at that very moment? It was the Moon of Turning Leaves, when the maples flared red and orange among the evergreens and the birch leaves turned gold.

Flann forced his attention back to the party. Servants brought water ices, lemonade, negus and small cakes after each dance. Flann took a lemonade.

"I understand you were at West Point," Abraham Van Buren said to him. "Could we have been there in one of the same years?"

"I'm afraid I didn't graduate," Flann admitted.

Van Buren's son seemed to lose interest in him.

The evening meal was set out on a long damask-covered table. Candles flickered in silver and crystal holders, throwing light onto gold plates that held beef, cold roast turkey, duck and chickens, fried and stewed oysters, blancmange, jellies, whips, floating islands, candied oranges, tarts and cakes.

A feast, he thought. The People have feasts, too, and dancing.

"So I called the cur out," the man next to him said loudly. "I'll not have a woman's name slandered in my presence. Scared him, you can bet. It's well known I've never lost a duel."

Flann saw another comparison in this, an open boasting of coups.

"Mr. O'Phelan," another man said to him.

Flann turned to the speaker. "I'm Bill Haviland. We heard you're just back from a year with the Indians." With a nod, he indicated a group of young men standing nearby. "Would you join us after the party? We'll retire to an oyster house or some such and listen to you tell of your adventures, if you're willing."

Flann's first impulse was to decline but he chided himself silently and accepted. The men first escorted several women home, then gathered on Pennsylvania Avenue. They drank from flasks of brandy as they walked four abreast down the avenue, singing and shouting.

"Isn't this a lark compared to what you've been through?" Bill Haviland asked, gulping brandy and offering Flann the flask. "We're off to a place called the Palace of Fortune."

"I don't care for a drink, thanks," Flann said. He knew the Palace of Fortune was a gambling hall. He did not feel like gambling, either.

He found he wanted only to be alone.

He saw one of the men pick up a stone from the road and hurl it at a building hidden in the shadows. There was the tinkle of breaking glass.

"Now you've done it," Bill Haviland called. They all ran away laughing.

Drunken braves behaved like this too, Flann thought.

When they were well ahead of him, he turned and made his way back to Fuller's Hotel.

The solitude pleased him.

Flann sat on the edge of his bed, his chin resting on his hands.

He smiled. He felt good. So many confusing elements had cleared for him during the evening.

And at that moment, Flann made a decision based on something President Van Buren had said earlier.

He had spoken of the Chippewa as savages in need of enlightenment. Flann knew that enlightenment

353

was the thing they needed least. Give them smallpox vaccination instead, for a start.

And if the United States government would not be generous enough to provide so small a thing, then Flann O'Phelan would provide it himself.

Somehow, he had to raise enough to finance vaccination for the Chippewa.

But he had no money of his own. Lawyers were still trying to untangle his father's estate and were quarreling about the settlement. Flann had to face the fact that he might not get any money from the estate for years, if ever. And Van Buren had no money for him.

Flann stood and began pacing. Damn it, he would raise the money. He'd collar every relative, every friend. He'd tackle his father's friends, too, and his uncle's. There was plenty of money in Boston despite the financial panic. He would persist until he made those who had money part with some of it.

The Chippewas would come first. They were his people. Then would come the Sioux, for they were no enemies of his. Yes, he would vaccinate the Sioux, too, in memory of Squirrel.

He could do more good for his adopted people by staying a white man. He saw that clearly now. He knew how to get his hands on white men's money to use white men's medicine to prevent a white man's disease. That was a start.

Later, if there were any way to influence the men in Washington to keep them from moving the Chippewa west, he would find that way.

Birch Leaf had chosen to stay with them.

She was lost to him forever, but he would work to save her and the Chippewa all his life. They were people, as good as anyone, no better, no worse. As good as Jackson, Van Buren and the men in Congress.

God help me, he prayed.

"Kitchi Manito," he said aloud. "Great Spirit, give me strength."

AMERICAN EXPLORERS #1

**A cruel test, an untamed land and
the love of a woman turned the boy into a man.**

JED SMITH

FREEDOM RIVER

****

Arriving in St. Louis in 1822, the daring, young Jedediah Smith
is confronted by rugged mountain men, trappers and bar-room
brawlers. He learns all too soon what is to be expected of him
on his first expedition into the new frontier up the Missouri
River. Making lifelong enemies and fighting terrifying hand-to-
hand battles, he learns how to live with men who will kill for a
cheap woman or a drop of liquor. But he learns more. Far from
the beautiful woman he left behind, in the arms of a free-spirited
Indian girl, he discovers the kind of love he never thought possible. *Freedom River* is the historical drama of an American
hero who opened the doors of the unknown wilderness to an
exciting future for an expanding nation.

Please send me _____ copies of the first book in the
AMERICAN EXPLORERS series, *Jed Smith: FREEDOM
RIVER*. I am enclosing $3.00 per copy (includes 25¢ to cover
postage and handling).

Please send check or money order (no cash or C.O.D.'s).

Name (please print)_____

Address_____ Apt._____

City_____

State_____ Zip_____

Send this coupon to:
MILES STANDISH PRESS
37 West Avenue, Suite 305, Wayne, PA 19087

A14   Please allow 6-8 weeks for delivery.
PA residents add 6% sales tax.

AMERICAN EXPLORERS #2

They faced 900 miles of savage wilderness
where a young man chose between fortune and love.

LEWIS & CLARK

NORTHWEST GLORY

★★★

Set in the turbulent 1800s, this is the story of the Lewis
and Clark expedition — and of the brave men and women
who faced brutal hardship and fierce tests of will. They encountered an untamed wilderness, its savage mountain men,
merciless fortune seekers and fiery Indian warriors. In the
midst of this hostile land, two lovers are united in their un-
dying passion. A truly incredible tale of love and adventure.

Please send me _____ copies of the second book in the
AMERICAN EXPLORER series, *Lewis & Clark: NORTH-
WEST GLORY*. I am enclosing $3.00 per copy (includes 25¢
to cover postage and handling).

Please send check or money order (no cash or C.O.D.'s).

Name (please print)_____

Address_____ Apt._____

City_____

State_____ Zip_____

Send this coupon to:
MILES STANDISH PRESS
37 West Avenue, Suite 305, Wayne, PA 19087
Please allow 6-8 weeks for delivery.
PA residents add 6% sales tax.

A14